Duty
on a
Lesser Front

ROB MCLAREN

This paperback edition published in 2021.
Lulu Publishing — www.lulu.com

A CiP record for this book is available from the National Library of Australia and the State Library of Queensland.

Text and illustration copyright © 2018 Rob McLaren
Graphic Design, typesetting and map illustrations by Matthew Lin
www.matthewlin.com.au

Paperback   ISBN 978-0-6484-716-3-9
E-book   ISBN 978-0-6484-716-4-6
Hardcover   ISBN 978-0-6484-716-5-3

Typeset in Bembo Semibold 12 pt

Duty on a Lesser Front
Acknowledgements

I sincerely thank the following people who generously enabled the creation of this book:

Andrew Koranski

Camilla Woods

Christopher Kelly

Daniel Burns

Daniel Flemming

David Matthews

Dominic Cook

Donald Maclean

Eva Servais

Frances Gates

Genevieve Rea

Graeme Hopgood

Grant Danby

Jo Wilson

Judy Clarke

Karl Schlobohm

Leida McLaren and Jan Couper

Mark Brady

Mark Brewer

Mathieu Degryse

Matthew Reeves

Michael Crowe

Michael Hunzel

Peter Cross

Richard Marsden

Richard Parkes

Rodney Cocks

Sandra Pope

Simon Coburn

Souella and Keith Walker

Steven M. Smith

Duty on a Lesser Front
Maps

Duty on a Lesser Front

Appendices

Prologue

Captain André Jobert clenched his teeth. His fingers lingered as he placed Corporal Arbod's cold hand onto the dead man's chest. Arbod's sightless, seared eyes, behind raw, half-closed lids, pierced Jobert's heart.

Beside the dull embers of the campfire, *Chasseur* Faure moaned as he rocked, crushing in his fist a corner of the blanket that covered his lower body. His eyes flickered toward the space his lower right arm and lower right leg ought to be.

Jobert and Sergeant Major Koschak lifted Faure onto his one leg to help him urinate. Too weak to stand, Faure had no ability, with his remaining left hand, to bring himself out of his underdrawers. With a forlorn sob, Faure urinated down his own leg. Tears oozed down through the filth on his pallid cheeks.

Jobert and Koschak lowered Faure beside the other wounded chasseur. Saint-Dizier, disembowelled by a spinning cannister ball, now writhed and kicked in the dirt.

'Captain Jobert, sir, he is my cousin.' Faure lifted Saint-Dizier's grimy hand to his lips. 'He is only nineteen. He deserves better.

Please, sir, a pistol? We show such mercy to our wounded horses, sir. Please?'

A vast weight slumped down on Jobert's neck and shoulders. Accusatory whispers gathered in the shadows. Jobert shrugged himself upright and gave Koschak a nod.

Koschak's mouth tightened. He turned to his bedroll and drew a pistol from his saddle holster. Sucking his breath through bared teeth, Koschak drew the ramrod and repacked the charge, opening the frizzen and checking the powder in the pan.

Jobert reached for Koschak's pistol and cocked the mechanism. As he bent to place the pistol in Faure's lap, Jobert kissed Faure's greasy scalp.

Staring at the fire, Faure calmed his breathing. He placed down his cousin's hand and took up the heavy cavalry pistol. His eyes on the flames, Faure placed the muzzle in his own mouth and fired.

Some chasseurs around nearby fires jerked in alarm. Some hung their heads, their faces in their hands.

Saint-Dizier squirmed at the pistol shot, crying out as his hand scraped at the mud to grip Faure's twitching fingers.

Jobert's hands trembled as he draped the stained blanket over Faure's body. *Did I fail them*, he thought? *What else could I have chosen?* 'I will stay with Saint-Dizier, Sergeant Major.'

Koschak retrieved his pistol from the widening pool of blood. 'No, you will not, sir.' Koschak glanced towards the other platoon fires. 'As a sergeant, yes, but not now as their captain. You lead them in battle. No! Go to bed. I will ... sit with him.'

'My wound will not let me sleep.'

'I care not, sir. Go.'

Jobert turned away into the darkness. He knew, when all was quiet, except for the snores of exhausted men and the soft footfall of the sentries, Koschak would pinch Saint-Dizier's nose then clamp down on his mouth until the writhing stopped.

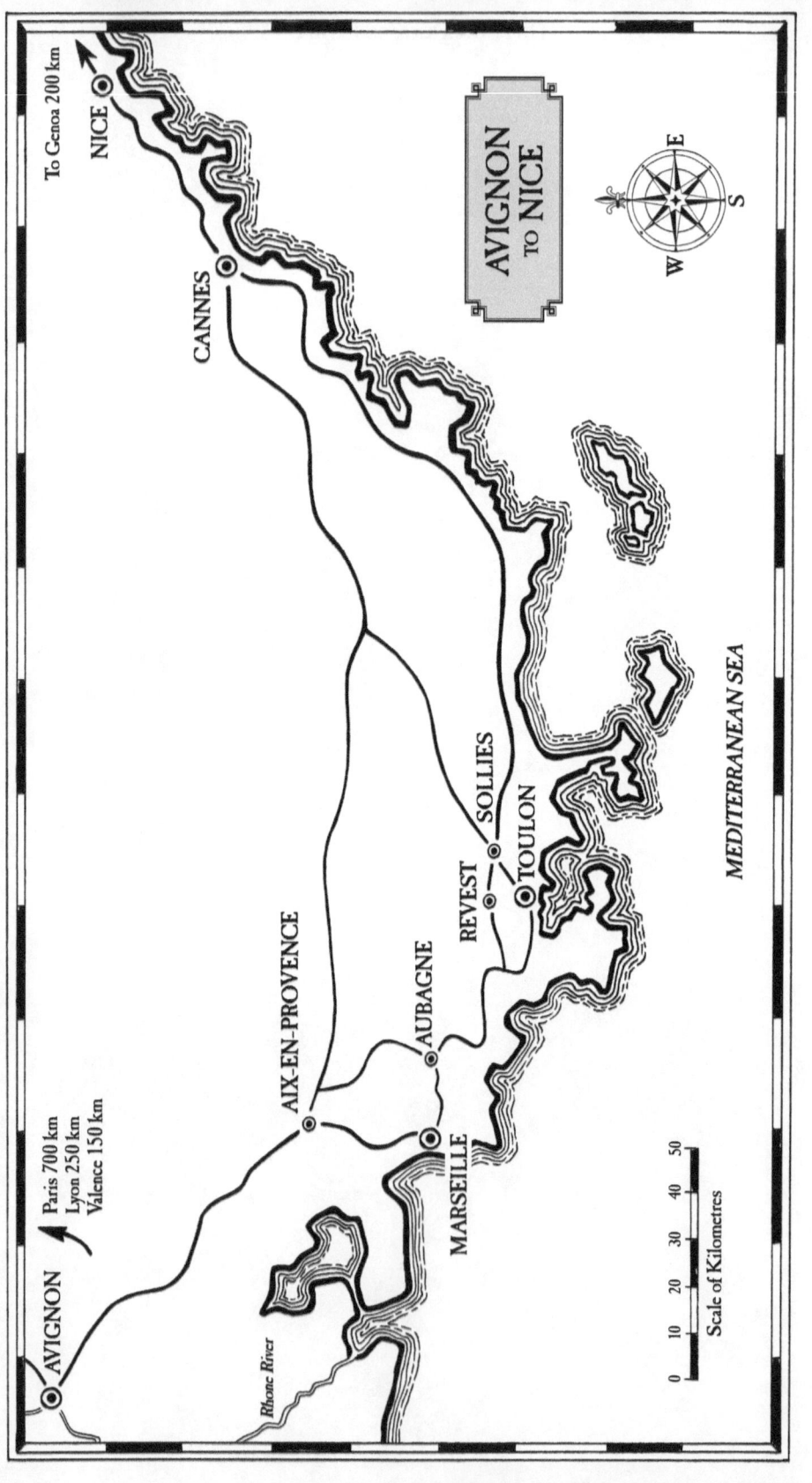

Chapter One

January 1794, Auvergne, France

André Jobert looked up from the cairn of black rocks that marked his grandfather's fresh grave in the family plot to the still, snow-covered slopes that surrounded him. The thick clouds blanketed the mountain sides, removing any view of the western heights of the Massif Central across the Allier Valley far below. Jobert's vision was restricted to the frozen granite and the snow-laden boughs within a few hundred metres.

The slowly drifting snow muted most sound. When one of the horses pawed at the crust of snow, crackling the frozen, dry grass and snorting a plume of thick steam, the noise punched the crisp air.

Jobert's gaze lingered on the pile of mossy stones, beyond the fresh grave, that pinned his father's bones. *You will never know how much I ...* Jobert expelled the sentiment away in a huff of steam, before looking towards his companion, a man he had known since childhood.

His lower face buried in an ice-encrusted scarf, Duque stared towards the black, silent pines. He sighed as his face turned back to the mound of ice-shrouded earth. He made the sign of the cross with the three remaining fingers of his right hand, his thick glove barely moving.

Jobert locked eyes with Duque for a moment. Duque tilted his head towards the descending slope. Jobert nodded.

A pulse of breeze rising from the valley floor whistled through the pine needles and swirled the snow in the air. Jobert let his horse pick his steps down the brittle, rocky slope, Duque by his side, away from Jacques Chauvel's grave to the huddled farms shrouded in the mist below.

'I have no desire for immediate cash, uncle,' said Jobert. 'I have no call to take my share of the estate. I live simply within my means. I am proud of our family's journey, and I wish to play my part in reinforcing that hard-won success.' Jobert spoke in German. An ancient rule since the family were itinerant drovers, and now a well-ingrained habit of the Chauvel family, only German was spoken within the house.

Yann Chauvel's eyes narrowed as he peered at his nephew. He then adjusted his wire-framed spectacles to squint at the document in his hand. 'Now, the last will and testament of my father, ... of Jacques Chauvel, directs the division of his estate into thirds. One-third to his sister Sophie, one-third to me and one-third to the children of his daughter. Here in one room are all those beneficiaries.'

Yann's daughter, Michelle, a tall woman in her early twenties, long hair pinned up into tresses, draped a knitted blanket across the waist of her great aunt Sophie. The elderly Sophie flapped a bony hand, tut-tutting over such fuss, but raised her slender arms and allowed Michelle to tuck the blanket.

Yann looked over his wire-framed spectacles at the faces illuminated by the flickering fire. 'Jacques' estate has grown, over thirty-five years, from nothing to a herd of two hundred and eighty horses based on five hundred and twenty acres, with a workforce of over forty men.'

Jobert gave his elder brother, Didier, a wink as he poured a myrtle-flavoured chartreuse, a local favourite, from a dark-glassed bottle into the small glasses of Yann, Michelle, Didier and himself. Aunt Sophie took a small splash in her coffee.

'In 1790,' said Yann, 'with the changes sweeping France, we acquired the land at a low price, but the interest rates from the lenders were high. That loan has a term of twenty years. The land is valued greater than the herd, so we pay an extreme rate of interest to cover the difference. Until the difference is covered, we cannot claim ownership of the land. The war over the last eighteen months ensures our artillery horses command a good price, but the sale of forty horses per annum barely covers the loan repayments and the needs of our workers.'

'Uncle,' asked Jobert, 'what part do the immense efforts of our dear aunt play in the family's endeavours?'

'Immense, indeed. Aunt Sophie's four workhouses are all owned in her brother Jacques' name —'

'The net profit from sewing uniforms is the equivalent to the sale of ten extra horses per annum,' said Michelle. She exchanged a curt nod with Aunt Sophie as she fussed with her skirt.

'Quite so, my dear.' Yann savoured his chartreuse.

Duque's family has cared for our family's herd for three generations. 'And what of the venture to extend our cartage capability with the Duque family?'

'Indeed, a third venture was undertaken in the last twelve months. The Republic's demand for cartage to supply the armies, and the subsequent income, cannot be ignored. Under the management of the Duque family, we are expanding in this area based on our forty-five-odd herd of three-year-old colts. Each March, the junior two-year-old colts become our senior colts. Since these new senior colts are still growing, one element of their schooling is to work as a team. By the end of the year's training, including their work under saddle, the colts are strong enough to pull a light load in pairs. Investing whatever is spare grows the fleet of wagons required.'

'Father, as you say, until the loan is repaid considerably, we cannot claim ownership of the land,' said Michelle. 'How does the combined income from these enterprises impact upon the loan?'

'At our current repayment level, we shall have access to the deeds by 1799,' said Yann. 'Drawn in 1790, little principal is repaid. We sit precariously. Any financial shock, and 1793 just past has threatened more than a few, will have our lenders pull the rug from under us. Jacques' estate, a family enterprise nearly fifty years in the making, is in a delicate financial position. The Republic provides good income through the demand for gun teams, cartage and the manufacture of uniforms, but our loan repayments leave no net profit. If any beneficiary of Jacques' estate decides to claim their share, the land and the herd would be sold. That sale repays the loans in full, with nothing left over, and have all the herdsmen dismissed. A meagre dividend for us all.'

The fire hissed and popped, giving reason for everyone to contemplate the hearth.

'Not only no dividend,' said Didier to the flames, 'our fortunes are entwined with the Republic's success on the battlefield.'

Yann shifted in his creaking chair and faced his nephews, sons of his long-dead sister. 'To that end, Aunt Sophie and I propose establishing a company in which there are four shareholders.

Aunt Sophie holds one-third, a second third to my estate, and a one-sixth holding to both you boys. If you concur, I propose to draw up company deeds whilst both of you lads are home on leave. We have the opportunity to consider signing them in the weeks prior to your return to your regiments.'

Jobert smiled grimly at Michelle and Didier. *We cousins now shackled tighter by our family's fortunes.*

A day of January sunshine was a rare treat on the upper slopes of Auvergne's Massif Central.

With the cloud cover absent, the sun rose over the ridges to the east by ten o'clock. As it skimmed the southern horizon, the watery sun warmed the household's spirits. After a family lunch, and before the sun set on the western heights across the valley by mid-afternoon, the brothers decided to escort Michelle down to the stables from the ramshackle farmhouse.

An icy wind raced south as the trio crunched through the snow arm in arm. Jobert felt Michelle's body jerk as a pistol fired from the vicinity of the stables.

'I hate that sound,' said Michelle. 'Even if it signals dinner-time for the horses.'

Jobert thought nothing of the standard practice to desensitise all military horses from the sound and the smoke.

Michelle leant her head on Jobert's arm. 'And what of Duque? How has he fared with his injuries since Jemappes? Will he return to the regiment as your groom? Or will he take a place in this cartage venture his father leads?'

Jobert shrugged. 'He has become adept with the remaining fingers the hussar's sabre did not remove. I raised the matter of re-joining his family with him, thinking I would require a new groom. Duque replied maybe one day, but not at the moment. He felt the venture had enough brothers and cousins involved. I think he enjoys the place he holds in my chasseur company as a respected horseman. All the perks of a non-commissioned officer without the responsibilities, perhaps.'

The three fell silent as they negotiated a length of slippery ice.

'What news of the de Chabenacs?' asked Jobert.

'Who?' asked Didier.

'A stunning noble woman André rescued from the Avignon revolt last year,' said Michelle, 'and her equally gorgeous mother.'

'Is the mother widowed and rich?' asked Didier.

Michelle glanced mockingly at Didier.

'Like many minor nobility,' said Jobert, 'destitute with the loss of land and title. The son commanded the junior company in my squadron before becoming a regimental *aide de camp.*'

'To answer your question, André,' said Michelle, 'both ladies are well, considering their unfortunate situation. With the Committee of Public Safety's new Law of Suspects, and the consequent rise in the number of executions in Paris, we all go about our lives with great care. The de Chabenac ladies are guests in our apartment, and they devote their daily energies to our women in the workhouses. I shall pass on your warmest regards, cousin, which I know will be appreciated. Valmai speaks highly of your dancing skills, of which I was unaware. No chance of ...?'

Jobert rolled his eyes. 'Of what? Dancing or marriage?'

Michelle winked at Didier. 'Surely one leads to the other.'

'Good grief, woman. Take a wife on a captain's salary in the middle of a war? You cannot be serious? I hardly stand still long enough to change my stockings, let alone fall in love.'

'Indeed! Preposterous notion.' Didier huffed. 'What of you, cousin? Are you close to marrying? How does Uncle Yann feel about your escapades as a single woman in Paris?'

Michelle's smile ceased. 'Paris in the grip of the Terror is not the place to consider courtship, let alone matrimony. My father is too aware of our need to survive and places his trust in me to secure my station, as all the women in our family have. No, with Aunt Sophie now seventy-five, my place is at her side. It may only be lace and braid we sew, but our production to fill contracts for military headdress is considerable. I will not lose all that to attend a husband.'

Jobert scowled across Michelle's wrapped head towards Didier. Didier grimaced an apology in return.

'Michelle,' asked Jobert, 'how can we assist the farm?'

Michelle stopped walking and disengaged her arms and wiped tears from her eyes. 'Stay safe. Come home.'

The brothers exchanged furtive glances. Didier shrugged. 'Perhaps allocate a small stipend from our salaries to the farm?'

Jobert shook his head. 'On your major's salary possibly. A captain's salary would certainly not allow it.'

'Then get promoted. Act recklessly brave in front of a Deputy of the People and be promoted to general. I am serious. All sorts of fellows are achieving it. Since 1791, our chance for rapid promotion is upon us.'

'Shut up, idiots.' Michelle stamped her foot, her face flushed. 'You are not with your hussars, or *chasseurs à cheval*, or what have you, now. Talk of reckless bravery somewhere else. A dead hero, cloaked in glory, will not help the farm ... though you might consider cartage contracts at a regimental level.'

Michelle's comment reminded Jobert of his close connection to Colonel Raive, now posted to the headquarters of General Masséna's division within the Army of Italy.

Michelle resettled her scarf around her freezing face, snuggled her arms into those of her beloved cousins and set off again for the stables.

Jobert cleared his throat. His brother and his cousin tipped their faces towards him anticipating some announcement. Jobert sought his words, reluctant to reveal his part in an armoury raid in Valence ten months ago.

'I ... I have three thousand francs to contribute to the farm. I wish to repay my grandfather for his gift of horses upon my promotions.'

Didier stopped in his tracks to stare at André. 'I beg your pardon, brother. That is over a year's salary for a captain. My word, you do live within your means.'

Michelle looked into André's stern eyes. 'Darling André, that is a lot of money. As father explained our situation, it is most welcome, of course. Are you sure you wish the farm to have it?'

Jobert shrugged. 'The new company's deeds described the ability to increase our shareholding by contributions, did they not?'

The three arrived at an outer gate to the stone stables. Unlinking arms to open the gate and usher their cousin through the muddy slush, Didier looked hard at André. 'What occupied you last year?'

'I told you. I joined one of the new chasseurs à cheval regiments and raised a company. My men were blooded screening Marseille and Avignon during their revolts.'

Didier stared with brows furrowed. 'But three thousand francs, brother? Did you benefit from the siege at Toulon?'

'No. Patrols, escorts, guides, and a few scraps here and there. We were lucky to come through reasonably unscathed.'

'But no glory, eh?'

Chapter Two

February 1794, Avignon, France

Jobert and the forty seated men looked down the long tables towards Colonel Morin, his glass raised in a toast.

'*Vive le République.*'

'*Vive le République.*' The response boomed back from those assembled.

'The 24th Chasseurs à Cheval.'

'24th Chasseurs.' The chorus patted the table with their free hands.

'To absent brothers.'

The room's mood changed in an instant. The young men's faces hardened with the memories of the regiment's first campaign prior to the new year. 'Absent brothers.'

Morin refilled his glass once more. 'Gentlemen, welcome back to the regiment. Let us now focus on our immediate task in this new year. With Colonel's Raive's promotion and his posting to General Masséna's staff, we welcome Lieutenant Colonel Spiccard as the regiment's second-in-command.'

'Hear! Hear!'

'We welcome our two new chiefs of squadron,' said Morin, 'Majors Fergnes and Clemusat. These well-deserved promotions are the result of uncompromised dedication from these fine officers. I wish to mention one of our brethren who has not received such honours. Captain Jobert, and his 2nd Company, gave excellent service to the regiment and France last year, in the face of the enemy in a number of exceptional situations, but he was not rewarded with promotion. I have chosen to acknowledge Jobert's actions with the granting of a small prize. Jobert, if you will?'

As Jobert walked the length of the dining tables to his colonel, each young officer eyed the small, calf-skin purse hefted in Morin's fist.

Jobert recognised the purse. It was identical to three purses he had acquired during a raid he had led to Valence last April. *We hear you, sir. Fight hard, my lads, fight hard for the 24th Chasseurs and France, and glory, promotion and gold will be yours.* Jobert expected the purse still contained fifty gold louis, equivalent to one thousand francs, or four months wages as a cavalry captain.

Morin rapped his knuckles on the table. 'Now, gentlemen, to our pressing task of marching the regiment three hundred kilometres from Avignon to Nice to join General Masséna's division within the Army of Italy. The natural frontier between France and Italy is the Maritime Alps. With its headquarters in Nice, the Army of Italy holds the frontier. Our Piedmontese enemies garrison fortresses on the French side of this natural boundary and threaten the Republic's sovereignty. With lunch about to be served, are there any pressing questions? No?'

Jobert drained his glass of *poire william*, his mind on the promise and the dangers of the Mediterranean coast.

Three caped horsemen entered from the tavern yard. The small kitchen's battered door admitted an icy gust. Jobert saw the fire in the hearth flare, and his valet, Orlande, scrabble to cover the soup kettle from the frozen strands of hay in the dusty cloud.

Orlande winced. 'Tea, sir?'

'Thank you, Orlande,' said Jobert, inviting the two other men to take one of the rickety chairs at the decrepit wooden table. 'What of your inspection of the company's remounts, Neilage?'

Lieutenant Neilage, 2nd Company's second-in-command, reaffirmed the curl of his red-blond moustache under his slim, pointed nose. 'Feet are fine and newly shod, sir. Manes are hogged. Standing in stables, the horses are putting on condition, more so under their new canvas rugs, so I have reduced the grain ration. Sergeants continue to lead their platoons out for daily exercise and for horses to pick at the winter grasses.'

'Did we receive a good price for manes?' asked Jobert. 'And what of regimental tasks in preparation to march?'

'Company funds are in a good state,' said Neilage. 'What constitutes our daily juggle is the requirement to man regimental work parties, loading ledgers and stores from headquarters and the contents of armouries and magazines into nearly sixty regimental wagons.'

'Where are our two troop commanders?'

'Lieutenant Colonel Spiccard has all the second lieutenants scribing the load lists for the regimental trains, sir.'

Jobert slid his eyes over the rim of his mug of tea from Neilage to Koschak. 'How do the men view our march to Nice, Sergeant Major?'

Company Sergeant Major Koschak removed his green *bonnet-de-police* from his hair bound back in a queue and allowed the heat from his wooden tea mug to warm his fingers. 'Some of our local lads are downcast they are marching far from home and sweethearts, sir. Of the four chasseurs who failed to report back for the muster parade, we retrieved three easily enough from their mothers' hearths. Others with itchier feet are keen to see more of the wider world.' Koschak's mouth tightened as he inspected the tea leaves at the bottom of his mug. 'I have adjusted their expectations by saying that the Austrian bastards on the frontier will be hard men.'

'Good,' said Jobert. 'We will not be as fortunate as Toulon.' *Barely a year under their belt, these lads still have far to go.* 'What else needs our attention, Sergeant Major?'

Koschak shrugged his broad shoulders. 'Naught else, sir. Just saddle, mount and march.'

By the spluttering light of pitch-soaked torches, under a freezing full moon, Jobert, Orlande and Moench huddled within the warmth generated by the three warhorses that surrounded them. At Rouge's nose stood Vert, Jobert's mount for the day, and Trumpeter Moench's grey gelding.

Distinctive from the mounted men around them, all trumpeters rode greys. Not only was Moench's gelding noticeable, Moench wore the dark-orange, or capucine, jacket of a regimental trumpeter, a complete reverse of the dark-green jackets of the remainder of the regiment. The reverse-coloured jacket combined with the grey horse indicated both the location of the trumpeter and the nearby presence of the officer they served.

Jobert observed Sergeant Major Koschak assemble the chasseurs, whilst the convoy commander, Lieutenant Neilage, liaised with the wagons detailed to 2nd Company. Leaning across Vert's saddle, Jobert watched his chasseurs lead their remounts out of the Avignon barracks stable for the last time.

'Happy to be back on the road, Moench?'

'Ooh, yes, sir,' said Trumpeter Moench. 'There are too many husbands in this town who want to cut my cock off.'

'Would shortening it a smidgeon be such a bad result?' Jobert winked at Orlande. 'You will not miss your hometown, Moench?'

'My little brother might.' Moench shrugged. 'I feel it is time to enjoy all the pleasures that Italy has to offer.'

Orlande pressed his spectacles back onto the bridge of his nose. 'Ah, lovely.'

'What about the kaiserliks, sir?' asked Moench. 'Will they be as tough as they say?'

Jobert scratched Rouge's ears. 'The Austrians will fight as hard as the Spanish and British we faced a few months ago. Since they have no fleet to escape in, the kaiserliks will stand their ground sure enough.'

Rouge pushed his muzzle into Jobert's ribs to scratch a bridled itch. Both Jobert and Vert shuffled to regain their balance. Jobert raised a warning finger at Rouge, at which the horse dipped his nose away.

Jobert owned a string of three warhorses, Rouge, Bleu and Vert. Today, Rouge was harnessed in the shafts of Jobert's light trap, a small two-wheeled cart that allowed Jobert to maintain a small store of water, an iron firebox, and a simple command marquee close behind the tail of the company. Bleu, rugged in canvas, was tied to the rear of the cart.

On campaign, Orlande rode the horse saddled in the shafts, able to abandon the cart should the situation require.

This morning, Orlande would drive from the cart's seat with a thick blanket wrapped around his legs. As Jobert's groom, Corporal Duque normally led Jobert's spare horse when his captain required it in battle, but today Duque drove one of the company's wagons.

Wheels squealed against laden axles and groaned on the compact gravel of the regimental square. Responding to the growled commands of their four platoon sergeants, with a jingle and clatter of bit chains, spurs, scabbards and slung musketoons, the chasseurs of 2nd Company mounted their horses.

Moench whistled the trumpet call *To Mess*, the signature tune of 2nd Company.

Young faces pinched with cold emerged from cape flaps and under helmet visors, whistling the trumpet call in response.

A strong southerly blew in from the Mediterranean, skidding clumps of low-lying grey cloud north towards the higher coastal ranges. Branches in the leafless orchards around Toulon rattled and scraped in the wind. The smoke from nearby kitchen chimneys eddied with the dust from the fallow fields in which 2nd Company had camped.

Observing the company and its train of wagons assemble on parade, Jobert and Captain Chabenac, one of Colonel Morin's aides de camp, breakfasted on Orlande's fried bread filled with poached egg and feta cheese, as their capes whipped around their legs.

Chabenac's clean-shaven face scowled as he watched Corporal Duque assist the squadron's *cantinière*, Madame Quandalle, and her son onto the back of a wagon. 'Is it for the best?'

Jobert wiped yolk and crumbs from his mouth with his thick glove cuff. 'My mother followed her brother up and down the Rhineland for seven years in the last war, darning stockings, replacing buttons and removing the lace of rank from dead men's sleeves. Madame Quandalle and her son served us well last year. She will make a fine cantinière.'

Jobert slid his eyes towards Chabenac as he reflected on his friend's boyhood of noble privilege. The execution of his uncle, the Comte de Chabenac. The mob's vicious beating of his parents, from which his father died. Deciding to remove the 'de' from his name thus publicly disavowing his nobility. When all Avignon society turned against his mother and sister in their moment of crisis, it was Jobert's family, a family of harness-makers and common soldiers, who provided charity and refuge.

'I have heard the Austrian is a doughty foe,' said Chabenac. 'Are you satisfied with 2nd Company's preparation?'

'No.' Jobert cast the dregs of his cold tea onto the ground and tucked the wooden cup into a deep pocket of his cape. 'There is still much to learn. I expect the Austrians will provide the severest school.'

On the improvised drill ground in the chill March wind, Sergeant Major Koschak stood rigid with a musket tucked under his left arm, the weapon's hammer snug in the crook of the left elbow, in the position of 'Shoulder Arms'. With the bayonet fitted to the musket's muzzle, the firearm, with a length of one hundred and thirteen centimetres, extended to become a weapon nearly one hundred and sixty centimetres in length.

'Sergeant Major, ready!' called Jobert.

Koschak stepped forward with his left foot, grasped the waist of the musket's stock with his right hand, the barrel with his left hand and positioned himself to fire.

'Lads,' said Jobert, projecting his voice to the troop of fifty 2nd Company chasseurs about him, 'you will note the fusilier is ready to fire. Sergeant Major, *en garde!*'

Koschak adjusted his stance, his knees bent, ready to thrust the bayonet if required.

'Take note that the right hand will provide the thrust to the musket,' said Jobert, 'and the left will guide the bayonet home. With the tip of the bayonet at the eye level of my horse, you will observe how my horse finds it difficult to approach the fusilier with his musket in this position.'

Jobert backed Rouge a few steps away from Koschak. 'Sergeant Major, at a mounted opponent, thrust!'

Koschak lunged, his left arm outstretched, the tip of the bayonet level with his eyes.

'Note the targets available to the fusilier. I spoke of the face of the horse, but the bayonet is easily parried by the horse's thrown head, leaving the fusilier vulnerable. Of greater value to the fusilier is the groin of the cavalryman, and just above that area, the abdomen. What protects the groin?'

'The saddle bow, sir,' said Chasseur Faure, 'with pistol holsters attached, and the horse rug and cape rolled under the shabraque.'

'Well done, Faure. The waist sash provides only limited protection to the abdomen. On initial inspection it appears that, in the outstretched arms of both opponents, the musket with the bayonet is longer than the sabre.'

Jobert side-stepped Rouge so that the tip of the bayonet rested against his ribs, and the tip of his one-hundred-centimetre sabre was still a good forty centimetres from Koschak's face.

'Observe, now, the wounding and death of the lazy chasseur

who chooses to slash at the fusilier.' With that, Jobert raised his sabre for a downward cut. As Jobert's arm swung the sabre above his head, Koschak leapt forward and again applied the tip of the musket to Jobert's ribs.

Jobert then sidestepped Rouge away from Koschak until only the tips of both weapons were touching.

'Aim your strike for the fingers of the fusilier's hands, especially the unprotected fingers of the fusilier's outstretched left hand. As we know from our fencing, the tip of the sabre and the tip of the bayonet are equal, for it is the parry that matters.'

Jobert nullified the threat with a gentle sweep of his wrist and a screech of blade on bayonet.

'It is the use of the horseman's nearside, or left, heel that signals the horse to sidestep towards the fusilier, thus creating the momentum of the strike. With the horse moving sideways, the bayonet tip parried, your blade glides down the barrel and slices off the fusilier's fingers, rendering him *hors de combat*. As the bayonet has no cutting edge and the sabre has a knuckle-guard to deflect both bayonet and barrel, the movement is achieved with complete safety to the horseman.'

Jobert's horse stepped sideways allowing Jobert to rest his sabre's edge on Koschak's bare fingers.

'Reform ranks and prepare to practise that stroke.'

As he broke a crusty bread roll over his steaming seafood *burrida*, Colonel Raive leant toward Jobert seated beside him, his eyes darting towards his dining companions. 'General Dumerbion is an interesting fellow.'

Jobert looked through the wavering candlelight at the young officers across the table staring eagerly towards the senior officers. Their keen eyes waited for the regiment's guests, and their host officers, to begin their soups, indicating they were allowed to begin their own meal. Far along the table General Dumerbion lifted his spoon and took a polite sip. This signal allowed the junior men to snatch up spoons and slurp.

'As the Commander of the Army of Italy,' said Raive, 'Dumerbion commands a force of forty thousand on paper, but effectively fields twenty thousand men due to rampant illness. He is quite canny. Having watched many of his peers executed by the People's Deputies, he asks the Deputies their opinion on how operations be conducted, and then complies with their advice. You will remember our citizen Deputy Saliceti from last year.'

Jobert slid his eyes in the direction of Raive's nod toward the sharp faced Deputy of the People Saliceti.

'Where do our Deputies derive such insightful military opinion for General Dumerbion?' Raive's eyes twinkled. 'None other than the Army of Italy's Chief of Artillery, our friend Brigadier General Bonaparte. With Austria's and Prussia's recent advance across the Rhine, young Bonaparte is advocating for an offensive into northern Italy to divert Austrian pressure from the Rhine. Desperate times these, Jobert. Paper money is worthless. The country is afflicted with famine and supply is woeful. Carnot, the Minister of War, is making noises for France to invade beyond our boundaries simply to feed the armies.'

'Speaking of supply, sir, my family is incorporating a small cartage business into the training of our colts. If they were seeking cartage contracts within the Army of Italy, where might they begin?'

Raive sucked his teeth and wobbled his head. 'For any supply extending back to the Rhône, army contracts originate in Paris. Local resupply contracts are well supported by local carters. The difficulty is when contracts are awarded, and the money paid, the material supplied is of inferior quality. What is more, the drivers are not paid, which results in the theft of those inadequate supplies.'

Raive considered Jobert a moment amidst the laughter, chatter and clinks of cutlery on crockery. 'Perhaps General Masséna and I would be glad of access to a small outfit, with a reputation for integrity, for the movement of key items both to and from Nice. If I placed an order for, say, wine for example, how might I arrange it?'

'My uncle has delegated the enterprise to the Duque family.' Jobert tipped his bowl to finish his soup. 'I will make Duque available to you as your agent.'

'Corporal Duque? Excellent! Then I am obliged, my dear fellow. Let us start with one load and grow it from there.'

'What of your new commander, sir, divisional commander Masséna?'

'Masséna is a sharp fellow. I enjoy working for him. He hails from the coast around Nice and knows the country well. Like us, a royal army sergeant major, he enjoyed rapid promotion in the volunteer infantry battalions that sprang up in 1791. With Saliceti promoting him to divisional commander, he now commands a force of six thousand men of four infantry regiments.'

'And what is the state of your battalions?'

The twist of Raive's mouth caused his moustache to flicker. 'The Minister of War continues to drive the amalgamation within each infantry regiment of one old, royal army battalion with two patriotic volunteer battalions. That amalgamation is now occurring here in Nice.'

'Is there any artillery allocated to the division?'

'A foot battery of six four-pounder guns and two six-inch howitzers.'

'And the 24ᵗʰ Chasseurs?'

'As Masséna is General Dumerbion's darling and leads all his operations here on the frontier, Dumerbion has allocated Masséna's division a regiment of chasseurs. You have seen a chart of the area, have you not? We sit south of the door to the vast Po River valley that flows east from the Maritime Alps to the Adriatic. To protect that entrance, our enemies hold a defensive line west of the Maritime Alps within the natural boundaries of France.'

'And what of our enemies?' asked Jobert.

'The Army of Italy faces three enemies. Twenty thousand Piedmontese in the mountains to the north, entrenched in a fortified line around the mountain fortress at Saorgio. Twenty-five thousand Austrians along the coast to the east. The British navy interdicts our coastal resupply to our south and intercepts our grain resupply from Genoa.'

As fresh carafes of wine were passed along the table, the young officers filled each other's glasses whilst soldiers removed the soup bowls.

'France secured the province of Savoy and the port of Nice in '92,' said Raive. 'But we failed to secure Saorgio. Early last year, the Army again attempted to take the fortress line that protects the high passes. The attack failed with disastrous results and our commanders executed. Hence the current general's well-developed sense of caution.'

Both Jobert and Raive leant back as a plate of fish in a fragrant wine and lemon sauce was placed in front of them.

'The use of cavalry in the mountains is currently a much-debated topic in the regiment,' said Jobert. 'What are Masséna's views on the use of the 24ᵗʰ Chasseurs?'

'The challenge for cavalry is that mountain soil is poor and there is next to no forage. Due to steep terrain, all movement is restricted to roads. The vital roads allow two carts to move past each other, so, at best, a battlefield frontage of a standard marching column, four horsemen or six infantrymen. But this is the exception, as most roads only allow one cart, or a frontage of two horses. Any bypassing of enemy positions can only be achieved on local village footpaths. Perhaps small groupings of horsemen can move rapidly and sustain themselves in such an environment, which gains some temporary tactical advantage, but the best use of the chasseurs is escorting artillery and resupply columns.'

'A platoon sergeant's war?'

'Due to the importance of the passes that need seizing, perhaps platoons commanded by colonels? But snow in the passes begins to melt. I suspect our friend Bonaparte has a scheme. He will feed it to Dumerbion via the People's Deputies. Masséna will be given his order to march, and the 24th Chasseurs will lead the way. I hope your men are ready, Jobert?'

Jobert's teeth ground his mouthfuls, his senses oblivious to the rich flavours.

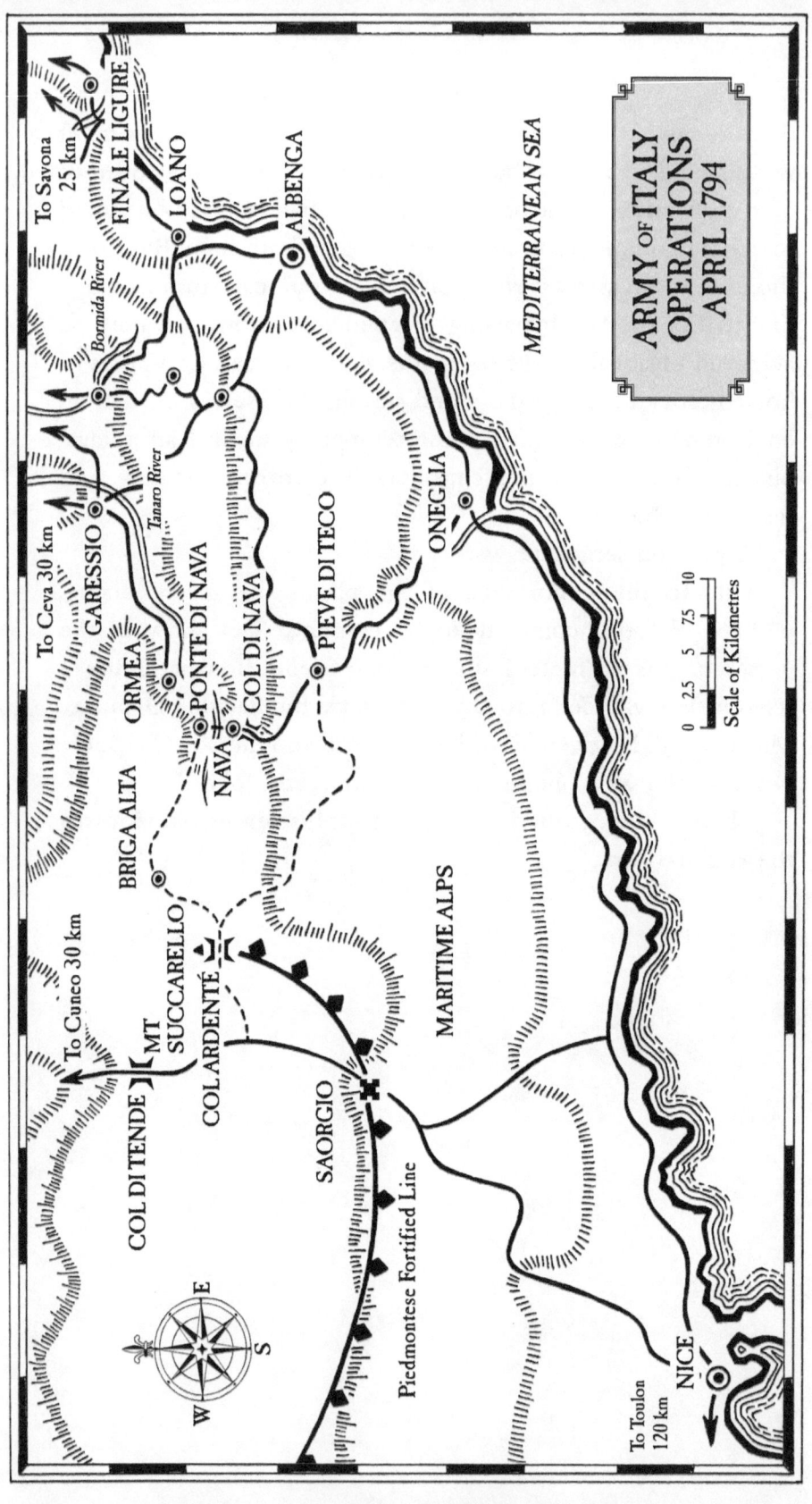

ARMY OF ITALY OPERATIONS APRIL 1794

MEDITERRANEAN SEA

To Savona 25 km

FINALE LIGURE
LOANO
ALBENGA
Bormida River

To Ceva 30 km

GARESSIO
Tanaro River
ORMEA
PONTE DI NAVA
NAVA
COL DI NAVA
PIEVE DI TECO
ONEGLIA

BRIGA ALTA

To Cuneo 30 km

SUCCARELLO
MT SUCCARELLO
COL DI TENDE
COL ARDENTE
SAORGIO
MARITIME ALPS

Piedmontese Fortified Line

NICE
To Toulon 120 km

Scale of Kilometres
0   2.5   5   7.5   10

Chapter Three

April 1794, Nice, France

A fire in the hearth and candles in the beams of the low-ceilinged tavern lit the terrain model.

'2nd Company, on parade, sir.' Jobert gave a respectful nod as he handed control of the assembly over to his commanding officer.

Colonel Morin stepped into the centre of the ring of smoky light.

'General Dumerbion has orders from Paris to expel the Piedmontese from French soil. General Dumerbion has selected General Masséna to spearhead that attack. General Masséna has requested I pass on how delighted he is that the 24th Chasseurs will lead his division into battle. The 2nd Company's role is vital to the Republic's success in this endeavour. From my close observation of you all, I believe wholeheartedly that every man, without exception, will do his best. Captain Jobert, your parade.'

Jobert stepped forward, his gaze passing with assurance across each face.

'Men, on this model of the Mediterranean coast before you,

you will note Mount Succarello, a dominating local mountain around which there are three passes across the range, the Col di Tende, the Col di Nava and the Col Ardente. Blocking the Col di Tende is the fortress at Saorgio. Over the Col di Nava, a road runs from Oneglia into the Tanaro River valley, which includes the towns of Ormea and Garessio.

'Consider the enemy. By defending the Col di Tende, the Piedmontese deny any movement over the Maritime Alps, into Piedmont and the headwaters of the great Po. To defend the Col di Tende, the Piedmontese hold a line of forts centred on Saorgio. The east flank of the fortified line extends to Mount Succarello. Beyond Mount Succarello, a string of isolated Austrian battalions is dispersed from the mountain down to Savona on the coast.

'General Dumerbion's plan is to secure the Col di Tende for France. The General will attack with three large columns. The first column will advance from Nice against Saorgio, attacking the fortress from the front, thus pinning the Piedmontese defence and their reserves.

'The second column, General Masséna's division – our division – will attack along the coast to Oneglia. General Masséna will then turn away from the coast and attack up and over the Col di Nava, enter the Tanaro River valley on the far side of the Alps and capture the towns of Ormea and Garessio.

'General Masséna will then reverse his advance west to Mount Succarello, break through the Piedmontese fortified line at the Col Ardente to secure the road between Saorgio and the Col di Tende, isolating the Piedmontese at Saorgio. The third column will advance along the coast beyond Oneglia to Loano, threatening the Austrians at Savona and diverting their reserves from the mountains to the sea.

'The 24th Chasseurs play a crucial role in General Masséna's success. Our 2nd Squadron is to lead General Masséna's division into every attack against the Austrians, with 2nd Company and 5th Company alternating as the divisional advance guard.'

The first into every fight. As they listened, the mouths of the 2nd Company men tightened.

'To begin with, 5th Company will lead General Masséna from Nice to Oneglia along the coast. We, 2nd Company, will lead General Masséna from Oneglia up and over the Col di Nava and into the Tanaro River valley.

'When 2nd Company turns north, taking the lead away from the coast, we will be followed by the 16th *Légère* Regiment. The 16th Légère have three light infantry battalions, not line infantry. They are chasseurs like us, but on foot. It is our job to find the enemy. It is the 16th Légère's job to attack the enemy.

'We will face steep hillsides and poor forage. Advancing on narrow roads and tracks means only small groups of chasseurs can patrol forward, and then only for a short time before being relieved by another small group.'

The grim commanders of 2nd Company studied the terrain model.

'This attack on the passes around Mount Succarello is so important that General Masséna wants Colonel Morin to be his personal eyes and ears as far forward as possible. Colonel Morin and I intend to lead the advance with one platoon and have Lieutenant Neilage follow with a reserve platoon. Lieutenant Voreille, your troop will provide those two advance guard platoons. Sergeants Pultiere and Bredieux will alternate at the head of the column with me, as ground and enemy allow.'

Second Lieutenant Voreille, Sergeant Pultiere and Sergeant Bredieux glanced at each other.

'But there are other vital tasks to be completed by 2nd Company. It is not enough that General Masséna has broken through the Austrians and outflanked the Piedmontese fortifications.

General Masséna must cut the road behind the Piedmontese holding the fortress at Saorgio. For the General's infantry to succeed, we chasseurs seek a path for the division up to the Col Ardente. Lieutenant Huin, that will be the task of one of your platoons. The division's artillery battery has a critical role in the ability of the 16th Légère to defeat any enemy positions encountered. Lieutenant Huin, your other platoon will escort the division's foot artillery battery.'

Huin nodded at the gravity of his independent tasks.

'Finally, Sergeant Major Koschak, our five company wagons will travel behind the advance guard platoons. Expect the regimental surgeon and a sergeant veterinarian to travel with your train.'

Koschak made a jot in his notebook.

Morin looked up from the model laid out on the floor to give Jobert a satisfied wink.

Jobert scanned his notebook pages. 'Men, we have only tonight and tomorrow to prepare. Are there any questions?'

Corporal Arbod raised his hand. 'What will the Austrians be like, sir?'

All eyes locked on Jobert.

'Sergeant Major Koschak and I were just discussing this very topic.' Jobert's face melted to a smile as his weight relaxed onto one leg. 'We both agreed we found the kaiserliks tough opponents at Jemappes. Yet we broke them. Sergeant Major Koschak and I also know you fellows. We feel absolutely confident that 2nd Company will triumph in the face of the enemy, just as we did at Toulon.'

Jobert pressed Vert to the side of the road and wondered at the length of General Masséna's six-thousand-man column.

For the last three days march to Oneglia, Jobert's 2nd Squadron was Masséna's vanguard. Captain Geourdai's junior 5th Company had led the march. In the approved style, Geourdai had set a file of four chasseurs to patrol two hundred metres ahead of his lead platoon.

In column of fours, and to the beat of hooves and clink of scabbards, bit chains and slung musketoons, Geourdai's lead platoon followed down the dusty coast road. Should contact be made with the Austrian outposts, Colonel Morin rode beside Geourdai, with his aide de camp Chabenac close behind.

Two hundred metres behind the lead platoon, the remaining three platoons of the 5th Company marched on the road, with two section flank guards weaving through the bleak, shuttered farmsteads. Within this larger group rode General Masséna, accompanied by his lead brigade commander, the lead regimental commander and the artillery battery commander.

Beyond 5th Company marched Jobert's own senior 2nd Company. Ninety-five men and horses tipped their faces away from the icy northerly wind which had brought the late snow falls to the Mediterranean slopes of the Maritime Alps. Wrapped in flapping chasseur-green capes, Lieutenant Voreille's troop led today, followed by the nine wagons of 2nd Squadron's train. Huin's troop acted as rear guard.

Another five hundred metres behind Huin's troop marched the remainder of Masséna's advance guard, five hundred blue-coated, bicorne-wearing light infantrymen, one of the three battalions of the 16th Légère Regiment. Then came the divisional foot artillery battery, the gunners marching beside their horse teams, two pairs of light draught horses pulling either the slim brass four-pounder cannon or the stocky six-inch howitzer hitched to a two-wheeled limber, or a long ammunition caisson.

One thousand metres beyond the advance guard, Masséna's remaining eleven infantry battalions – a mixture of light and line infantry distinguishable by their blue or white trousers respectively – and their trains, stretched out for over ten kilometres.

Jobert's face whipped around when he heard musket fire from the direction of Oneglia. His leg pressed Vert back onto the road, and a muscular squeeze through his saddle lifted Vert into a canter towards Geourdai's platoon.

Morin, Geourdai and Chabenac had already cantered forward to the chasseur patrol. Jobert and his eternal shadow, Trumpeter Moench, sank in their saddles to bring their warhorses in beside them.

'Austrians on the bridge, sir,' said the 5th Company corporal, pointing into the shallow valley in front of them.

All the officers extended their telescopes and surveyed the scene.

A wide, but shallow, stream raced down from the coastal hills on their left and into the grey, froth-whipped Mediterranean on their right. Over the rocky stream squatted a solid stone bridge. Beyond the bridge and a few thatch-and-timber hovels rose the yellow and white-plastered buildings of Oneglia, chimney smoke from evening fires eddying between the brown-tiled roofs.

Above the whip of the wind, the rattle of drums sounded as the Austrians beat *To Arms*. The bridge guard, a one-hundred-man company of Austrian fusiliers in black, visorless, leather helmets, white tailcoats, white trousers and long black gaiters, raced to assemble.

Morin collapsed his telescope. 'Geourdai, advance 5th Company to the bridge and secure the near side. Jobert, locate a crossing point upstream, then descend on the flank of the bridge from the far side. Chabenac, pass my compliments to General

Masséna and inform him of the situation. Pass on that I suggest the guns be brought up to secure the bridge before sunset. Go!'

Shortening his reins, Jobert saluted as he pivoted Vert over his hocks, then pressed his bay gelding to leap from a halt to a fast canter over three hundred metres, past 5th Company with its retinue of senior officers, to 2nd Company.

2nd Company's Neilage, Koschak, Voreille and Huin were alerted by Jobert and Moench cantering towards them. '2nd Company,' called Koschak, 'stow capes, musketoons ready.'

Jobert's eyes were wild and his nostrils flared as he prepared for the anticipated violence. 'Over the lip of the rise runs a river, a bridge and Oneglia just beyond. An Austrian company holds the bridge. 5th Company is to take the near bank. The lead infantry and the guns are coming forward. 2nd Company is to cross the river and flank the bridge. Voreille, take your troop now and find a crossing point. Go! Sergeant Major, clear our train off the road for the infantry and the guns to pass. Huin, column of fours, follow me. Trot, march!'

As Huin's forty-five-man troop surged onto farm paths beside the road, one of Masséna's aides de camp, the commander of the 16th Légère and the battery commander, all three now appraised of the situation by Chabenac, galloped passed 2nd Company to find their units further down the column. On the heels of the chasseurs, the French infantry's drums thrashed out a high tempo beat as bellowed commands prepared the five hundred fusiliers of the advance guard battalion for the assault.

Following farm lanes into the miserable, dusty wind, Jobert and Huin's troop wound their way towards the grey stream swirling in its wide, shallow bed. Ahead, Jobert observed Voreille's troopers trotting here and there, inspecting places on the bank where horses could descend, and yelling to mates who had already crossed the freezing water and found paths up onto the far bank.

Voreille waved his gloved hand at Jobert's fast approaching column of fifty horsemen.

'Voreille,' called Jobert, 'leave a platoon to hold both sides of this crossing. You bring a platoon in column to my left rear as flank guard.'

Glancing to see Voreille's nod of acknowledgement, Jobert led the troop down the bank where Voreille's guides indicated. The neat column of horsemen with a frontage of four broke into an inelegant gaggle of ones and twos. Horses dropped their heads and picked their way across, the icy water splashing their bellies and swirling over the men's booted ankles. The horses then leapt up the stony shelves to the fallow fields and leafless olive groves on the far bank. As they ascended the banks to the snarls of the section corporals, Huin's wide-eyed chasseurs reformed in the files of four riders to recreate the 'column of fours' formation which allowed the fastest movement.

'Huin, form column of troop, walk, march!' yelled Jobert over his shoulder. Moench repeated the command with hand-signals. Huin's troop formation spread wider and wider to the left, from a frontage of four men to a 'column of platoon', a frontage of twelve men, all the way to 'column of troop', a frontage of over twenty horsemen in two ranks. The river tumbled on their right. On their left the silent cottages of the town stacked on the rising slope.

As Jobert twisted to confirm 2nd Company's formation, Moench tucked his grey gelding just behind and to the right of Jobert. Moench sucked and squeezed his lips, numb from the bracing wind, in anticipation of the trumpet calls required, and rubbed his trumpet's mouthpiece on the ribs of his braided dolman jacket.

Musket fire erupted downstream.

'Sabres!' called Jobert, satisfied that Voreille and his platoon had taken their post on his left rear.

Short-barrelled musketoons clattered as they were released to swing on their cross-belt clips. Steel blades drawn from brass scabbards gave an evil hiss into the gusting wind. Thick gloved hands clutching at cord-bound grips rested the sabres' pommels onto the chasseurs' right thighs.

'Shorten your reins, lads,' called Koschak. 'Up around their fucking ears.'

'Trot' was signalled along the line.

Except for a few outlying cottages obscuring his view, Jobert observed the length of the road from the bridge on his right to the gates of Oneglia on his left.

Bounding back by half-company, the Austrian bridge guard company was retiring from the bridge in good order, as the dark green figures of 5th Company darted on the far bank. Across the river on the far slope, the lead battalion of blue-coated French light infantry descended at a fast pace towards the bridge.

Two Austrian fusilier companies formed a fire line at Oneglia's gate. A third company marched towards the bridge to support the bridge guard.

Screams from the Austrian column on the road mid-way from gates to bridge, as they spotted Jobert's flanking chasseurs, turned into the insistent thrash of Austrian company drums. Expecting to receive a French cavalry charge, the fusilier company executed a flawless transformation from column to square.

Until alerted to the threat of French cavalry, the Austrian company had marched six fusiliers abreast. In response to their drum's insistent order to form square, the first quarter of the company moved outwards to form a three-rank frontage approximately eight men long. The middle half of the column faced left and right to form the sides of the square. The final quarter of the column simultaneously pressed forward to connect the two sides with the rear side of the square, before turning to face out. The front ranks knelt and, to create a horse-proof hedge, pressed their musket butts into the ground by their knees and held their bayonet-tipped muskets outwards at forty-five degrees. The two ranks behind readied their muskets and prepared to fire.

Jobert was surprised when the Austrians fired a volley whilst 2nd Company was well over two hundred metres away. Over the deep rumble of two hundred hooves behind him, he was hard pressed to hear any balls zip past at that extreme range, considering the Austrians fired into the prevailing wind.

Then Jobert understood the reason for the volley as the white-coated fusiliers reloaded. *The bridge guard is now alerted to our flanking threat.*

The Austrian drums from the square at the mid-way point pounded out the order *Form Square.*

Jobert judged the distance from 2nd Company from their target, the retiring bridge guard. *Two hundred metres, well out of musket range but twenty seconds on a galloping horse. Only enough time to discharge one musket volley.* Vert's swinging gait brought Jobert closer to his enemy. Now was the time for his decision.

If the bridge guard either freeze due to indecision, or break and run for the mid-way square, we charge. Why not add a little pressure? 'Moench, sound *Advance.*' Moench's trumpet screamed the command.

The bridge company halted and, due to the relatively small size of the unit, smoothly formed square, as had their sister company. *I would attack either squares with both 2nd Company and 5th Company, but not with Huin's troop only.* Jobert thrust up his sabre and signalled 'Halt'.

Non-commissioned officers yelled. Men shivered with the bitter winds on their backs. Impatient horses threw their heads.

Far over on his right, Jobert watched a 5th Company troop trot across the bridge, followed by a company of light infantry.

The troop halted unsure of Jobert's movements. A square of Austrian infantry is safe from a small group of French chasseurs à cheval, but they were extremely vulnerable to the French infantry about to cross the bridge. Jobert took in the sun sinking toward the western skyline over his right shoulder knowing Colonel Morin's purpose was to secure the bridge. The capture of the town would occur tomorrow.

'Lieutenant Huin, return to Voreille's crossing, form column of fours to the left, walk, march!'

With the chasseurs now turning their line away from any commitment to charge, the Austrians, remaining in square, withdrew towards the gates of the town.

To form square so composed and then to alert its sister company to the flanking threat, indicated to Jobert the Austrian company's disciplined steadiness. *As our first encounter, such skill requires acknowledgement.* Jobert trotted forward to within one hundred and fifty metres of the Austrian square. Saluting the square, Jobert brought the hilt of his sabre up to his lips in salute and then swept the blade back, his hand by his hip, the sabre's blade describing a line towards Vert's muzzle.

An Austrian officer, the black and yellow plume of his black bicorne whipping in the breeze, pushed his way forward through the close-packed ranks. Standing clear of his front rank, with sword drawn, he reciprocated Jobert's compliment.

Both men brought up their sabres to their lips in unison and completed the movement.

Chapter Four
April 1794, Pieve di Teco, Italy

The soaking, miserable drizzle excited Jobert. *This is always the best weather to kill.*

Rain kept the defender indoors. Rain outside gave rise to a fire inside and the opportunity to while away the hours cooking a cheery broth. Cooking fires created smoke which lay in the hollows and the low ground, revealing the location of the cosy prey.

Rain caused the defender's bored sentries to be uncomfortable and careless, whilst the aromatic smoke distracted their attention. The ability for a sentry to listen to the sodden world was reduced by the plips and plops from boughs and tent flaps onto capes and helmets. Rain caused hands and feet to become sodden and stiff. Rain seeped into the working mechanisms of the musket, either via the pan or down the barrel to the rammed charge, despite the best efforts of the most disciplined fusilier, increasing the likelihood of misfire.

In the rain, the hunter moved with swift stealth across the mud-softened earth and timber underfoot. Senses heightened by cooking-fire smoke, the hunter's fear of being shot-at diminished knowing wet powder would fail to warn the sentries' warm and drowsy comrades.

After four hours in the saddle from Oneglia, Jobert tickled the base of Bleu's shorn mane and looked down into the broad valley of Pieve di Teco. As the junction of three valleys, the main valley ran west to east guiding a small, rocky river to the sea. The minor valleys allowed snow-fed streams to join the small river and the road from Oneglia to wind north towards the Alpine peaks shrouded in low, wispy clouds.

Around the fertile intersections of streams and river nestled a series of villages and farms, all connected to the major road by fords and bridges. Each village was cloaked in smoke, the rain pressing the smoke against the walls of the squat stone houses.

From their vantage point on the upper slopes of the valley, Jobert, Morin and Chabenac saw no movement within the villages and the farms with the naked eye. They chose not to draw their telescopes and scrutinise in more detail, knowing their lenses would fog over.

An abrupt movement from the chasseur patrol descending the slope two hundred metres ahead caught their attention. The chasseurs signalled 'infantry'.

'Platoon stow capes, ready!' said Sergeant Bredieux to his platoon.

As hurriedly as sodden gloves and frozen fingers allowed, the platoon unbuttoned their capes and lashed them to their saddle bows. Musketoons emerged from beneath protective capes for butts to be held steady on the men's right thighs.

'Bredieux, trot, march!' said Jobert. 'Moench, signal trot march for Lieutenant Voreille to bring the rest of the platoon forward.'

Following Morin and Jobert, Sergeant Bredieux's platoon

soon closed the distance to the scouts ahead.

'Austrian sentries, sir,' said rain drenched Corporal Arbod.

Four white-clad, black-helmeted soldiers ran down the road towards the village bridge. At least three more descended the slope away from the road, through the gaunt trees, to the gurgling stream well below.

'None of them fired, sir,' said Arbod. 'No signal of our arrival.'

'Jobert,' said Morin, 'if there is an Austrian battalion in the town, the main bridge will lock the centre of their defences. Look to position yourself on the far bank by flanking crossing points. Chabenac, inform the 16th Légère of our intent. I shall wait for General Masséna.'

'Follow me! Trot, march!' called Jobert.

Trotting is a balanced, two-beat gait where the horse extends its stride to increase the speed. Squelching down the muddy road, Jobert's troops maintained a fast trot to overtake the fleeing Austrian sentries. Faced with an uphill scramble on one side, to be sabred down on the road or leap over the stone walls into the bare groves beneath, the harried Austrian fusiliers chose to depart the road downhill. Before he leapt the wall, a fierce-looking Austrian sergeant with a bristling black moustache, bellowed in German, 'Fire! Fire to warn the bridge company.'

'He wants his men to fire.' Jobert threw up his right hand to signal halt. 'He wants to warn the company on the bridge.'

'Follow them, sir?' asked young Voreille.

'No. I have an idea.' *Will we be fast enough to fool them?* 'Have Neilage bring Sergeant Pultiere's platoon forward to join us. Moench, fetch Sergeant Major Koschak to me now.'

As Bredieux's platoon clattered to a halt, Moench peeled his grey warhorse from the column and ascended the hill at the canter.

Through the trees, muskets fired by the stream. Perhaps a half-dozen shots, each with a pause between, signalled the village.

Now lower down the slope, and within the trees lining the road, the chasseurs had lost their vantage point and the village or enemy ahead were obscured. Yet they heard Austrian drums explode as they beat *To Arms*. Within moments Jobert looked up the slope to see the French infantry cresting the hill while their drums beat *Double March*.

Koschak and Moench cantered down the hill to join Jobert and the company's officers.

'Listen in, lads,' said Jobert, projecting his voice to the soldiers around him. 'We are now Piedmontese volunteers re-joining the Austrians. Voreille, split Pultiere's platoon. Place a section in front of our train and a section behind. Sergeant Major Koschak, command Bredieux's platoon in front. On arrival at the bridge, form line, and face back up the hill as if you are to delay the French advance. Give all your orders in German, Sergeant Major, understand?' Koschak returned an affirmative nod. 'I will take Pultiere's platoon and train across the bridge and into the village. Nobody speak, understand? No French, lads. Hear me? No one speak French when we close with the Austrians. Now, follow me! Trot, march!'

Jobert saw Bredieux's troopers glance left and right at their comrades, in their toe-to-toe formation, wide-eyed with alarm. Growled expletives from their section corporals had the chasseurs gathering their reins to press their impatient remounts into the trot.

The leafless trees thinned at the base of the valley, the stream by the Oneglia road roared as it met the little river bearing east. Emerging into the open, Jobert saw two Austrian fusilier companies having formed a fire line beyond the low stone bridge and three more companies marching to join them. An officer on horseback, the battalion commander wearing a plume-adorned bicorne and white jacket, rode at the head of the column.

'Moench, signal walk march,' hissed Jobert from the side of his mouth.

'Company, walk, march!' Jobert called in German. 'Lieutenant Koschak, form line and face the French.'

Koschak saluted.

Jobert gave a cheery wave towards the Austrians on the bridge.

'Form column of platoon, at the halt!' called Koschak in German. 'About face!'

Neilage and Pultiere with the section ahead of the five company wagons and Voreille's section behind, maintained their silent walking column, musketoons resting on thighs, towards the now five hundred Austrians forming an imposing three-rank line on the far bank of the river. In the centre of the fire line squatted two three-pounder cannons, loaded and aimed by a dozen brown-coated artillerymen and white-coated fusiliers.

Jobert squeezed Bleu into a gentle canter towards the bridge and approached the Austrian battalion commander.

The major blinked hard and licked his lips at the approaching cavalryman.

In the icy rain, Jobert drew up to the Austrian and saluted.

'Good morning, sir,' said Jobert in German. 'Captain Chetcuti of the Legion of Savoy, at your service. You are aware of the French approaching. The drums you hear are a battalion of ragged volunteers with a brigade struggling to keep up. We have impeded their advance since before Oneglia.'

The major looked at an elderly captain beside him. The Austrian captain's suspicious stare never left Jobert, his forehead creased in concern.

'Good morning, sir,' said the battalion commander. 'Major Leitzer of the Purn Regiment. Do the French advance with artillery?'

'Guns, sir? Not that I have seen. How might I support your defence, sir?'

The rattling French drums beyond the treeline held the Austrian major's attention. 'What was your regiment again, sir?'

'The Legion of Savoy, sir. Piedmontese volunteers.' Jobert pointed downstream. 'I suggest I place my train on the far side of the village and regather my company, cross the stream perhaps down there using the cover of the trees, and then take the French in the flank, sir?'

The sound of drumming and marching feet grew louder.

'Very well. Have the line break ranks to let them pass.'

Alarm showed in the eyes of the old captain.

'Company, advance!' called Jobert in German.

As Pultiere's platoon and the five wagons passed close by the tall wheels of the two artillery pieces, Jobert yelled, 'Lieutenant Koschak, retire your line, sir.'

Moench looked about wide-eyed, conscience of the simmering glare of the Austrian captain now snarling to a likewise sullen sergeant major.

'At the walk, in front of the French, Lieutenant Koschak,' called Jobert. 'This is not the place for unseemly haste. Well done the Purns. Do not let the bark of the French dogs unsettle your aim.'

As Jobert's fifty-odd horsemen departed the riverbank they passed the two limbers and two caissons serving the two Austrian cannons. The horse teams faced away from the gun position at the bridge towards the town. The four grey-jacketed, unarmed civilian drivers appeared anxious as they twisted in their saddles and watched the events behind them unfold.

As the chasseurs entered the steep streets, the beat of French drums and marching feet were amplified amongst the timber buildings. Local men and women, faces strained with fear, raced to close shutters and gather children and animals inside.

Two more Austrian companies advanced through the village. Company officers looked up in surprise to see green-clad horsemen blocking the street.

'The French are coming,' cried Jobert to the Austrians. 'Form line at the bridge. Clear the streets for the Purn Regiment. Hurrah for the Purns!'

Voreille's troop passed the infantry and pressed on at a fast walk and reached the far side of the village.

'Company, halt!' Jobert called to his men in French. 'Duque, secure our wagons in that tavern yard. Fall out!'

'Sir, riders!' called Duque.

Jobert looked up the slopes at the rear of the village where Duque pointed. Two white-coat horsemen, probably battalion aides, galloped north with the news of the French advance.

'Troop, about face! Sabres! Column of fours, walk, march!'

As the chasseurs rode their horses back down the street, the village walls distorted the cacophony of the drumming from both the Austrian line and the approaching French column.

Taking cover behind the last of the buildings in the narrow streets before the bridge, Jobert signalled halt and observed the scene.

Two hundred metres beyond the edge of the buildings the Austrian battalion covered the bridge with two four-hundred-man fire lines in three ranks, creating great wings over one hundred metres long, either side of the two patient cannons levelled across the bridge.

Three hundred metres beyond the bridge, emerging from the treelined slope in the drizzling rain, a company of blue-coated French skirmishers darted towards the riverbanks, taking cover behind trees, shrubs, boulders and low walls.

At the entrance to the road sat mounted French officers. Jobert expected Masséna and Morin rode in that group. Jobert had seen French commanders handle French volunteers for two years now. Acting on instinct, the drum-enraged fervour must unleash a battalion charge, particularly in the rain where the bayonet triumphs over the volley.

But, on this occasion, no such action. Instead, three artillery limbers rolled forward. Within sixty seconds, the teams turned about and delivered their four-pounder cannons to face the Austrian line. Preloaded with canister, the French gunners stood to their guns, matches lit.

The Austrian gunners screamed at their battalion commander. *They are loaded with canister for our infantry, not ball for our guns.* As for the infantry, Jobert saw the Austrian line was prevented from charging the unlimbering gun teams, blocked by the river, as the narrow bridge disallowed any forward movement. At three hundred metres, the imminent fire of French canister would be devastating.

The head of the French infantry column emerged from the tree line, the soldiers howling *La Marseillaise* over the sound of their thrashing drums.

A visible ripple of fear shuddered through the Austrian battalion. *Our deployment is occurring far too fast for them.* The mounted Austrian major looked left and right. He slumped in the saddle at the sight of more green-clad horsemen, Geourdai's 5th Company, crossing the rain-swollen river downstream.

As Jobert gathered his reins, Moench rolled his lips to warm them. 'Form troop line! Trot, march! Moench, sound *Advance.*'

As Moench's trumpet call tore through the rain, the old infantry captain screamed expletives and shook his fist at the two ranks of horsemen, over twenty-men wide, assembling up-hill between the battalion and the safety of the village's buildings.

'Halt!' Jobert kept his sabre high in the air in case he needed to drop it to order the charge.

The chasseurs shortened their reins. Horses threw their heads.

The Austrian gun team drivers' eyes bulged with fearful surprise as they raised their hands to show they were unarmed.

Austrian fusiliers half-turned in their packed ranks. The Austrian major spun his nervous horse and looked to Jobert.

The scene descended to silence, except for the spattering of rain on shoulders and faces.

The major turned to his battalion. 'Battalion, open order, march! Ground arms!'

The battalion looked at him. They looked to each other. Then feet shuffled to open the ranks followed by the clatter of muskets dropped into the mud. 'Form column to the left, left turn! Quick march!' The Austrian battalion cleared the egress to the bridge.

The battalion commander spurred his skittering horse across the bridge towards the knot of French officers by the treeline. General Masséna rode forward and accepted the Austrian's sword.

A freezing northerly pushed thick clouds across the face of an icy full moon.

Jobert straightened his mud-encrusted uniform and stepped through the low doorway into the wavering firelight. Despite his exhaustion, Jobert drew himself up to salute the senior officers in the room. The faces of General Masséna and his commanders turned unsmiling towards Jobert, their own eyes ringed with the signs of fatigue. 'Tell me of Ponte di Nava, Captain Jobert.'

'I have drawn a sketch in my notepad, sir. The Tanaro River runs west to east with banks one to two metres high, the river runs high and fast with snow melt, perhaps one metre deep and ten metres wide.

'The north-running road winds down from Nava to the bridge. The bridge is stone, wide enough for two carts and is quite high above the level of the Tanaro, perhaps three to four metres. Once the road crosses the bridge, it branches at a T-intersection inside the village.

'The majority of the village of Ponte di Nava lies on the northern bank. There are several two storey stone buildings in the village, with a few timber homes on the southern bank. There is a row of stone buildings behind the main street, perhaps accessed by a rear lane running parallel to the east-west road.'

'You have given me a good feel for the town.' Masséna rubbed his eyes. 'What of the enemy, Jobert?'

'A Hungarian battalion, sir, Austrians in tight blue breeches, occupy the town. Two companies skirmished on the southern bank, two companies worked east and west of the bridge on the far northern bank. Another two companies were sighted on the slopes to the rear of the town.

'In the centre of the town, at the T-intersection, there are three six-pounders, with dozens of their brown-jacketed artillerymen. The battery stands in a compressed front over one hundred metres beyond the bridge. All three are laid to cover the bridge.'

Masséna squinted at Jobert. 'Six-pounders? You feel quite certain?'

'I know Austrian six-pounders from Valmy and Jemappes, sir.'

'Were you able to identify the Austrian battalion's own battery, a pair of three-pounders?'

'No, we were not, sir.'

'Anywhere to site our guns?'

Jobert blinked away his fatigue. 'There is a small apron perhaps two hundred metres from the outer buildings, three hundred metres from the bridge that will accommodate three to four guns of the battery.'

Masséna snorted. 'Our four-pounders place themselves four hundred metres across the bridge from the enemy's six-pounders?' Masséna's eyes darted across the page from Jobert's notebook and the maps that covered the table to the assembled commanders in the smoky, stuffy room. 'Gentlemen, what I desire more than the bridge itself is the road east to Ormea. When I look at Jobert's sketch I feel the 16th Légère has three options. One, to conduct a frontal assault over the bridge into the mouths of the enemy's guns. Two, to assault across the river on the right, Ormea-side of the bridge. Jobert, can you describe the ground for this easterly, or north-easterly, approach?'

'We found no paths that allow that approach, sir. Except to go down beneath the bridge into the river and cross under the fire of the Austrian left.'

'Very well, what of the left approach on the western, or Briga Alta side, of the bridge?'

'There are difficult goat tracks on that side. Much of the time the tracks move under such low vegetation that crawling on hands and knees is required. Hence my state of dress. But there may be a fourth option, sir.'

'Indeed?'

'We found more goat tracks going further west along the southern bank for three hundred metres. The tracks become footpaths allowing a man to stand. The footpaths arrive at a simple ford allowing men, but not horses, passage across the river near a hamlet with a chapel. The chapel stands on the Briga Alta road about four hundred metres west of the T-intersection. One kilometre further west we found a horse-capable ford.'

'On any other piece of ground, for a divisional flanking man-oeuvre, quite simple to achieve. But here? Allow me to reflect on that option, thank you, Jobert.'

Dismissed, Jobert shuffled back into the shadows and stood beside Colonel Morin and Masséna's other commanders.

Masséna turned to his lead regimental commander, the commander of the 16th Légère. 'Colonel, your thoughts at this stage?'

'I have two battalions at your immediate disposal, sir. With what is known, and with the intent of minimising exposure to the Austrian battery laid across the bridge, I will secure the southern bank of the Tanaro. I will concentrate all the sappers from my regiment to clear these western tracks, allowing one battalion descent into the river to assault the town from the west. Once a foothold on the far bank is achieved, I will send my second battalion, under the bridge as Jobert suggests, and seek a way to cross on the eastern flank.'

Masséna rocked his head as he evaluated the plan, then looked up to his artillery captain. 'Captain, how will your guns support the infantry assault?'

'I, too, seek to minimise the exposure of our guns to Austrian fire. I will unlimber the four field guns to support the assault into the southern outskirts. I will then push the guns forward, tuck them in behind the buildings and gain crossfire onto the stone buildings on the far bank thus supporting the infantry's movement across the river. I will site my pair of howitzers to target the rear of the village where the enemy's reserves will shelter.'

'Gentlemen, I feel exceedingly confident.' Masséna's eyes burned with confidence. 'The assault is to commence at midday.'

In the smoky shadows, Morin spun to face Jobert. 'Jobert, gather Voreille's troop tonight. At first light follow these footpaths you have discovered down to this chapel and assemble on the far bank. Locate yourself there by midday when the infantry assault.'

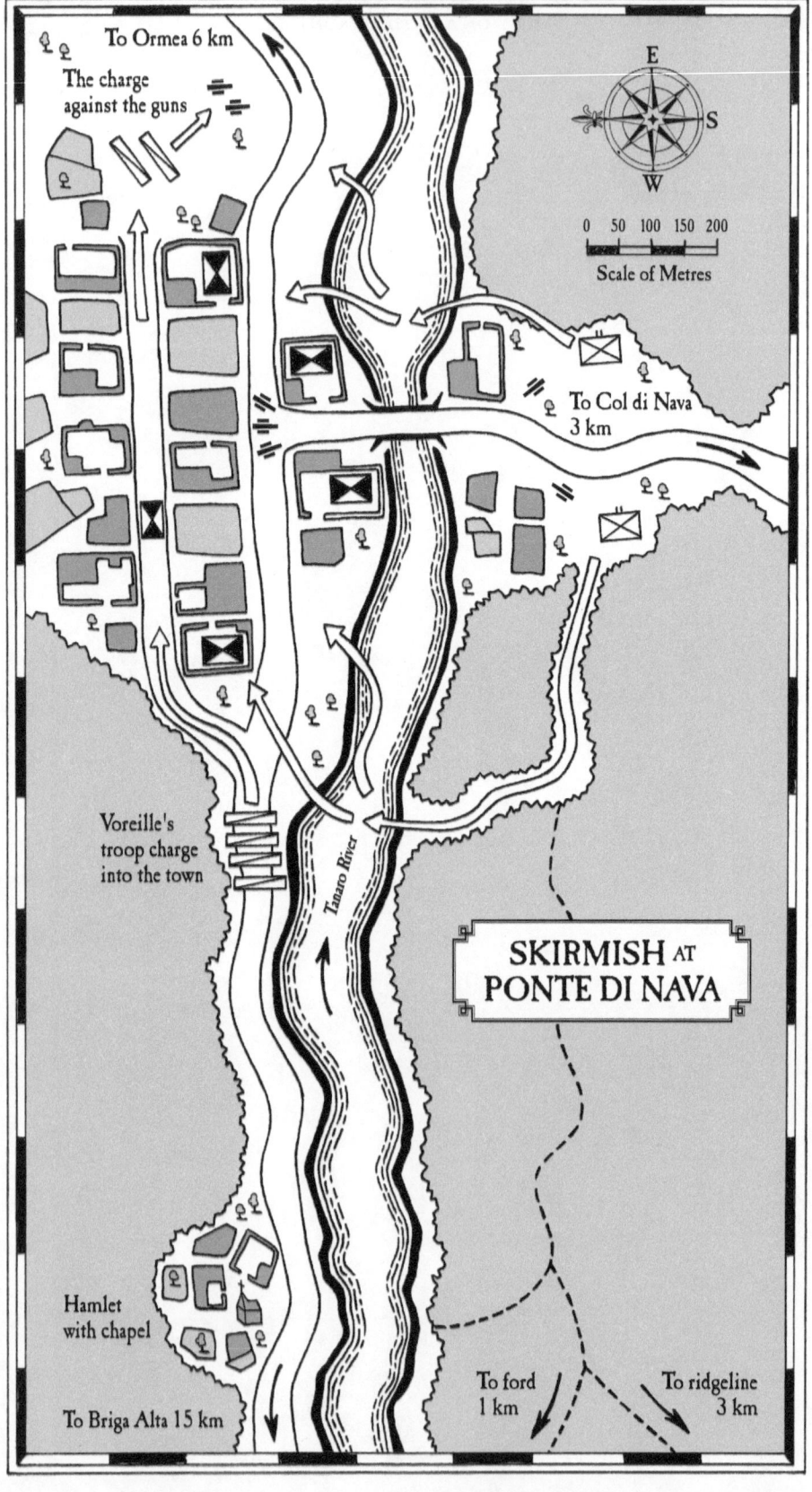

To Ormea 6 km

The charge
against the guns

To Col di Nava
3 km

Voreille's
troop charge
into the town

Tanaro River

SKIRMISH AT
PONTE DI NAVA

Hamlet
with chapel

To Briga Alta 15 km

To ford
1 km

To ridgeline
3 km

E
S
W

0 50 100 150 200
Scale of Metres

Chapter Five
April 1794, Battle of Ponte di Nava

Jobert, Moench, Pultiere and three chasseurs descended the paths of gluggy sand, winding through the drooping pine branches, heavy with early morning rain. Midway down the flanks of Mount Succarello, a line of sheer granite cliffs divided the upper and lower slopes. Tight ravines allowed the ancient forest path to link the higher ridgeline with the Tanaro River below. As Jobert's foot patrol emerged into the heavily vegetated lower slopes, they heard distinct musketry, probably the clash of the skirmishers, over one thousand metres to the east. As they continued to descend, the gurgling of the Tanaro River, increasingly heard but not yet seen, drowned out the sporadic fire.

If patrolling the Tanaro's banks yesterday was tiring for the chasseurs, it had become an even longer night.

Once Morin obtained Masséna's permission for the venture, it took three long hours for the chasseurs to hand over the piquet line to a company of light infantry. A two-hour, pitch-black climb followed, in freezing light rain, back up to the village of Nava. There was a great deal of midnight movement within Nava as the two 16th Légère battalions prepared for the morning's assault. Further on to the farms above the Col di Nava, the march was achieved more easily as the roads were clear of infantry.

The chasseurs had less than two hours rest before retightening girths. Then, one by one, each man leading his horse, with packhorses and remounts of the forward dismounted patrol following, they stumbled along the faint footpath into the mist-enshrouded pine forest.

As a general rule, a horse could traverse terrain where a man could walk without requiring his hands to assist him. Once a man needed to reach out and scramble over logs and boulders or climb a slope, the terrain was regarded impassable for horses. Today's path allowed men to walk and lead horses, yet the progress of the single file of men and horses down the rocky, twisting slope was tedious.

Well in advance of the horse column, the lead chasseurs signalled to Jobert that the river was in sight. Above the rushing current in the river, an intense fusillade was soon followed by the boom of artillery. Jobert opened his watch. Twelve o'clock. He looked up to see the scouts' signal and waved for them to continue.

As Pultiere's patrol descended the bank and waded into the freezing stream, musketoons and cartridge boxes held high, the individual explosions of cannon fire echoed up the valley. As the sodden troopers waved from the northern bank that all was well, the head of the horse-column emerged from the straggling thorns lining the forest edge.

It took another hour to bring the horses down the paths, allow each to drink and cross to the other side.

From the road on the northern bank, sharing a crust of bread with Morin, Chabenac and Moench, Jobert looked up the flanks of Mount Succarello they had just descended and marvelled at the thick pines and the massive cliffs they had meandered through.

The cannonade intensified above the rolling musketry.

'Our artillery has joined the chorus,' said Morin, taking the opportunity to empty his boots of river water. 'Jobert, march east to the sound of the guns. I expect we will find elements of the 16th Légère on the outskirts in the process of flanking the village.'

Jobert turned to his assembled commanders. 'Pultiere, lead us the one thousand metres to the chapel. Sergeant Major, secure the chapel for our packhorse section. Voreille, with four hundred metres to the village of Ponte di Nava, we will take a dismounted patrol forward to assess. Mount, musketoons ready, column of fours, trot, march!'

The troop column trotted one thousand metres to the chapel in under ten minutes. The sound of gun and musket fire from the village intensified despite the clatter of over two hundred hooves on the gravel road. The smoke of spent powder, smelling of sulphur, wafted up the riverbed, overcoming the mist clinging just above the roaring torrent.

The act of securing the hamlet in which the small stone chapel sat was swift. The few local peasants anxious of the fighting to the east, scurried terrified indoors when the column of horsemen entered their hamlet from the west.

Jobert drew his sabre and took a silver-inlaid cavalry pistol from his saddle holsters. 'Voreille, Pultiere, dismount a section patrol and follow me.'

Creeping further down the verges of the road, the chasseurs soon connected with a company of light infantry, whereupon they were directed to an elderly captain with a thick, drooping moustache.

'Good afternoon, captain,' Morin introduced himself. 'What

is your situation? My chasseurs are keen to join the fight.'

The infantry officer saluted. 'Our battalion is struggling to cross the river under Austrian musket fire from the village's western buildings. Within the riverbanks, we are under their guns. My company is to hold the road. I will take you to an observation position of the Austrian defence.'

The chasseur patrol moved forward to the edge of the infantry defensive perimeter hugging the tree-lined strip between road and riverbank.

The captain, kneeling amongst a knot of saturated fusiliers, indicated towards the western outskirts of Ponte di Nava. 'As you see, sir, the kaiserlik guns cover the main road entering the town from the south, the east and the west. You see their ammunition caissons tucked into the lanes between the build-ings. Their guns are well fed.

'My sister companies throw themselves at the buildings full of kaiserliks fusiliers. We are receiving crossfire from the build-ings at the rear of the village. You see down the rear lane how the Austrians are transferring more of their companies to this side of the village. My chief of battalion has sent word to our other eastern battalion that the Austrians are shifting their reserves to the west. Thus, our sister battalion begins the assault to the Ormea-side of the bridge.'

As stray musket balls zipped unseen overhead, Morin, Jobert, Chabenac and Voreille considered, with their telescopes, the Austrian six-pounders firing south across the bridge. Morin and Jobert collapsed their glasses and exchanged determined glances. Chabenac and Voreille put away their telescope with pensive looks.

'I am not sure there is anything a body of cavalry can achieve here, sir,' said the grizzled infantryman. 'Surely you will not charge the guns?'

'No, not directly,' said Morin, then turning to Jobert, 'but if we moved down the lane behind the road, would it not threaten their guns? Would it cause their battery to depart?'

'But, sir,' said the infantry captain, 'that lane is a crush of kaiserliks moving to this end of the town. What is more, our howitzers now have the range to the lane with their shells.'

'My friend,' said Jobert, 'if you were marching your company in column down a tight lane, would you accept a charge by horse? For that is what we will do. May I request your company discharge a fusillade as we come up to provide a modicum of concealment prior to us dashing across to the rear lane?'

The veteran captain considered the grimly confident faces around him. Only Moench, dutifully trailing Jobert, continued to stare at the smoke-enveloped village with blinking trepidation.

'There we have it,' said Morin. 'Chabenac, take a message to the commander of the 16th Légère and the battery commander that I lead a troop of chasseurs into the rear of the town with the intent of threatening the guns.'

Chabenac looked down into the freezing river with a grimace.

Morin, Jobert and the patrol returned to the waiting chasseurs.

'Mount!' called Jobert, swinging into Rouge's saddle. 'Commanders in! Voreille, lead Pultiere's platoon into the rear lane behind myself and Colonel Morin. Sergeant Major, leave the section with the packhorses here. Move forward as we advance further into the village.'

'Regimental surgeon,' added Morin, 'yourself and the sergeant veterinarian are to accompany Sergeant Major Koschak forward.'

'2nd Company, sabres!' Jobert gathered his reins. 'Give point, boys. Parry the bayonets to slice fingers and faces. Do not slash. On me! Trot, march!'

The men from the 16th Légère company scrambled to the side of the road and gawped in awe as the column surged forward. As the chasseurs passed, the light infantry cheered. The explosion of infantry muskets around the horses was deafening. The resultant gun smoke was trapped within the roadside trees and pressed low due to restrictions of the lane in the valley.

'Moench, sound *Charge!*' The trumpet blared the insistent call.

The thunder of two hundred hooves was distinct against the violent eruptions of musketry.

With a leap, Rouge extended into a gallop. Morin and Jobert covered the two hundred metres from the French lines to the smoke-engulfed village in less than fifteen seconds. Although the Austrian infantry were protected within the stone buildings, they were unable to produce any devastating volleys. In column of fours, Voreille's fifty-man troop was less than one hundred metres long. As the last man, Neilage entered the town ten seconds after Morin and Jobert.

Although a few Austrian muskets fired at the galloping horsemen erupting from the thick smoke, the screams of alarm spread through the town sharply enough. Behind Neilage, a full-throated roar from the blue-jacketed infantry erupted as companies struggled up the riverbank to charge in the wake of the green-clad horsemen.

Once in the rear lane, Jobert let the press of a company of Austrian fusiliers check Rouge's stride.

At the head of the column, the company commander and his drummer disappeared beneath Rouge's flashing hooves. The column was six men wide, each astonished face framed by the squat leather helmet and the white powdered curls above the ears, the open mouths under black moustaches.

The Austrians were not able to bring their muskets to the ready position before Jobert was slicing through the first face.

Jobert leant forward in the saddle, his vulnerable groin protected by his holsters, rolled cape and canvas horse rug, covered in thick sheepskin, with sabre arm outstretched, elbow locked, blade to the right. Jobert screamed, teeth bared, as Rouge's ploughing momentum drove the steady blade across ears, eyes and cheeks deeper into the column.

Homes on high terraces, accessed by steps, were on the left side as they pressed east down the lane. Stairs descended the tight lanes between tall stone buildings on the right. The white-jacketed, blue-trousered Hungarian fusiliers roared at each other, and soon the column disappeared down the lanes, between the buildings fronting the river, towards the main road.

Jobert's head jerked up as a demonic squeal sounded just ahead of him. A black blur plunged amongst the packed fusiliers. The Austrians recoiled to avoid a French howitzer shell hissing at their feet.

Within the shell, the quickmatch fuse found the packed powder at the shell's centre. The resulting explosion felled as many men with its blast, as did the shell's thin iron case fragmenting into hundreds of spinning blades. Receiving the full blast, over a dozen men were scythed down in an instant. The smoke-filled gap allowed others to turn, slip on the wounded and run.

In the road below, between the buildings, the grey-jacketed artillery drivers were yelling. They slashed at their teams to move the caissons and limbers out of the infantry crush. The brown-jacketed artillerymen started to limber the guns in response.

With three stone buildings on his right and two timber houses on his left, Jobert would soon be clear of the lane and on the eastern side of the village.

Another fizzing shell squealed into the horsemen somewhere behind Jobert.

The explosion caused long groans from the wounded horses. Jobert parried a bayonet then twisted to look back on Pultiere's platoon. Pultiere and Voreille were just behind him, with white-faced Moench, trumpet in hand, sabre swinging on his sword knot, sandwiched between them. 'Voreille! Pultiere! On me!'

'Eyes front, sir!'

Rouge shuddered, reared and screamed.

Jobert rolled his wrist over to deliver a quick cut at a young, bewildered face. The blade bit into flesh, the weight of the falling soldier taking Jobert's blade back behind him as Rouge lurched forward. Jobert felt the blade come free, and he swung his sabre in a practised motion to 'give point' once more.

Rouge hesitated to move forward. Jobert urged him with knees and heels. Rouge bounded forward into a canter with a deep groan.

The grunting and swearing of the soldiers driving the twenty-four horses of the Austrian half-battery were clear to Jobert as he passed the final laneway beside the last stone building in the village.

Two rapid explosions reverberated. A cloud of gun smoke obscured the end of the rear laneway.

Who? The battalion's own three-pounders? Where? Jobert emerged from the last buildings on the rear lane and looked down the slope towards the roaring river.

Through the smoke haze, the six teams of the enemy's six-pounders defined the road as they dashed east to Ormea. Beyond the frantic gun teams, a solid-white, three rank fire line of Austrian fusiliers on the verge of the road fired down into the river, as companies of the 16th Légère's first battalion struggled across the freezing torrent. Incessant screaming filled the lulls between the fusillades.

Two more violent explosions caused Rouge to throw his head and sink back on his haunches.

On a terrace just above the road but below Jobert, the Austrian battalion's own two three-pounder guns fired across the river towards buildings on the southern bank. Jobert saw artillery drivers and Hungarian fusiliers in support of the guns pointing up towards the horsemen forming two ranks behind him.

Where is Morin? Surely I must charge? To fortify his commitment, Jobert extended his blade towards the two cannon and the twenty-odd men crewing them. 'Voreille, Pultiere, form column of platoon, trot, march!' Jobert's voice was hoarse due to the smoke. Moench pressed his grey gelding in beside Jobert. 'Moench, sound *Charge!*'

The artillerymen were one hundred metres from the chasseurs' line. The supporting infantry heaved to wheel the guns' trails around and face the cavalry threat above them. The gunners bawled at each other as they loaded their guns while the barrels were moving. The closest gun loaded ball. The farthest loaded canister. Neither crew had time to load ball and case to be 'double-shotted'.

With the crazed howl of madmen, the chasseurs spurred their agitated, resistant horses down the steep slope.

The gun commanders adjusted the rear-screws to elevate their barrels. Their barrels were too low, their targets too high.

The rocks on the slope had the horses dropping their heads to pick their way at the trot. Rouge was stepping short, despite Jobert's urging thighs.

Jobert watched the first gun's firer step forward with his smouldering portfire. Jobert dropped his sword onto his sword knot and swept up his musketoon.

The closest gun fired at fifty metres to the chasseurs' line. Jobert saw the black streak ricochet, covering him in stinging spray of gravel and powder, before howling past his right boot.

Cacophony. Muskets firing. Hooves striking. Torrent splashing. Men screaming. Screaming in frustration. Screaming in pain. Twenty metres.

The Austrian ventman took his finger off the vent of the second gun, the firing tube was thrust into the breech vent. The Austrian firer touched his portfire's quickmatch to the smouldering slowmatch wrapped on the nearby linstock. The quickmatch sputtered into life.

Jobert cocked and shouldered his musketoon. *Rouge, you prick, extend your trot if you will not canter.*

In his peripheral vision Jobert glimpsed an artillery officer, bicorne, brown tailcoat, yellow waist sash, raise his pistol at Jobert. To the side of the gun the artillery firer swung his portfire towards the powder-packed firing tube extending from the vent.

At ten metres, Jobert fired at the gunner's chest.

In that moment, his face seared in excruciating pain. His vision lost to a burst of red light.

The cannon roared just beyond his right stirrup.

Jobert found himself blind on a swerving horse. Habit caused him to drop his musketoon onto his cross belt and shorten his reins. Rouge moved sideways beneath him. In a well-practised movement, Jobert flicked his wrist to swing the tip of his sabre onto his boot to catch the grip. All around him there was screaming.

'Cut the pricks down!' shrieked Pultiere. 'Cut them all down!'

Rouge had stopped moving. Jobert stood still in the middle of a melee. *Oh shit, I cannot open my eyelids.* Fire raced down the side of his cheeks. Blood filled his mouth. Jobert's guts churned with nausea.

'Moench, sound *Rally!* Moench?' He pressed his left gloved hand to his eyebrow and peeled open his left eye. The pain was so intense he vomited down his chest.

All he saw were green-clad men, mounted and dismounted,

hacking brown and white jackets and bleeding meat. The thwack of steel crunched on bone and on steel. The grunts of labouring men, the blowing of terrified horses. The thud of bodies, man and horse, ramming each other out of the way. The panting moans of the wounded and those being carved.

'On me!' someone called nearby.

Neilage? Somewhere. 'Neilage! Neilage?'

Jobert dropped his sword and used both hands to open his left eye. His right eye was in extreme pain. Rouge stood quite still the whole time, and only took steps as he was buffeted by the movement of other horses.

Bredieux called from somewhere under him. 'Lieutenant Neilage is forward, sir.'

'Bredieux! What is happening? I cannot see.'

'Stay where you are, sir. You have a face wound. You are safe where you are. Our infantry are pushing through.'

Jobert groaned through the pain. He looked down the slope to the writhing bodies on the road and the river tumbling blue-jacketed bodies in pink-tinged waves as the water pulsed over the rocks beneath.

A line of mounted chasseurs stood guard on two Austrian ammunition caissons, Morin and Neilage at their head. Their immobility in sharp contrast to the dismounted mayhem swirling on the road beyond them.

French infantry scrambled up the banks and onto the road. White-jacketed Austrians were firing, or scrambling along the road further down the valley, or parrying French thrusts with their bayonets.

Jobert pressed Rouge to pivot so he could look up the hill, but Rouge resisted the command. Jobert twisted in his saddle and peered up the slope they had charged down.

The ground around the silent guns was strewn with blood, shit and brown cloth. Around the guns sat, or walked, blood-soaked chasseurs, their horses standing unattended, reins hanging in the mud, shuffling together in their discomfort. Voreille, both pistols in hand, held back chasseurs keen to butcher the unarmed, grey-jacketed artillery drivers. Sergeant Pultiere was identifiable as one of the few still walking among the dead and wounded with his sabre. With malicious method, he plunged his sabre into every Austrian corpse with a two-handed action.

At the mouth of the guns Jobert struggled to make out a wide mound of steaming meat and brown fur. His strained vision was dizzying. Beyond the steaming mounds, lay a large grey sack covering horses' legs.

'Bredieux! Bredieux?' Jobert rasped a spray of blood.

'Sergeant Bredieux is ... fuck, sir, dismount,' said Duque close by.

'Duque, I cannot see.'

'You do not need to see to dismount.'

With a tight grip on his saddle, Jobert swung down beside Rouge.

'Duque, I need to piss, I cannot hold it.'

'You do not need to see to piss either. Go on, I have you.'

Jobert was barely able to reach into his underdrawers to pull himself clear of his breeches when he urinated, due to the shock, down his own leg.

'Duque, who is in command? What has happened to the troop? Are we safe? Where are the fucking kaiserliks? The fucking pain ... I cannot think.'

'Sir, listen.' Duque gripped Jobert's shoulder and shook him firmly. 'We have the village. The enemy have gone. Our infantry has formed line to hold the Ormea road. Colonel Morin and Lieutenant Neilage have Sergeant Bredieux's platoon formed up to support the infantry. Lieutenant Voreille is regathering Sergeant Pultiere's platoon.'

Jobert faded with shock. 'Duque! Duque?'

'I am here, sir. Rouge has taken a bayonet in the chest.'

Jobert peeled his left eye open. He gagged at the nausea his action created. Jobert's vision swam, but he made out a flap of Rouge's flesh, the size of two hands together, hanging from Rouge's chest. Duque was struggling to lift the horses' head and examine the wound.

Jobert pressed his forehead to his horse's withers. *Not Rouge, not today.* 'He caught it in the street. He was a bastard to force into the trot down the slope.'

Duque grunted in response, as he attempted to strap Rouge's wound with a roll of bandage from the portmanteau at the rear of Jobert's saddle.

'Corporal Duque,' said Koschak from somewhere nearby, 'will Rouge return to camp or —'

'Absolutely yes, Sergeant Major. I will lead him to camp.'

'Thank you, Duque.' Jobert felt his tears dribble into his cheek wound.

'Ooh, fuck, sir! That is a nasty one,' said Koschak.

'Who? Me or Rouge? What is my wound? I cannot see.'

Koschak twisted Jobert's face in his gloved hands and removed Jobert's helmet. Jobert moaned as a pulse of pain surged into his right temple now that his scalp was free of the helmet's headband.

'Your face has burst open under your right eye,' said Koschak, 'and the whole side of your head is swollen. That is why you cannot see.' Koschak hefted Jobert's bent musketoon hanging on his cross belt. Jobert squinted to see the indent in the barrel.

'Did it misfire?' asked Jobert.

'No, the barrel was struck by a ball.'

'I nearly had the second gun's firer. I got my shot off, but some prick's shot has gone wide, hit my barrel, kicked the musketoon into my face.'

'That will do it. Just a moment, sir, I need to provide some soldierly guidance. Sergeant Pultiere! Stop that bullshit and come here now! Oh, for fuck's sake man, wipe the bastard of a thing before you return it to the scabbard.'

Pultiere quivered with anger, tears carving patterns down his grime-encased face. 'Those arseholes slaughtered my platoon, Sergeant Major.'

'Shut up, Sergeant Pultiere, and listen. One, get your men on their feet and gather your horses. Two, gather both limber and caisson teams, any loose horses and all their drivers. All ten drivers, hear me, Sergeant? I will remove one of your fingers for any one of those grey-jacketed cocks who fails to arrive in camp tonight.' Koschak pumped two thick fingers into Pultiere's broad chest.

'Yes, Sergeant Major.'

'Now, have you searched that mess to see if there is anyone alive? Wheel the limbers around to pick up our boys and strip the horses of all saddlery and equipment.'

Jobert spat blood. 'And Pultiere, strip the kaiserlik gunners of their satchels and purses.'

Pultiere stumbled away to roar oaths at his stunned men.

'Sergeant Major,' said Jobert, 'the first gun fired shot and the second fired canister. What hit us? Take me there.'

Koschak nodded towards Vert besides Duque's mount. 'Duque, help me get him up.' Koschak remounted his bay warhorse and took one of Vert's reins and led Jobert back to the muzzles of the guns.

Jobert spat continuously into his left hand to create enough moisture to clean the crusty serum from his left eye.

As they approached the macabre scene, Jobert watched the company farrier and the sergeant veterinarian shoot four wounded horses with their pistols. Standing horses folded with a great wheeze. The lying horses quivered momentarily after the shot, then relaxed, their service to the Republic complete.

'The canister has taken about seven in the front rank, about twenty metres out from the gun's muzzle,' said Koschak. 'It looks as if three men were taken by the blast. Another four wounded are being loaded onto the limbers.'

As chasseurs lifted the torn body of Faure, Jobert involuntarily clenched his jaw to suppress a groan, only to release a punch of pain throughout his head and throat. One chasseur vomited as Faure was settled onto the artillery limber.

The regimental surgeon turned from supervising the lifting of the crushed and moaning bodies from beneath the peeled horse carcasses to peer up at Jobert's bleeding face. 'Captain Jobert, sir, there are a number of minor wounds such as yours, but the four here are serious. Two will not survive long. I will return to the chapel and attend to the other three or four.'

'If I had shot my man the gun would not have fired,' said Jobert.

'Take him to camp, Duque,' said Koschak. 'Follow Lieutenant Voreille and Pultiere's limbers. I will follow up with Bredieux's platoon.'

Jobert now saw a grey corpse crumpled in on itself like a pair of folded socks, the front hooves scarcely emerging from the headless chest. 'Duque, is that Moench's horse?'

'It took that ball in the chest.'

'Moench?'

'He is walking, but he is hurting. Moench was rolled up and stepped on as everybody rode over him. His worst injury is his broken fiddle.'

The follow-on French companies were marching into and through Ponte di Nava. Duque, leading Rouge and Jobert mounted on Vert, picked his way through the crowded main road at the tail of Pultiere's Austrian prisoners.

Surrounded by an escort of Huin's chasseurs, four limbered French four-pounder crews yelled and whipped their way forward. As an old habit, Jobert always looked to the brands on the artillery horses left, or nearside, shoulders to determine if the animal was from his grandfather's farm. But in this afternoon's watery sunshine Jobert's vision lurched in a sickening blur.

Nearly two thousand men, Austrian and French, moved, or lay motionless, throughout Ponte di Nava. Men crumpled to sit, slouched to piss, or squatted to shit wherever they found themselves. The wounded writhed, whimpered and grasped. The dead were flipped over to have their possessions rifled. Water in the canteens of the dead and wounded held the greatest value.

Officers, both commissioned and non-commissioned, bellowed in French, German or Hungarian to overcome the stupor that follows combat, to get men moving, to re-establish order, to recover the wounded, to prepare for counterattack.

Columns of prisoners stripped of their jackets, shirts, satchels and shoes shuffled towards the bridge. Blue-jacketed captors laughed at the spoils bulging from their backpacks. Prisoners carried both French and Austrian wounded. The wounded slouched against the two prisoners who held two muskets as a makeshift chair.

Abandoned horses stood trembling, their noses pressed to comforting flanks. Some with broken legs swinging within the skin's envelope. Some adjusted their feet entangled in the loops of their own intestines.

Local people huddled in family groups in doorways.

Light infantrymen, alone or in pairs, ducked in and out of broken doors ransacking the homes and stores.

Breaking jars and bottles. Swearing.

The occasional shot was fired.

A dog barked. Toddlers bawled. A woman screamed.

Chapter Six

Jobert hissed in agony through his spasming throat. To grit his teeth was unbearable.

He dispersed the excruciating pain by clenching every muscle in his body. The sergeant veterinarian and the regimental surgeon adjusted their stance as Jobert shifted their weight with his straining arms. Koschak leant his muscular bulk onto Jobert's ankles as Jobert arched his spine and dug his spurs into the dirt.

Being pinned, the queasy childhood memories pulsed though him remembering the castration of colts. Jobert expelled the reminiscence with a groan, his eyes popping to focus on the grey clouds above.

Duque removed his fingers from Jobert split cheek, just under his right eye. Jobert gasped for breath and gathered his frayed willpower to not soil himself.

'I feel the fractured cheekbone, sir,' said Duque looking up at the regimental surgeon, 'but I cannot feel any bone splinters.'

'Well done, Duque,' said the surgeon. 'Then clean the wound and dress it.'

'I have brandy and a shaving brush,' said Duque, holding up the items.

'Just the thing. Hold on, Jobert, this will sting like the devil.'

Choking on his scream, Jobert's eyes bulged from their sockets as he drove the back of his skull into the blankets on which he lay, as Duque dribbled brandy into his wound. His fingers dug deep into his thighs as the bristles of the shaving brush flicked away the embedded grit. When Duque finished, Jobert's breathing was laboured and tears ran down his cheeks.

'Excuse me, gentlemen, I need to stretch my legs.' Jobert staggered away and braced himself against a tree to urinate.

'Hurry up, Jobert, we have not finished with you,' said the surgeon. 'Where did you learn your skills, Duque?'

'I am most interested in healing injured horses, sir. Captain Jobert's uncle was a sergeant veterinarian and is most adamant about vinegar, soap or brandy when handling horses' wounds, difficult births and castration. We seem to have the best healing results in the valley.'

'There are certainly some interesting papers and anecdotes about it all. Have you considered studying the veterinary arts at Alfort?'

Duque squinted at the suggestion.

'As for your men, Jobert,' said the surgeon, 'you lost a man on the way into the town. You have three musket ball wounds, of which only one required amputation. Whilst in the lane, your men received six minor bayonet wounds to thighs and arms. All sewn and dressed. No thrusts to anyone's belly, which is pleasing. The howitzer shell caught only the horses. Your trumpeter, whose horse was felled by the ball, is badly bruised but nothing broken.

'The canister spread across seven men in the front rank. That the gun was unable to elevate further saved the second rank. Three perished in the blast. Two on either side of the three,

Arbod and Saint-Dizier, are in a bad way, sorry, and will not last the next two days. The two outer men received wounds to the lower arms and leg on the side closest to the muzzle. I have amputated Chasseur Faure's arm above the elbow, his leg above the knee. The other fellow had clean fractures and was splinted. He will return to the company in two months. Now, what happened to you?'

'I was aiming my musketoon when I was shot at,' said Jobert. 'My musketoon shows that it was hit in the barrel. That kicked the weapon into my face.'

'Indeed, you have a fractured cheekbone, but no splintered bone and the wound is clean. Can your tongue feel any loose teeth?'

Jobert shook his head. *I hurt too fucking much to find out.*

'Shall I apply the hashish oil and honey now, sir?' asked Duque, digging into his saddle portmanteau.

'You carry laudanum and honey?' asked the surgeon.

'The captain's private stock, sir.'

'We cannot suture while it is so swollen. Allow the swelling to reduce for a day or two. Keep the wound covered in honey and a boiled bandage. I want to suture the wound, but I am needed forward with 5th Company.'

'Corporal Duque can sew him, sir,' said the sergeant veterinarian. 'You should see his needlework on Captain Jobert's horse.'

'How many horses have you sutured, Duque?' asked the surgeon.

'That horse is my fourth.'

'Are you happy with that, Jobert?'

Jobert shrugged.

'If you sew him, Duque,' said the surgeon, 'lie him down and sew him sitting above his head, otherwise if he sits while you stitch, as you would a horse, you will pull the skin unevenly. No matter how much pain he says he is in, give him only two drops of laudanum in his tea per night before bed, and no more.'

'I now need to brace for Duque's needlework tomorrow?' asked Jobert.

'My dear fellow,' said the regimental surgeon, 'the tickle from stitching is the least of your worries. Your immediate threat is fever. If Duque has cleaned your wound and applied honey, all bodes well.'

The throbbing pain in Jobert's swaddled face was so intense he could not sleep. Unsettled that there was nothing to alleviate Rouge's sutured chest, Jobert distracted himself by sitting with the dying and the wounded. Pultiere's platoon had built a fire for their dying and wounded mates, the men visiting as their duties allowed. By late into the evening, only Jobert and Duque remained with the twelve wounded.

Corporal Arbod was hit by the canister blast. As one of the better horsemen upon his arrival in the regiment over a year ago, Jobert liked young Arbod. Over those thirteen months, Jobert, Arbod and a few hand-picked others had schooled the poorer horses to improve their movements. Now, Jobert held Arbod's hand as he died, as Duque dribbled hashish oil mixed with goat's milk into Arbod's throat. The left side of Arbod's face and chest was flayed and his jaw blown away. Arbod was thrown so far by the cannon's blast that his spine and ribs had broken. His breathing was shallow and difficult against the bubbles of mucous.

The opium relaxed the injured chasseur. Duque shifted with discomfort as he packed away his medicines in a captured

Austrian satchel.

Jobert knew Duque too well. 'What is it?'

'The regimental surgeon said I might consider Alfort?' Duque looked up slowly and observed Jobert's reaction.

'Yes, of course. You would make an excellent veterinarian. Why ever not?'

'Your uncle had said at Christmas it is worth reflection. He said it was a four-year course of study.'

'I imagine, if your application was successful, entry to the School would be July or August next year. Make the commitment, Duque. I know you will excel. I will submit your application to Lieutenant Colonel Spiccard on our return to Pieve di Teco. Yes?'

Duque stood and looked across to the next campfire and the soldiers who awaited his evening ministrations.

'Yes, I suppose.'

Jobert and Koschak listened to the muted voices of the sentries moving amongst the horses.

'Were the wounded bathed and their underwear washed today?' asked Jobert.

'Yes, sir, their shirts and drawers were dry in time for the sunset burials.'

Jobert's face tightened at the memory of Arbod's, Faure's and Saint-Dizier's naked corpses being lowered into the shallow graves.

Jobert hung his head. 'Did I ... go too far?'

'When?' Koschak hunched over the campfire's flames and poked the embers with a long stick. 'In Toulon, when we stole canvas for our horses, or saved a fleet? When we bullshitted our way behind a kaiserlik fire line and captured them? Or the other day when we caused one battery to flee and captured another, saving a battalion from destruction?' Koschak swept his baleful green eyes from his intense inspection of the meagre flames to pierce Jobert's melancholy. 'You have done nothing that we are ashamed of.'

Corporal Duval, the sentry commander, ducked under a tent line and into the dull glow. 'Just reporting all clear, Sergeant Major.'

Over the wind in the pines and the churning of the River Tanaro, two horses screamed from the horse lines, their hooves pounding as they kicked out at each other in the dark. The three men's heads spun towards the ruckus.

'Piss off, Duval, it is never all clear,' said Koschak. 'Nine days ago, on the bridge outside Oneglia, an Austrian corporal reported "All clear", moments before 5th Company charged over the hill. A week ago, in the rain above a bridge, another Austrian reported "All clear", only to look up and see you, Colonel Morin and Captain Jobert trotting forward. Three days ago, in the morning's mist at Ponte di Nava, some kaiserlik reported "All clear" just before the shots rang out. No, Duval, it is never all clear. If it is silent, then we are threatened with attack. Is it not ideal for an enemy to approach under the squeals and stomps of unsettled horses and the roaring of a narrow river?'

'Yes, Sergeant Major.'

'Which horses are unsettled?'

'When we sited the horse lines, the Austrian teams are tied closer to our horses and now they are bitching.'

'Put one of your sentries amongst them and calm them.' Koschak jerked his head towards the darkness, returning the soldier to his duties.

As Duval stepped back from the wavering fire light into the inky dark, Sergeant Pultiere ambled towards the fire, buckling on his sword belt and rubbing his unshaven jowls to awaken himself for duty. Pultiere snorted back phlegm and swallowed as he buttoned his cape.

Although his gaze remained on the fire's coals and twigs, Jobert's face turned towards Pultiere. 'Fetch me Sergeant Pultiere.'

Pultiere's eyes narrowed at the request and his brow furrowed.

'You heard me,' said Jobert. 'Fetch me the Pultiere who cut down the Marseillaise rebels at Aubagne last year, who rode at my side to encircle two Spanish companies at Sollies, who stood firm at his post in the inferno of Toulon's docks, who brazenly walked his platoon through the middle of an Austrian battalion a week ago. Fetch me that Pultiere.'

Jobert shoved at a burning branch.

'Do not, I say, bring the surly bastard, charading as a sergeant of chasseurs, that is moping around this camp. Not the miserable creature bemoaning the loss of his men. A bruised and limping Moench I accept, bleating about the dents in his trumpet and that his fiddle was crushed. But Pultiere, no! Bring me the Pultiere who led his brave platoon into the mouths of an Austrian battery and saved a trapped battalion from assured destruction.'

The poked embers hissed at their disturbance. Jobert turned stiffly and looked Pultiere in the eye. 'That is the Pultiere we want by our side.'

Pultiere tightened his lips and blinked into the fire. 'I am here now, sir.'

In the morning, three days later, the mist-enshrouded valley exploded with the pounding of drums.

The Tanaro River towns of Ormea and Garessio were secured by Masséna's first infantry brigade. The three thousand men from Masséna's second brigade had crushed in around the river-banks of Ponte di Nava the day before, and now they formed their long columns for the march up to Mount Succarello.

Jobert formed 2nd Company on parade to salute the column as it proceeded on the next phase of the operation. The steepness of the slopes around the chapel and its village restricted 2nd Company to a dismounted parade on the terraces above the road.

With Jobert's 2nd Company earmarked for rearwards escort duty, and 5th Company still holding the French army's eastern outpost line beyond Garessio, troops from the 24th Chasseurs' reserve squadron were called forward. A platoon vedette from 3rd Company led the column. These fresh chasseurs gaped at their regimental brothers on the terraces above the roadway.

Although 2nd Company had bathed and washed their under-clothing, they still looked ragged. Their uniforms, of braided dolman jackets and tight Hungarian breeches were shabby, torn and ill-fitting. The green of the men's uniforms was as grey-brown as Moench's faded dark-orange jacket. The chasseurs' browning cross-belts for their cartridge boxes and musketoon cried out for white pipeclay. Their calf-high boots were dull from immersion in river mud and fireside ash. Their leather helmets were misshapen from the constant river mist and the helmets' crests had descended to mere tufts.

Of greater concern to the passing chasseurs was the sight of the bandaged men, in particular the chasseur who had a lower arm amputated following an Austrian musket ball breaking his forearm.

Now a week since the fight for Ponte di Nava, Jobert remov-ed his bandages for this morning's parade. His face was swollen with a black and yellow bruise, with a livid crimson 'mouth' held together by black thread beneath his slitted right eye.

General Masséna led the brigade column with Deputy of the People Saliceti by his side. Saliceti was a slim, sharp-faced young man, who wore a broadbrimmed hat bedecked with tricolour plumes, and a wide tricolour sash about his waist. Attired in a sober black frock coat, Masséna looked Jobert in the eye and touched the brim of his simple black bicorne in response to Jobert's sword salute. 'How is your company this fine day, Jobert?'

'We are well rested, sir, and eager to continue the advance.'

'Good grief, Masséna,' said Saliceti. 'Here are the heroes of the Republic. Let me address them.'

Both Masséna and Jobert's eyes momentarily locked in a flicker of alarm. Then their eyes jerked elsewhere. *Idiot.* Any expression of concern over another of Saliceti's Jacobin diatribes caused a blaze of embarrassment across Jobert's chest.

Jobert was certainly not allowing this befeathered rainbow to bore his men with the righteousness of the war, the suffering of France's families, the insidious threat of royalists, the delivery of the benighted Piedmontese from the evils of monarchy, et cetera. *I can have that rubbish at any back street theatre in Nice, seated for my troubles and with a bottle of something pleasant no less. Indeed not. 2nd Company has work to do.* Jobert's eyes slid along the three thousand infantry crammed onto the tight roads ready for today's march up Mount Succarello.

'2nd Company,' called Jobert. '*La Marseillaise!*'

'*Arise children of the fatherland,*
The day of glory has arrived,
Against us tyranny's
Bloody standard is raised.'

'Ah, perhaps, citizen-deputy,' said Masséna, 'shall we address the men once we have taken Saorgio. You see how keen the men are to achieve the victory the Committee has asked of them.'

'Listen to the sound in the fields,
The howling of these fearsome soldiers
They are coming into our midst,
To cut the throats of your sons and your women.'

'Yes, citizen-general, forgive my passion.' Saliceti bowed his head. 'I am imbued with martial fervour at the sight of these determined fellows. Yes, let us continue.'

'To arms, citizens,
Form your battalions,
Let's march! Let's march!
Let an impure blood
Water our furrows'

As he pressed his horse forward, Masséna cocked an eyebrow at Jobert in farewell.

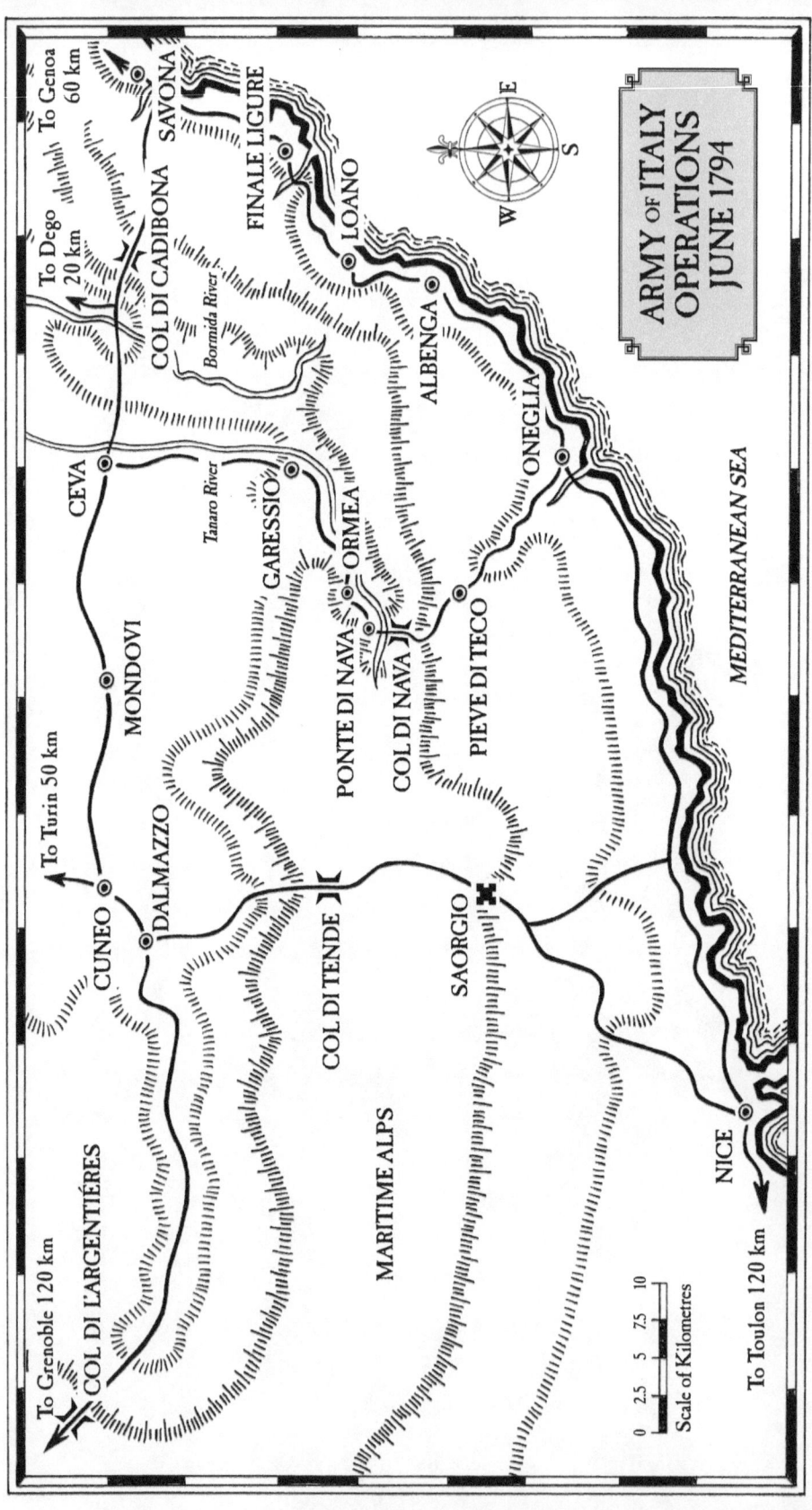

ARMY OF ITALY
OPERATIONS
JUNE 1794

To Genoa 60 km

To Dego 20 km

SAVONA

FINALE LIGURE

COL DI CADIBONA

LOANO

Bormida River

ALBENGA

CEVA

GARESSIO

Tanaro River

ONEGLIA

MONDOVI

ORMEA

PONTE DI NAVA

To Turin 50 km

DALMAZZO

COL DI NAVA

PIEVE DI TECO

CUNEO

COL DI TENDE

SAORGIO

MEDITERRANEAN SEA

MARITIME ALPS

To Grenoble 120 km
COL DI L'ARGENTIÉRES

NICE

To Toulon 120 km

0 2.5 5 7.5 10
Scale of Kilometres

N
W   E
S

Chapter Seven
May - August 1794, Oneglia, Italy

Jobert adjusted his scabbard and sat on a rickety chair within Lieutenant Colonel Spiccard's Oneglia office. The thin curtains pulsed in the fresh coastal breeze. An orderly chasseur poured fresh coffee.

'You went shopping in Marseille?' Spiccard's dark eyes betrayed no emotion.

Jobert considered the blond, boyish second-in-command as he accepted an aromatic cup. 'We obtained new gloves and re-soled the company's boots, sir.'

Spiccard slumped back in his armchair. 'How did you afford it?'

'From our share of the sale of Austrian equipment from the battalion we bluffed in Pieve di Teco and the Austrian horses and artillery purses we took at Ponte di Nava.'

'Hmm, Ponte di Nava.' Spiccard's face twisted as he drummed his fingers on the desktop. 'Yes, it is quite disturbing how desperate the infantry regiments are to purchase captured clothing and equipment. How was your convoy of the four hundred divisional remounts that were unable to move by coastal shipping?'

'It worked out well in two respects, sir. First, the supply contractors had two hundred and eighty horses for collection in Marseille —'

Spiccard snorted with disgust.

'Second, I brought a wagon convoy with us with the regimental issue of salt and vinegar. Not just the regiment's, sir, but divisional headquarters' issue as well. Otherwise, it too would have come up by coastal shipping.'

Spiccard's lop-sided sneer curled into a smile. 'You know that supply never arrived here thanks to the British navy. Where did you find the wagons?'

'Are you aware my family has a cartage contract with General Masséna, sir?'

Spiccard arched his eyebrows. 'I am vaguely aware. Something about your corporal groom. The fellow you have recommended for the veterinary school at Alfort?'

'Yes, sir. Our families have a long connection. My groom's family manages the enterprise on behalf of my uncle.'

Spiccard shrugged indifference as he sipped his coffee. 'You are a cunning sod, Jobert. That explains Colonel Raive including General Masséna's personal recommendation within your man's application. So, what of your fortuitous convoy?'

'Good fortune, sir, allowed us to connect with the convoy bringing up supplies for the general's cellar, and the wagons were able to accommodate the extra cargo.'

'At the general's expense, I hope?'

'Hence my inclusion of the headquarters' supplies, sir.'

'Our ridiculous supply situation, whether we are hamstrung by the British navy or our own supply contractors, brings me to my news. With Saorgio and Col di Tende secured last month, we are to advance back into Piedmont.'

Spiccard refilled both coffee cups.

'Our erudite chief of artillery Bonaparte has devised a scheme whereby our Army of Italy works with the Army of the Alps to conduct a combined advance; the Army of the Alps strikes east at the Piedmontese, whilst we attack their flank and secure the fortress at Cuneo and the supply arsenals at Mondovi.

'The Deputies have endorsed the plan and General Dumerbion has sent his recommendation for the plan to Paris. General Masséna's division, based at Ormea, acts as a flank guard to the Col di Tende approach and aims for Mondovi. In line with our standard monthly rotation of squadrons, Colonel Morin has brought up 1st Squadron into the screen to anticipate the advance routes. Now that you and Geourdai have returned, 2nd Squadron will act as reserve and 3rd Squadron will return from Ormea and Garessio to escort divisional convoys.'

'Do you wish us to move forward to General Masséna's second brigade at Pieve di Teco, sir?'

'No, you will base yourself here in Oneglia. Supply and forage are better by the coast, and if the depth brigade moves forward, you are a three-hour march from them. Moreover, after your ... unnecessary losses at Ponte di Nava I would have you close by.' A spasm in Jobert's purple scar caused his cheek to twitch. 'I acknowledge your bias for action, Jobert, but I doubt your soundness when it counts.'

On this humid June day, no breeze stirred Lieutenant Colonel Spiccard's office curtains. Yet Jobert watched a puff of air pulse a languid ripple through a strand of dusty cobweb. Having saluted Colonel Raive from General Masséna's headquarters,

Jobert, Geourdai and Koschak were invited by Spiccard to pour themselves tall glasses of cool water mixed with fresh lemon juice.

'The Army of the Alps has secured the Col de l'Argentiéres,' said Spiccard. 'But the Minister of War has vetoed any further advance into Piedmont. This new order from Paris is racing forward to General Masséna and Colonel Morin.'

'Why, sir?' asked Jobert. 'Were not our supply problems so pressing that Minister Carnot approved the scheme?'

'It appears the resources are needed on the Rhine. There were some alarming reverses with the northern spring offensive. Perhaps, you have a clearer understanding, Colonel Raive, sir?'

Raive swished stray lemon pips around his glass. 'To open the campaigning season, our armies in the north attempted to raise the allied siege of our fortress at Landrécies. Austrian and British cavalry squadrons charged our recruit infantry. We had eight hundred killed, four hundred wounded and lost three guns for their eighty casualties. On a second occasion, the allied cavalry killed seven thousand, routed twenty thousand and took forty-one guns. Needless to say, the allies maintain their grip on Landrécies. We have lost Menin, Courtrai and Ypres. So far, the allies' counter-offensive is succeeding despite General Pichergru's victory at Tourcoing and his subsequent capture of Charleroi.'

Jobert set his teeth and squinted at the floorboards to control his breathing. The litany of military disasters that was served upon France in the last two years seemed overwhelming and the consequences to the Republic unfathomable.

Raive's eyes resumed their customary sparkle. 'There is another matter. That is why I have asked Sergeant Major Koschak to join us. Has anyone heard the expression "tumble out of our mountain dens like the demons from hell and flood the plains of Piedmont", or words to that effect?'

Everyone's faces twitched with recognition.

'Lieutenant Colonel Spiccard?' asked Raive.

'General Morin used the expression at his orders.'

Raive turned to look at Geourdai.

'Yes, sir, I heard Colonel Morin use those words,' said Geourdai.

'Did you repeat that expression?'

'No, sir.'

'Really? Jobert?' asked Raive.

'Yes, sir, I also heard Colonel Morin say it. I repeated that phrase during my orders to my company.'

'Sergeant Major Koschak?'

'Yes, sir, Captain Jobert used that expression.'

'And who attended those orders, Sergeant Major?'

'The company officers and sergeants, sir.'

'I also heard that phrase,' said Raive. 'It was first expressed by the commander of the 16th Légère Regiment at General Masséna's orders which I attended along with Colonel Morin. General Masséna repeated the evocative expression.' Raive smiled as he looked at each in turn. 'Curiously, that same phrase is relayed back to us by our agents within the Austrian forces in Piedmont. Moreover, a secret royalist courier coming from Avignon was intercepted carrying a cipher with the same phrase. We have been aware of a royalist agent, a spider of indeterminate size, operating from Avignon for some time.'

The four men of the 24th Chasseurs remained immobile. The turn of conversation hinted at treachery and summary execution.

Raive poured himself another cup of lemon water from an earthenware jug beaded with dew.

'Last year, after our raid on the Valence armoury to secure our sabres, we learnt of the existence of the agent, or agents, centred in Avignon. As we know with spiders, they spin many strands of web in which all sorts of information, insects large and small, are trapped. Not one insect satisfies any spider, all scraps are taken in. Not all information is digested by the spider, who in turn, passes it on to feed larger and larger spiders.

'Then with the Marseille uprising last June, two pieces of information appeared to connect the 24th Chasseurs into the Avignon web. First, we learnt from rebel prisoners taken by your companies that they expected a certain size of escort with then Captain, now Brigadier, Bonaparte's powder convoy. At that time, we spoke together, and felt assured that this particular fact could only have come from within the regiment.

'Second, after Avignon's uprising, it was you who reported, from the rebels, that they knew the strength of the force that held the road between Marseille and Avignon and had received this knowledge from Avignon. At that time, we all agreed that information originated from within your two companies.'

Jobert, his breathing quite shallow, watched Raive closely. *The implications of Raive's theory under the Law of Suspects, if reported to Saliceti, ensures Geourdai's and my immediate execution.*

'If we sweep away the webs with a large broom,' said Raive, wafting his hand, 'the spiders will retreat then re-emerge and respin their webs. We need patience and vigilance in seeking particular threads of web. Reflect for a moment that our regiment is unlike any other in the Army of Italy. Our regiment is the vanguard of General Dumerbion's leading division. Any questions General Masséna has in achieving General Dumerbion's wider plans, it is our regiment that reveals the answers. Our junior officers and sergeants are privy to vast schemes well ahead of their implementation.'

Raive's eyes lost their merriment.

'I ask you to observe the fellows in your companies. But I warn you of certain failure. Our investigation will fail if we use motive as our source of inspiration. Let me demonstrate the pitfalls. We know Avignon was a papal state for five hundred years, returning to France in 1791. We know our regiment was raised from an existing Avignon regiment, the *Chasseurs Volontaires*. How easy it is for anyone to point the finger of guilt at Colonel Morin, as the commander of the previous regiment and well connected into Avignon society. Or condemn Captain Chabenac, or as he was known, de Chabenac, a member of a family of minor nobility, his father murdered by the republican mob, and the successor to the title the Comte de Chabenac were the monarchy returned. Why not accuse Neilage and Huin, members of wealthy families within the Avignon business community, to all outward appearances increasing their family wealth by the removal of the aristocracy, but perhaps with hidden agendas?'

Jobert's brow furrowed with concern as he attempted to anticipate the outcome of Raive's address.

'The Law of Suspects,' said Raive, 'enacted September last year, provided the Committee of Public Safety the official mechanism to detain and execute any person once a reasonable case for royalist motive is argued against them. The Law of Suspects is the grand sweep of the large, but, alas, ineffective broom. That approach is not for us. My friends, eschew motive and seek opportunity.

Jobert's tongue pulsed to lubricate his dry throat.

Raive took another sip. 'Let us examine the insect in this case; the phrase "mountain den, demons from hell, flood the plain". The thread leads from General Masséna's orders, quite innocent you will agree, to the junior officers and sergeants within our companies. We then tease out two other ends of the same thread. One in Piedmont and one in Avignon.

'We all agree that it is a most reasonable argument that those threads could have entered Piedmont and Avignon by many, many ends emanating from this division. But I return to our shared deductions from last year, that I suspect there is an informant, or informants, within either 2nd Company or 5th Company, or indeed, both. There is a very real chance that no actual thread emerges from 2nd and 5th Company at all, gentlemen. This is what I commission you to determine. Hence our need for patience and vigilance in seeking opportunity and avoiding the intrigue of motive.

'Now, why have I chosen you? First, each of us joined the 24th Chasseurs from existing regiments distant from Avignon. None of us, that I can determine, are associated with Avignon. Second, we are all ex-royal army. We have differing views on some of the more rigorous measures employed by the Republic's current government, but I feel quite confident none of us accepts the return of the monarchy and the aristocracy. Am I correct?'

The four chasseurs shifted in their seats uncomfortably, eyes flickering to one another, grunting their assent.

'This is the basis of my trust in you on this grave matter. Allow me to repeat my requirements. Observe your men. Ignore any regimental fellow outside of your companies. Seek opportunity. Avoid distraction by possible motive. Someone is talking, for we have proof someone is listening.'

The cool August southerly blowing in from the Mediterranean was a welcome respite on the dust-encrusted faces of soldiers and remounts. As 2nd Company sweated in their woollen tail-coats, helmets and thick gloves, the wind cleared away the fine powder churned by horses' hooves that had enveloped the mounted formation.

'Sir, Captain Chabenac approaches,' said Moench.

Jobert glanced at the aide trotting down the valley's rocky slope.

Within a few lengths of Jobert, Chabenac sat deep in his saddle and brought his soaked gelding to a halt. 'News from Paris, Jobert. Robespierre is overthrown. The Terror is at an end.'

'Moench, sound *Commanders In*.'

Neilage, Koschak and the two second lieutenants wheeled their horses away from their manoeuvres towards the shrill trumpet call.

'Gentlemen, short halt in place,' said Jobert. 'Captain Chabenac has news from Paris.'

'News has reached the regiment that the Dictator is overthrown,' said Chabenac. 'The National Convention has assumed control of the government.'

The young officers rocked back in their saddles. Neilage curled his moustache. 'This will not bode well for any friends of Robespierre.'

Voreille's freckles flushed with excitement. 'To think the regiment dined with the Dictator's brother in March.'

Huin appeared unflustered. 'What of Saliceti and Bonaparte, sir?'

'Saliceti has arrested Bonaparte and charged him with treason,' said Chabenac.

'Good grief! The loss of another capable fellow,' said Neilage. 'Will some of the more extreme measures cease, such as the Law of Suspects or the seizure of grain crops without payment?'

Chabenac shook his head. 'I am sorry. I am unaware.'

'Sir, what caused the coup?' asked Huin.

'It appears the threat to France has evaporated with a decisive battle in Belgium. General Jourdan defeated the allies near the village of Fleurus. He flew a hot-air balloon which provided observation of the entire battlefield. The Austrians have evacuated Belgium and the British have withdrawn their expeditionary force. General Jourdan has entered Brussels and annexed Belgium for France. Forces within the National Convention felt the 'revolutionary dictatorship' had ... served its purpose and was now no longer required.'

The faces of the three young officers became quite animated, as further questions for Chabenac welled to the surface.

'Very well, gentlemen.' Jobert raised a gloved hand. 'Thank you, Captain Chabenac. Our soldiers await. Let us complete our exercises and discuss the latest Paris theatre over dinner. Take post, gentlemen. Moench, sound *Assembly*.'

The three junior men resumed their places alongside the column of chasseurs. The chasseurs closed the lids of their water gourds and regathered their reins in response to the trumpet's call.

Koschak's steady green eyes slid across his sunburnt face. 'You doubt Captain Chabenac's news is good news, sir?'

Jobert pushed up the brim of his helmet and wiped sweat from his brow. 'First, since the Bastille five years ago, this is France's sixth form of government. From monarch to National Assembly, Legislative Assembly, National Convention, Dictatorship, and back to National Convention. What next?'

Koschak's face tightened as Jobert looked him in the eye.

'Second, eighteen months ago, you and I were at Jemappes, Sergeant Major. They called that a decisive battle when we rode into Brussels. Then last year the allies returned, and we lost it all. With Jourdan's victory at Fleurus, Belgium is again ours.' As Jobert adjusted his helmet on his forehead, the peak shaded his scowl. 'At some point in the future the allies will return, and we will lose Belgium. Then we will march north to Brussels once more for another decisive battle. Mark my words.'

Jobert rubbed his grimy fingertips across Michelle's lavender pages. He imagined a world far from his, where curtains wafted and the carpet's pattern dappled in the sunlight as his cousin's quill inscribed her words.

Paris
29ᵗʰ July 1794

Darling André,

Robespierre has been overthrown in a coup. The resultant executions of anyone connected to the Jacobins is overwhelming. We all feel the hundreds, if not thousands, of people slaughtered here is more than at any time during the last five years. The chaos in the streets are scenes from hell. Yet they inform us the Terror is over. No one dares go outside. It is a danger to go outside to collect water from the pumps or empty our chamber pots.

But Paris is truly mad. Whilst the threat of abduction is ever present, messages still get through from our friends. You will not believe me when I relate what these messages reveal. Parties! Yes, Valmai and I are inundated with invitations to card evenings, recitals and dances. There is a great expectation of levity and frivolity with the removal of the Dictator.

The mention of Chabenac's blonde sister caused a twist in Jobert's chest. He closed his eyes as memories of her slim shape twirled around him at a ball. *How long ago was that ball?*

The Ministry of War is bringing out a new variation of the hussar's mirliton cap, as opposed to procuring another batch of what is issued to the hussar regiments. We were awarded the contract for dressing the underlying leather shells, for all twelve regiments of hussars and twenty-four regiments of chasseurs à cheval. For us, that is thirty-thousand individual caps we are to sew in regimental colours. Yes, you will soon be rid of those smelly old leather helmets with their scruffy crests. I believe these smart new mirliton caps will be issued to the regiments next year.

Jobert snorted at the prospect of the corrupt commissary delivering anything ever. *And why am I forced to look like a bloody hussar?*

What marvellous news that Duque comes to Paris next year. You know I cannot help myself, as I will make discreet enquiries with my friends who are connected to the Veterinary School. It will be wonderful to see him again – no, not like that!

Didier writes that the 1ˢᵗ Hussars were transferred to the Army of the Alps. With pressure on the northern armies alleviated following Belgium becoming ours, and the Republic still at war with Austria on the upper Rhine and Italy, his regiment marches to Grenoble. Perhaps, like last year, we all might come together at grandfather's farm to celebrate the New Year?

Write to me this minute,
We love you ...

Jobert soured at the thought that there was no prospect of returning home. *Unless so wounded that ...*

The morsel of fish on Jobert's fork made slick curves in the wine and lemon reduction sauce. The languid Major Fergnes twirled a long-stemmed wine glass in his muscular fingers. 'You appear distracted, Jobert. These humid August nights?'

Jobert returned the dripping fork with the cooling fish to his plate. 'Ah, no, not at all, sir. The evenings here on the coast are more pleasant than those in the mountains.'

'Then the tiresome rotations of duty, perhaps?'

'Again, no, I appreciate the monthly change of tasks. April in the vanguard of the advance. May escorting the remounts up from Marseille. June in reserve for the "flood" into Piedmont. July scouting that steep country north of Ormea. Now August has 2nd Squadron escorting convoys, warm sea breezes and pleasant dinners.'

Fergnes leant forward on his elbows and wiggled his wine glass at Jobert. 'Then what captivates your thoughts, my friend?'

Jobert squinted for answers in the weave of the linen table-cloth, the right side of his face still twinged from the scar under his eye. 'Something odd occurred as we returned to Nice today. I saw a face in the crowd and the incident irks me.'

'How so?'

Jobert's eyes lowered to the table, his mind visualising a scene in his head. 'The convoy column was held up in the crush of the crowd. My attention was caught by a fellow hopping up onto a railing ledge hoping to cross the street through the convoy and the crowd. By his ragged brown or grey homespun, he was perhaps a local labourer. He turned and looked in my direction. Here is the curious thing. I felt as if our eyes locked momentarily.'

'Perhaps it was love?'

'I felt I knew who it was, but I could not place him. He showed no emotion when he saw me. I feel he held my eye because he recognised me. My eyes flicked down due to a movement of my horse, then back to the fellow in less than a second, yet I swear, he had disappeared in that instant.'

'How curious.' Fergnes reclined to sip his wine.

'Indeed. I looked for movement in the crowd and there was nothing to show for where he had gone. So, while I enjoy dinner, I seek to place his face.'

Fergnes swallowed the last of his wine. 'I hear Voreille continues to pay court here in Nice?'

Jobert blinked as he returned to the present. 'The love-struck fool had a girl in Avignon over whom he pined. His distraction irritated me.'

'Distracted or envious?'

'Why waste your time in love when you can pay for it by the hour?' Jobert frowned at his indiscretion. *Careful, he has a sweetheart in Avignon.* 'Anyway, I am now thankful Voreille has found someone local with whom he can play the gallant.'

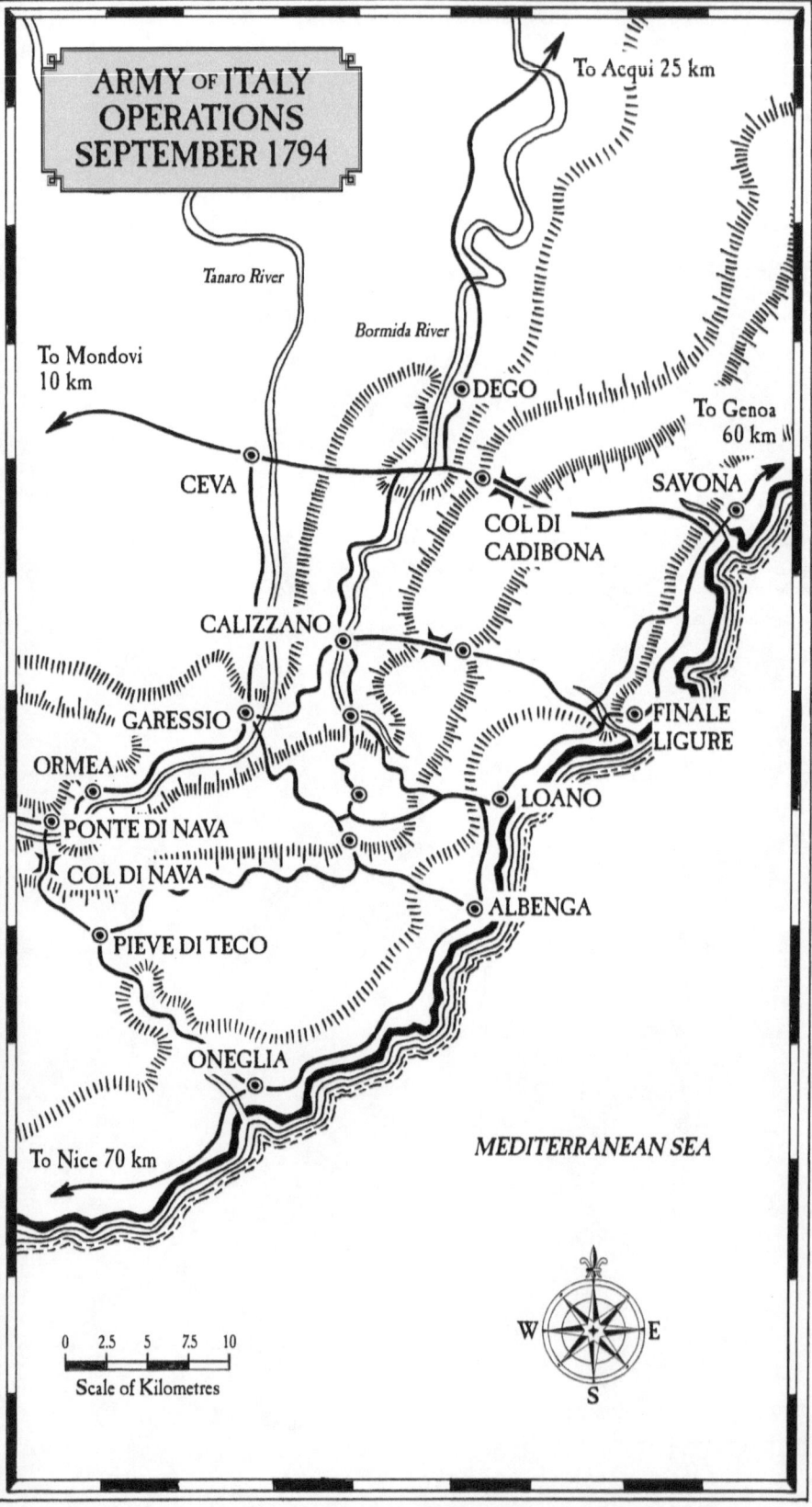

Chapter Eight

September 1794, Oneglia, Italy

Jobert and Geourdai were ushered by Spiccard towards a table covered in maps and charts. Jobert's eyes moved with familiarity along the Tanaro River valley with its towns of Ormea and Garessio. He traced his fingers down the parallel Bormida River valley to the east, with the key towns of Calizzano and Dego and the massive Austrian arsenal at Acqui further north. 'Ah, look Geourdai, the Col di Cadibona allows access between Savona on the coast and the headwaters of the Bormida.'

Geourdai studied the map.

Spiccard tapped the chart with a pencil. 'Look here, gentlemen. The Austrian Army is concentrating from Acqui into the Bormida Valley. We expect their intent is to capture Savona and disrupt our trade with Genoa. Their operations are proceeding slowly, as they coordinate with the British navy. General Dumerbion has accepted a plan of Bonaparte's to hold the Austrian coastal advance at Loano and counterattack with Masséna's division out of the Tanaro Valley and into the Bormida Valley —'

Spiccard looked up under his blond locks to catch Geourdai throwing a puzzled glance towards Jobert. Jobert rolled his eyes in response.

'Is there a concern?' asked Spiccard. 'Am I interrupting a private exchange, gentlemen?'

'Excuse me, sir,' said Jobert. 'Has Deputy Saliceti not arrested General Bonaparte on a charge of treason?'

'Ah, our Chief of Artillery is released. Citizen Saliceti arranged it when it was obvious the Army of Italy was incapable without him. Might I continue without further interruption, Jobert?'

Jobert suppressed his curiosity of the political intrigue to re-sume his impassive attentiveness. 'Forgive me, sir.'

'General Masséna has orders to advance from Garessio to Dego on the Bormida River. As I understand it, 1st Squadron is reconnoitring the routes out of the Tanaro Valley and over the ridgeline to Calizzano in the Bormida Valley.'

Spiccard's finger tapped on the port of Savona. 'Once Dego is secured, it is critical that General Masséna assault down onto Savona through the Col di Cadibona. Jobert, take 2nd Squadron to Garessio as reserve. You have a few days to prepare, then report to Colonel Morin, before Masséna's advance.' Spiccard's dark eyes remained fixed on the town trapped under his finger. 'Keep in mind, 2nd Squadron will act as advance guard when the division sweeps down onto Savona, through the Col di Cadibona, and assault the Austrians in the flank.'

The mongrel doubts us. Jobert jotted this final detail into his notebook.

On the road north-west out of Oneglia, a salty southerly cleared the dust from between the grinding hooves of the marching squadron. Neilage urged his horse in beside Jobert's Rouge. 'Excuse me, sir, may we join you?'

Jobert shifted Rouge's shoulder with a squeeze of his leg and allowed Neilage and Koschak to ride side-by-side on the narrow road. He looked across at both of them. *They have been chatting. Something is up.*

'Ponte di Nava, last April, sir, was a grim affair,' said Neilage. 'Two months ago, we returned to Ormea as the divisional screen. When we marched through Ponte di Nava, Voreille's troop was quite morose. I observed a deep sense of despondency, sir, when we visited the graves at the chapel.'

'I remember.'

Neilage glanced towards Koschak. 'I feel the men need to put that occasion behind them, sir, especially as we march toward further action.'

Jobert's jaw bunched. 'Your thoughts, Sergeant Major?'

'I have spoken to Sergeant Pultiere to keep a close eye on his lads, sir. Perhaps, the men may respond to a few words on what we gained that day, not what we lost.'

Later that day, having marched down to the Tanaro River, Jobert diverted the company column through the back lane of Ponte di Nava, where they had charged the Austrian infantry. Downcast villagers slunk back into the shadows of their shattered homes. 2nd Company squeezed into column of fours within the ball-scarred terrace.

Jobert stood in his stirrups.

'Who was with me when we charged down this lane five months ago? Who rode with me when we broke the enemy's reserves? On that day I rode this horse, a horse impaled upon an Austrian bayonet. Who chased the kaiserlik guns which stopped our infantry from crossing the river?'

The chasseurs shifted in their saddles under Jobert's searching gaze.

'You and me, 2nd Company! We achieved this feat of arms together.'

Jobert led the column of ninety horsemen to the end of the lane. At the edge of the village, 2nd Company formed column of platoons with Pultiere's platoon leading, just as it had before it charged the pair of Austrian three-pounders.

'Sabres!' called Jobert. Steel sabres hissed from the brass throats of their scabbards.

'Who was with me when we charged a pair of guns massacring our infantry?' Jobert flinched as an icy twinge sizzled along his scar. 'I was wounded in this place. Who else received a wound in this place?'

Jobert looked at Moench. 'Who lost their horse in this place?'

Jobert stared at Pultiere. 'Who lost brothers in this place?'

Jobert's extended sabre tip followed his malevolent glare along the length of the ranks.

'Who was with me when we cut those gunners down? Those kaiserlik gunners will never leave this place. No one returns to this place and remembers them. We sold their horses and re-soled our boots. We sent their purses home to the families of the brothers we lost. You and me. We achieved this, you and me.'

Jobert, resting his sabre pommel on his right thigh, turned Rouge down the slope and led the chasseurs to halt on the place where the guns had cut down their mates before they were captured. 'To our brothers who stand guard on this place of honour, salute!'

As the Tanaro River thrashed and gurgled over the slippery rocks, every man swept his sabre's hilt up to his lips, then dropped the blade-tip towards his horse's nostrils before sweeping the blade up again.

'Moench, sound *To Mess*.'

The last notes of the trumpet call bounced off the stonework to be absorbed by the stunted pines drooping over the river's bank.

Jobert pressed Rouge to a place where he could review the passing of the company. '2nd Company, you and me! To our next battle and our next victory. Form column of fours, walk, march!'

1st Squadron and Masséna's lead brigade found the Austrian main force a few kilometres south of the village of Dego. Excitement buzzed through the ranks of 2nd Squadron upon news that 1st Squadron's screen had encountered a company of Austrian light horsemen, or *chevau-léger*.

Now, all around 2nd Squadron, the air filled with the crunch of tramping shoes, the drumming and shouts of the second infantry brigade marching forward to the sound of the guns.

Both companies of 2nd Squadron departed the dusty road and dismounted along the shallow banks of the Bormida River. Second Lieutenants Voreille and Huin moved amongst the clusters of drinking horses, patting remounts' necks and exchanging quips with the men. Spurs scraped on rocks and scabbards clattered. The chasseurs filled their flasks, tightened portmanteau straps and girths, as horses stretched their necks and nipped an extra bite of lush river weeds. Madame Quandalle, her ankle-length skirt tucked high into her apron strings, wobbled on the rocks as she refilled tin cups, tied to her apron, with *grappa* for the chasseurs. Standing along the road, the wagons' teams received bucketed water, as Koschak ensured the trains' water barrels were filled.

With the expectation of imminent battle, Jobert and Geourdai gathered their company officers about them. 'Before we disperse, men,' said Jobert, waving a half-eaten apple towards the approaching Chabenac, 'let us hear Colonel Morin's requirements.'

Chabenac, blackened by gun smoke, leant from the saddle and guzzled Moench's offered flask. 'Colonel Morin sends his compliments. General Masséna has an Austrian division to his front. Beyond the hamlet that we see, a wide plain exists upon which, 1st Company reports, the Austrians are drawing up at least two regiments supported by a battery of foot guns. Four battalions have come up in line, with two battalions in reserve. With our lead brigade debouching onto the plain as we speak, General Masséna is attacking with three regiments forward, and one regiment in reserve with the 15th Dragoons.'

Chabenac was interrupted by the loud clatter of over six hundred iron-shod hooves and the urgent snarls of sergeants. A squadron of the 15th Regiment of Dragoons marched past at the walk, in the wake of the infantry. The dragoons, clad in green jackets, white breeches and tall black boots, confirmed the charges in their dragoon muskets, too busy to look down from under their peaked, bronze helmets with flowing horsehair manes and acknowledge the chasseurs.

'Colonel Morin has fresh orders for the 24th Chasseurs.' Chabenac resumed his briefing once the dragoons had passed. 'The companies of 1st Squadron are supporting the division's flanks. 2nd Squadron must join Colonel Morin and form on the left of the division's reserve line, between the 15th Dragoons and the river.'

Cannon fire erupted from beyond the hamlet. 'The lead brigade is exchanging compliments, sir.' Jobert fed his apple core to Vert. They all looked up to a crescendo of drumming. 'Is that all, as the infantry are advancing?'

The crackling of ragged musket fire beyond the hamlet distracted everyone.

'Our infantry skirmishers are engaging the Austrian outposts,' said Jobert. 'Men, beyond the hamlet, there lies a plain. General Masséna is attacking three regiments up, with our 1st and 4th Companies supporting the division's flanks. In the division's second line, the general has his reserve regiment, the 15th Dragoons and us. We are to form on the left of the reserve line, 5th Company forward, 2nd Company back. Those kaiserlik chevau-léger are out there somewhere and are desperate for a sound lesson in horsemanship. Squadron trains will remain here upstream of the infantry in the hamlet.'

The cannons roared again, followed by fever-pitched cheering. 'The infantry are charging. Questions? No? Moench, sound *Assembly*. Form column of fours, walk, march!'

From the chaotic hustle and bustle amongst the boulders and reeds of the riverbed, the one hundred and eighty veterans of 2nd Squadron mounted, squeezed their remounts into a walk and smoothly formed column.

The column passed through the ball-riddled hamlet, the opening scene of the day's battle. Local peasants dashed to put out fires, small knots of infantry herded goats and geese whilst others gathered French and Austrian wounded around a few surgeons and a growing group of moaning casualties by the riverbank.

Beyond the hamlet and its encircling olive and citrus groves, the expected plain was a pall of gun smoke as the lead chasseurs caught up with the rear of the column of green-jacketed dragoons. The river swept away to the left and the road from the hamlet to the village of Dego curved right. Not that the far side of the valley was visible as a light easterly breeze caused the thick, acrid haze, from the combat to their front, to drift from right to left.

'Voreille,' Jobert called, as it became apparent that the dragoon column was forming in a line formation, 'take a section escort, go left of the dragoons, find Colonel Morin and report back. Geourdai, form column of troop. Huin, place vedettes on the river somewhere on our left and a vedette to maintain contact with the dragoons.'

Soon enough Voreille's patrol moved back through the field of ripening wheat and wafting expended cartridge papers. Voreille reported Colonel Morin was just ahead as the musketry intensified well off to the right. Jobert found Morin and Fergnes surrounded by aides, trumpeters, surgeons, grooms with spare horses, and an escort section of chasseurs.

'Gentlemen,' said Morin, 'the Austrians are withdrawing their fire line. The current battle seems a contest for Dego well off to our right. General Masséna has directed two infantry regiments to clear the town. Beyond Bormida and west of the town, a small promontory lies across our front, sloping down from the hills on our left. At the tip of the promontory, an ancient fort overlooks the town. The 16th Légère is flanking the fort and clearing the heights. Fergnes, take 2nd Squadron, ascend the heights and support the left flank of the 16th Légère. Chabenac, inform the dragoons and then General Masséna of our departure forward.'

Chabenac saluted and trotted his horse into the swirling yellow-grey gloom.

'Jobert, how are you arrayed?' asked Chief of Squadron Fergnes.

'Squadron in column of troop, sir, 5th Company leading,' said Jobert. 'Are the enemy chevau-léger upon the field, sir?'

'No, not since early this morning,' said Fergnes. 'Jobert, form column of fours to cross the river, form column of platoons as we ascend and prepare to form column of troop as we reach the summit.'

Jobert clenched his teeth as he saluted. *Old friend or not, I do not need you, a green chief of squadron, to tell me how to handle my men.*

In the drifting smoke, infantry drums thrashed out a new beat as orders changed. As the lead files of the chasseur column scrambled up the rocky banks to the cheers of infantry stragglers clustered by the river's shoals, Geourdai's lead patrols, scouting ahead of the column, urged their horses to canter up the slope.

'In what formation did your regiment ascend, sir?' Jobert called to an infantry officer, coordinating the gathering of wounded at the water's edge.

'In regimental line, sir, three battalions in attack column.' An increase in musket fire sounded from the top of the ridge. 'Our skirmishers have found whoever is on top. Good luck, sir.'

'Form column of platoons,' cried Geourdai.

Chabenac returned up the hill.

'Chabenac,' said Colonel Morin, 'convey my compliments to the Colonel of the 16th Légère and inform him our squadron is forming on his left.'

Chabenac tugged on the reins of his sweating horse, who resisted the command to follow the trampled spring grasses in the wake of one-and-a-half thousand infantrymen, instead stretching out his neck and chomping a mouthful of clover.

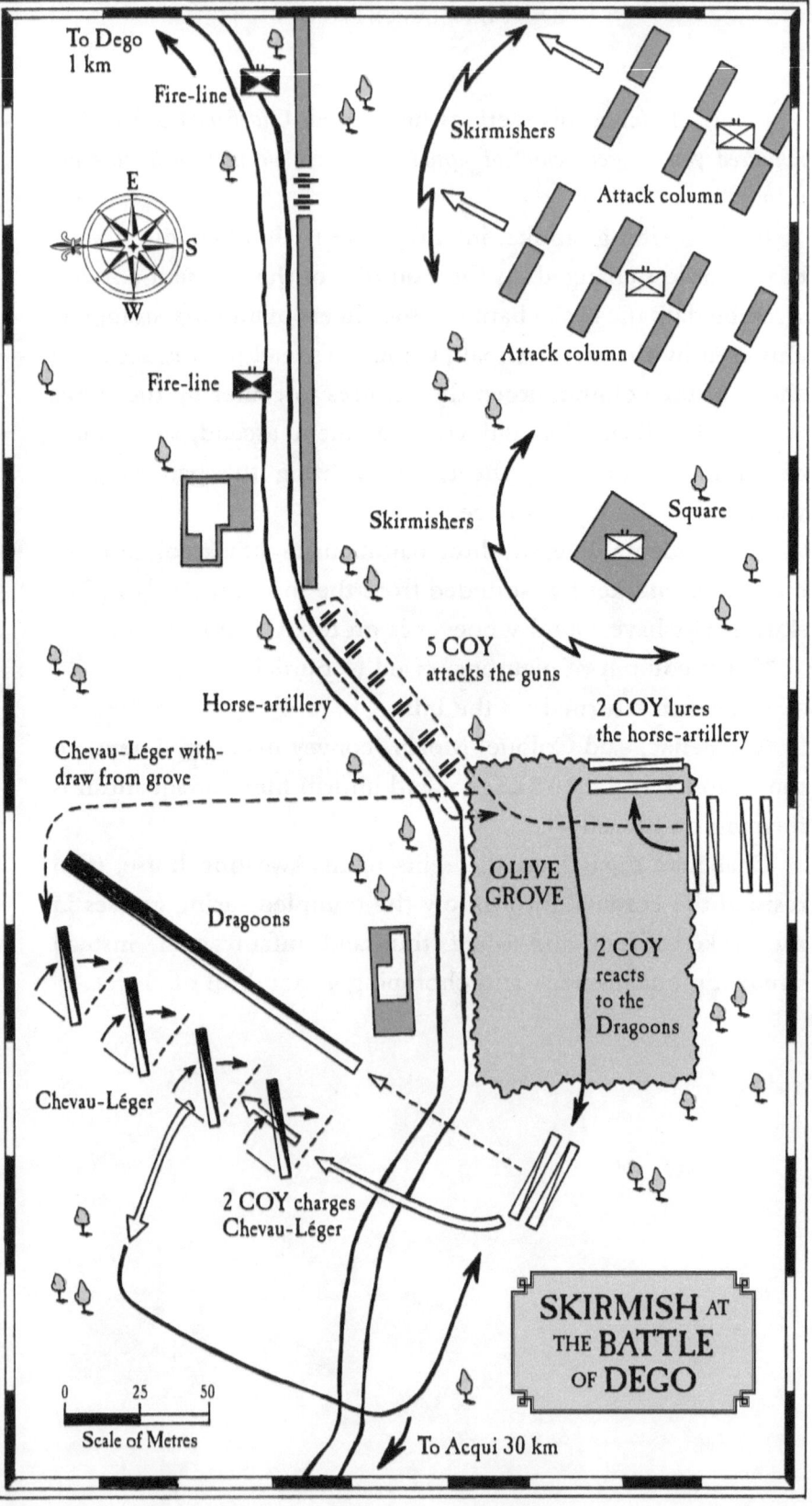

To Dego
1 km

Fire-line

E
S
W

Fire-line

Skirmishers

Attack column

Attack column

Square

Skirmishers

5 COY
attacks the guns

Horse-artillery

2 COY lures
the horse-artillery

Chevau-Léger with-
draw from grove

Dragoons

OLIVE
GROVE

2 COY
reacts
to the
Dragoons

Chevau-Léger

2 COY charges
Chevau-Léger

0   25   50
Scale of Metres

SKIRMISH AT
THE BATTLE
OF DEGO

To Acqui 30 km

Chapter Nine
September 1794 - Battle of Dego

Infantry drums rolled on the crest above. A heart-felt roar sounded from the ranks of the light-infantry regiment. As the cheer died away, sporadic skirmisher fire increased.

'We see the Austrian line ahead, sir and the flanks of the 16th Légère,' reported Geourdai's lead scouts.

Jobert peered into the smoke as 2nd Squadron crested the rise.

'2nd Squadron, form column of troop at the halt. Geourdai, vedettes out.'

The promontory was six to eight hundred metres wide before it fell away. A roadway ran its length, marked by occasional low, solid farmhouses and stunted hedges. The lead troop of 5th Company faced a large, dense olive grove beyond which the end of the Austrian fire line, a long white-grey smudge, was just visible.

'Officers forward,' called Morin.

The drums of the nearest French battalion changed beat from that of the advance to an intensely insistent beat.

'Sir, they are forming square,' said Jobert. A flank battalion forming square reduces the power of the regimental assault and becomes an immediate target for an Austrian bayonet counter-charge.

'Who is causing that? Surely, not us!' cried Morin standing in his stirrups to gauge the visibility back to 5th Company's front rank.

Jobert noticed a ripple of movement in the exposed lower trunks of the grove's trees. Hundreds of horses' legs, their torsos and riders concealed by the low smoke-enwrapped branches. *The bastards.* 'Sir, chevau-léger in the olive grove!'

'5th Company, sabres! Trot, march! Sound *Advance,*' called Morin. 'Fergnes and Jobert, have 2nd Company follow at the walk.'

A volley from the Austrian line against the French infantry advance swallowed them in smoke. Jobert and Fergnes moved their horses to the flank as 5th Company's four ranks of twenty-plus chasseurs trotted forward and disappeared amongst the smoke and the olive leaves.

Harsh cries and musket fire bellowed from within the grove. A trumpet blew *Charge.* The low branches consumed the rear rank of Geourdai's company. The trees soon swallowed the cries of 5th Company's pursuit of the chevau-léger.

'Sir,' said Jobert to Fergnes, 'I suggest taking one troop within the grove and keeping the rear troop out, then place ourselves on the right of the line to maintain observation of the 16th Légère's attack.'

'I quite agree. Make it so.'

2nd Company kept their musketoons ready, the butts resting on their right thighs. Within the grove, nothing was seen but the leaves, the fruit and the high probability of being swept from the saddle by numerous low branches.

As Jobert and Fergnes stood at the east face of the orchard towards the infantry, the nearest French battalion rolled its drums, and opened its ranks and reformed the assault column, fifty men wide and twelve ranks deep.

At Vert's hooves lay a fallen Austrian chevau-léger shot through the side of the face. The Austrian soldier's green tail-coat with red and black facings and white trousers tucked into calf-high boots were similar to the chasseurs' in-barracks dress uniform. The black leather cap had a small red and white plume on the side and a brass regimental badge on the front.

'Jobert, who is this now?' asked Fergnes.

A white-coated Austrian officer cantered towards them.

'Gentlemen, my colonel requests you hold your line,' the exasperated Austrian declared in German. 'The French are coming out of square. De Kerpen's battery will not unlimber if you abandon his flank.'

The officer jabbed with his sabre at the blue-jacketed battalion swallowed in a billow of grey smoke from a volley further down the line. Fergnes' eyes were wide with alarm as he looked to Jobert.

'Forgive me, sir, de Kerpen's battery?' Jobert asked the Austrian.

'Yes, the horse artillery, sir —'

The Austrian swung around and addressed the officer with the sword, not the fellow with the musketoon on his thigh. His eyes swept across the dead chevau-léger at their horses' feet, then flicked back to the green-panted soldiers about him, their helmets crested and none with red and white plumes, no one with white, powdered curls above their ears. The colour drained from his face as he shortened his reins.

Jobert thrust his levelled musketoon towards the officer's chest, cocking it with his rein hand and fired. The ball tore through the man's sternum and ripped its way through his spine. The Austrian, goggle-eyed and slack-jawed, was punched out of the saddle and dead before he hit the ground.

'Duval, come here.' Jobert reloaded his musketoon. 'What is in the kaiserlik's pockets are yours. What is on his horse is mine. Take the horse to Duque in the rear rank.'

Somewhere deep in the grove came the trumpet call to *Rally*.

'2ⁿᵈ Company, right wheel at the halt, walk, march! Moench, sound *To Arms*. Voreille, wheel the troop to the right, as if we are to charge the French battalion coming out of square.'

2ⁿᵈ Company's front troop surged forward in a right wheel.

'Jobert, what did he say?' cried Fergnes. 'What is going on?'

'The Austrian horses were to check our flank battalion in square, sir, so they might be harvested by an Austrian horse battery. The battery will not unlimber its guns until the battalion is in square, sir. I will show the Austrian line that we are preparing to charge the French battalion. The horse battery will commit to unlimbering. Then we attack the battery as it comes up.'

Fergnes blew hard in agitation as he stared at the French infantry reforming column.

'Yes or no, sir?' asked Jobert.

'Jobert, you are threatening the destruction of the 16ᵗʰ Légère's flank.'

'Not if 2ⁿᵈ Company causes the artillery to commit to unlimbering. We then launch 5ᵗʰ Company into the battery's flank, sir. Voreille, bring Huin's troop in behind. Moench, sound *To Arms* until that battalion —'

Musket fire zipped into the branches close by, fired by screaming and pointing French skirmishers wrapped in wisps of yellow-grey smoke. The battalion drums pounded the order to reform square, as Moench's trumpet call cut through the smog.

Geourdai led 5ᵗʰ Company at the trot through the lanes between the trees. 'Colonel Morin is injured. His horse was shot,' reported Geourdai. 'He is protected. The surgeon is attending him.'

'Geourdai, who did you pursue?' asked Jobert.

'At least a squadron of chevau-léger.'

'Sir, the guns!' Moench pointed along the face of the grove.

Over one hundred metres from the three chasseur officers, and over two hundred metres from the French light infantry, a battery of Austrian horse artillery trotted forward out of the gloom and formed a fire line.

Five six-pounder cannons and one seven-pounder howitzer, each towed by limbers behind a four-horse team, turned into a line extending from the edge of the Austrian infantry's fire line toward the edge of the olive grove. The six ammunition caissons, supporting each gun, began turning into a parallel second rank.

The howls of the French infantry skirmishers to the new threat ceased their long-range fire into the grove.

Geourdai, eyes wide, looked from Fergnes to Jobert. 'Charge, sir?'

Fergnes blinked. 'But you are in column of fours.'

Jobert ground his teeth. *The lace of a major on your sleeve but not yet faced artillery. Seniority, be damned.* 'Those guns are already loaded, sir. They will fire on the infantry within one minute of unlimbering. Go now, sir, you have their flank.'

The Austrian limbers turned away from the French, leaving the trailing barrels pointing, double-shotted with ball and canister, towards the hapless, bellowing French square. The mounted Austrian officers and gun sergeants gesticulated to hasten their teams' manoeuvre.

'Unleash us, sir,' said Geourdai.

Far along the olive grove, six crews of brown-jacketed artillerymen leapt from their padded seats on the guns' trails, rammers, firing tubes and portfires in hand.

Fergnes sat erect in the saddle. 'Sound *Charge!* 5th Company, on me!'

Squadron and company trumpets overlapped their shrill, insistent call. The 5th Company chasseurs roared away through the lanes of trees.

'Huin, vedettes out,' ordered Jobert. 'One to follow 5th Company to know what lies north of the road. One vedette to the far, western edge of the grove.'

As the tails of 5th Company cantered out of sight, Colonel Morin and escort arrived through the trees. Morin's lower right leg was splinted with cut branches, and he gripped his pistol holsters for balance as he rode. Morin's sleeve was torn, blood trickled from the bandages wrapping his right ear and neck. His face was pale, lips trembling as he held back the rising nausea from shock.

'Who is charging whom, Jobert?'

'An Austrian horse battery has unlimbered on the 16th Légère's flank, sir. Major Fergnes has taken 5th Company into theirs.'

The screams and bellows of French chasseurs and Austrian artillerymen penetrated the fringe of trees.

'Captain Jobert, sir! Austrian cavalry, sir!' cried Corporal Duval, approaching from behind Morin's retinue. 'Beyond the grove there is a road, sir. White jackets, black bicornes, big horses.'

'Dragoons!' spat Morin. 'Well sited behind the horse guns. They will have 5th Company in the flank. Have at them, Jobert!'

'Neilage, form column of fours to the left, trot, march! Exit the grove on the western edge.'

Jobert dropped his musketoon onto his thigh, drew his sabre before lifting Vert into a canter down a lane between the trees.

A single cannon blasted from the horse artillery line on the eastern side of the grove.

The smoke had dissipated on the far side of the grove from the infantry combat, perhaps due to the olive trees' canopy and the increasing slope in the stronger breeze. Slowing Vert to a walk, Jobert peered out through the branches.

Less than two hundred metres away, across the road, were two imposing ranks of Austrian dragoons facing along the road to the east. Jobert estimated three hundred, possibly a small regiment, but more likely a large squadron. The white-jacketed enemy dragoons sat alert under their tall, black bicorne hats, pommels of their drawn swords resting on their right thighs, watching the French charging into the horse battery while a group of officers standing to the front of their ranks gestured towards the far end of the grove. *Just keep standing there, you idiots.* Another horse gun roared on the far side of the grove. 'Moench, signal form column of troop to the right at the halt.'

Jobert led Bredieux and the column at the trot out from beneath the grove's shadows into a field of ripening wheat. Vert and the other lead horses lowered their heads to bite at the wavering seed heads, but soon jerked their heads erect at the grunted oaths, tugged reins and clenched legs of their riders.

On 2nd Company's right, at two hundred metres, the flank-men of the Austrian dragoon line were pointing at them and roaring with alarm. On their left, a dragoon vedette, now separated from their main body, fired their pistols in warning.

'Bredieux, right wheel into line, at the halt. Sabres!'

A squadron of dragoons does not extend such a courtesy as to present its flank every day, and the dragoon commander was not appearing to take any action to forego 2nd Company the pleasure.

'Sir!' called Moench. 'Look there! The chevau-léger.'

Jobert swivelled further around. The rallied Austrian light horsemen walked their disciplined, green-jacketed ranks in behind the wall of dragoons. It took a moment for the chevau-léger troopers on the right of their line to scream and point towards the French chasseurs.

Jobert hesitated as his mind raced to foresee the outcome of his eighty men charging into nearly five hundred. *Why are the dragoons frozen? Is 2nd Company clear of the trees?* Jobert extended his little finger from his sabre hilt and shortened the reins in his left gloved hand.

A trumpet screamed from the centre of the Austrian horsemen. The chevau-léger commander brooked no hesitation as his dragoon peer had, as the chevau-léger ranks swung towards them. The Austrian light horsemen formed column of troops. Jobert clenched his teeth. *The chevau-léger will hit us in the flank if we charge the dragoons.*

Jobert's eyes flickered as he calculated the angle and time to reform his ranks to accept any charge from the chevau-léger. *The angle is possible. But there is no time. Act now. Or flee.* 'Moench, sound *To Mess*, then *Charge*. Bredieux, Pultiere, form column of fours to the left, canter, march! On me! Now!'

Jobert lifted Vert into an extended gallop on a right lead. Koschak's bellowed 'Follow! Follow! Follow!' over Moench's blaring trumpet.

2nd Company's orderly north-facing line's left extremity melted into a roaring, galloping swarm.

Two hundred metres to the enemy. Twenty seconds to impact.

The two ranks of Austrian chevau-léger broke into four 'gates' and swung toward the French threat. Their left-hand men squeezed along the rear rank of the now cheering, yet stock-still, dragoons.

Jobert saw the chevau-léger commander spin his horse and face his men. One hundred metres. Ten seconds on a galloping horse.

The chevau-léger front rank erupted with cries as they dropped their musketoons and drew sabres, in the face of a torrent of thundering Frenchmen.

Jobert stood in his stirrups, clenched the saddle with his thighs, thrust his sabre arm forward, elbow to the right, and locked eyes on the chevau-léger commander wheeling his skittering horse to face front.

'I want you, you fucking kaiserlik turd! I want you!' Jobert screamed his rage into his core, his sabre tip aiming straight at the brim of the Austrian's helmet along the powdered curl. The Austrian, wide-eyed with dread, flicked his blade to parry.

Too late.

In less than a gallop-stride, Jobert's blade sliced through the man's right temple and eye, the hilt punching into the Austrian commander's cheek as Vert hurtled past.

In the blink of an eye, the chevau-léger trumpeter appeared beyond his commander, raising his trumpet and covering his face. Jobert pressed with his right knee to keep Vert's shoulder up, dipped the tip of his sabre, avoided the lanyard dangling from the trumpet and felt the blade cut into the man's underarm, the hilt skimming his ribs.

Jobert's eyes were on the front rank three strides away. Jobert picked his man, a single Austrian soldier, one man in the middle of a rank of twenty-five. 'You! I want you!'

With his reins held short just behind Vert's outstretched ears, he reached as far forward from the shoulder, giving the impression he was launching himself from the saddle.

The Austrian soldier's eyes bulged as he saw the madman flying towards him, followed by a horde of howling French savages. In short succession, he saw his major and the trumpeter fold back in their saddles as this human tornado, on his careering horse, scorched past them. *Your reins are too loose. Go on, push your horse to the right.* The soldier's corporal screamed beside him and he raised his sabre to parry the incoming hammer blow.

Jobert saw the man step his horse across, saw the gap appear on the other side. Jobert flicked his eyes to the next man along as he shoved his stirrupped toe into Vert's left shoulder, tipping Vert's nose into the space. The next man along did not see the change and did not raise his blade to parry as his horse shied away from the collision.

Jobert whipped his hilt in front of his face, flicked his blade to point out to his left. Jobert's roar of fury was more akin to a strangled croak. As Vert punched through the narrowest of gaps between the horses' hips, Jobert's one-hundred-centimetre blade slashed across the face of the initial trooper on his left.

As Vert emerged into the four strides between the front and second rank of the lead Austrian troop, the chevau-léger were still walking their horses into the wheel. For the closest men to this mounted avalanche, Jobert's appearance, along with Pultiere, Duval and Koschak on his heels, occurred on their half-right.

The Austrian troopers took their horses further to their left. With no time to check his stride, Vert thudded into the overlapping horsemen. Vert groaned from the impact and dropped his hips to decelerate. Raising his head and thrusting his extended face across the nearest soldier's saddle bow, Vert's reckless momentum snapped the neck of the Austrian horse.

Jobert punched out with his left rein hand and parried the unprepared sabre blade of the man he rode over. With his own sabre biting deep into the next man's arm, the hilt of the sabre thudded into the man's upper arm held firm against his body. Pain seared through Jobert's crushed knuckles causing him to bellow.

Vert stumbled over the first soldier's horse collapsing under his front hooves. One Austrian rein had looped over Vert's neck and Jobert's own reins and was pulling Vert down. Jobert dropped his eyes and swung his blade to his left. As he brought the sabre down in a swift arc on the taut leather, he flicked his eyes to the terrified Austrian trooper being absorbed into the earth as his dead horse rolled over him.

In the moment that Moench's horse thumped hard into Vert's rump, another Austrian collided with his shoulder. The impact knocked Jobert's boot from his right stirrup. An Austrian horse's nostrils snorted under Jobert's right armpit. Jobert gripped hard with his left thigh to stay in the saddle.

'Sir! Parry high!'

Jobert allowed the momentum of his blade to sweep past his left boot, then with a distinct press of his right wrist and elbow, the sabre flashed up to sit above his helmet peak pointing out over Jobert's right shoulder. A heavy Austrian blade clanged onto his own, a hair's breadth from his right ear, smashing the top edge of his sabre onto his right shoulder.

Jobert wheezed from the blow, folded to his left, drew his blade over his head in a wide arc, knowing his opponent's sword was extended, whipped his sabre tip around to the right for it to slice into the man's underarm.

The Austrian, probably a sergeant major or officer from behind the rear rank, hissed at the strike. Vert and the Austrian's horse regained their feet and leapt away from each other. As Jobert looked up to bring his sabre front, a green blur flashed past in the short distance between himself and the Austrian, only to reveal a headless chevau-léger torso rocking back in the saddle, arms relaxing to drop both reins and sword.

More horsemen pressed past Jobert. He saw Bredieux, Pultiere, Duval and Koschak hacking into the Austrians in the next rank, the first rank of the second troop. All around him, horses were spurred forward by riders, both Austrian and French, howling like demons. Within a moment, the fourth rank was breached, as a trumpet called close by from his right.

Flexing his stinging right knuckles within his sabre's hilt, Jobert again hooked the little finger of his sabre hand to pull short his reins. Cries of 'About turn' in German caused Jobert to look hard over his right shoulder. The Austrian dragoons turned to face him at less than thirty metres. 2nd Company's gaggle of roaring lunatics were about to have their flank crushed by a solid white wall of dragoons.

'Out! Get out! Moench, sound *Rally*!' Jobert twisted in his saddle to confirm his order was heard. Moench nodded as he fought to gather the reins of his agitated white mare and put his trumpet to his lips.

In the crush of horsemen, the momentum stalled and the outcome hung in the balance.

For the Austrians, the soldiers completed the command of wheeling to the right in troop. Their full attention was on the backs of their front-rank man or, possibly, turning their heads to the right to confirm their dressing of their wheel from the inside man. Raging death erupted on the half-right. Each man's sabre was blocked by the next fellow who was right and slightly forward of him. For most, safety lay over their left shoulder as the man on his left was beyond his left hip. The simple and immediate choice was to peel their horses away to the left. For the deeper ranks, they beheld the vision, six-horse lengths in front of them, of the forward troops melting towards them bellowing 'Run!'

For the unruly French mass, the first half-dozen men found the gaps in the Austrian front rank and raced through. Those behind were forced to slow, causing follow-on chasseurs to ride wider and smash into the flank-on chevau-léger. As the centre of the mass carved out a wider channel, so the speed of those at the centre subsequently increased. With their rage now tinged with the terror of abandonment, the chasseurs barged their horses through the fleeing mass of Austrians to stay with their company-mates.

In the moment it takes for a dense flock of large birds to change direction, three hundred men of both nationalities bellowed, kicked and slashed to find a path to safety.

Moench fought for breath to wheeze out the notes for the *Rally*.

Jobert stood in his stirrups and willed his shattered throat to scream 'On me!' as he swung his sabre in a circular motion above his head and jerked harshly on Vert's bit to check his racing pace.

Austrian soldiers avoided the towering berserker, with eyes popped, teeth bared, nostrils flared in extreme anger, blade slicked black with blood.

In the haze of wheat dust and gun smoke, just behind Jobert and Moench, a trotting column of fours formed. Regardless of section and platoon order, each chasseur raced to join the growing column, each sergeant and lieutenant signalling the rally by twirling their sabres in the sky.

As the ground around him cleared of galloping chevau-léger, and chasseurs cantered to join their column, Jobert searched the cloying dust for any indication, trumpet calls, screamed commands, pounding hooves or flashing sabres, of a wave of charging dragoons. Sensing no threat, perhaps the dragoons were blind to their prey as they were to him, Jobert sought any orientation to the east-west ridgeline road.

'Huin, lead the rally at the walk. Find the road, return to the grove and Colonel Morin. Moench, sound *Rally* again.' *What has the smoke done with those bastard dragoons?*

Since the battle, 2nd Squadron had spent two days and two nights screening Masséna's division north of Dego.

A light September rain swept down the Alpine valleys as the officers gathered at Fergnes' headquarters, a ramshackle stone-walled cottage whose thatched roof leaked and unswept chimney forced the smoke from the meagre fire to cloud under the low beams.

Chabenac flipped the pages of his notebook. 'General Dumerbion has ordered the Army of Italy to withdraw to a defensive line in preparation for winter. General Masséna is withdrawing his division from tomorrow. The 24th Chasseurs are to withdraw to Oneglia via Savona. Colonel Morin has ordered 1st Squadron to support the rear-guard. 2nd Company is to escort the prisoners to Savona and 5th Company will escort the wounded. Jobert, you and Geourdai are then to return to Ormea by the end of the month to assume screen duties in October. Questions?'

'Why are we withdrawing?' asked Jobert.

'From what I hear,' said Chabenac, 'we have a desperate supply situation. Our supplies that come down the Rhône and onward from Marseille are at the mercy of the British navy. Resupply of grain from Genoa is again intercepted by the British by sea and the Austrians by land. No one, except General Bonaparte, believes we are in any fit state to secure the enemy's arsenals in Piedmont. The word at Masséna's headquarters is that we are to comply with Minister Carnot's directives that the Republic's emphasis is on the Rhine. General Dumerbion has convinced the Deputies to discontinue the campaign and has ordered us back into a defensive line for winter.'

'The arsenals of Acqui are just seven hours march along this road.' Jobert held up his hands in bewilderment. 'I —'

'How is Colonel Morin?' asked Fergnes.

'He is well and in good spirits, sir,' said Chabenac, 'but he returns to Nice to convalesce. Masséna has conferred temporary command upon Lieutenant Colonel Spiccard.'

'What of attacking down through the Col di Cadibona onto the Austrian flank at Savona?' asked Jobert.

Chabenac's brows furrowed as he looked to Fergnes with uncertainty. 'I apologise, I do not understand. We still hold Savona. The Austrians were never able to lay siege. I have not heard any mention of an attack. Why?'

Jobert exchanged a glance with Geourdai, then shook his head imperceptibly at Geourdai's raised eyebrows. 'It is nothing.' *Why had Spiccard emphasised the task?*

Jobert felt he was overthinking the situation. At the very least, Savona will yield a hot bath.

Chapter Ten
November 1794, Oneglia, Italy

A sense of unease grew in Jobert's gut.

'Jobert,' said Spiccard, 'Colonel Morin is to become the Prefect of the department of Vaucluse, based in Avignon. I am to command the regiment. Lieutenant Colonel Clemusat is to step to regimental second-in-command. I was displeased with your escapade at Dego, yet, based on seniority, you are next for promotion to chief of squadron. What say you? Mind now, I will not accept further disappointment.'

You miserable turd. 'You honour me, sir. I humbly accept. Ah, congratulations on your promotion, sir. What progress of Colonel Morin's wound?'

'Colonel Morin's leg mends slowly, but he is well.' Spiccard draped backwards across his chair, a sneer curling his cheek. 'We must adjust to these circumstances. With 2nd Squadron returning to convoy escort duties, and your promotion, it is an ideal time for the fellows to settle into their new roles. It is my intent to offer command of 2nd Company to Geourdai.'

A cold dread gripped Jobert's ribs. He shifted in his seat.

Spiccard stiffened. 'Is there any reason that I should not?'

'None whatsoever, sir. Geourdai is an excellent choice.'

Jobert recognised his discomfort. *I am leaving 2ⁿᵈ Company.*

'It is my intent to offer command of the junior 5ᵗʰ Company to Neilage,' said Spiccard. 'Again, your thoughts on such an appointment?'

'I have no objection, sir. Neilage is well prepared for command. He has served as company second-in-command prior to the uprisings in Marseille last April.'

'I believe Voreille and Huin capable as company seconds-in-command for 2ⁿᵈ and 5ᵗʰ Companies respectively.'

Jobert swallowed against the dryness in his throat to focus on the emerging possibilities of subsequent promotions.

'Despite Voreille's seniority, sir, I feel Huin is the steadier of the two and the better man to support Neilage in his first command. Voreille has had eighteen months solid experience as a troop commander and would excel under Geourdai's guidance. Sir, had you considered Sergeant Major Koschak for company command? His performance is exemplary.'

Spiccard raised an eyebrow at the alternative. 'I might consider Koschak if I saw him in a company second-in-command position for six months.'

'Koschak would eat the duties of company second-in-command for breakfast, sir,' said Jobert. 'I argue that his ability places him ahead of Huin and Voreille.'

'I feel comfortable in him assuming the second-in-command of 5ᵗʰ Company, ahead of Huin. Inform me this afternoon when I confirm second-in-command and troop commander appointments. I will announce all promotions on parade tomorrow.'

'Sergeant Major, a quiet word if I may?'

Jobert looked under the lines of drying laundry. Bedrolls filled the floor of the room. The only seating was at the kitchen table.

'Just between you and I for the moment, Colonel Morin has been promoted back to Avignon and Colonel Spiccard now commands the regiment. With Clemusat now the regimental second-in-command, I am now chief of squadron with Fergnes.'

'Just between you and I, sir, the news is all through the lines. Congratulations, sir.'

Jobert snorted. 'Of course it is. Thank you. Geourdai is to command 2nd Company and Neilage is to take 5th Company. I put forward that you would make an excellent company commander and Colonel Spiccard agrees. Spiccard feels you are most eligible following a short stint as a company second-in-command. A job, you and I know, you would perform on your ear.'

Koschak jerked his head towards Jobert, his face perplexed.

'I feel uncomfortable with that, sir. Excuse me, sir, this is not what —'

'Koschak, your pay rises from four hundred francs per annum to nine hundred as a lieutenant and over two thousand as a captain.'

Koschak clenched his eyelids shut. 'I reject it, sir, all of it, sir. Thank you, sir, but no.'

Jobert blinked as he searched for words. 'Koschak, you baffle me. I could not imagine the men responding to a finer chasseur commander than yourself.'

'Maybe so, sir, but that is not what I want.'

Jobert's fingers stroked his pursed lips. 'Spiccard will offer you the role of second-in-command of 5th Company this afternoon, under Neilage. And you will say "No"?'

'That is correct, sir. I say, and will say, "No".'

'Very well, there we have it.' Jobert stood and turned to leave.

'What about you, sir?'

'Me?'

'As chief of squadron, sir? Who is your squadron trumpeter? Will you take Moench?'

Jobert's brow furrowed in confusion. 'I had not thought about it. I was preoccupied with 2ⁿᵈ Company. If Moench wanted to —'

'Wanted to? Moench is a private soldier, sir, he will go where he is fucking told.' Koschak's sullen glare was direct. 'Who will be your squadron sergeant major, sir?'

Jobert released his breath and lowered his eyes. 'Ah, I am very thankful, Sergeant Major Koschak, for having you by my side these last eighteen months. I have appreciated your steadfastness as we have brought 2ⁿᵈ Company along. I have … we have … we work well together.'

Koschak mumbled as he straightened his jacket.

Jobert shuffled as he combed his fingers through his short hair. 'Koschak, I would be obliged if you became my squadron sergeant major.'

'I am at your service, sir.'

A knife butt rapped the head table. Readying himself for toasting, Jobert tipped a slosh of *rosolio* from a jug into his cup.

'Gentlemen, charge your glasses and be upstanding,' said General Masséna. '*Vive le République.*'

'*Vive le République,*' responded the officers and guests of the 24ᵗʰ Chasseurs.

'It is with heavy heart,' said Masséna once all were seated, 'that I announce the promotion of Colonel Morin to become the Prefect of the department of Vaucluse.

'Since I was blessed with the attachment of the 24th Chasseurs à Cheval to my division, Colonel Morin has proven a wise counsellor and a good friend. Whilst most learned commanders, including our enemies, eschew the use of cavalry in mountainous country, due to Colonel Morin, I am thoroughly convinced of the value of small packets of cavalry in the screen, supporting the movement of artillery and ensuring vital supplies reach us and our wounded are hastened to care. His contributions have enhanced the division's fighting mettle and enabled us to defeat our enemies at every turn.

'Colonel, on behalf of the division, thank you for your depth of knowledge, your tireless application and your sincere friendship. I wish you the best of luck in your new assignment. Gentlemen,' Masséna raised his glass, as the officers resumed their feet, 'Colonel Morin!'

Morin leant heavily on his cane as he stood.

'Sir, gentlemen, thank you for your kind words. It is with great pride I claim that I was a brother of the capucine. It is with great sadness that I depart the ranks of such a fine regiment. I was granted a singular privilege to raise the regiment eighteen months ago. At that time, I demanded each man give his best. What I have observed daily is that every soldier in this regiment has exceeded what I expected. For that I am humbled.

'I congratulate Colonel Spiccard on his assuming command of the 24th Chasseurs. I take delight in passing on the custodianship of such a battle-hardened regiment to such a dedicated soldier and good friend. It is an immense honour to have ridden into battle with you all. On behalf of the Republic, I thank every man in this hall for his service to France. I look forward to dining with every one of you when you next visit Avignon. Gentlemen, the 24th Chasseurs à Cheval.'

'24ᵗʰ Chasseurs,' the room boomed back.

'To absent brothers.'

'Absent brothers,' rumbled the subdued response.

'Colonel Morin,' said Spiccard, who had remained standing, 'I echo General Masséna's sentiments, that it is with heavy heart we see you depart our ranks. I am aware of the importance of your new post and know Avignon is well served by your keen eye and your firm hand in her government.

'I am deeply honoured to take up the mantle of Commanding Officer of the 24ᵗʰ Chasseurs à Cheval. I step into big boots. But safe within the strength of our brotherhood I am not daunted.

'I shall announce a number of key promotions. I welcome Lieutenant Colonel Clemusat as the new regimental second-in-command. I welcome Major Jobert as the new Chief of Squadron, alongside Major Fergnes.

'I welcome Captain Geourdai as the commander of 2ⁿᵈ Company, supported by Lieutenant Voreille as company second-in-command. I welcome Captain Neilage as the commander of 5ᵗʰ Company, supported by Lieutenant Huin as company second-in-command.'

Jobert waved his cup to Geourdai and Voreille across the table, radiating sincerity from his flushed face.

'Each of us who are incorrectly dressed this evening,' said Spiccard referring to the incorrect stripes of rank on the cuffs of those just promoted, 'will make amends by supplying all the liqueur this evening to our guests and brothers.'

Jobert and the men around him roared and stomped with delight.

'Can this be repaired before the wedding, Orlande?'

Jobert and Orlande huddled over the moth damaged felt of Jobert's dress bicorne.

Orlande pressed his spectacles onto the bridge of his nose. 'Sufficient repair, sir, that all of Avignon's eyes will remain on Major Fergnes' bride.'

'Hmm, sweet Marguerite. I am unsure what attracts Fergnes more. The lady's flashing eyes or that her father is a metal merchant.' Jobert rummaged in his footlocker to inspect the scuffs on his green Moroccan leather dress boots. 'Were you able to post my letter to my brother?'

'I did, sir. I feel confident it will arrive in good time for you both to meet in Avignon. Speaking of family, sir, I sense Duque is eager to return home.'

Jobert frowned at the display of his best uniform and all associated accoutrements laid out on his bedroll. 'I will miss Duque.'

'As will I, sir. We three have ...' Orlande swept his red forelock back only for it to flop once more across his forehead. 'He will return from his veterinary studies soon enough. I have kept a jar of preserved apricots for our last ... our dinner to-gether before you both depart. Have you decided on your new groom?'

Jobert shrugged. 'Madame Quandalle's boy is not an option. I was not much older when I assumed such duties, but I was not required to follow my officer onto a battlefield until I was fifteen.' Jobert's vision blurred to a countryside an ocean away, and his fingertips brushed the hilt of a small dagger he kept in his left cuff. 'Tulloc is my choice, as he has served as an apprentice farrier to the company this last eighteen months and is a proven marksman, but I will finalise those arrangements on my return.'

Orlande rubbed at a mark on Jobert's dark-orange waistcoat.

'Have you heard, sir, that Major Fergnes now seeks an apart-ment in Nice for his bride. *Mademoiselle* Marguerite's cousin, Mademoiselle Camille, will accompany her. I hope Captain Geourdai will find comfort at such news.'

'Geourdai's desire for Camille cannot be realised due to the paucity of his income.'

'With you on a major's wage, sir, how soon until wedding bells ring for you?'

'Hah! It is the wealth of Fergnes' family, and hers, that makes love possible. Fergnes secures accommodation in Nice, and then maintains the expense of home and servants. Good grief, I can-not imagine the cost of furnishings. How can Fergnes serve both his wife and France? The truth is he cannot, no man can.'

Jobert bristled as an enigmatic smile warmed Orlande's face.

'You know quite well, Orlande, I have not stood still long enough to fall in love. Moreover, stationed in bleak Oneglia, with six thousand hungry troops ravaging the countryside, the ladies, whether whores or maidens, are scant. A most unlikely environment for engaging any eligible Madame Jobert. I have observed Geourdai and Voreille burdened with constant distraction, hoping any approaching aide carries a letter of ardent love. I elude such bother. I remain content with feminine company for an evening or two on my visits to Nice.'

Orlande smoothed the lapels of Jobert's full-dress tailcoat. 'But love will cross your path, sir, and demand satisfaction. How will you address love then?'

'It is all beyond me, Orlande.' Jobert's fingertips strayed along the inlaid details of his dress sword belt. 'Should love challenge me, I will probably dishonour myself and run.'

Chapter Eleven

December 1794, Avignon, France

'Stand to arms! The bridal party approaches.'

Jobert and Chabenac turned towards Fergnes and his bride, each fixing a serene smile to his face.

'Gentlemen,' said Marguerite, 'you will not sneak off and discuss cannons and Austrians and whatnot. Not today.' Marguerite waved a slender, white arm towards the flickering light of massive chandeliers. 'Who can believe it is twenty months since we all met here in Madame de Rossi's magnificent ballroom?'

Marguerite then turned to a blonde woman in her early forties, whose calm blue eyes drifted across each officer in the party. Her lips curled as if they were about to bestow a kiss. 'Madame Berland, may I introduce the officers of Fergnes' regiment?'

'Simon de Chabenac!' said Madame Berland. 'My goodness how you have grown!'

Chabenac bowed with a graceful flourish. 'Madame, it has been too long. Are you quite well?'

'Come, tell me of your adventures.' Madame Berland took

both of Chabenac's hands in hers and led him away from the group.

'Oh, darling André, we are so delighted you could attend,' said Marguerite. 'Oh, my goodness! Is it seemly, even as a married woman, to kiss a man with such a scar?'

Fergnes offered his hand to Jobert. 'Kiss only the scar-faced brigands at your wedding feast, my sweetness, and then no other.'

'Congratulations, Fergnes,' said Jobert. 'My sincere best wishes for your life together.'

Fergnes cocked his head to one side, appraising Jobert with his dark eyes. 'My congratulations on your new lace. Forgive my absence, I had much to attend to here.'

'There is nothing to forgive. As the snows close the passes, December in Oneglia is forlorn. I was appreciative of the journey here.'

Fergnes took two glasses of champagne from a passing tray. 'I hope the taverns you, Chabenac and Geourdai travelled through will be repaired in time for your return. Allow me to beg your forgiveness further. I have taken rooms in Nice for Marguerite and her cousin Camille. I have asked Spiccard if I might attach to the squadrons on escort and reserve duty until domestic matters settle.'

Jobert recognised if one chief of squadron was based in Nice, then the other, himself, was forever on duty at the bleak outposts. 'My wedding gift to you both.'

'Thank you, my friend.' Fergnes winced with relief. 'There will always be a room for you whenever you call.'

A smile flashed across Jobert's face, as he thought of the obliging ladies at whose establishment he preferred to stay when visiting Nice.

'How have you found the new role?' asked Fergnes.

'Chief of squadron? Winter duty with no cavalry in the divisional screen is both idle and grim. The villages around Garessio were plundered in April, their crops and groves stripped during the summer. Now the villagers and the infantry are starving. Separated from 2nd Company, I admit to feeling disoriented. Why ask?'

'Be ready to adjust to the new rank. I found myself intruding on the responsibilities of the company commanders. Having just handed over 1st Company, I found myself stepping on toes.'

'Then I forgive you detailing how my company at Dego crossed the Bormida and ascended the slope.'

Fergnes opened his palms upwards. 'There you have it. Well done on identifying my deliberate mistake. Speaking of Dego, thank you for … your assessment of the Austrian horse artillery.'

Jobert was tapped on the shoulder with a folded fan.

'Jobert,' Marguerite asked, 'do you remember my cousin Camille?'

'Most certainly. Mademoiselle Camille, how do you do?' Jobert lifted his chin to avoid the temptation of her figure.

Camille's calm, dark eyes slid across his tanned face to linger on the brown scar. 'Have you heard we are to join you in Nice, Jobert?'

'Most welcome news. I hope you ladies are preparing to host a deluge of young officers.' Jobert winked at Fergnes who rolled his eyes at the thought. 'Camille, where is your gallant escort? The way Geourdai speaks of you, I am surprised to not see him in constant attendance.'

'Here he comes now,' Camille smiled without humour.

Geourdai beamed his lop-sided grin as he joined them, some inner delight causing him to bounce upon his toes.

'Major Jobert, sir, an old friend awaits you in the library, and requests you attend him at your earliest convenience.'

Jobert's eyes adjusted in the dim library, the firelight from the hearth dancing on the burnished timber wall-panels. The smell of ancient parchment and leather-bound books was overlaid by the sweet tang of cigar smoke. Jobert peered about the room to discern the source.

'Major Jobert, no less,' growled the harsh voice of Jobert's old friend, Avriol. 'My warmest congratulations, dear fellow.'

'General Avriol, sir.' Jobert stifled his shock as he strode across the room and shook Avriol's hand. 'What a most pleasant surprise. How wonderful that you attend.'

Avriol replaced a volume back onto the shelf. 'Do you still have de Guibert's *Essai général de Tactique*?'

'Of course, sir.' Jobert smiled at the thought of Avriol's parting gift last December. 'I consume it section by section, as my company is rotated back to our depot for a month in reserve. I enjoy de Guibert's ideas. His tactical concepts align with my experiences in the north two years ago, but there is little immediate use to a company commander on goat tracks in the Alps.'

'Hah! A company commander no longer, eh.' Avriol slapped Jobert on the shoulder. 'I shall send you Bourcet's *Principes de la Guerre des Montagnes*. Come, armagnac? It is particularly good.'

As he poured them both a large measure from a cut-glass decanter, Avriol's intense eyes squinted at Jobert's scar. 'What have you there?'

'An Austrian gift.'

Avriol drew on his cigar. 'May I share my thoughts on your new rank, one old sergeant to another?'

'Please, sir.'

'It is fair to say that attention to company detail was the cornerstone of our lives as non-commissioned officers. Perhaps you and I excelled in such, and that led to our promotion in the old army and becoming officers in the new. When I departed the comforting routines of the company, as a chief of squadron, I chafed at the bit as I watched new men, like Fergnes and Chabenac, struggle with what I knew intuitively. No longer was I to implement those details, as either sergeant or captain. Now I was to guide with patience. I found that hard to adjust to. I fought the desire to knock fellows out of the way and get company details attended to properly and promptly.'

'You fought that desire well, sir. I never sensed anything from you but patient guidance.'

'Oh, no, you, Geourdai and the other sergeants who had become officers were a joy. I suppose I warn you of a potential distraction in your new role. The colonel of a regiment of chasseurs à cheval, having received his orders from a divisional commander, breaks that wide-ranging task into sub-elements allocated to his squadrons. The colonel takes one squadron and entrusts the other two to both his chiefs of squadron. You, young Major Jobert, now complete the task to achieve a key element in the general's plan. This must occupy your mind now. How will the ground confound or enhance the general's plan? How will the enemy's actions threaten or advance your senior commander's options? No longer run your eye across girths, cartridge boxes or bit-chains.'

Avriol poured them both another armagnac. 'But enough of all that. I know you will shine. Down to business.'

Avriol waved his hand at a small table upon which sat a short stack of documents.

'You remember that last night in Toulon? When a squadron of Spanish dragoons abandoned their horses in the naval precinct prior to them embarking? And you and I sent word to Geourdai

141

to fetch the horses away before the city burnt? I sold those two hundred horses. Spanish blood, mares in particular, commands a good price. Indeed, an exceptionally good price. I have seventy thousand francs for you to divide amongst 2nd Company.'

Jobert's face twisted in alarm, and he reeled back in his chair at the size of the sum.

'Indeed,' said Avriol. 'We bagged nearly two hundred horses, dragoon remounts as well as quality chargers abandoned by the admirals, the senior officers and their aides. After costs, I divided the prize between Geourdai's and your companies, Colonel Morin and myself.'

'But seventy thousand francs, sir,' said Jobert, 'divided amongst the company, that is the equivalent of each of my chasseurs receiving a second lieutenant's annual salary.'

Avriol passed across an envelope. 'The fortunes of war, my lad. I have lodged the funds here with the de Rossi family. Here is a note of withdrawal for the amount. I believe there remain company families, who have lost their sons, grateful for the windfall.'

'Puh! Half the company will desert.'

'You will manage it.' Avriol drained his glass and turned to the decanter. 'Now, finish those dregs. There is more.'

'More?' Jobert raised his eyes from his own glass to look at Avriol.

'Morin and Geourdai have received their share of the horse sale. That business is concluded. This next discussion is just between you and me.'

Jobert blinked.

Avriol maintained Jobert's gaze and licked his lips. 'Again, that last night in Toulon, were you of the understanding we were saving the French Mediterranean Fleet from destruction?'

Jobert scowled. 'Yes, sir.'

'And are you still of that opinion? That we saved twenty-five

French warships?'

'Yes, sir.'

'Then you are wrong.'

Jobert blinked but remained still.

Avriol's intense eyes narrowed. 'When the British and Spanish secured Toulon on the 27th of August 1793, they captured sixty French warships. Those warships became the property of the British, Spanish, and in due course, the Sardinian and Neapolitan navies. Our enemies removed twenty of their ships in the four months before our final attack. Aided by the deception to which you and I were party, our enemies were only able to scuttle sixteen of their ships in their haste to abandon the port. When the sun rose on the 19th of December, France had captured twenty-five intact enemy warships and was able to salvage eleven vessels burnt to the waterline in the shallows beside the wharves.'

'We captured twenty-five enemy warships, sir? Not saved twenty-five French —'

'Correct. What is the market price for a captured warship, Jobert? Hmm? It is cheaper to pay prize money for a captured ship than pay for a new ship to be laid down, fitted out and crewed. Hmm? Three hundred thousand gold louis. Our little Spanish demolition party of twenty-one captured seven-and-a-half million louis' worth of warships.'

Jobert froze. He wanted to swallow but was not sure he could move.

'Now,' said Avriol, 'how is such a prize divided when an enemy ship is captured at sea? The admiral who commissioned the voyage receives a healthy slice. The captain of the successful vessel and every member of the crew receives their share. The rule of thumb is a man who participates in capturing a prize ship expects to receive a purse equivalent to ten years of his current wage.'

Jobert narrowed his eyes in disbelief. *Am I to receive two-hundred-and-fifty-years wages?*

Avriol smiled without humour. 'The Ministry of War has reviewed the matter and has declared the distribution of prize money. Rest assured knowing Deputy Saliceti, the Admiral, Saint-Joséph and quite a few influential gentlemen in Paris have received a most generous purse to ensure the review process achieved a satisfactory conclusion.'

As Avriol flicked his cigar butt into the fireplace, Jobert ran his eyes over Avriol's finely woven jacket, its silver buttons, his richly brocaded waistcoat, the heavy silver fob chain, the lustre of the leather of his well-stitched shoes.

'Paris has recognised that the eighteen men of the 24th Chasseurs capturing twenty-five ships-of-the-line is a most exceptional circumstance. In their infinite wisdom, they have determined that we accord a prize equivalent to the capture of *four* ships. Yes, each man from 2nd Company who participated will receive a sum equivalent to *forty* years wages. Now, Paris admonishes us to be fair, for a naval man to capture four ships warrants an entire lifetime at sea. We are, on reflection, most fortunate in our serendipitous selection for the affair. Would you not agree?'

Jobert's heart raced as he attempted to lick his bone-dry lips but found his tongue would not move. Trembling, he blew out a deep, slow breath.

Avriol passed further documents to Jobert.

'Now, Jobert, you are responsible for the division of the monies to your men, some twenty-five thousand louis. Here is a note of account with the Treasury of the Republic. You will receive this money, I assure you. How you transport it and store it requires some thought which I leave to you. I also have a draft breakdown of the funds for each man, for your review as you see fit. You will note on that list before you, Jobert, you personally receive some five thousand louis. If you were wise, purchase yourself an annuity from which you receive an amount every year equivalent to the salary of a colonel of cavalry for the rest of your life.'

Jobert looked at the crisp, yellow page, his limbs leaden. As he looked up from the page, Jobert found the strength to close his mouth and swallow hard.

As Jobert closed the library door, the merriment of the bridal reception was jarring.

He pressed his hand to his full-dress chasseur-green tailcoat and confirmed the safety of Avriol's documents within his inner pockets.

In a situation when quick money is to be made, I am a reasonable judge of options. But that is for one or two hundred francs, not one hundred thousand francs! I need to think this through. I need to leave. I need to find Didier as he arrives either today or tomorrow. I must take my leave of Fergnes and Marguerite!

A sudden 'hurrah' from the wedding revellers caused Jobert to turn. Men cheered and women squealed as someone within their circle performed an impressive dancing leap.

'Again!' cried Marguerite.

Jobert saw a green chasseur uniform launch high into the air to land in the middle of the audience. Jobert peered past the throng and identified Geourdai. Then another dancer, dressed in white silk, leapt even higher, spun and landed with cat-like softness on the marble floor. The growing crowd erupted with pleasure.

Marguerite clapped with exhilaration, giddy with champagne

and excitement. As she stepped back, Jobert saw the white-clad dancer, folded with gentle grace on one knee on the floor, hand extended in homage towards the bride. Highlighting the white silk suit, pink and sky-blue bows, on shoes, cuffs and queue, hinted at tricolour virtues on this blissful day.

The dancer raised his head, his face serene.

Jobert froze.

Jobert recognised the face from Nice.

Inoubli.

The dancer was Inoubli, an Avignon dance instructor.

Just after the 24th Chasseurs was raised, as recruits and re-mounts flooded into the Avignon barracks, Madame de Rossi had invited the officers of the new regiment to a ball in this very hall. At that time, a certain degree of anxiety ensued, as many of the new officers were ex-sergeants and sergeant majors of the old, royal army, and were concerned they did not know how to dance at a society occasion. Prior to the ball, Jobert improved company funds by providing dance lessons at a local tavern. Inoubli had instructed the steps of the *gavotte*, the *bourrée* and the *allemande*.

Now, here was Inoubli at an Avignon society wedding. That was not unusual. What caused Jobert's discomfort was that it was Inoubli's face he had seen in the crowded streets of Nice in August.

Inoubli in Nice?

Jobert looked away from the revellers. *Am I sure? It must have been. Very well, Inoubli was in Nice. But in the garb of a labourer? A man renowned for his colour-coordinated silks.*

Jobert remembered his and Inoubli's eyes locking in that moment. *Inoubli looked at me. He recognised me, but he did not acknowledge me. His face as serene then as it is now.* Jobert frowned. *Would the man even remember me after three or four dance lessons?*

'Forgive me, Major, you look as if you have seen a ghost.'

Jobert's gaze returned to the parted lips of Madame Berland. 'Are you quite well, sir? I know that many of our warriors become quite disoriented in an environment of perfume, music, champagne and soft curls.'

'Forgive me, Madame, it may well be as you describe. The sudden change from ...' Jobert shook his head. 'Perhaps I need to retire.'

'Where are you staying? No matter! Wherever it is, it is horrid.' Madame placed both her gloved hands on Jobert's chest. 'I insist you take my coach to my home. A room is ready. Your baggage will be collected from your current lodgings.'

Jobert fought the desire to take her in his arms. 'No, Madame, you are too kind —'

Madame Berland placed a gloved fingertip to his lips. 'No, sir, enough. I will have my coach brought up. In the Alps you protect me. In Avignon, I will refresh you.'

Chapter Twelve

'Major Didier Jobert-Chauvel.'

Jobert placed his coffee cup down on the inlaid side table beside his plush upholstered chair and stood.

Didier moved smoothly across the carpeted salon in his well-tailored light-blue dolman jacket and tight breeches of the 1st Hussars. His smile flashed beneath the handsome sweep of his thick moustache, his dark hair combed back into a bound queue.

The hussar uniform included an extra jacket, the heavily braided *pelisse*, with cuffs and collars edged with fur. Maintaining the fashion of all hussars, Didier's pelisse was draped raffishly across his left shoulder and kept in place by a decorative cord.

'And here we are. Congratulations, Major André Jobert.'

Jobert snorted with a half-smile and wrapped his elder, but shorter, brother in a tight hug.

'Jobert-Chauvel?'

'What? Can I not honour my grandfather?'

Didier frowned as he took Jobert's jaw in his gloved hand

to peer at Jobert's scar on his right cheek. 'My affectation pales before this. You will obviously stop at nothing to attract the ladies. You look quite becoming. I must have one. Wherever did you have it done?'

Jobert flinched as an icy sensation crawled across his cheekbone. 'In April, an Austrian ball struck my musketoon whilst I was in the act of firing.' He calmed the scarred skin with his fingertips.

Didier winced. 'You are very thin, brother. Did the wound bring a fever with it?'

'No.' Jobert was surprised at the description. 'More than likely, the abysmal supply situation.'

'Does your regimental officer's mess dine so poorly? Is there not —'

'We have no mess at the present.' Jobert waved his hand to dismiss the conversation. 'Our squadrons are dispersed and always on the move. It is as good as it can be.'

A footman appeared at Jobert's elbow. 'Excuse me, gentlemen, may I offer refreshment?'

'Coffee for two, please,' said Jobert.

'*Armagnac?*' Didier smiled at the steward.

'Certainly, sir, and cake?'

'Why not?' Didier's eyes followed the footman as he departed, then allowed his eyes to drift about the sumptuous salon. Three young officers lounged in deep chairs by the fire and two others were engaged in an earnest conversation over cards by the window. 'What a convivial situation. How long have you been here?'

'Just last night. I met Madame Berland at the wedding's reception, and she invited me to stay.'

'And did you have ... a pleasant evening?'

It was Jobert's turn for a half smile. He nodded slowly. 'Most pleasant, thank you. You will be extended an invitation at lunch.'

Didier flapped his hand and focused his attention on the selection of small cakes, as the footman poured coffee from an exquisite silver pot.

'Your hat, sir?' asked the footman of Didier, referring to his hussar headdress, the mirliton cap.

'No, if you please, pass it here,' said Jobert, reaching forward for the tall sky blue and red hat. 'Michelle wrote of a contract the family has won to dress the new mirliton.'

Jobert took the tall cylindrical hat, tapering to a flat top. Along one-side was fixed a long, triangular regimentally-coloured pennant, in Didier's case, sky blue and red. On the peak of the hat, a long sky-blue feathered plume rose, tipped with red.

'The flame, as it is known,' Didier pointed at the extended triangle of cloth, 'can be worn long over the shoulder, or wrapped about the cap, one way or the other, highlighting one regimental colour or the other, dependent on occasion.'

'Michelle wrote some thirty-thousand are required to be issued in the coming year.'

'Huh!' scoffed Didier. 'The family will deeply appreciate the receipt of the revenue, but we will see about the timeliness of the issue of the new headdress. Have you received news from her?'

'No, not since the fall of Robespierre.' Jobert handed the mirliton back to the footman. 'Doubtless, Yann will have her most recent mail. Are you still going up to the farm? Will Michelle leave Paris to join you?'

'No, Michelle will stay in Paris with Aunt Sophie. Yes, I will spend a few weeks with Yann. And Duque will join me on the journey up to the Auvergne, I believe? Veterinary school, I hear? How marvellous. Moreover, what of these confounded cartage contracts with the Army of Italy that have completely taken over the colts?'

'Yes, Duque will accompany you up to the farm.' A humourless smile bent Jobert's lips. 'Yes, he will attend Alfort midyear, until then he will study under Yann. As I understand, we have established a supply of fine wines to Masséna, one of our divisional commanders.'

Didier slumped in his chair. 'Then that gentleman has a most particular palate and entertains lavishly. I had a contractual opportunity within the Army of the Alps and was informed all twenty wagons were absorbed with trade from Paris to Nice. If they are taking wine to Nice, I assume they have a return load. If so, what the hell is it?'

'I am unaware. That is for Yann and Duque's father to manage. My hands are rather full with regimental duties. I assume, since the venture generates revenue for the family, and schooling for the colts, that it is a welcome outcome.'

Didier drained his armagnac balloon. 'Then I shall enquire upon reaching home.'

'There is something I wish you to take home to Yann.' Jobert passed across a thick key on a looped string.

'More prudent savings, brother?'

'First, I have a few more items for my collection.'

'What? Your museum? Whatever now?'

'They are nothing. Please just place the package in uncle's storeroom.'

'Come now, you know I envy your collection. I never think to have one of my own. What is to be added?'

'A musketoon with a bent barrel.' Jobert rubbed the scar on his cheek. 'And my old plumes with my company pom-pom. Enthralling, I am sure.'

Didier tilted his head in confusion. 'And this key?'

'Duque has the strongbox. Three thousand francs.'

'André!' Didier sat up, looking exasperated. 'It was unfair you kept a secret about three thousand francs you conjured last year, and now you magic another?'

Jobert raised his hands. 'Last year I was involved in an affair in Valence, where I skimmed a trifle from a vast Royalist hoard.'

'Lucky you. This year?'

'My colonel awarded me a prize of fifty gold louis resulting from the regiment's good work at Toulon. The other two thousand francs are from the sale of an Austrian horse I took in combat.'

'Two thousand francs? Whose horse was it? The Emperor's?'

Jobert shrugged. 'Fine horses in the Alps are a rare commodity.'

Didier stretched his highly polished toe of his calf-length riding boots to nudge Jobert's shin. 'Come now, darling brother, well done.'

'There is more.'

Didier set his lips and tilted his head.

Jobert retrieved a letter from an inner pocket. 'There is five thousand more.'

Didier drew in his breath.

A half-grin twisted Jobert's scarred cheek. 'Five thousand gold louis more.'

Didier recoiled, his mouth forming an expletive. His abrupt movement and look of alarm attracted the attention of the others in the room. 'One hundred thousand francs?'

Jobert smiled at his brother's reaction under hooded eyes. 'Yes. The sum is of benefit to us all, Didier.'

Didier searched his brother's face, shrugging to invite Jobert's explanation.

'You know I was part of an enterprise to minimise the destruction of Toulon's fleet last December, yes? As a result, twenty-five ships were saved. Or so I thought.'

Didier remained attentively still as Jobert continued. 'Our navy had a fleet of seventy in the Mediterranean, of which sixty were captured by the British and the Spanish. As I now understand, those sixty ships became prizes of the enemy and joined their navies. The coalition removed twenty of their new ships, destroyed sixteen in their last night in Toulon. I was part of the capture of twenty-five enemy warships.'

Realisation dawned on Didier's face. He leant forward, elbows on knees, mouth agape, eyes flickering, calculating. 'As I understand, a man makes ten years wages from the capture of one prize. And you captured twenty-five?'

'Paris has determined that we be compensated as if we had captured four ships. More than any naval man could ever hope for in a lifetime of service at sea, they say. One hundred thousand francs. Five thousand louis. Forty years of earnings for a captain of cavalry.'

Didier rocked back, his hands to his mouth, then lurched forward and squeezed Jobert's knee, before collapsing back again. 'What is your intent?'

'Reduce the exorbitant farm loan so that our family holds the title. The balance paid to reduce the mortgage. It is all in the letter to Yann.'

'This event is as pivotal as grandfather receiving the initial tenancy.' Didier stared at the envelope in his hands. 'Or the opportunity to purchase when his colonel's family fled. Whatever will you do next, dear brother?'

Jobert swallowed his armagnac in a gulp. 'Tomorrow I travel for two weeks to my starving village in the Alps and take up duties as commander of the regiment's divisional screen.'

Didier sat forward on the edge of his seat. 'Are you ambitious, André? Look at your Avriol, Bonaparte, Victor and Masséna. I observe the rapid promotions around me, and my chest burns with desire to grasp any opportunity for advancement. Is that wrong?'

'No, it is not wrong. France is at war with Europe and now is our moment to shine. Or die. Though, in discussion with my infantry friends, the time of rapid promotion has passed. Victor and Masséna were royal army sergeants who joined the volunteer legions in 1791 and were voted to battalion command.'

'I was voted from captain to major when I joined my new legion.'

'Yes, but your regimental colonel commanded his cavalry regiment as a regiment. In '92 and '93, infantry battalions, commanded by their majors, were dispersed into various brigades. If a major, such as Victor or Masséna, excelled in front of a People's Deputy, such as Saliceti, of course they skipped over the rank of regimental colonel to become brigade general instead. Now, with Minister Carnot's amalgamation of the battalions into permanent regiments, the days of sergeants becoming chiefs of battalion one day and becoming brigade generals the next are well over.'

Didier sulked, scoffing the last two pieces of cake. 'Avriol and Bonaparte were not infantrymen.'

'That is correct, they were not. They held headquarters appointments to incompetent generals, acting in independent commands under the eye of friends of Robespierre. With the guillotine removing many incompetent generals and all of Robespierre's connections, the ability for a Deputy to advance a promising staff officer is much diminished. Should the Republic spawn another dictator, then pounce to join his staff.'

'Oh, shut up, little brother. I ought to punch you. I need more armagnac.' Didier slouched in his armchair and looked about for a footman. 'You say you are not ambitious, yet you seize opportunities which net you sabres and battleships. We all have our secrets, André, what are yours? I believe father, or perhaps grandfather, has said something which is now the burr in your blanket.'

'Major Jobert, sir, the young officers are here.'

The icy February rain sheeted down on the Mediterranean coast, creating a lake of slop around the meagre regimental billets and stables on the outskirts of Oneglia. Jobert looked past Koschak standing in the door frame to the four hunched men clutching capes and sabres, trudging across the churned slush towards the leaking porch.

Freshly promoted from sergeant, Second Lieutenants Pultiere, Yinot and Bredieux saluted.

The fourth bedraggled figure, Second Lieutenant Peugeot, had arrived from the *École Militaire* in Paris. The boy's rain-streaked face was framed by black curls and topped by his saturated bonnet-de-police. Jobert had noted that Peugeot's face was in attentive motion seeking information, like a hunting dog always scenting the air.

'Lieutenant Peugeot,' said Jobert, 'you are not required at this meeting. I have directed all saddlery and harness lifted off the stable floor if it floods. Ensure my command is executed by your sergeants. That will be all.'

Peugeot gripped his wet cape about his shoulders to re-enter the deluge.

The newly promoted senior officers of 2nd Squadron were positioned around a long kitchen table. Chief of Squadron Jobert sat in the centre with Squadron Sergeant Major Koschak to his left and Captain Neilage, 5th Company, scratching documents with a quill, to Jobert's right. Voreille and Huin, seconds-in-command of 2nd and 5th Company respectively, sat with detached expressions at either end of the table.

'As for the rest of you,' said Jobert, 'I shall award duty officer for a week to any man who babbles about the 8th Hussars' recent escapades in Utrecht. Contain any youthful excitement about charging across ice and capturing the Dutch fleet for the dinner table.'

In the trains of the new lace upon their sleeves, consistent reminders rumbled to adjust attitudes to their new rank. Invited to sit, the junior officers rummaged in their tailcoats for notebooks and pencils.

'There is an outstanding item of 2nd Company business to conclude,' said Jobert. 'A reward is allocated to all ranks of the company resulting from our part in the capture of Toulon. The money allocated is in part from the sale of the captured Spanish horses and for our part in the securing of our warships.'

Bredieux shifted in his seat. Jobert knew Bredieux, as a Saint-Nazaire fisherman, understood the prize associated with captured vessels.

'This morning Captain Neilage, Sergeant Major Koschak and I have reviewed and confirmed the amounts to be distributed to each man. We have allocated a purse to each 2nd Company chasseur who enlisted in March 1793 and was on the company roll in the last days of Toulon. Any man who died during that period, his family will receive his purse. Any man who was invalided out of the regiment will also be sent his purse.'

Koschak rumbled an acknowledgement of those now gone.

Jobert lowered his face and inspected his palms but saw only a parade of ghostly faces. He straightened his shoulders, shrugging the dead and maimed from his immediate thoughts. 'I now have two tasks for you all. First, each of you will be allocated one thousand gold louis.'

Pultiere, Yinot and Bredieux all slumped and frowned, their mouths open, their breathing slowed.

'If you are wise,' said Jobert, 'you will purchase an annuity. An annuity of this magnitude will provide you an annual income equivalent to the current salary of a lieutenant, not second lieutenant, but lieutenant of cavalry, for the rest of your life.'

Jobert had seen this same expression of utter disbelief, or the expectation someone would declare this whole proceeding a joke, some hours earlier this morning, on Neilage's, Voreille's, Huin's and Koschak's faces when they were allocated two thousand louis for their part in the venture.

'You have three broad options. First, receive the original amount to spend as you will. Second, receive the interest from the annuity to supplement your, or your family's, current income. Third, leave the interest to compound with the principal to increase the size of your asset.'

Yinot looked vexed at the implications.

'Major Fergnes, Captain Neilage and I are well versed in arranging annuities.' Jobert nodded reassurance. 'I urge you to visit any one of us to discuss how. The money is now in Paris under the watchful eye of my agents, members of my family. I need each of you to inform me of your requirements once you have reflected on your options. It is a large prize. The situation demands your careful consideration.'

Jobert looked to the page upon which Neilage's bobbing quill raced. Satisfied with the notetaking, Jobert gave each second lieutenant a harsh stare.

'I spoke of two tasks. The second is to support our chasseurs, those below the rank of sergeant in late December '93, to digest the enormity of their windfall. All corporals at that time, all chasseurs who were selected to enter Toulon with us that last night and all members of the 'Spanish water-cart', and that includes Madame Quandalle, are to receive one thousand francs, or the equivalent of one year's wages for a lieutenant. All chasseurs who were not members of the Spanish demolition party will receive five hundred francs or equivalent to a year's wages for a company sergeant major.'

Jobert scowled as he lent back. 'Your task, young officers,

which Sergeant Major and I shall monitor closely, is to support your chasseurs so that they shield their prize from cards, whores or the keg.'

Jobert broke his uncle's wax seal and unfolded the yellow paper.

5th February 1795

André,

Didier has arrived safe, told me your news and passed me your strong box. My congratulations on your recent promotion and good fortune. I have received your contribution of three thousand francs. Find enclosed a receipt for your records reflecting the increase in your shareholding.

I have reflected for some time on your offer of five thousand louis. Didier and I are of the opinion that we accept your generous offer of one thousand louis to reduce the loan to secure the title. The elimination of the interest repayments will cause a most beneficial re-allocation of income. Thank you.

Didier and I are of a similar view that we decline your ridiculous offer of the remaining four thousand louis. Generous but ridiculous.

Jobert creaked on the stool by the hearth.
'All is well at home, I hope, sir?' asked Orlande.

We both counsel you most strongly to purchase an annuity. Didier informs me such an asset provides the annual salary of a lieutenant colonel of cavalry. I impress upon you the wisdom of this course of action. How you dispose of the annual dividend is then up to you. Allocating part, or all, of such funds to the farm is but one option.

Duque, Didier and I have discussed the matter of consolidating the money from the Treasury and the de Rossi family that is allocated to your discretion, that is, the entire five hundred and seventy thousand francs. We are of the opinion that the funds be temporarily moved to within the family accounts in Paris, and then dispersing those funds as you have directed in your letter. Once the snows abate here, Duque and I will travel to Avignon and then Paris and attend to the matter.

Didier requested I inform you of the details of the current cartage contract with Colonel Raive of the Army of Italy. Every six months, five wagon loads of fine wine are to arrive in Nice, and five wagon loads of furniture are transported from Nice to Raive's agents in Paris.

The income of this cartage, after costs, is equivalent to the sale of eight extra horses to the artillery. I have made quite sure this contractual obligation has no detrimental impact on the well-being and schooling of the colts prior to their sale to the artillery. On the contrary, the size of loads and the distance travelled strengthens the tendons and bones …

'Orlande, is there time for a walk before dinner?'

Without waiting for an answer, Jobert thrust the letter into his waistcoat, snatched at his cape and shoved open the door.

Chapter Thirteen
March 1795, Oneglia, Italy

Six hundred chasseurs à pied of the 3rd Battalion, 16th Légère Regiment had formed an infantry fire line in three ranks. The battalion had deployed forward a company of eighty men, forty pairs in two lines of skirmishers, providing a two-hundred-metre screen to the front and flanks of the battalion. The first skirmish line deployed at one hundred metres from the front rank of the battalion, the second line was positioned mid-way. Despite the cold Mediterranean wind, Jobert knew it would be warm for the men in the ranks within their allotted half-a-metre spacing.

General Masséna had approved a scheme where each of the three battalions of the 16th Légère were exposed to the effects of attacking cavalry, supported by the three squadrons of the 24th Chasseurs. Today, the final battalion was to engage in a series of demonstrations with Geourdai's 2nd Squadron, devised by the 16th Légère's colonel and Jobert.

As the skirmishers scampered to their positions, the fire line was extended to create an artificial requirement to aid the demonstration; four ten-metre gaps to allow the cavalry to pass through.

A trumpet call demanded everyone's attention.

The eyes of infantry skirmishers and fire line alike were attracted to a slight crest in the white plain.

A knot of green-jacketed cavalry, the head of a column, rose out of the near-horizon and, within two minutes, built a battle-line along the crest. At four hundred metres, the cavalry was well beyond the recognised range of a battalion's effective fire at one hundred metres.

Two minutes after the first crested chasseur helmet appeared above the horizon, the line had extended and *Charge* sounded. Geourdai flattened his sabre to give point. One minute later, charging at the trot, sabres extended, bellowing abuse at the infantry, the line swept around the knots of stationary skirmishers. One minute later, the trotting chasseurs roared through the lanes within the line, looking down on the excited fusiliers jeering back at them.

Rally sounded. The mounted men dropped to a walk, formed column and moved back up and over the slope.

A paradiddle on the drums caused the chatter to cease and all attention returned to Jobert. 'Four minutes. From column to line then charge. Generous, perhaps? Certainly, while no smoke obscures your vision. At four hundred metres, your front-rank is only thirty seconds away for a galloping horse. In the next approach, no warning. Skirmishers beware! The chasseurs are ordered to ride you down if they catch you.'

Once agitated skirmishers were set, a rumble built on the far-side of the plain's slight crest. Without warning, the chasseurs crested at the trot already formed in line with sabres drawn.

The battalion roared with enthusiastic alarm. Drums rolled *Outposts In*. Skirmishers ran headlong to the fire line.

No sooner had the skirmisher line dissolved, *Charge* sounded.

2nd Squadron's remounts leapt to a gallop at one hundred and fifty metres from the line. With sufficient time for a battalion to fire just one volley, if ordered to fire, the thundering horsemen covered the distance in a frightening ten seconds.

If the infantrymen had enjoyed the rush of two hundred cavalrymen trotting towards and through them in four minutes, then this next demonstration was unpleasant in the extreme. The shock was palpable as the bulk of seven hundred kilograms of man and horse, flashed through the lanes at face level, chasseurs and trumpets screaming as horse's lungs grunted and hooves thundered.

The indiscernible pointing blades, unable to be identified let alone parried, sliced through the hoof-flicked gravel.

The reverberations through earth and air inspired the fusiliers themselves to howl.

Hearts leapt from one thousand chests, human and equine.

Rally sounded. 2nd Squadron transitioned to the walk, formed column and moved around the fire line to return over the crest.

A roll of the drums subdued the hubbub in the packed ranks.

'Two minutes from sighting their approach to your front-rank,' called Jobert. 'Infantry in line cannot receive cavalry. Can the battalion form square in less than two minutes?'

The battalion accepted the challenge with a roar of enthusiasm.

'Battalion, close the gaps!' ordered the battalion's commanding officer. 'Beat *Skirmishers Out*. Battalion, fix bayonets! Load!'

Two blank cartridges were in each fusilier's cartridge box. Heart rates soared at the intensity of the drumming. Snarled warnings from the sergeants in the rear rank focused each fusilier on the drill of loading his musket.

'Present! Fire!'

The signal for the cavalry to advance once more engulfed the fire line in a cloud of acrid smoke, reducing observation to less than three metres. Fear swept through the ranks as a ripple of musketry sounded beyond the stinging haze and the skirmishers were heard to scream 'Cavalry!'

Each man's face craned towards the centre of the line to see if the chief of battalion had ordered the drummers to beat *Form Square.*

Every second counted.

Cries of 'Cavalry!' from the ranks, in case the chief of battalion was unaware of the threat, were intermingled with bellows of 'Eyes front! Load!' The drums thrashed the order to form square.

Gripped with the surge of adrenalin, infantrymen turned, yelled and stumbled to bend the line into the sides of the square. The noise of the drumming intensified as the six hundred bodies enclosed the sound.

The three ranks shuffled to become four ranks. The new first rank protected the three firing ranks from the horses by kneeling, planting their musket butts into the earth and causing a hedge of bayonets to blossom.

While those forming the sides of the square staggered into position, beyond the yellow-grey gloom, trumpets howled *Charge.*

Yelling intensified as the eighty skirmishers barged to safety through the dense human mass.

Through the smoke, the soldiers were only able to see their feet and their comrades beside them as they built the rear wall of the square. Behind them, on the side of the square facing the cavalry, muskets exploded in an ascending scale of intensity. The fire caused a crackle of further firing from around the other three sides of the square although no order was given.

Within the compressed bodies of six hundred men, in a square formation not more than twenty-five metres wide, the 'Hold fire! Hold fire!' bellows of the sergeants were overwhelmed by an incoherent animal roar around them.

The fusiliers' eyes jerked outwards through the smoke and found, a mere two metres away, the instant and alarming appearance of tossing horse heads, shuffling hooves, flashing sabres and the discord of maniacal chasseurs.

No sooner had these monstrous apparitions appeared in the gun smoke just beyond musket length, a rallying trumpet called the intimidating wall of horse flesh and steel to disappear back into the dusty gloom.

The fusiliers were left trembling and babbling with intense excitement.

The drums demanded silence.

The smoke cleared and revealed the one-hundred-metre-long line of chasseurs now retired to the low ridge. Jobert cantered Bleu slowly around the square's perimeter once calm was restored.

'Three keys to surviving cavalry,' yelled Jobert. 'One, form square. Two, front ranks kneeling with bayonets ready. Three, fire on command.'

Jobert's hips sunk Bleu to a halt. 'Just now, you fired without an order. A horseman can kill you faster than you reload. 3rd Battalion, maintain your fire discipline. If you fail, the cavalry will cut their way into your square.'

A rumble of chatter from the tight ranks caused a burst of invective from the sergeant majors to ensure silence.

Jobert stood in his stirrups and pointed to the chasseurs on the ridge. 'Cavalry will attack with half of their available force. The second half will echelon behind the first, approaching at an angle across ground not obstructed by downed horses. Watch now! More tricks to ensure your destruction. Mounted skirmishers will force infantry skirmishers to withdraw. Moench, sound *To Mess*.'

The fusiliers craned their necks and watched. The battalion's captains and lieutenants scribbled in their notebooks.

Just as the notes began to float on the air, a quarter of the chasseur line broke forward. The swarm of horsemen, musketoons raised, cantered around the flanks, and within two minutes had surrounded the square. To the fusiliers' surprise, the surrounding chasseurs started an intermittent fire of blank cartridges.

Jobert skipped Bleu back into his canter around the faces of the square. 'You fusiliers are an easy target in your dense ranks. Their gun smoke blinds you.'

'Battalion, ready! Present!' cried the chief of battalion.

The rumble of trotting horses became apparent through the mist of gun smoke generated by the mounted skirmishers.

Charge sounded.

Within ten seconds, forty galloping horsemen of the front rank flew by the square. The whoosh of hurtling great bodies caused the blue-jacketed infantry to press back upon themselves. Two seconds later the second rank flashed by, adding to the intense sensation by firing their pistols.

Five seconds later, the second half of the cavalry thundered past, the firing of blank cartridges caused curses from the infantry. The infantry was surrounded by a green-jacketed whirlpool, cantering just beyond the tips of the front rank's bayonets, explosions of musketoon and pistol fire, smoke and expended cartridge paper swirled in their faces.

Rally sounded. The chasseurs removed themselves from the proximity to the square, trotting to form a column on their commanders.

The infantry jabbered with exhilaration, breathless at the intensity of the throbbing, dust-raising experience.

Jobert trotted close to the front-rank bayonets in a counter-clockwise motion. '3rd Battalion, who here would have held his fire in that situation? Who noted the direction of the cavalry's encirclement?'

'From our right to our left, or counterclockwise, sir,' shouted a grenadier captain.

'Correct. It is easy for cavalry to fire to the left. Yet very difficult for you to fire back as he passes. Even more so here at the corner of the square.' Jobert halted at one corner of the formation. 'How about you fellows beyond the corner on the next face, are you comfortable with my position?'

The fusiliers muttered at the intimidating position over their right shoulder.

'Turn around so that you face toward Major Jobert,' the chief of battalion ordered.

The infantry watched, with suspicion, as the final troop of the squadron approached Jobert's corner location in column at the walk.

'Now for the *coup de grâce*. You were encouraged to fire by skirmishers. You were assaulted by four ranks of horsemen. If your commander had ordered a volley at the first wave, the follow-on attack, unimpeded by casualties, would have taken immediate advantage of your unloaded muskets.'

Jobert pressed Bleu forward to the barricade of bayonets. 'Observe now, the ease of cutting into a square. The kneeling bayonet holders are the prized target of the circling horsemen. Assume just one man was struck down. Excuse me, you there, lad, stand up and step out of the square!'

As the fusilier created the space in the front rank, Jobert guided Bleu's face into the gap, and the fusiliers shuffled away at the intrusion.

'In the space of one man, I avoid the distraction of bayonets at the eye level of my horse. It is now difficult for our friends here to stand firm, or kneel, with the bulk of my horse imposed upon them. My sabre reaches the second rank on my left and as far as the third rank on my right. My sabre cuts toward the tip of the square's corner on my right, a place in the square reserved for your officers. My point of weakness is my left ribs, which another cavalryman is trained to cover.'

Koschak pressed his remount forward, and three more men stepped out of the square. The tight packed ranks rocked as Jobert stepped Bleu forward, Koschak close by his left hip. Bredieux stepped up to widen the breach.

'Gentlemen, our friends here beneath me are finding this particularly uncomfortable. Within the time it has taken me to take three cuts, my horse is now emerging beyond your fourth rank.'

Jobert stood in his stirrups and looked down at the glowering faces around him. 'My natural compunction is to cut my way out to the right, through the four ranks that I now stand behind. If I become *hors de combat*, my horse will thrash uncontrolled amongst you all. If the horse is killed outright, its great weight will also widen the breach in your ranks.'

Jobert's eyes roamed over the six hundred surly men packed beneath Bleu.

'Our tactics have encouraged you to flee or fire. You have stood firm in a maelstrom of hooves and blades. You have fired according to your commander's orders. That will not impede us. We fire at your kneeling bayonet-holders on the corners. A small group of dedicated enemy cavalry, as erudite as your own grenadiers, now pounce upon a crack in your fortress. For a cavalryman to break an infantry square, even in death, the honour and the glory will be forever theirs.'

Chapter Fourteen
April 1795, Oneglia, Italy

Jobert and Geourdai sat rigid on their hardbacked chairs.

The door opened, admitting Colonel Spiccard and a gust of chill air. 'Colonel Raive, gentlemen, forgive me. Once enwrapped in the warm embrace of the regimental accounts I find it ever so difficult to take my leave. Colonel, how may we assist you?'

Raive slicked his moustache with the back of his finger. 'Gentlemen, I call to order the most virtuous Society of Alpine Web Unravellers. Jobert and Geourdai, prior to General Masséna's advance into the Bormida Valley last September, do you recall orders to advance down through the Col di Cadibona to attack the Austrians in the flank at Savona? As the regimental reserve, that was to be your task. Did you repeat that in your orders to your companies?'

'No, sir,' said Geourdai.

'Yes, sir,' said Jobert.

'Hmm, so why did you, Jobert, choose to tell your fellows?' asked Raive.

Sensing a trap, Jobert's grim face opposed Raive's light-hearted smile. 'Colonel Spiccard had specified it as a task, sir. Should I be rendered *hors de combat* I desired my commanders be aware of the wider scheme.'

'Did you ever refer to the task to anyone outside of your company?' Raive noticed Geourdai's eyes flick towards Jobert. 'Hmm? Who, Jobert?'

'On only one occasion,' said Jobert. 'Following the battle of Dego, sir, when ordered to withdraw I raised the matter of the task with Fergnes and Chabenac. I noted that it caused confusion when discussed.'

Raive's eyes sparkled. 'We have had word back from our agents within the Piedmontese and the Austrians. That task, that phrase, was received by our enemies. It possibly contributed to the Austrian decision to withdraw from Dego and not to commit laying siege to Savona.'

Raive's smug grin was absent from his eyes. 'That phrase "advance from Col di Cadibona and attack the Austrian flank at Savona" was deliberately provided only to 2nd Squadron. It is reasonable to assume our web now begins in 2nd Company. Your command now, Geourdai, I believe. Which men went across from 2nd to 5th Company with the recent promotions?'

'Only Captain Neilage, Lieutenant Huin and Second Lieutenant Yinot, sir,' answered Geourdai.

Raive jotted the names into his ever-present notebook.

'Excuse me, sir, may I ask a question? asked Peugeot. 'Is it correct that your regiment mutinied during the Revolution?'

Every other diner at the long table became motionless,

dripping spoons hovering between bowls and lips.

Until that moment, Jobert was enjoying the celebration of his thirtieth birthday. The fire warmed the small farmhouse kitchen. Madame Quandalle's *sangiovese* flowed in his veins. Orlande's vegetables, stuffed with herbed rabbit, sat in his belly. The aroma of brandied apricot dumplings filled the air.

Candlelight danced with every roar of laughter and every palm slamming the table. Excited conversation delved within the dividends of last June's victory at the battle of Fleurus. The recent peace with Prussia, the establishment of the Batavian Republic centred on Brussels, the imminent alliance with the Netherlands, the peace negotiations with Spain. Speculation soared with the revitalised Toulon fleet engaging with the British off Genoa and Austria's withdrawal beyond the Danube, due to last week's defeat on the Rhine.

Then young Peugeot asked his impertinent, if not dangerous, question.

'What did you just ask me?' Jobert searched the young man's face for any hint of malice and found only unblemished cheeks flushed with wine.

'Forgive me, sir … we were discussing —'

'How old were you when the Bastille was taken, Peugeot?'

'Twelve, sir.'

'Do you understand the Republic you offer your life for?'

Peugeot's nervous gaze leapt across the hard men around the table. The crackle of flames in the hearth the only sound in the room.

'Such events occurred within a context, Peugeot.' Jobert poked at the remnants of his dinner with his spoon. 'Where do I start?'

Geourdai tapped his wine cup on the table. The candlelight quivered. 'Once upon a time, the king wanted more money,'

'Hah! Very well, then.'

Everyone relaxed. Cups were filled.

'Once upon a time, the king wanted more money. Having bled the bourgeoisie white, the king sought greater input to his treasuries and called for the Estates General in May of '89. From this emerged the National Assembly, the true government of the constitutional monarchy of France.'

In no mood to give a lesson in recent history, Jobert scowled as he mulled over what was relevant.

'Now, all of these happenings were irrelevant to me. As a soldier, Peugeot, I was not represented at the Estates General, neither were any skilled or unskilled labourers or peasants. Up until this moment, the chasseurs of my regiment and I were loyal only to the king of France and subject to his laws. Overnight, I became a citizen of the nation of France. The laws of the king were no longer the laws of the land.'

Across the candle flicker, Koschak traced the rim of his cup with his fingers. 'Do you remember, lads? In that moment, everybody held onto their gold, nobody spent a sou, nobody received their pay, nobody made anything or grew more food. Everyone in France stood still. What would happen next?'

Faces downcast with individual memories looked up for Jobert to continue.

'We knew other regiments had mutinied,' said Jobert, 'or deserted *en masse*, or dissolved with a sizeable portion of men following their officers to their estates, or even beyond the realm. We heard of the clashes occurring between the royal army and the new National Guard. At the fall of the Bastille, at least half of our officers abandoned the regiment for their estates. The drastic erosion of rights in the lives of our officers had no great bearing upon us. Regimental life went on without them as it had always done. For those in the ranks, some were excited, most were anxious. Day after day, reported event after event, we waited for our king and our government to provide clarity, and, day after day, none came. Then one day, Peugeot, enough was enough.'

Jobert shifted with discomfort. *Am I making excuses for six years ago?* His refilled cup slid towards him.

'We had suppressed riots in the past. Pitchforks, crowbars and cobblestones are simple enough to parry. You focus on laying the flat of your blade onto shoulders and backs while ensuring your horse was not cut. The people were disobedient subjects of the king's law. Our duty was to protect the warehouses and the silos.' Jobert's eyes slid the length of the table to Chabenac. 'The property of the nobility and the clergy.'

Chabenac's frozen face focused on the curl of flame.

'The winter of 1789 was harsh. Food supplies evaporated or were under tight guard. Two squadrons were called out to suppress a food riot, armed only with sabres so no man would desert with a musketoon. On arrival, the local National Guard battalion of four hundred men had formed a protective fire line. The starving townsfolk stood with their torches, pitchforks, hammers and river stones. The Guard had no uniforms, apart from their tricolour rosette in their hats, they were as motley a gaggle as you might ever hope to see. There were as many pikes and spontoons as there were hunting rifles and fowling pieces. More swords than bayonets.'

Leaning back to have his platter removed by Madame Quandalle, Jobert remained slumped, his eyes flickering across the scene in his mind.

'Our colonel drew us up in extended battle line, sabres drawn. They were in line, not square. They stood no chance if we charged. Every man of us knew this was going to be a massacre. The crowd started to heckle and jeer. A party of officers demanded the withdrawal of the Guard. The chasseurs in the ranks looked left and right in alarm, to sergeants like me, and turned around in the saddle and sought direction from the sergeant majors behind the rear rank.'

Jobert's fingers flexed. His left hand gathered imaginary reins. His right wrist flexed under the weight of an invisible sabre. 'The officers posted behind the rear rank ordered "Eyes front". The officers posted in front started to turn around. The colonel was beside himself with rage, raised his sabre, nodded to his trumpeter who put his horn to his lips.'

Jobert's head jerked over his shoulder to the shadows by the wall. 'Then one of the sergeant majors in the rear rank started screaming "Stand fast, all ranks, stand fast". Then all the sergeants and men, all of us, started screaming "Stand fast, stand fast". The colonel's trumpeter sounded *Advance* and we were all screaming "Stand fast".'

Jobert's cheeks flinched at the spectral movement in front of him. His throat was dry. 'The officers in the front rank launched forward only to wheel around when it was obvious no one was following. One of the sergeant majors pressed forward, with some chosen men around him, and ordered "About face". He even got one of the trumpeters to sound *About Face*. So about we went.'

Jobert gulped at his wine. Three men leant forward to refill his cup. 'My men were all looking to me. Everyone was terrified. We had all just brought great dishonour on the regiment. We were all to be hung. Officers I knew well made personal appeals, threatening us with the noose. For me, a soldier's brat born on the regimental dung heap, I had known these officers all my life. I trusted and respected nearly all of them, especially those officers that had not abandoned us for their estates. I shall not forget the betrayal stamped on their faces.'

Everyone at the table was silent.

'What happened on return to barracks?' asked Geourdai.

Disoriented by his memories, Jobert searched the keen faces around him. 'Prior to that morning, indeed, for months, a core group of sergeant majors and sergeants reinforced the need for routine, discipline and calm. This committee persisted in reassuring the officers of our loyalty to the regiment. This was not a lie. We were loyal to our colours. For many, it was the only home we had ever known. Ashamed by the scandal, the officers made their own way back to their residences. Many departed for their homes, never to be seen again. We seized armouries and magazines on return to barracks. Indeed, the Paymaster, the Treasurer and the Wagonmaster all absconded that evening with the regiment's pay.'

Snorts of disgust along the table puffed on the shortening candlesticks.

'We sent a delegation to the regimental second-in-command, the most senior officer remaining with the regiment that evening. In the spirit of the National Guard, we decided to vote for our officers. Only ten of the dozen officers who wished to remain with the regiment were retained, only two of them from the petty nobility and no aristocrats. The thirty-odd other officers' positions were filled by the senior non-commissioned officers.'

Bowls of Orlande's apricots were slid along the table from Madame Quandalle's tray.

Jobert cupped his warm bowl in his hands. 'I woke that morning as a sergeant. I went to bed that night as a lieutenant company second-in-command.'

Chapter Fifteen

Jobert raised his eyes from the month-old Paris broadsheets as Voreille stepped into the small kitchen.

'Excuse me, Captain Chabenac, sir,' asked Voreille, 'is there any mail for the company?'

Chabenac glanced up from Geourdai's chess board. 'Sadly, no. I asked before I came up and was told the mail was sent three days ago with the squadron trains.'

Voreille failed to mask his disappointment from Jobert's glance.

'Do you require more paper, sir?' asked Orlande, pouring fragrant *sciacchetra* into Geourdai's wooden mug.

'No,' said Voreille. 'If there is nothing else, Captain Geourdai, sir, I shall retire.'

Jobert frowned at Voreille's sharpness. Geourdai leant forward to study the pieces on the board.

Voreille clenched his jaw. 'Captain Geourdai, sir?'

Geourdai fingers wiggled in consideration of his black bishop. 'Yes? No. Good night.'

Jobert glared as Voreille shut the door with a soft thud. 'What is his problem?'

'No mail from his sweetheart, sir,' said Orlande as he poured Jobert a cup of the dry honey and nutmeg wine.

'Does he not know how to comport with these women?' Chabenac shook his head. 'I genuinely tire of acting the Hermes for his Eros.'

Orlande moved the candle to place a plate of *focaccia* at Chabenac's elbow. 'His desire for paper is inexhaustible.'

'Thank you, Orlande. It appears these women live only to aggravate him. Was he not confounded by his previous love?'

'Previous, sir?' asked Orlande.

'Prior to this maid in Nice, did he not have a sweetheart in Avignon?'

'It is one and the same girl, sir. Anissa.'

Chabenac looked up at Orlande. 'The same girl? The girl from Avignon is now in Nice?'

'Who?' said Geourdai, committing to move his black bishop. 'Anissa? From Avignon? Not Anissa the whore from across the lane by our 2nd Company tavern?'

Orlande reset his spectacles on his nose. 'Yes, sir. The girl has lived in Nice at least a year.'

'And he writes to her?' asked Geourdai. 'For two years?'

'Yes, indeed, sir.' Chabenac swept a knight to remove Geourdai's bishop. 'I take it you are acquainted with the lady?'

'Only from dance lessons,' said Geourdai, his dismayed focus on the chessboard.

Dance lessons? A shiver of dread ran down Jobert's spine.

Orlande swept back his errant red fringe. 'Do you require anything else, gentlemen?'

'Stop!' Jobert's growl caused Geourdai and Chabenac to twitch from their game. 'Orlande, Voreille writes to a prostitute named Anissa? A woman who provided our dancing partners when we convened dance lessons in the Avignon tavern?'

'Yes, sir.'

An ugly crease twisted Jobert's scar as he folded his news-paper. 'Voreille has written to her for two years? Since we departed from Avignon for Marseille in May '93?'

'Yes, sir.'

'And she has since moved to Nice? When did she relocate to Nice?'

'Last May, sir, after you were injured.'

Jobert looked at the others. Orlande remained patient. Jobert saw a deeper realisation dawning on Geourdai's face.

Chabenac remained puzzled. 'This makes no sense. What would a girl from the back streets of Avignon write to a young officer for two years? What of the cost of the post? Is she expecting him to lift her from the gutter? Whatever does he write about? His undying love?'

Jobert stood. 'Orlande, fetch Sergeant Major Koschak here, with Moench and Tulloc. Geourdai, where are your pistols?'

'In the room I share with Voreille, sir.'

'Sir? What —' Chabenac was silenced with Jobert's raised finger. Chabenac blanched when Jobert drew a slim pointed dagger from his cuff.

'Chabenac, wait here. Orlande, go now. Geourdai, on me.'

Jobert opened the door and entered the narrow hallway, then opened the door to Geourdai's and Voreille's quarters.

Voreille sat in his shirt sleeves, linen breeches and stockings, writing a letter on a small desk by the light of a solitary candle. He stood whilst steadying his ink pot. 'Ah, how can I help you, sir?'

'Do you correspond with a woman named Anissa?' asked Jobert through gritted teeth. 'Is this woman the harlot who assisted us with our dance lessons in Avignon?'

Voreille blushed. 'Yes, sir.'

'Has this woman relocated from Avignon to Nice? And if so, when did she relocate? And why?'

Voreille looked puzzled. 'I assisted her last May, sir, to care for her sick aunt.'

Boots sounded in the hallway.

'Moench! Tulloc!' called Jobert to the men in the corridor. 'Saddle horses for Sergeant Major Koschak and I to ride to Pieve di Teco. Then bring Lieutenant Voreille's horse here. Move!'

As he turned, Jobert revealed to Voreille the dagger he held. 'Lieutenant Voreille, I place you under arrest. I demand your parole.'

Voreille's face paled. 'Sir, I do not understand. You have my parole, sir. How may I assist you?'

'Geourdai, take his sword and pistols. Voreille, is that a letter to Anissa now?' Jobert thrust out his hand. 'Give it to me.'

Voreille scrabbled to pass the unfinished letter to Jobert. Geourdai pressed past to draw Voreille's pistols from their saddle holsters.

'Sergeant Major,' said Jobert without interrupting his inspection of the letter, 'search Lieutenant Voreille's belongings for letters.'

Voreille turned to his equipment packed about his bedroll on the floor. 'Sir, my letters are all contained in a waterproof wallet in my portmanteau.'

'Remain absolutely still, Voreille! Sergeant Major, continue your search.'

Koschak was thorough, as he searched Voreille's saddlery and portmanteau, every item of his clothing and boots, even patting Voreille's body through his shirt and breeches. Only the wallet was found as Voreille had described.

Jobert opened the thick wallet, packed with letters.

'Voreille, you are under arrest, and I have your parole. Geourdai has heard you give it. Disgrace and dishonour await you if you break it. You will accompany Sergeant Major and I to Pieve di Teco. If you disobey my exact commands, Sergeant Major Koschak has my explicit order to cut you down.'

Jobert and Koschak stood ready a few steps behind Voreille. Jobert stood at ease, the fingers of his right hand stroking the handle of the dagger in his left cuff. Koschak held a cocked pistol and his sword hung from his wrist by the sword knot.

Standing at attention, Voreille's vision fixed on the wall behind Raive's desk.

Raive, flanked by two four-candle holders, sifted through the pile of letters before him and scribed on a paper by his elbow. Every now and then he placed down his quill and shuffled back through letters he had already read, mumbled and then made further annotations.

Quite some time passed before Raive placed all the letters back in the oilskin wallet, then placed the wallet to one side. He spent further time reviewing his summary and making extra notes.

Finally, Raive reclined in his high-backed chair, removed his spectacles and smiled at the three men in front of his desk. 'Do you write to your parents, Lieutenant Voreille, as you write to Anissa?'

'Only occasionally, sir.'

'Why?'

'Anissa seems to understand the life of a soldier. My parents do not.'

'Your father is a doctor in Caen, is he not?'

'Yes, sir.'

'Write down his name and address in Caen.'

'Sir?'

'Do as you are ordered!' said Jobert.

Voreille trembled as he took up the quill, barely able to dip the nib in the ink well. His breathing was shallow as he scratched the required information on the paper. He looked at Raive beseechingly as he stepped back to his place of attention in front of the desk.

'Thank you, Voreille,' said Raive. 'You met Anissa in Avignon at the time of the dance lessons? When 2nd Squadron was ordered to Marseille, did you bid her farewell?'

'Yes, sir'

'And you told her where you were going?'

'Probably, sir, yes.'

'Had you lain with her prior to leaving for Marseille?'

'Ah, no, sir.'

'Have you ever lain with her?'

'Ah, no, sir.'

'Never in two years? Had you sought to lie with her?'

Voreille's shoulders slumped. 'Sir, I feel this ... yes, sir. Often, sir.'

'Has she ever allowed you more simple intimacies?'

'Yes, sir.'

'Lieutenant Voreille, have you ever lain with any ... person?'

Voreille's breathing was laboured. Jobert saw tears well in Voreille's eyes. 'No, sir.'

Raive found something in his notes worth staring at. 'Anissa describes in her letters how much she loves you. Do you love her?'

Voreille's jaw quivered. 'Yes, sir.'

'She writes of Juno. Who is Juno?'

'My mare, sir.'

Raive noted Jobert's affirmative nod.

'Once you parted, did you write to her from the vicinity of Marseille?'

'Yes, sir.'

'Did she write back to you whilst you were outside of Marseille?'

'Yes, sir.'

'How did you receive her letters?'

'Through the aides de camp, sir.'

'Your letters here are dated since the beginning of 1794. Where are the letters for 1793?'

'I destroyed them, sir.'

'Why?'

'Because I returned to her in Avignon over the winter before the regiment deployed to Nice.'

'She writes of "our friend". Who is "our friend"?'

'Master Inoubli, the dance master in Avignon.'

Jobert closed his eyes as a wave of nausea pulsed him.

'When did Anissa move to Nice?' asked Raive.

'Ah, last May, sir, after we returned from Ponte di Nava. When the company rotated to escort duties.'

Raive looked to Jobert. Jobert nodded.

'Why did Anissa move to Nice?' asked Raive.

'To care for her sick aunt, sir.'

'How often did you visit Anissa in Nice?'

'Each time the company was placed on convoy escort duty, sir.'

'May? August? November? And this year? February? And, I imagine, December and January while the regiment was in winter lines.' Voreille nodded to each of Raive's dates. 'Have you met Anissa's aunt, Voreille?'

'Ah, only once, sir.'

'Describe her aunt, please?'

'Anissa's room was dark, sir. The lady was in bed under her

blankets. She wore a night cap. I remember a thin nose and sunken cheeks. She coughed unbearably, so I kept my distance. From then, Anissa insisted on meeting at a tavern while her aunt slept.'

Raive paused to make another note on his page at his elbow. 'I see from Anissa's letters she describes her excitement in the description of "demons from hell tumbling out of your mountain dens to flood the plains of ... Lombardy". Why express such excitement?'

'It was to flood the plains of Piedmont, sir, not Lombardy.'

'I stand corrected.' Glancing at Jobert, Raive hid his smile with a knuckle smoothing his moustache. 'Did you provide her with such a thrilling phrase?'

'I may have, sir.'

Jobert exchanged a glance of despair with Koschak.

'I note another interesting passage from her letter last September,' said Raive. 'She is fascinated by the colours of the vine leaves in the Col di Cadibona in autumn. Anissa writes of her desire for your safety when you approach the Austrians at Savona. Why approach the Austrians there?'

'As our company commander at the time, Major Jobert, had 2nd Company prepared to advance down through the Col di Cadibona to assault the Austrians in the flank at Savona.'

'That seems exciting. Perhaps you felt a little anxious?'

'A little, sir.'

'And you shared those feelings of the impending operation with Anissa?'

'Not our plan, sir, just the possibility of visiting Savona.'

Raive reviewed his notes. 'Lieutenant, would you agree, as a chasseur officer of a sabre squadron in the vanguard of the Army of Italy's most aggressive divisional commander, General Masséna, that you have quite an insight into the comings and goings of the entire Army?'

Voreille shuffled. 'Ah, possibly, sir, ... yes.'

'And here you are, that very junior officer with a box seat within the Army's theatre, informing someone of those evolutions?'

'No, sir, not at all. I was careful never to specify our battle plans, sir.'

Raive's amenable demeanour evaporated. 'Is Anissa blackmailing you, Lieutenant Voreille?'

Voreille recoiled. 'No, sir!'

'Can you see that if she retains your letters, she will have built up a considerable case against you? To either blackmail you or denounce you under the Law of Suspects. Would you agree, sir?'

Voreille convulsed as the blood drained from his face.

Jobert again looked to Koschak, to which Koschak rolled his eyes. *Despite my efforts, things have slipped my notice and I have endangered my men. My inattention has risked everything.*

'You would agree that with our conversation this morning,' said Raive, 'plus these letters, supported by these witnesses, I have a strong case to present your treason to Deputy Saliceti. Yes? You understand you would be shot within the hour. Voreille, do I have your parole?'

Voreille raised his spasming chin and pressed his quivering shoulders back into the position of attention. 'Yes, sir.'

'Sergeant Major Koschak, take Lieutenant Voreille to my quarters and detain him there. Bind him if you feel it necessary. Lieutenant Voreille, without any sign of fuss, accompany Sergeant Major Koschak to my rooms. If you disgrace yourself in any way, you will be taken to the cells in chains.'

Voreille shuddered.

'Sir!' Koschak braced in the position of attention. 'Lieutenant Voreille, salute. Lieutenant Voreille, follow me outside, sir.'

Raive tinkled a small table bell once Voreille and Koschak had departed.

'Jobert, please sit. I will send for coffee. You understand the case exists for you to be shot as well. This was occurring under your command for two years.'

Jobert lowered himself into the chair, his eyes never leaving Raive.

'What I feel we have here,' said Raive, 'is a lovesick fool on the verge of blackmail, if he shakes himself free of his stupor. If he is in a conspiracy with Anissa, then he is masterful at hiding it. Here was I monitoring the mail to Avignon, and not the mail to Nice. Well played.'

'I have a piece of news that will assist your investigation, sir.' Jobert swallowed hard in a bone-dry throat. 'I saw Inoubli in Nice last August.'

'Really? Our friend Inoubli? How fascinating.' Raive consulted his notes before adding a quick scribble. 'Our friend asks this, then much later our friend asks that. The dance master is our spider. Or one of them. Now where do I know the fellow?'

'Following the provision of dance lessons to the regiment's officers, he attended Madame de Rossi's ball.'

'Yes, yes, but I feel there was another occasion?'

'He attended the regimental dress parade to which we invited the Avignon merchants and suppliers of our uniforms and equipment. Inoubli wore a capucine silk suit whilst accompanying the Mayor of Avignon.'

'Yes, that is right. Marvellously hideous costume. He has access to senior officers, to society events and to the administration of the city. And now our Colonel Morin's relocation to Avignon sends a new tremor through Inoubli's web. What an interesting fellow? And you say you saw him in Nice in August? When? Just after Anissa's move to Nice and prior to our advance along the Bormida River to Dego?'

'And then again at Fergnes' wedding last December.' Jobert's voice was hoarse.

'Of course, a prominent social function is his natural habitat. Though, I shall check Inoubli's whereabouts in August last year, as August is the height of the Avignon season. Surely society missed him in the three weeks he needed to race to Nice and back.'

As coffee was served by a staff orderly, Raive reviewed his notes.

'I am most impressed by Anissa's questions. Her pages and pages of questions. She enquires, with care and persistence, about the towns Voreille passes through to determine the routes taken and garrisoned. Whether he sees girls prettier than her to understand the impact of the passage of troops through the villages. The food he is eating to determine supply. The well-being of his horse to determine distance. When was he planning to visit next to determine the nature of the regiment's rotations? Impressive insight for an untravelled girl from the back streets of Avignon.'

'Shall I arrest her, sir?' asked Jobert.

'No. I shrink from disturbing our pretty Anissa, as this will send our spider scuttling underground. I feel assured she is another desperate woman seeking extra cash. I feel certain she is not the only honeypot set to catch young fools. I was always intrigued that our agents with the Austrians attached to the Piedmontese were just as well informed as the Austrians emanating from further down the Po in Lombardy. Inoubli may provide that piece of the puzzle. The Avignon and Nice couriers feed Piedmont, not Lombardy.'

Raive waved a letter at Jobert.

'Extrapolating from her questions and the single example that we have of his responses, there is now no doubt of what the Austrians are aware. Our reduced numbers due to the growing number of sick in the overcrowded villages, the complete absence of reinforcements to this lesser front, the egregious state of supply, and command confusion as our commanding generals come and go.'

Raive smiled over the top of his coffee cup.

'Jobert, we now have a conduit to the Austrians. Would it not please us if they jigged to our tune? We must prove if the Austrians act on such information. We need to inform our esteemed enemy that an opportunity has arisen, which, if they act, will be to their advantage. If we see they tap their toe to such a simple melody, then we are positioned to play them quite a dance.'

'What of Voreille, sir?'

Raive's moustache curled in a sinister half-smile. 'I intend to test his mettle. Voreille will now act for General Masséna as a divisional aide de camp. I will keep a close eye on him and direct the content of his letters. What a thrill that will give our Inoubli at his man's ascendency. Jobert, if Voreille is of any use to us, he needs to clear his head. I would be obliged, sir, if you might arrange an appropriate lass to reveal the bewitching mystery to him.'

Chapter Sixteen
May 1795, Oneglia, Italy

Jobert's and Geourdai's pencils were poised over their notebooks, while Spiccard lounged in his chair.

Raive beamed at his audience. 'I have just returned from the Army's headquarters in Nice where our deception plan is authorised and arrangements finalised. Deputy Saliceti is most keen for the scheme's success whereby we pass information to the enemy via Anissa and Inoubli. This subterfuge is a drama of three acts. In each of the three acts a convoy is escorted the three hundred kilometres from Toulon to Savona, ten days march, with Nice at the half-way point.'

Spiccard flapped a hand to interrupt. 'I request a priority of divisional grain rations if these remounts are to travel without rest for sixty days.'

Raive made a note in his pocketbook.

'2nd Squadron will proceed to Toulon and escort a powder convoy to Savona,' said Raive. 'In Toulon you will receive a dummy load of empty crates and one crate of cannon balls. Twelve-pound balls.' Geourdai raised his eyebrows to Jobert at the mention of ammunition for the heaviest calibre of field artillery. 'In Nice, you will contrive to spill those balls where all will be seen. You will hastily regather what you have so carelessly disclosed and continue to Savona. You will then travel back to Toulon and escort two twelve-pound batteries.'

Spiccard gave a derisive snort. 'Two twelve-pounder batteries? In Toulon?'

'No, not quite,' said Raive. 'The second act now requires the escort of eight twelve-pounder limbers and eight gun carriages, but only one twelve-pounder barrel. The other seven barrels, under their canvas tarpaulins, are logs crafted to appear authentic. On arrival in Nice, in another act of poor discipline, the tarpaulin will come away from the actual brass gun barrel momentarily confirming the calibre of the guns. For the third and final act, once returned to Toulon, you will reassemble the eight-gun battery and travel a second time to Savona.'

Jobert grimaced at the idea of three six-hundred-kilometre round trips. *Better as a part of the solution than be shot for my naivete of Voreille's stupidity.* 'What of Voreille, sir?' asked Jobert. 'Is it he who contacts Anissa each time the convoy passes through Nice?'

'Voreille now answers to me,' said Raive. 'Voreille will pass messages of my creation to Anissa in Nice. He shall report to her of the movement of two foot batteries of twelve-pounder cannon to Savona. If he obeys and we succeed, there is redemption for him. If he fails, he is aware of the severe punishment to be visited upon himself and his family. There will be six opportunities to pass information to Anissa, and at least one, if not two, opportunities for the Austrians to strike.'

'To ambush us, sir?' asked Jobert.

Raive tilted his head to regard Jobert. 'Yes, Jobert, that is why I have chosen the best men. If the Austrians strike at the convoy, then we have won. We have proven we can pass false information through to the Austrians, and we then begin to infiltrate Inoubli's network. Further, the kaiserliks must not identify the seven wooden barrels wrapped in canvas. It is vital the fraud remains secret.'

Jobert set his teeth but did not break eye contact.

Spiccard disrupted the tension with a languid smile. 'Jobert, you will take Chabenac. If you are ambushed, he is to get away and inform us of your ... our success. You will also take the regimental surgeon. By my reckoning, the first battery escort will be on the road when it becomes 3rd Squadron's duty as convoy escort. Would it not be wise to maintain that consistency? What is more, Fergnes is the chief of squadron for all convoy escorts this year.'

'Yes,' said Raive, 'I quite agree that consistency is important, but Fergnes must take his bed for two months in Nice. The affair needs Jobert and Geourdai who both understand what is at stake, especially fighting to protect fake gun barrels. Yes, Major Jobert?'

Jobert pressed his notebook closed and raised his chin. 'I am at your service, sir.'

'The Republic is obliged, sir.'

The sun had not risen, yet the streets of Nice were full of citizens streaming to the wharves to greet the morning's docked fishing fleet. Sellers of vegetables and fresh bread lined the laneways to take advantage of the passing trade gathering the day's groceries.

The crush of people around the convoy hid Anissa from Jobert.

Pushing through the morning shoppers was the convoy of eight false ammunition wagons, each paired with a wagon from either 2nd or 5th Companies' trains. With a platoon of over twenty chasseurs surrounding each pair of wagons, there was very little chance that Jobert would see Anissa in the crowd.

But Voreille was well positioned to identify her as he rode beside the escorting horsemen. Keeping his eye on Voreille, Geourdai rode between the fourth pair of wagons and the fifth, ready to give the signal to Koschak.

Koschak drove the second wagon of the fifth pair. By his side lay a rope attached to a release pin which held the box of twelve-pound round shot firmly shut. A sharp tug would release the hinged side for ten cannon balls to drop onto the road.

Jobert and Moench rode behind Koschak's wagon. Jobert's sheepskin shabraque pulled back to reveal the handles of his loaded and cocked pistols, their finely engraved, silver inlay glinting from the first rays of the rising sun.

'Hey there!' Geourdai caused his horse to skitter sideways into the crowd, the agreed signal to begin. *Voreille has raised his hat to Anissa somewhere in the crowd.*

Jobert saw Koschak twitch his muscular shoulders and heard the metallic click of the release catch. Ten balls rolled from the rear of the wagon, crashed onto the cobblestones of the street and rumbled towards the roadside gutters.

'Stand fast!' bellowed Jobert, drawing a pistol. 'Corporal Duval, dismount your section and retrieve those balls. Moench, sound *Halt.*'

Moench's trumpet call split the morning air.

A barefoot urchin dashed from the crowd.

The slim boy, Madame Quandalle's son, scooped up a loose cannon ball that had come to rest in a pile of horse manure, and sprinted across the street with his slippery prize, dodging the other pedestrians as he disappeared down a side lane.

Jobert fired his long-barrelled cavalry pistol well above the darting child. The lead ball cracked the stonework on the alley's wall. The crowd screamed and drew back. The chasseurs levelled their muskets at the crowd.

'Get your backs into it, lads,' called Koschak, standing on the driver's seat. 'Collect those balls and keep moving.'

The snarling chasseurs barged their way into the crowd, pushing the townsfolk back with their threatening musketoon muzzles, to collect the wayward iron shot.

As the back gate of the wagon was refastened and the canvas cover retightened, Geourdai brought his horse smoothly in beside Jobert's Vert.

'Did she see?' asked Jobert.

'Voreille said she did.'

'Then onto Savona. Moench, sound *Advance*.'

Two weeks since the loose cannon balls had rolled across the street in Nice, Jobert faced his grim-faced, saddle-weary chasseur commanders.

'There is a traitor within the Army of Italy and the People's Deputies are hunting him.' Jobert's eyes paused on Voreille. 'As part of that hunt, Deputy Saliceti has chosen us, based on General Masséna's recommendation, to assist. For our part, we will escort two batteries of twelve-pounders from Toulon to Savona. If the Austrians attack the convoy, the plan has worked, and the Deputies will have identified their spy.'

The thirty commanders of 2nd Squadron shuffled and folded their arms, their eyes flickering nonplussed glances.

'Our convoy has only one real twelve-pounder brass barrel. The other seven barrels are timber.' Jobert emphasised with a slap on the fake wooden barrel against which he leant. 'Wrapped in canvas and mounted on a gun carriage, the brass and timber barrels are identical. For this traitor to be identified and elim- inated, we hold that secret close.'

The men mumbled their discontent.

'Shut it, lads,' said Koschak, 'and listen in.'

Jobert squared his shoulders and his face soured. *I only desired to lead my men with honour, to keep them alive as best I can, but now all is in reverse.*

'If the Austrians attack us they will use a combination of Italian partisans and some form of elite force, such as their jaeger troops, to infiltrate the mountain paths by night. We have patrolled those mountains and we know good troops get through. We proved it at Ponte di Nava a year ago, did we not? We know the difficulty of infiltrating cavalry and the impossibility of infiltrating artillery any larger than one or two three-pounders. We are likely to be paid compliments by highly competent light infantry.'

With a grim smirk, Jobert bent forward and looked each fellow in the eye. *I must now lead them into a massacre to cover my shame.*

'We will defeat their methods by a number of our own. First, the convoy will travel at night and bivouac in open country by day. Moving by night will severely diminish the Austrian's ability to bring effective fire against us. Second, the length of the convoy. 5th Company will always lead the convoy with one troop as advance guard and one troop with Guns 1, 2, 3 and 4. The gun with the brass barrel is Gun 4. 2nd Company is always at the rear of the convoy with one troop as rear guard and one troop with Guns 5, 6, 7 and 8. Our column, from the start of Gun 1's section to the rear of Gun 8's section, measures about five hundred metres long, with forty-five chasseurs leading and another forty-five chasseurs following up. A most difficult target, no matter how competent the enemy infantry.'

A ripple of gruff confidence pulsed through the seasoned sergeants and corporals.

Five days later, the early June evening brought clouds of insects around the few glass-enclosed lanterns along the narrow, stifling Nice streets. Soldiers and citizens tumbled into, or out of, the dimly lit, rowdy taverns a few lanes back from the wharves. In the shadows, whores and their customers whistled and cat-called to the forbidding chasseurs escorting the long, rumbling convoy. Although the chasseurs clustered around their gun carriages and followed wagons as ordered, Jobert had arranged that, tonight in Nice, very few men rode close beside the real twelve-pounder barrel of Gun 4.

Tonight, the huge five-hundred-and-fifty-kilogram barrel jolted snugly in the gun carriage's trails. In action, the barrel elevated or depressed by pivoting on its trunnions in grooves carved in the gun carriage. When the barrel's trunnions were shunted back into a second set of grooves in the trails, as it was now, the gun was transported without its muzzle swinging down into the dirt. Koschak had arranged for the ties of the canvas cover to be undone, exposing a third of the brass barrel, now shimmering as it passed the few street lanterns.

'Oi! Move through quickly, there,' shouted Koschak.

A slim, feminine shape, a shawl draped over her head, emerged from the shadows to cross the street between the gun and the two chasseurs following.

With the trailing wagon blocking his view, Jobert squeezed Bleu to a trot for a few paces and observed the ruckus.

The woman grabbed hold of the brass barrel and shuffled to keep up with the moving gun. A dull glint in the torchlight revealed a knife in her grasp.

'Stand clear!' yelled Koschak.

A screech of metal on metal sounded from the gun's muzzle.

Jobert saw the woman wrench the wooden plug, the tampion, from the mouth of the gun. By sealing the muzzle of the gun, the tampion, kept in place by a thick leather strap, not only ensured dust or rain did not enter the bore, but if the gun was loaded whilst moving, the ball and charge would not fall from the muzzle.

'Cut her down!' roared Jobert.

Jobert and Koschak drew their sabres and pressed their horses forward anticipating her escape.

As the woman tugged the four-and-a-half-inch thick wooden cylinder free, her shawl fell away from her shoulders, dragging her bonnet with it and her long dark hair cascaded down her back. Koschak thrust his sabre at her chest. She ducked under the barrel, dropped her knife but scooped up her shawl. With a flourish, she twirled the shawl in the face of Koschak's horse, then, as the horse threw its head, she dodged under the barrel again. With her skirt hoisted in one hand and tampion tucked under the other arm, she sprinted for a dark side lane.

Jobert pressed Bleu and extended his sabre to block her movement. The woman hurdled a stack of empty fruit crates and disappeared into the darkness.

'She cut the tampion strap, sir. She stole the tampion,' said Koschak. 'Sergeant, secure the tarpaulin on Gun 4.'

Voreille cantered up and halted beside Jobert. 'Someone took the tampion, sir?'

'A woman, Voreille, an exceptionally athletic woman. With

the tampion in her possession, there is no doubt as to the calibre of the gun.'

Jobert extended his sabre to pick up the fallen bonnet. 'Recognise the bonnet?'

'Yes, sir. Shall I ask Anissa about the bonnet?'

Jobert cut two nicks into the bonnet's brim with the tip of his blade. 'No. Look for this bonnet with its two small tears when you see her next, but never speak of this with her.'

Jobert threw the bonnet into the gutter.

Waves slapped on the hulls of Oneglia's fishing fleet, drawn up on the beach, as 2nd Squadron trooped past Raive and Jobert.

'We know Anissa has the hard evidence to support Voreille's indiscreet prattle,' said Raive. 'She tracked down Madame Quandalle and her boy and purchased the stolen cannon ball. Now she has the tampion which confirms the calibre, there is no doubt.'

'Voreille recognised the bonnet as Anissa's on the evening the tampion was taken,' said Jobert. 'When we passed back through Nice after escorting the first battery, he visited her and saw both the same bonnet and the tampion strap brazenly hanging from a hook over Anissa's hearth. Do you regard that as a little too bold?'

'You said the figure who removed the tampion moved fleetingly. Perhaps the actions of a focused and limber young woman? Perhaps the movement commensurate with a leaping dance-master?'

'Inoubli in Nice?' asked Jobert.

'Yes, we have identified Inoubli in Nice. Fergnes has emerged from his supposed sickbed by night and prowled the back lanes. Fergnes knows Inoubli well enough. Perhaps Inoubli reinforces to us that Anissa is our main suspect by leaving such items plainly in view. Perhaps he waits for Voreille to act, hoping Voreille reveals whether we are aware of their deceit.'

'So, I did see Inoubli in Nice,' said Jobert.

'I have made discreet inquiries with our Colonel Morin in Avignon. Inoubli was in Avignon all of last August. Colonel Morin confirms Inoubli was never absent at that time.'

'I saw him. I am assured of it.'

'I believe you. Morin is unaware Fergnes saw Inoubli in Nice last month. I will check with Morin if Inoubli was in Avignon on the same date.'

'What? Two Inoublis? Twins?'

Raive shrugged. 'Either that ... or a remarkably fast horse.'

As the squadron escorted the last of their convoys, hooves of the column were wrapped in hessian, curb chains and spurs removed, scabbards wrapped so as not to clank against stirrups, wheel hubs rolled on greased axles.

'You believe our message has been passed, sir,' said Jobert. 'Do you feel the Austrians will act?'

Raive stiffened in the saddle. 'Are they ready?'

'Our counter-ambush drills are sound,' said Jobert. 'We have talked through and practised every contingency we can imagine. Every man has ridden the route four times. I am now blessed with two hundred experts in counter-ambush techniques.'

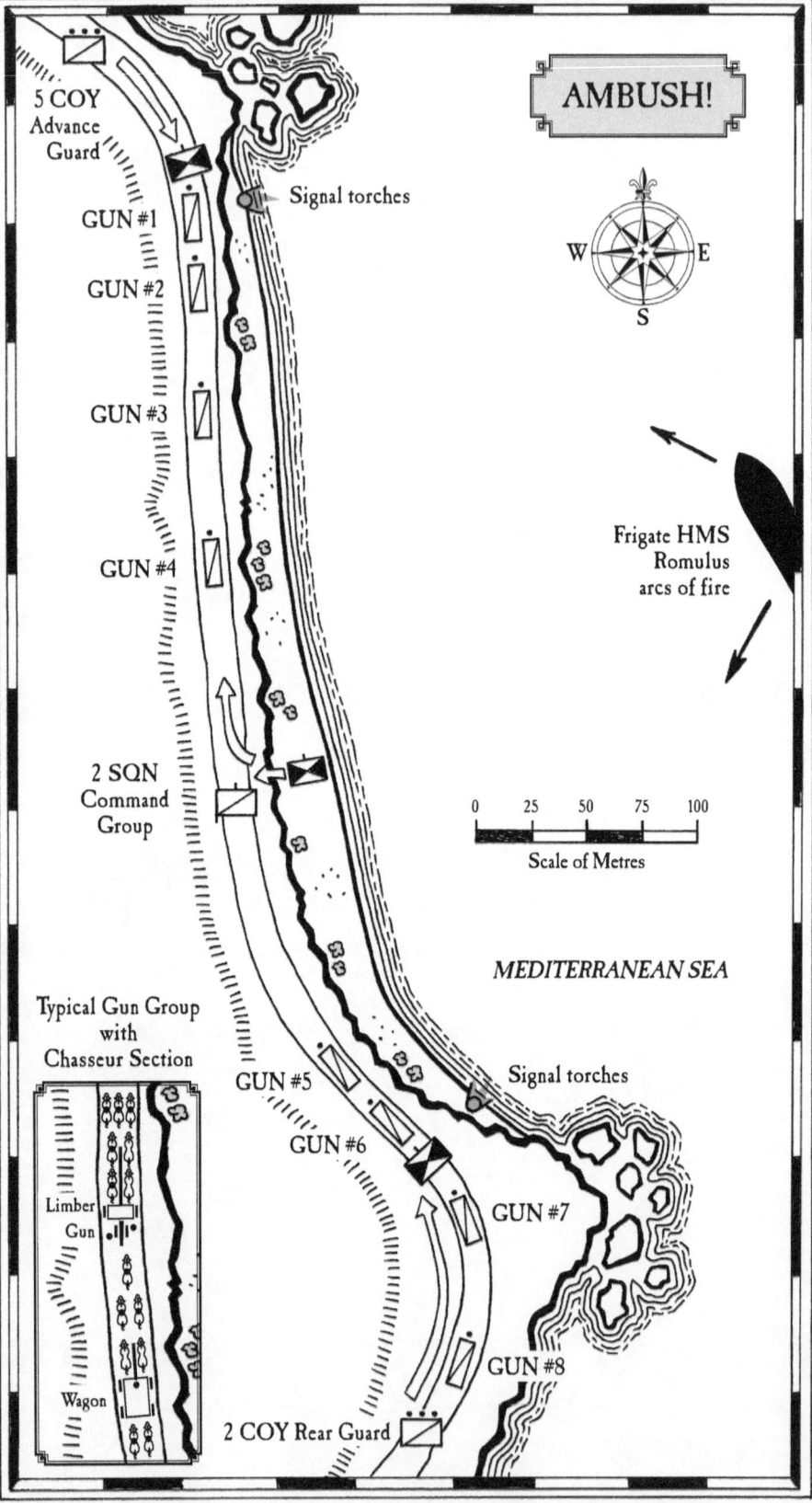

AMBUSH!

5 COY Advance Guard

GUN #1

GUN #2

GUN #3

GUN #4

2 SQN Command Group

Signal torches

W · E · S

Frigate HMS Romulus arcs of fire

0 25 50 75 100

Scale of Metres

MEDITERRANEAN SEA

Typical Gun Group with Chasseur Section

GUN #5

GUN #6

Signal torches

GUN #7

Limber Gun

Wagon

GUN #8

2 COY Rear Guard

Chapter Seventeen
June 1795, Savona, Italy

The column followed the Oneglia-Savona road as it clung to the cove's shoreline ten kilometres from Savona. At this point, the roadway was not more than eight metres wide, measured from a gutter that ran along the base of a slight cliff face to the lip of a two-metre embankment which led down to the rock-strewn beach.

The moon had set early on this warm, clear night in late June. Salty star-lit darkness engulfed the squadron. Jobert strained to hear any movement above the column on the cliff. A section flank-guard followed the trails along the top of the escarpment, but Jobert could not detect them. After midnight, Neilage's 5th Company shot a wayward donkey. *With two hours before dawn and entry into Savona I do not need another false alarm.*

The gentle rhythm of both waves slapping on rocks and the plodding of muffled hooves was shattered by the piercing shriek of a whistle blast.

Gloved hands gripped the waists of musketoons tight.

Guts turned to ice.

'Moench, sound *To Arms!*' cried Jobert, shortening his reins on Vert.

On the whistle's signal, one hundred dark-clad Austrian infantrymen threw off their capes and stood up amongst the rocks littering the beach.

Fifty men fired their muskets at the shadows on the road above them.

Their musket balls thwacked into the men and horses leading Gun 1.

At the volley, three torches, with their bases shoved deep into the beach sand, flared into life.

The other fifty fusiliers sloshed through the tidal pools and clambered up the slight shelf onto the road.

'Gun 1! Gun 1!' cried the rehearsed French, identifying the location of the attack.

The Austrian infantry struggled onto the road, shuffling in the dark to form a fire line facing the cliff face. Lit torches were flung forward illuminating the struggling and thrashing wounded men and horses. Shadows of mounted and dismounted men melted into the darkness towards the centre of the column.

A trumpet signalled the impending assault of the French advance guard.

The Austrian commander discerned shouting within the French column stretching away to his left, but of greater concern was the scream of the trumpet and rumble of hooves shrouded somewhere along the dark road to his right.

He formed his company, barking his commands in a Balkan tongue never spoken in the imperial courts of Vienna.

As the muffled hooves and wheels of the French column thudded and crunched above his head, another Austrian company commander responsible for placing in the rear blocking force, heard the shrill whistle four hundred metres down the beach to his right.

The forward block was going in.

The Austrian captain suppressed his feelings of dread and blew his whistle as hard as possible.

Another one hundred fusiliers shrugged off their cape disguises and stood.

Again, fifty fired at the shadows and reloaded.

Three more staked pitch torches burst into flame at the edge of the lapping waves.

Then the sodden company scrambled forward to the road's edge with the distinct rattle of hobnailed boots and clanking slung equipment.

'Gun 7! Gun 7!' screamed the French above them.

A French trumpet call tore into the star-lit night to the company's left, signalling the assault of the French rear guard.

Having thrown extra torches to reveal the mounds of French dead and wounded on the road, the Austrians shuffled amongst the standing and lying horses, trapped in their traces. Having faced howling Ottoman warriors, the Austrian veterans clenched their teeth and gripped their muskets tight as they formed line against the oncoming French.

As Moench blew *To Arms*, Jobert swelled with the surge of cold hatred and clarity of vision that came from entering a fight.

An Austrian whistle from the front of the column had resulted in a roar of musketry, a burst of torch light from the beach and the sound of movement up onto the road. Jobert heard 5th Company's trumpet response of *Reveille* to the repeated cries of 'Gun 1'.

To the rear of the column, another whistle, another powerful volley, more torches springing alight amongst the waves which reflected the shimmering light, more movement onto the road.

Cries of 'Gun 7' was the response to which 2nd Company's trumpet sounded.

Aware of both the fury of the fighting growing at the front and rear of the column, Jobert knew that Neilage's and Geourdai's reserves were in the best position to deal with it. All the commanders, gun commanders and reserve commanders, had talked of nothing else during the past thirty days.

Koschak's shadow moved near Jobert toward the shoreline edge of the road. Koschak fired his musketoon into the shadows beyond which caused a cry of pain from the sloshing waves. 'They are on the beach! They are beneath us! Dismount! Ambush right!'

As they had rehearsed, the squadron command group reacted with purpose to the initial surprise. Jobert heard Orlande unhitching Rouge from the shafts of Jobert's trap and untying Bleu to walk free. Other horsemen gathered, mounted and dismounted about him.

'Koschak, Chabenac, Voreille, Duval and your second, move rearward to Gun 6.' Jobert was intent on projecting calm authority to what they had rehearsed. 'Orlande, Huin, Tulloc and your sniper mate, come with me forward to Gun 3.'

A dull explosion sounded far out across the water.

Jobert's mind froze as he tried to comprehend.

'A gun? How?' Chabenac's voice wavered in the dark.

'No, a warship!'

A hurtling, whooshing object sped across the waves to strike the head of the column, resulting in the screams of horses.

Then another gun far out on the water fired.

Eight hundred metres off the shore, stably anchored fore and aft, rode the dark, low shadow of His Britannic Majesty's thirty-six-gun frigate *Romulus*.

On sighting the Austrian torches erupt into life, describing her left and right of arc, the number-one gun of *Romulus'* thirteen port guns, fired the first of three rounds. In the one hundred seconds between firing the initial shot and ready to fire the second from the first gun, the other twelve eighteen-pounders on the portside issued ripple fire down the length of the gun deck. The ripple fire repeated its deadly rhythm, every eight seconds, until every gun had fired three rounds, one chain-shot and two ball, in five minutes.

While the monstrous eighteen-pounders fired from the gun deck, on the upper-works five portside nine-pounders contributed their weight of fire in sequence to the guns on the deck below.

The projectiles flew through the still night for eight seconds before ripping into their four-hundred-metre-long target, striking evenly somewhere in the darkness between and above the torches marking the shoreline.

On the road above the rocky escarpment, 2ⁿᵈ Squadron was struck with fifty-four giant hammer blows every eight seconds.

The initial round fired from each of the *Romulus's* eighteen-pounders was chain-shot.

Eighteen-pounder chain-shot, two halves of a hollow iron ball joined by a length of stout chain, designed to strip the rigging from an enemy ship, twirled and tumbled across the gentle Mediterranean waves before severing pairs of horses standing flank-on to the frigate, into quivering, wet chunks, flinging both their great screaming bodies and their riders against the cliff wall.

Hit by either chain or ball, limbers, gun carriages and wagons detonated into a storm of splinters, spinning shards skewering any man or horse close by. On the cliff face, having struck any part of the convoy or not, the chain-shot slapped to rest.

Not so the incoming solid shot.

The deep hiss of the flying ball swept away flesh or timber in an instant. With a resounding crack, the ball pounded into the cliff face to shatter the rock into a lethal spray of gravel, then ricochet to strike the unwary a second time.

Every eight seconds, about twenty-five to thirty metres apart, progressively down the column, the giant hammer struck.

Jobert faced Vert towards the gunfire. 'Dismount! Unhitch the teams! Face the horses towards the beach!'

Jobert heard the explosion from the rock face behind him and cringed as the stinging shower of shards hit, before he felt Vert collapse beneath him.

A round shot had amputated Vert's nearside foreleg at the shoulder, skimming the inside of Jobert's left stirrup, cutting the saddle's girth straps, then slicing through the near-side hock to remove Vert's hindleg.

Vert collapsed with a scream.

Jobert thumped onto the road.

The ball had struck the wall, rolled down the face and bounced clear of his right shoulder. If the near-exhausted ball had scraped Jobert, its residual velocity would have torn his arm from his body.

As Vert wheezed and groaned from massive blood loss, he tried to stand without success. Jobert dived for Vert's neck and pinned the horse's head to the ground and ceased Vert's thrashing. Jobert drew a pistol from his holster, then roared with madness as he cocked the hammer, found Vert's temple with the muzzle and fired.

Shivering with insane rage, Jobert stood and reloaded his pistol, then took the second pistol from under his sheepskin shabraque. He was aware that the others had already departed to their battle-stations as ordered.

A sizzling hiss raced towards him.

Jobert threw himself down onto the road. Struck by a nine-pound round shot, Jobert's two-wheel trap exploded into fragments in the darkness.

Jobert stood again and, satisfied that Orlande, Rouge or Bleu were no longer in the vicinity of the demolished timber frame, strode towards the sounds of fighting at the front of the column.

As the last great eighteen-pounder boomed, the *Romulus* fired a rocket. The rocket's smoky trail arced towards the top of the cliff face before exploding in a huge red flare above the beach-side road. The shifting illumination revealed to Jobert a stark jumble of timber vehicle frames, to which horses stood tethered and rounded mounds of bodies, large and small.

The rocket was not for illumination.

It was a signal.

'Gun 5? Gun 5?'

Koschak and his squadron party scrabbled their way through a herd of abandoned remounts. The horses snorted as they smelt the familiar scent of unwashed horsemen moving between them. The chasseurs' discussions had often centred around their concern for their beloved horses if they had to dismount and fight. One contingency, the situation that played out tonight, was to herd the horses together away from the firing, on the basis that the sooner the ambushing enemy were slaughtered, the safer the horses would be.

The cannon fire from the warship had already passed down the column, and the terrifying pounding was approaching steadily once more.

'Gun 5 here, Sergeant Major,' called a chasseur sentry. 'Gun 5's section is at Gun 6.'

Koschak fumbled past further dead or wheezing horses, tripping over harness chains, slipping in slick pools of unseen blood and viscera, until he discerned dim shapes kneeling in the dark ahead. Koschak grunted with satisfaction that the huddled forms wore only the one white cross-belt of a cavalryman barely visible in the starlight, not the criss-crossed white webbing of an infantryman.

'Gun 6? Who is in command here?'

A pipe-bowl glowed in the dark. 'Bredieux, Sergeant Major. The enemy are around Gun 7. They are dark-clad, not white-coat Austrians, probably British Marines. 2nd Company are pushing them back this way. That fucking warship's fire approaches from the head of the column. I have scouts at Gun 5 to let us know when it is our turn to be hammered. Otherwise, I have moved the horses forward with the scouts. I have both sections from

Guns 5 and 6 here, minus two scouts, fourteen men on parade, Sergeant Major.'

The grunted effort to slash and the resultant cries of 2nd Company's fight was close. Musket balls zipped by in the dark.

Without warning, the night transformed into an eerie red gloom.

Appearing forty metres ahead of Koschak and his wide-eyed chasseurs huddling around Gun 6's shattered limber were the backs of a line of enemy fusiliers, brown-jackets criss-crossed with white belts.

'Then we make our stand here at Gun 6. Lieutenant Voreille, sir, move to Gun 3 to report our situation to Major Jobert. Duval, fire at the figures by the torches on the beach. Captain Chabenac, sir, the way forward is blocked. For your message to get out you need to either scale the cliff or escape down onto the beach.'

'Thank you, Sergeant Major,' said Chabenac. 'I hear Captain Geourdai and Lieutenant Pultiere roaring like bulls. I am content to wait for 2nd Company.'

Koschak watched the flare's light fade on the backs of the enemy line. 'Gun 5 and Gun 6, stand up, musketoons, ready!'

The chasseurs cocked the hammers on their musketoons and tapped their cartridge boxes ensuring the box was firm on their right hip when they needed to reload.

'Present!'

Shuffling to take aim on the fading image of the enemy to their front, they saw fusiliers turning around in the flare's final glow and look back at them.

'By sections, Gun 5, fire!'

The Austrians screamed as the volley tore into their backs.

Koschak heard the scraping of the ramrods returning to their brackets from the first volley. 'Gun 6, fire!'

Somewhere in the night another whistle squealed.

For the Austrian commander of the rear blocking force, the assault by the French was intense. His men were unable to set their positions amongst the dead horses. After the initial Austrian volley, the French had closed swiftly in the darkness and the engulfing gun smoke. Very few of his fusiliers were able to reload, forced to defend their line with the bayonet, thus firing was intermittent and less than an effective deterrent.

The French cavalry had dismounted and pressed forward with sabres extended. Men on both sides were screaming in shock, reeling back, slashed or stabbed in the dark. The Austrian captain saw the rage in the faces of the French sabre line only metres apart from his own wavering line, their gradual advance like some ancient phalanx, thrusting their curved blades into the Austrian wounded as they disappeared under the advancing boots.

More concerning, the Austrians had not yet found any cannons amongst the wagons of the column.

Without warning, the flare burst and bathed the scene in dull red light.

The drifting flare revealed musketoons and pistols thrust forward from the French second rank that fired into the faces of the Austrian fusiliers. The exhortation from the French commanders bellowed above the laboured effort of parrying and stabbing. The interminable trumpet scream was silenced mid-call with a musket shot.

Yet the Austrian line fell back, or jumped down onto the rocks, fusiliers scampering amongst horses standing or lying, thrashing or still.

A volley fired from behind tore into his men's backs.

'Break ranks! Get down on the beach!' cried the Austrian captain.

A third whistle blast sounded from the centre of the column.

In response to the signal rocket, and their own whistle blast in the centre of the ambush, a third company of dark-clad Austrian fusiliers shrugged off their capes and stood.

None fired.

Instead, they advanced across the rocks, up the shore-line embankment and onto the road, where they too threw lit torches and illuminated the remnants of the French column on the road. The company faced a silent, empty roadway, abandoned moments before by the French central squadron group.

Musket fire and the savage screams of combat were far away on the left towards the rear block.

On the right, stood or lay horses and wagons that had survived the frigate's five-minute bombardment. A column of dark shapes disappeared into the night towards the firing from the forward block.

'Look there, captain,' called the Austrian battalion commander. 'A gun. Spike it. Guard toward the rear of the column with half the company. I will take the other half towards the forward block.'

'Commander Gun 2? Commander Gun 2?'

Jobert cringed under the explosion of spinning rock shards as another invisible ball thumped into the cliff wall only to bounce and crunch heavily on the road soon after. Jobert, Moench, Huin, Orlande, Tulloc and Tulloc's sniper-mate pressed forward, each man gripping the belts of the man to his front, tripping over iron cannon balls lying in the gutter, bumping roughly into wounded men at the base of the cliff face.

'Gun 2 here, sir,' a voice called from the outline of an over-turned wagon.

'What is the situation, Gun 2?'

'Gun 1 is lost forward of us, sir. We hear skirmish fire from 5th Company, otherwise nothing is moving. An enemy company has formed across the road, separating us from 5th Company. They have an outpost near Gun 1's limber. They are not in white, sir, and speak neither Italian nor German.'

'Hungarian or British, no matter. How many men on parade?'

'Two scouts forward, sir, and thirteen with me now from Gun 1 and 2.'

'Listen in, lads,' said Jobert, 'this is where we stand. Huin, return to Gun 3. Bring up your Company Sergeant Major and his seventeen men. Bring Gun 3's wooden barrel with them. Take all loose horses back towards the centre. Place two sentries to watch the centre of the column.'

A loud pop caused them all to look up as a wobbly red star shone above them.

Twenty metres ahead of him, Jobert saw the abandoned Gun 1 attached to its limber behind at least two horses standing in their traces as they were left. Brown-jacketed men, with white cross belts, either knelt by the tall wheels of the field gun or scurried towards the front of the column. Beyond the gun's team lay mounds of dead horses and the four short ranks of enemy fusiliers, with a frontage of twenty-five men extending from cliff face to beach.

Another whistle squealed from the centre of the column.

'Tulloc?' called Jobert. 'Take post here. Those torches at the water's edge are aiming marks for that fucking warship. Knock them down. Moench, sound *Reveille*! We need to get 5th Company moving again.'

As Moench sounded the long notes of *Reveille*, signalling 5th Company to attack, Lieutenant Huin and the reinforcements from Gun 3's and Gun 4's sections gathered about Jobert.

'Major Jobert, sir, kaiserliks are coming up the column from the centre. Coming this way in strength.'

We are to be crushed by the approaching 'hammer' onto the blocking 'anvil' at the head of the column. Jobert knew the disoriented, disordered group of enemy soldiers were groping their way forward along a column, albeit strewn with casualties, a column that his men knew intimately. *Attack the approaching 'hammer'.*

'Listen in, men. Yinot, with Gun 1's section, watch forward to Gun 1. The rest of us, Gun 2, Gun 3 and Gun 4, on me. Form fire line rearward towards Gun 3. Move! Those shithead kaiserlik bastards have massacred our horses with a warship. Are you ready to return the compliment?'

'Fuck yes, sir!' roared the chasseurs.

The flare snuffed out, returning them to darkness.

Chapter Eighteen

As the red flare danced and rocked above them, Neilage and Yinot knelt on the road at the head of the column with their dismounted chasseurs, kneeling and firing in loose skirmish order around them.

Following the enemy's initial whistle blast, 5th Company had reacted with immediacy as they had practised. With Neilage's trumpeter ordering the attack, the chasseurs wheeled around and pressed their trotting horses to engage the shadowy forms clambering up from the beach to block the road.

The Austrians had fired on the charging chasseurs, bringing down the leading men and horses. Leading the charge, Neilage was wounded, balls slicing his thigh, shoulder and ear, as his horse collapsed dead onto the road.

As they had practised time and again, the chasseurs knew the enemy infantry were at their most vulnerable once they had fired. That was the time to crush them with iron hooves and steel blades. The chasseurs screamed to move forward, around the few fallen horses riddled with shot, blocking the road, but to no avail.

With Neilage rendered *hors de combat*, Yinot ordered the chasseurs dismount and move into a skirmish line amongst the corpses of the horses against the four ranks of enemy fusiliers blocking the road from cliff to sea. While the five-minute naval bombardment tore into their company mates beyond the unmoving wall of fusiliers, enraged by the cacophony of piercing screams from men and horses and eruptions of disintegrating rock and wood, 5th Company's chasseurs roared at each other to maintain the fire against the Austrian ranks.

For their part, the dark barricade of Austrian fusiliers continued to close ranks as the wounded were punched backwards from French musketry. With hard-earned discipline, the Austrians held their volley for any further French cavalry charging out of the darkness.

Neilage, now hastily bandaged, shuffled in beside Yinot in the wobbling red haze. 'What is our situation?'

'There is a company in four ranks separating us from Gun 1, sir. Our initial strength was forty-four. Minus the flank-guard on the cliff above us, our horse-holders and our losses from the initial charge, the advance guard now has twenty-three. Twenty-three against half their company in the two ranks facing forward.'

Neilage willed his pain-induced adrenalin to keep his focus. 'But our skirmish fire is reducing those ranks. Our brothers are trapped. They have no option but to fight to the last. We will not stand by and have them and their horses massacred by that monstrous warship.'

As the wavering light encouraged an increase in 5th Company's erratic fire, a musket volley exploded causing a cloud of gun smoke to erupt beyond the Austrian fire line. Then a trumpet sounded *Reveille*, 5th Company's pre-arranged signal to attack.

Neilage struggled to stand as his thigh wound cramped with pain.

'Jobert wants us to attack. Our boys are standing firm. We must get through. Attack their flank against the cliff. Force them back down onto the rocks. Sound *Reveille*. 5th Company, on me!'

Geourdai's 2nd Company slew their way through the remaining Austrians of the rear block to join Koschak's gun section survivors.

With the breakthrough, Chabenac availed himself of two spare horses and sped for Oneglia.

Reformed by the light of the frigate's intermittent flares, 2nd Company surged on behind a berserk Pultiere, through the loose remounts to receive a devastating volley from the half-company of Austrians holding the centre of the column around Gun 4. Geourdai's exhausted but enraged chasseurs pressed forward as the Austrians shuffled backwards.

The Austrians were conscious that behind them the other half-company that had pressed forward was struck by violent fire from the French survivors amongst the column's wreckage. Now the half-companies regathered and formed a defensive line, back-to-back and ferried their wounded to the shoreline, firing as individuals at the sparks of the French skirmishers in the dense cloud of acrid smoke.

For their valiant part, Neilage's assault had managed to convince the Austrian forward block to withdraw towards the beach. The enemy fusiliers still dominated the area around Gun 1 with their lethal musket fire, so 5th Company and Jobert's gun sections were unable to link up.

The whole affair had devolved into small knots of survivors, both French and Austrian, strung out along the route of the column, all semblance of order lost. Small stands of wounded men of either side lay in blood and shit, breathed the stench of gun powder and cooked flesh, entrusted themselves to the few fierce leaders who demanded they maintain their vigilance into the inky blackness and directed their fire at the slightest movement.

It became obvious to all that nothing would be achieved in the dark.

The next phase of the battle might erupt in the faint light of predawn. In sight of each other's skulking shadows, both Austrians and French heaved broken vehicles and horse bodies to form a barricade against the mutually expected dawn attack.

Ammunition was distributed from the smashed wagons. Water flasks were gathered from the surrounding corpses.

Above the moans, grunts and whimpering of the wounded, the French heard the frigate's long boats creeping into the beach. Rumours of enemy reinforcements were whispered amongst the fatigued and blood-soaked chasseurs of 2nd Squadron.

'Soldiers of France! Soldiers of France, can you hear me? Hold your fire. We seek to parley.'

The eastern horizon promised a swift sunrise in less than an hour's time. Barely discernible in the gloom, four enemy soldiers emerged from the lip of the road and the rocky beach.

Jobert tucked his two engraved pistols into his sword belt. Aided by the outlines of swords or muskets, Jobert identified two officers by their bicornes, one British Marine and one brown-jacketed Austrian, and two flanking fusiliers, with white flags attached to their bayonets.

'Sir, I am Lieutenant Tapping of His Britannic Majesty's Royal Marines, and may I introduce Major Urosevic, of the Holy Roman Emperor's Grenzers. Major Urosevic speaks only limited French.'

Jobert gave a sullen nod. 'Major Jobert sir. Do you speak German, Major Urosevic?'

Urosevic bowed his head. 'I do, sir.'

'How may I be of service?' asked Jobert in both French and German.

'If you observe down onto the beach, sir,' said Tapping, 'you will note we have withdrawn our troops to the frigate.'

Jobert peered down into the morning mist and saw not more than thirty or forty slumped forms, silhouetted in the purple haze, with capes around their shoulders. Out on the water, the black frigate crouched, ready to strike.

'We have only a few men attending to our wounded,' said Tapping. 'We request a short truce to gather our wounded in the light before returning them aboard.'

Jobert rubbed his whiskered jowls, feeling the grime and scabs of blood, either his or someone else's.

'I will only grant a truce if you assure me the ship will no longer fire on us this day.'

Tapping stiffened as the grey light revealed the mounds of bodies and the shattered frames of wagons and limbers.

'Our action is complete, sir. You have my word that the Captain of His Majesty's frigate *Romulus* will not fire if you allow us to remove our wounded.'

'The *Romulus*, hmm. Gather your wounded. At first light my men will despatch our horses that your warship butchered.'

Tapping bristled, then sagged. 'Then we are agreed, sir.'

Tapping returned to the rocks, waving to his party by the shoreline. Jobert saw long dark boats emerging from under the stern and the bow of the warship, rowing hard for the beach.

'Excuse me, Major.'

Jobert turned back to Urosevic and the two escorts. The three burly, moustachioed Austrians looked over the grim scene without any visible discomfort.

Urosevic scanned Jobert's grime-encrusted features. 'Where were the gun's barrels? I lost many good men to spike one gun.'

'We delivered the battery to Loano, as ordered. These were just spare limbers for Savona.'

'Huh!' The Austrian's shoulders sagged with the false revelation.

'How did you conceal yourselves amongst the rocks?' asked Jobert.

'We sat in the water with our capes over our heads.'

'I see the blue trousers of Hungary, sir, but your brown jacket is unfamiliar.'

Urosevic tilted his head to the side as he appraised the French cavalryman with dead, unblinking eyes.

'Imperial Grenzer infantry, sir. Croatian and Serbian frontiersmen who guard our Imperial Majesty's borders against the accursed Ottomans. Until next time, Major.'

Chapter Nineteen

The low morning sun cast long shadows over the cliff-face. The road beneath was a scene of quiet misery.

Through the stench of blood, split intestines and roast meat, chasseurs carried the wounded to the surgeon on the cliff-side of the road while others rolled dead horses over the drop onto the beach's rocks, or placed the dead in a long line, and stripped them of their clothing and equipment.

Jobert slumped against Bleu. 'We will replace the cart, Orlande. Our next one will be much better. Just as you like it.'

Orlande looked up from his broken spectacles. Jobert held his eye with a questioning look.

Orlande raised his chin, his mouth creasing into a sad smile as he patted Rouge beside him. 'I have packed as much as I found from the cart as well as Vert's portmanteau, sir. We have had worse, have we not?'

Jobert summoned a reassuring nod as he tightened the straps of his portmanteau behind Bleu's saddle. Bleu pawed the blood-wet road, threw his head and snorted with discomfort at the butchered horses strewn on the rocks beside him. With swift discretion, Jobert wiped his tears on his upper sleeve as he looked across the saddle to the crumpled mass of meat, hide and bare teeth that was Vert.

As Jobert hoisted his scabbard and moved to join Koschak, Geourdai and Neilage conversing further down the road, he noticed two near-brown jackets locked in embrace. To Jobert, it appeared an Austrian grenzer was comforting a dying mate. About to summon a chasseur and get the prisoner back to his work of burying the dead, Jobert observed a chasseur's helmet beside the soldier.

The jackets were not grenzer-brown, but trumpeter's capucine.

Jobert stiffened as he watched Moench rock the lifeless body of his younger brother, Geourdai's 2nd Company trumpeter, in his arms. Jobert watched Bredieux approach with two chasseurs and nurse the crushed body out of Moench's grasp, taking the dead soldier for stripping and burial.

Moench collapsed onto the gravel and howled in anguish.

Jobert knew he needed to remain focused and engaged, otherwise he too would succumb to his exhaustion and emotions.

His heart leapt when a gun fired from the frigate.

Jobert spun and saw the British warship moving towards the rising sun in full sail. *A gun salute, perhaps.* He spat at the despised ship and turned back to his commanders.

All three, Koschak, Geourdai and Neilage, raised their chins, clenched their jaws and looked at Jobert with hooded, red-rimmed, lifeless eyes.

'First and foremost, have the wounded horses been dispatched?' asked Jobert. 'Then security? Are vedettes out?'

Geourdai looked down as he gave Jobert an imperceptible nod.

'Then have you accounted for all your timber gun barrels?'

Neilage adjusted his weary shoulders, cradling his blood-soaked bandaged upper arm. 'Gun 1 was found wrapped in its canvas undisturbed. Gun 2 took more than one hit as we only found splinters in shredded canvas. Gun 3's trail was hit and the barrel thrown clear. The brass barrel of Gun 4 was spiked by the Austrians.'

Jobert turned toward Geourdai.

Geourdai twisted his mouth. 'Gun 5's limber was hit, the barrel flung into the ditch. Gun 6 was shattered by a direct hit. Gun 7 and Gun 8 never entered the ambush. I see the occasional red-coated British Marine amongst the dead, but who were the brown-jackets?'

Jobert's eyes followed the departing warship. 'The Austrians were Grenzers. Tough bastards from the Ottoman frontier. They waited for us by sitting in the sea with capes over their heads. From what the Austrian battalion commander said, they only found the one brass barrel. Did Chabenac get away?'

'Yes, sir, west to Oneglia,' said Geourdai.

'Huh! So much for Raive's and Saliceti's bullshit scheme. What about us? Parade state?'

Geourdai's lips quivered as he fidgeted with his notebook.

'The squadron began the convoy with one hundred and ninety-five, plus your squadron group of six, which includes Chabenac and the surgeon.' Geourdai took a deep breath. 'The squadron has lost forty-four men, sir, and has fifty-eight horses dead or destroyed. As for wounded, everybody is bleeding, sir.'

'Have we lost officers? Sergeants?'

Geourdai's mouth twisted in sorrow. '2nd Company has lost Lieutenant Pultiere, sir.'

'Argh ...' Koschak shoulders sagged.

Jobert's lips quivered at the news of the big man's death.

Neilage sniffed and spat. 'Huin will probably lose an eye.'

Koschak's jaw spasmed. 'Many of our dead have been bayon-

eted after wounding. The prisoners said they were ordered to
...'

Jobert closed his eyes as he breathed to contain his sadness.
'Our wounded? Our horses? Prisoners?'

Koschak snorted the mucus that comes with tears and spat
noisily into the dust. 'From the surgeon, we have about sixty
men incapable of parading for duty. About fourteen will not
survive their wounds. About seventeen, if they survive the
bone-saw, will not return to the regiment. And the other thirty-
odd, broken bones and badly cut up, if they are not taken by
contagion, will return to the saddle in six weeks. With the
triage complete, the surgeon is about to perform his arts. He
recommends we take a bath in the sea to cleanse our wounds.'

Jobert glanced at the frothing crimson waves pulsing amongst
the horse corpses tumbled onto the rocks.

Koschak continued to flick through his notebook. 'As for
horses, sir, the squadron has lost sixty. One hundred and forty
remain to provide a battleline of about ninety and the remaining
fifty as teams and packhorses. Of the convoy's eight wagons
and eight limbers and gun carriages, four wagons survived the
bombardment and we can assemble six carts from the remaining
limbers and gun carriages.

'We have used all our spare water that survived the gunfire.
There is a village a little way back. I will refill from their wells.
I have placed all our vinegar and brandy with the surgeon. I
have redistributed ammunition to the men then stockpiled the
little remaining bread, tentage and farrier's stores. I have work
parties gathering saddlery and harness stripped from the horses.
The sergeants have stripped the dead, theirs and ours, and are
bundling the weapons, clothing and equipment onto packhorses.'

Koschak hawked and spat again. 'We only secured a dozen
prisoners found lost along the beach, who are now digging
graves. Once the work is completed, our chasseurs are to clean

weapons and resharpen sabres, before bathing in the sea.'

'Hmm. Two extra tasks,' said Jobert. 'First, burn those fucking barrels to boil water for the surgeon and tip the brass bastard into the gutter. Second, collect the balls that were fired at us. I would like to find a way to return them, to either the British or the Austrians, in the same fashion they were presented to us.'

A chasseur sentry, approaching from the outposts on the headland, pushed his tired horse to maintain a canter down the road. 'Major Jobert, sir! Gunfire, sir. Gunfire from Savona. Much bigger than Ponte di Nava last year, sir, and at least as heavy as Dego.'

Geourdai and Koschak swore.

Jobert looked to the eastern horizon. 'The Austrians are attacking Savona. We need to depart immediately. How many wounded? How many vehicles? How many spare horses? Where is Moench? Neilage, have your trumpeter sound *Commanders In*.'

Feeling the weight of sadness on the three haggard chasseur leaders beside him, Jobert swallowed hard against his barely contained emotion. '2nd Squadron has been butchered from two hundred sabres to just over ninety. With over forty dead and around sixty wounded, with a long night behind us and a long day ahead, this is how victory feels. Savour it!'

The officers and sergeant majors of the squadron command group gathered. They flopped to sit on the blood-stained road.

Jobert chased flies from his dirty face and contemplated wasted, ripped men sitting on the white gravel. 'Men, this is just how the Austrians want us to feel. They want every Frenchman to feel as we do, so they can march unopposed from Savona to Paris. We know nothing undoes the grief we feel for our lost brothers. We know a bath, a meal and sleep will remove our fatigue. But we know, in this moment, our men need us to cast our fatigue aside, so we can march them to safety.'

Jobert sunk wearily and squatted on one knee in front of the group who wriggled to straighten their postures to one of soldierly determination.

'It is now six o'clock. We have marched through the night to win a fierce fight, but we cannot rest. The guns we hear to the east are the Austrians seizing Savona. We need to get our wounded off this road and far from Savona as we can. If the Savona garrison cannot hold, within the next two to three hours, this stretch of road will be a flood of men and vehicles. Those withdrawing columns will attract a swarm of Austrian cavalry; chevau-léger, hussars, dragoons and horse artillery.

'As we have done for the last two months, 5th Company is our advance guard and 2nd Company is our rear guard. Captains Geourdai and Neilage, raise a troop in the saddle for immediate service. Four ten-man sections, two sergeants, one troop officer, a marksman and his mate, you and your trumpeter. How many is that? Forty-seven per company?'

Geourdai and Neilage nodded as they scribbled.

'Geourdai,' said Jobert, 'with Pultiere's loss, Peugeot will act as troop officer for 2nd Company. Who will you take, Neilage?'

'Second Lieutenant Yinot, sir.'

'Good. What train can be composed for them, Sergeant Major?'

'Lieutenants Peugeot and Yinot, sirs,' said Koschak, jabbing his pencil at their notebooks inferring they take notes. 'Sixty cartridges on the man. We will refill water from wells on our march out. There is no bread available. Ensure there is a bandage roll, even it is not boiled, in each portmanteau and two spare shoes on the saddle. Each company will take two packhorses. No food, no ammunition, no tentage. Take two platoon horse-lines and casks sufficient for one hundred litres of water. I will also provide a few litres of brandy or vinegar for wounds.'

'The rest of the squadron will form four packets,' said Jobert, 'and manned by our walking wounded. The first in order of march are our seventeen severely wounded and the regimental surgeon. Lieutenant Huin, this is your command.' Huin's eye wound was heavily bandaged. He twisted his neck to see the page on which he wrote 'Sergeant Major, men, horses, vehicles, stores?'

'Lieutenant Huin, sir,' said Koschak, 'all the wounded will keep their bonnet-de-police, portmanteau, cape, shabraque and bedroll on them. You will take the remaining four company wagons, four drivers and eight horses.'

'Orlande will be of assistance to the surgeon, and will join your packet with his packhorse,' said Jobert. 'Second in order of march, our stores commanded by Company Sergeant Major 5th Company. Composition, Sergeant Major Koschak?'

Koschak consulted his notebook. 'You will take three of the carts we have rigged from limbers and gun trails, with three drivers and six horses. There is no grain, a small amount of bread and no spare ammunition. You will load a spare one hundred litres of water, all tentage stores, the two remaining platoon horse-lines, the farriers' stores, any remaining pieces of harness and side chains and the recovered cannonballs. There are no spare shoes, so strip the spare shoes out of the extra saddles.'

At the phrase 'recovered cannonballs', grimy faces angled towards Jobert.

'I want to find a way to return those iron balls,' said Jobert, 'to either the British or the Austrians, in the style they were gifted to us. Third in order of march are our fourteen palliative-wounded, under command of Lieutenant Bredieux.'

Bredieux chewed his pipestem and looked steadily at Koschak.

'Lieutenant Bredieux, sir, your wounded will also keep their bonnet-de-police, portmanteau, cape, shabraque and bedroll with them. You will take the remaining three carts rigged from limbers and trails, drawn by our dozen prisoners, no horses. You are assigned six dismounted guards. Each man to carry two pistols as well as his musketoon, portmanteau and bedroll.'

'Fourth packet in the order of march,' said Jobert, 'the most capable of the wounded, spare horses and remaining stores, commanded by Lieutenant Voreille.'

'Lieutenant Voreille, sir, by my calculations you have about ten or eleven men with you and around twenty-five to twenty-seven horses. So, ride one, lead one or two. On those horses, pack around seventy-five spare saddles, musketoons, sabres and helmets, and the portmanteaus, bedrolls and clothing of our lost brothers. As you are following our dying men, you will also take the picks and shovels from the tentage stores.'

Voreille tightened his lips as he looked up from his notebook at Koschak's scowling face.

Corporal Duval approached Jobert sitting in the middle of the dusty road. The man's sunken, exhausted eyes were slits in his filthy face. 'Excuse me, sir, we have collected twelve chain-shot, twenty-four big round-shot and thirteen smaller balls. Keep searching for more, sir?'

Jobert jotted the information into his tattered notebook. 'No. Return to your platoon, lad.'

Jobert withdrew his fob-watch. 'It is approaching half-past six. Advance guard, we depart at eight o'clock. We should arrive in Finale Ligure by eleven o'clock, and Loano, where we set off from last night, as late as two o'clock this afternoon. Go now and assemble your commands.'

A pistol signal from a chasseur sentry caused everyone's faces to jerk towards the road that curved beyond the headland of the cove. A group of green-jacketed French dragoons trotted into view, their long, horse-hair manes flowing from their brass helmets, the dust swirling around their hooves in the cool morning air. Jobert recognised a dragoon captain, an aide for the commander of the French coastal division, with an escort of four dragoons.

The dragoons' faces flicked about in alarm as they looked down on to the near-sixty horses' corpses rolled onto the rocks, the incoming tide sloshing around the discarded bodies in a thick red soup. They pressed their nervous mounts through the congealing black puddles, raising clouds of sticky, early-morning flies.

The dragoon officer saluted the stained chasseur chief of squadron who blocked his path. 'Is this the site of the gunfire before dawn, sir? Who struck at you?'

'A British frigate fired a broadside, then assaulted us with three companies of Austrians. What of the fire we hear from Savona?'

'Savona is under attack by at least two Austrian divisions. Riders are coming in from the valleys to the north and reporting Austrian columns are moving down the Bormida and Tanaro river valleys to flank us. My divisional commander has only one of his brigades in the city. The other brigade has regiments behind us at Finale Ligure and Loano. The forward brigade has orders to withdraw to Loano. They will be through here soon, sir, with the Austrians hot on their heels. You must excuse me, sir.'

'Of course, see to your duties, sir.'

The aide de camp looked at the long line of wounded being loaded into the wagons and gun limbers.

'Good luck, sir.'

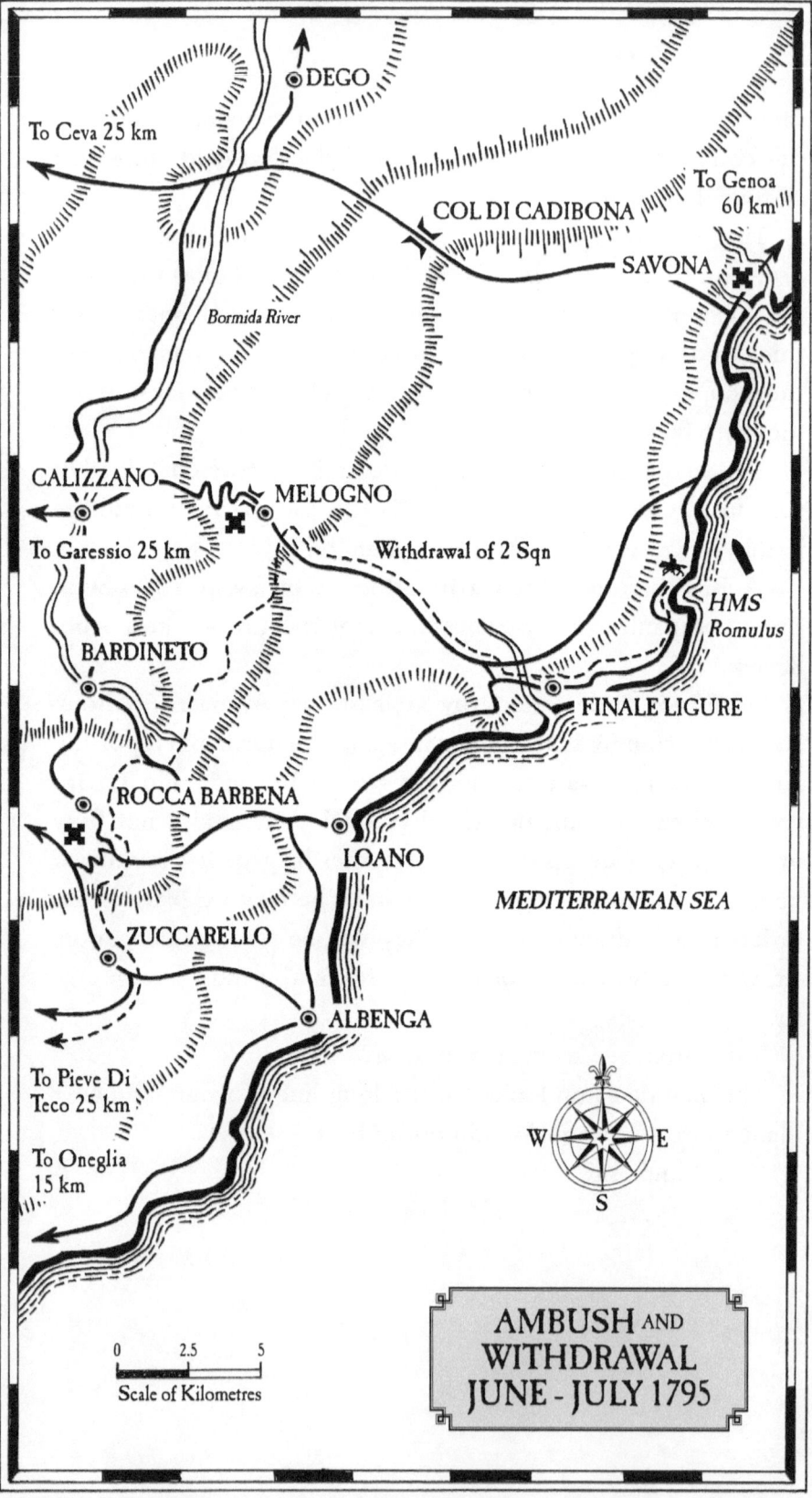

DEGO

To Ceva 25 km

COL DI CADIBONA

To Genoa
60 km

SAVONA

Bormida River

CALIZZANO

MELOGNO

To Garessio 25 km

Withdrawal of 2 Sqn

HMS
Romulus

BARDINETO

FINALE LIGURE

ROCCA BARBENA

LOANO

MEDITERRANEAN SEA

ZUCCARELLO

ALBENGA

To Pieve Di
Teco 25 km

To Oneglia
15 km

W E

S

0   2.5   5

Scale of Kilometres

AMBUSH AND
WITHDRAWAL
JUNE - JULY 1795

Chapter Twenty

June 1795, Finale Ligure, Italy

Jobert saluted the commander of the brigade defending Finale Ligure.

'Good morning, sir. Major Jobert, chief of squadron with the 24th Chasseurs à Cheval.'

The general turned from his entourage and ran his eye over Jobert's filthy and torn uniform, then swept his gaze across the wagons of wounded passing on the road into the town. '24th Chasseurs? Masséna's division?'

'My squadron was escorting a convoy to Savona, sir, when we were broadsided by a British frigate on the coast road ten kilometres from Savona.'

'I heard. Are you aware that the Austrians have broken through at Savona? The brigade from Savona is ordered to withdraw to defend Loano. I expect the head of our Savona column within the next hour or two. It is reasonable to assume our column will be accompanied by enemy cavalry. My brigade has one regiment here at Finale Ligure and the other preparing the defence at Loano. As I have only three battalions at my disposal, and a motley collection of cannon to support them, I require your chasseurs to assist my rear guard until the Savona column has passed through.'

Jobert raised his chin. *Show no sign of disappointment.* 'I have a company of chasseurs at your immediate disposal, sir.'

'I am obliged, sir,' said the brigadier general. 'As you see, west behind the town a great headland sweeps down to the sea. The coast road enters the town then turns inland and ascends the steep headland. Having reached the top of the ridgeline, the road turns once more towards the sea to descend to Loano. On top of the ridge there is a junction with a road that runs north to Melogno and Calizzano. That vital junction is held by a company guard from the left-flanking battalion. As well as a cavalry vedette forward of my left flank's outposts back toward Savona, I require a second vedette north along the Melogno–Calizzano road.'

'I shall place one troop of chasseurs on the Savona road, sir, and the other troop on the heights towards Melogno. It is now eleven o'clock. The screen will deploy by midday.'

'Very good, Jobert, then I shall delay you no further. You will find the flanking battalion, the 1st Battalion of the 45th Ligne, through the town, across the bridge and along the river.'

Jobert trotted Bleu after the chasseur trains and reached the head of the column of the squadron's wounded.

'Lieutenant Voreille,' said Jobert, 'our remaining sabres are now pressed into the defence of the town. Take the convoy home. Loano is ten kilometres, or three hours march, over this headland.' Jobert swept his hand toward the great peninsula above Finale Ligure. 'You ought to arrive by two o'clock. A defensive position is prepared for Loano, so it is not the place to rest the wounded but ensure you refill your water in the Loano valley. Press beyond Loano and stop at dusk. Tomorrow, Oneglia is then only thirty-five kilometres away. Go now, before you are caught by the head of the Savona column.'

'Yes, sir. Is this all my fault?'

Jobert watched the wagons roll past with groaning men in the searing midday sun, the pain of their morning amputations and hurried sutures fully upon them, the viscous dribble of bodily fluids dripping from the carts into the churned dust. He spotted Huin, eyes blindfolded in a swaddle of spare stockings, head jolting puppet-like to the jarring of the wagon.

Jobert blinked back the pressing emotion that hung on the heels of his tiredness. 'I admit I was outraged at your appalling lack of judgement with Anissa. I give thanks that your stupidity was revealed before Inoubli alerted the kaiserliks to the slaughter of thousands. But this?' Jobert flicked a finger toward the wounded, breathing through gritted teeth. 'No, this is not your fault. We were as ready for the ambush as we could be. But now, you must atone by leading the kaiserlik shitheads into an ambush of our design. Enough. These men need you focused, Voreille. See to your command.'

Infantry work-parties sweated to increase the heights of stonewalls overlooking the long, broad ford straddling the thrashing, grey stream. The column of dusty horsemen ambled to a halt. The chasseurs had eyes only for the water. The agitated horses stamped, rocked and pawed.

'1st Battalion, 45th Ligne?' asked Jobert.

The infantry chief of battalion appraised the dishevelled, unshaven and exhausted men who towered above him on their raggedy, listless mounts. 'At your service, sir.'

'Sir, my company of chasseurs is to join your defence,' said Jobert. 'Your brigade commander has directed me to place an outpost forward of you here towards the Savona road. He has also directed me to place an outpost on the Melogno-Calizzano road up on the ridge. I would be obliged, sir, if you share with me your dispositions.'

'My battalion is thinly spread, sir. I hold two fords three hundred metres apart and secure a road junction on the headland above us. I have an outpost line four hundred metres beyond the river out toward the treeline on the slopes to our east. My grenadier company holds a farm at the road junction on the ridge. What of you, sir? Have you just come from Savona? What news, sir?'

'Forgive me, sir, with a river at your back, I must water my horses and fill my men's water flasks.'

The infantry major cocked his head to one side. 'I imagine you have a decent farrier in your midst. In exchange for tacking shoes on my horse, would you and your men accept an offer of a river bath under the protection of the 45th Ligne?'

A smile creased Jobert's hollow cheeks. 'Fetch your horse, sir, and I shall fetch my soap.'

Jobert lifted Bleu's shoulders and stepped his forequarters across towards the squadron's commanders around him. 'Koschak, bathe the men and water the horses. I want us on parade and ready to move in one hour. Neilage, march 5th Company to the top of the ridge and establish an outpost on the Melogno road. Geourdai, establish observation of the Savona road forward of the infantry piquet line. Prepare to withdraw through this battalion if you are pressed by the enemy.'

'Sergeants, on me!' Koschak bellowed. 'Water the horses. Refill all kegs, bladders, gourds and flasks. Unsaddle. Groom horses' backs, as these horses have been under saddle for eighteen hours. Bathe and change into the underclothing we were saving for our arrival into Savona. Be quick about it. Tulloc, tack a set of shoes on the good major's horse. Take shoes out of your, my or Moench's saddle. Duval, see to Major Jobert's horse and your own before you bathe.'

Jobert dismounted and unstrapped his long, cylindrical portmanteau from behind his cantle. Looking away from Duval's scowl, Jobert watched the 2nd Squadron trains ascend the headland road with their sorrowful cargo.

'When is our Savona column expected?' asked the infantry major at Jobert's elbow.

'Within the next hour or so. The rear of the column is two or three hours behind that. The enemy cavalry ought to be expected then.'

Jobert followed the straggle of chasseurs and horses walking down to the bathing area on the riverbank.

Propping his musketoon and portmanteau on the rocks beside the tumbling grey river, Jobert removed his helmet, two cross-belts and sword belt. He then unbuttoned his jacket, tugged off his boots, peeled off his breeches, drawers, stockings and shirt. He winced at how atrocious his crotch smelt.

With a bar of soap, Jobert squelched across the slimy rocks and squatted in the stinging cold stream. He huffed as he ladled the chill water onto his chest, head and shoulders, then lathered his bristly face, armpits and groin. He wet and soaped his hair, his fingernails scratching the matted filth from his scalp. He ran his tongue over the grime coating his teeth and resolved to clean his teeth if time permitted.

Once clean, Jobert allowed himself a moment of luxury by stopping.

Just stopping. Squatting naked in the middle of a river in the middle of a battlefield.

In that moment of indulgence, Jobert's weary mind was engulfed by a tumult of images: Vert's torn corpse; the terrified, stoic faces of the chasseurs he held firm as the surgeon cut, sawed and sutured; the nodding, bandaged face of Huin; Moench clinging to his lifeless brother. He swooned to his deep desire for a hot bath, a wholesome dinner and a soft bed.

Only by immersing himself under the freezing water were these distractions expunged.

Aware that chasseurs were saddling horses, Jobert rose from his swirling, icy bath, blotted himself dry with his putrid shirt and retrieved clean underclothes from his portmanteau. *My breeches and jacket are so encrusted with sweat, dust, gun oil and blood that they could mount Bleu all on their own.*

Now, smelling of soap and with fresh underclothes against his clean skin, the overwhelming craving to sleep was unbearable. Jobert knew each man in the squadron felt this irresistible siren-song, and he and his officers had to hold it at bay until sunset.

Jobert stood at the road junction on the crest of the ridge-line above Finale Ligure. He scowled at the headland's road disappearing over the crest towards Loano. The road was clog-ged with Savona's dust-churning wagon traffic. Columns of downcast, clanking infantry. Knots of civilian men, women and children struggling with their loads and animals up the incline.

Jobert's attention returned to the rolling forests and farmland that lay below him, east of Finale Ligure.

'Bastard of a day, sir. Here …,' said Koschak. Koschak's hands trembled with fatigue as he passed Jobert two small, mottled plums in exchange for Jobert's telescope. Koschak surveyed the rear-guard of the Savona column entering the outskirts of Finale Ligure. Beyond the hovels and cottages that fringed the town, Koschak swept the glass across two French infantry battalions forming a fire line either side of an eight-gun foot battery. A third blue-jacketed battalion column raced towards the sanctuary of the town. Green-jacketed, long-maned French dragoons trotted from the treelines and formed behind the fire line.

Koschak lifted the glass and peered at small groups of more green-jacketed cavalrymen emerging with hesitation from the forests into the cleared fields. 'There they are, the dirty little kaiserlik cocks.'

Wiping tart plum juice from his chin's bristles with the soiled cuff of his heavy glove, Jobert looked up and saw an Austrian chevau-léger squadron working as a skirmish screen four hundred metres from the French infantry. A second squadron trotted into the fields escorting a six-gun horse battery.

French guns began to fire.

'Look! A third squadron is seeking their flanks toward the river,' grunted Koschak. 'Three squadrons, huh?'

'There is probably a fourth squadron back in the trees. Eight hundred sabres.'

Koschak whistled. 'Captain Geourdai will not stand long then? Four hours to the sunset of this bastard of a day. What are your expectations of tonight and tomorrow, sir? I ask because the men are desperate for sleep.'

'The Savona column will clear this junction by sunset. The kaiserliks will bring their infantry up from Savona tomorrow. The Austrians know the importance of this ridgeline junction to the success of the French rear-guard defence in the town below. Once rested, I expect the chevau-léger will become active after midnight. If the Austrians march from Savona at first light, they ought to arrive here by nine or ten o'clock. An enemy column descending from Melogno would flank our defence of Finale Ligure.'

Koschak jerked his chin at Moench snoring in the shade of his grey mare and Bleu, both horses tethered to his boot. 'I went out to Lieutenant Yinot's piquet to kick the arses of those dozing off. Back at our camp, the hour of shut-eye did nought for the lads, but they did find food. Goose and onion soup tonight. And they are roasting a goat for tomorrow. I have no doubt Captain Geourdai will have squeezed the locals down there for 2nd Company's bread. If we are going to face those pricks tomorrow, I will have all ranks shave tonight. The time for looking like a shower of shit is over. But, sir ...'

'Hmm?'

'Will our wounded be safe on the far side of Loano by now? Will Captain Chabenac have made the sixty kilometres to Oneglia by tonight?'

'More than likely. But our news is nothing compared to the alarm of the Austrian advance.'

Chapter Twenty-One

A sentry gripped Jobert's stockinged toe and shook it.

Rousing an exhausted man by shaking his shoulder was a sure way to be punched, or worse, elicit a shocked cry which could alert enemy scouts lurking nearby.

Jobert awoke with a groan. Muscular pain flooded his consciousness. Twisted in his grimy blankets, he rolled over onto his elbows and knees, his head on his forearms, and attempted to stretch the discomfort from his lower back.

'Sir, are you awake?' Each chasseur was drilled to ask the question in case drowsy officers fell back to sleep in the middle of a vital message.

Jobert grunted.

'Piquet, sir.'

This time yesterday morning, we were minced by a British frigate. 'Piquet, yes. Go to bed.' In the dark, Jobert fumbled on his boots and staggered to fold his bedroll into a saddle-pad.

Jobert maintained the habit of taking the last duty-officer piquet of the night. On any other morning rising before reveille allowed him to gather his thoughts while he massaged Bleu's back and loins with his curry brush. Or it provided an opportunity to chat with the sentries as they roved.

This morning, Jobert first woke Tulloc to saddle their horses for the day and to put on a kettle of tea. He then stood with the outlying piquet to watch the thickening mist creep up the headland's forested slopes. As the cloud of clammy fog rose with the morning's warming air, Jobert saw the enemy chevau-léger slither up the steep slope towards the farm at the junction. From his post, Jobert observed the flank of a company skirmish screen, fifty pairs of men some ten metres apart, in two lines, their frontage extending two hundred metres into the hazy hillside scrub.

The French grenadier company garrisoned were waiting. Fire poured from the farm at the intersection.

The pairs of Austrian skirmishers shrank back.

Jobert turned to a nearby sentry. 'Silent reveille. Now!'

Jobert guessed at the enemy's intent. If the chevau-léger maintained their disciplined stealth to the farm's flanks, they would soon isolate the defenders. Moreover, cause alarm to the French in Finale Ligure below by creating the belief that any escape over the headland was denied. With the infantry holed up inside the farm, any traffic, foot, horse or wagon, on the road alongside the farm's stout walls blocked the infantry's line-of-sight to the chevau-léger and thus the traffic was at the mercy of Austrian sniping.

Jobert determined a simple plan. He strode into the squadron's camp to address the puffy-eyed officers shuffling in the ash of the small central fire.

'Dismounted chevau-léger are attempting to seize the junction farm. Yinot, maintain a section at our observation post along the Melogno road. Neilage, take a platoon patrol one hour further down the road towards Melogno than our observation post. Koschak, with 5th Company's remaining section, secure the camp here and the packhorses.

'Geourdai, provide me a platoon in the saddle in fifteen minutes. I will set a mounted skirmish line around the junction farm. Geourdai, take your other platoon as a dismounted skirmish line out from the camp toward the junction. Threaten the flank of the chevau-léger's skirmishers if you reach that far.

'Peugeot, arrange a four-man escort for yourself. Take a message down to the brigade commander in Finale Ligure. Inform him that despite the fire from the ridge, the junction is resolutely held, and the road is open to any traffic directed to ascend at his convenience. Repeat the message.'

Peugeot responded.

Jobert scrutinised the dull faces around him in the gloom. 'Questions? No? There will come a time to discuss yesterday. But a new threat arises today and face it we will. Moench, sound *To Arms!*'

Twenty minutes later, Jobert led the 2nd Company platoon at the trot, sabres drawn, pistols firing, trumpet blaring, down the Melogno road toward the junction farm and the descent to Finale Ligure just beyond, until they passed through the farm's gates.

'Sir, we are surrounded,' said the commander of the farm's garrison, an unruffled captain of grenadiers. 'A company of Austrians has cut routes south to both Finale Ligure and Loano. A second company east of us plays cat-and-mouse over the slope beyond the road. Another company north-east of us, towards your chasseur camp, attempts to wrap around our north.'

'Our extravagant entrance has dispersed those third flock of birds back to their eastern slope,' said Jobert. 'You have identified three companies of dismounted chevau-léger. So, we are faced with two enemy squadrons, with a reserve company somewhere down the slope. My advice is to hold the farm with one half-company and set a skirmish line to clear the Finale Ligure road with the other.

'I have twenty sabres to support that line. With only their musketoons, the kaiserliks face our muskets, bayonets, hooves and sabres. Our first sweep will ensure the junction is not surrounded, and then, working together, we will establish your skirmish line on the road so that any traffic passes safely to Loano.'

'Surely, sir, they will just duck over the lip of the crest, and then return once we move past? This game will absorb us for hours.'

Musket fire rang out from the farm's walls and upper storeys.

'The Austrian main column from Savona could arrive by nine o'clock,' said Jobert. 'With the stout rear-guard action that I expect your regiment will deliver, I foresee us maintaining our part in the game until midday. What say you? The enemy is lingering beyond our gate. Who seeks the honour of showing the Austrian cavalry how dismounted skirmishing is performed?'

The sun was clear of the shimmering Mediterranean horizon by the time the grenadiers secured the road, enhancing their marksmanship at the scurrying Austrians amongst the stunted pine on the thorny slopes.

Late in the morning, the French piquet reported a white flag of truce hoisted on an Austrian musketoon.

Jobert pressed Bleu a little further down the slope and maintained the authority that height conferred.

A green-jacketed chevau-léger officer, a handsome young man with a thick black moustache, distinct in black bicorne with red and white plumes, puffed up through the rocks and bushes. 'Lieutenant D'Onofrio, of His Imperial Majesty's Regiment of Chevau-léger de Kerzy, at your service, sir.' The Austrian suppressed a grimace.

Distaste at my appearance, I am sure. Jobert knew his uniform was matted with filth, with his ripped, blood-stained jacket with buttons missing, leather cross-belts cracked and worn, a misshapen helmet with a tattered crest, with scuffed and splitting boots. 'Major Jobert, 24th Chasseurs à Cheval. And I at your service, sir.'

D'Onofrio raised an eyebrow, his gaze flicking between the lace on Jobert's sleeve and his musketoon. 'My colonel has a request, sir. Last September, a squadron of my regiment had the honour of crossing sabres in the field with a regiment of chasseurs à cheval outside of Dego. Was that the 24th Chasseurs?'

'It was, sir.'

A malicious smile spread under D'Onofrio's moustache. 'Your regiment had the best of us that day. My colonel is most keen to repay the compliment. I look forward to us meeting again soon.'

Artillery began to boom in the valley to the east. Every Austrian and French head turned down and faced Finale Ligure below. The Austrian main force had arrived.

At eleven o'clock, a cannonade announced the Austrian assault upon Finale Ligure.

By one o'clock, the French infantry had quit the town below and ascended the ridgeline.

'Any enemy movement on the Melogno road, Jobert?' asked the brigade commander.

'I have a patrol one hour down the road, sir, and no word yet.'

'The Austrians will have secured the Finale Ligure bridges below by now. The slope of the road will stop the infantry pursuing, but the chevau-léger? What tactic of yours allows us a clean break from them?'

'I suggest, sir, the slope is too steep and the road too narrow for cavalry to break your anchored battalion fire line. The first volley, calmly delivered, will clog the road with downed horses, and no matter the élan of the cavalry, your line will remain unthreatened. I expect enemy infantry infiltrating to form on your battalion's flank will cause the line to relinquish the junction.'

'Yes, thank you, Chief of Squadron, I know that. I ask of your experience as to the disposal of their cavalry once my infantry retires.'

Jobert straightened his bearing. 'My response begins with how much infantry, and possibly artillery, is required to shift your battalion. Then how much road space such a force requires to ascend the slope. Then the chevau-léger will follow that column, and once clear, deploy on the ridge beyond the junction farm, before committing to any pursuit. I believe it is my chasseurs' presence on the Melogno road that will present a severe flanking threat to their assaulting infantry. The immediate demand of any supporting cavalry will be to remove my force before pursuing your infantry, sir.'

Jobert, expecting further rebuke, remained upright in the saddle, his eyes front, his chin raised and his face impassive.

The brigade commander raised his eyebrow as he turned and looked at the line of chasseurs enclosed in the treeline along the Melogno road. 'You hold that location, Jobert, and you will be separated from us.'

'But I will have gained you time, sir. I will rejoin you later by taking mountain paths.'

'As you would have it. Good luck!'

The Austrians did infiltrate a battalion to the flank of the defending French. Any threat from Jobert's chasseurs was neutralised by an Austrian battalion forming square to block the Melogno road beyond the junction farm.

'Geourdai,' said Jobert, 'we are of little use to our withdrawing infantry now. We shall retire from here while our horses are fresh and before the chevau-léger ascend. The first march is to Melogno fifteen kilometres away, yes? Three hours march, or two if we trot. What say you, Geourdai?'

Geourdai wobbled his head as he considered the options. 'The Austrians may have already secured Melogno, coming down from the northern valleys via Calizzano. Having said that, we know how many goat tracks these mountains hide.'

Jobert sensed where the most immediate threat lay. 'If we march for Melogno we will be followed. It is probable a squadron of chevau-léger will clear the route towards Melogno. They are motivated to return the compliment we paid them at Dego. Geourdai, find Neilage's patrol. Column of fours, trot, march!'

Chapter Twenty-Two
June 1795, Melogno, Italy

In the hour before sunset, the light dimmed within the alpine forest road to Melogno. As he had done for the last two months, Neilage led the two-hundred-metre column of chasseurs. The warning of 'Infantry!' was whispered down the column.

'The kaiserliks have Melogno?' Jobert departed Geourdai and the rear-guard to trot Bleu forward to Neilage. As always, Koschak and Moench followed.

At the head of the column Jobert found Lieutenant Yinot and the sergeants ensuring all musketoon cartridges were well packed. Further up the road, Jobert saw Neilage returning at the trot from a mounted chasseur holding three horses. The three dismounted scouts were somewhere forward of that.

'The outer cottages of Melogno are ahead.' Neilage grunted through gritted teeth. Jobert glanced at Neilage's oozing bandaged thigh. 'There is an Austrian infantry outpost too busy collecting firewood to notice us. They have not signalled. No one is beating *To Arms*.'

'Only the chevau-léger from Finale Ligure know we are on the road, not the infantry at Melogno,' said Jobert. 'We need to get off the road. Moench, signal silence to the column. Neilage, reverse the column to Geourdai. Sergeant Major, take the column into the forest. Sweep away our tracks coming off the road. We will ambush any kaiserliks following up. I need to understand the country hereabouts. Yinot, there are cottages near the tail of our column. Impress a local into our service. Take a child hostage to ensure his enthusiasm.' Jobert saw the flicker of discomfort in an exchange of glances between Neilage and Yinot. 'Just do it, Lieutenant Yinot. The survival of all of us is worth more than any inconvenience we might impose on a local peasant.'

An hour later in the dark forest, as Moench plucked a soft, gentle tune on his treasured fiddle, the chasseurs puffed on their pipes, or chewed on slivers of cold, roast goat, underneath their remounts' muzzles, awaiting the order to either form column or unsaddle. Their commanders knelt in the smoke of the camp's only small fire.

Geourdai approached along a forest path leading down the slope from the Melogno road. Geourdai adjusted his sabre and musketoon and squatted amongst the others. 'I have just watched a chevau-léger squadron column move toward Melogno, past our exit from the road. It is pitch black up on the road, but the moon will rise in an hour. If they come back tonight to search for where we broke track, they will need torches. 2nd Company is ready to take them if they come.'

'Good, but that is unnecessary,' said Jobert. 'Yinot, what news from our captive?'

'Sir, our peasant suggests our next march is to Bardineto. He says the Austrians arrived in Melogno around midday. With the Melogno-Bardineto road held by the Austrians, our man is confident he can guide us through the forest paths to Bardineto.'

Jobert blinked into the fire. 'If the Austrians departed Calizzano today to secure Melogno, they will have done the same for Bardineto. Just as the kaiserlik infantry collecting firewood were not expecting any French advancing from Finale Ligure, why would any Austrians expect a French column to approach Bardineto from Melogno? Our immediate threat is the chevauléger.'

Jobert evaluated the nervous peasant in the rough-spun tunic. A shivering, tear-streaked boy clung to the man, and due to the man's hands bound behind his back, the child waved mosquitoes from his face with a twig of pine. 'How long until Bardineto by night march? We need distance between ourselves and the chevau-léger.'

'This man says he knows the country well, sir,' said Yinot. 'Some two, or three hours, through the forest to Bardineto.'

Leading horses under the heavily scented pine boughs along the moonlit track, the chasseurs marched up-ridge and down-dale in single file for ten dreary kilometres.

Four hours later, the order to 'unsaddle and tether' was greeted with appreciative expletives from the soldiers. With a solitary campfire to orient the sentries to the duty-officer and the impost of double-piquet security, quiet soldierly curses hummed through the insect-laden air, as the squadron's commanders gathered and evaluated their situation.

'Anyone?' asked Jobert.

Geourdai shook his water flask to find it empty. 'There is no one behind us, sir.'

Neilage passed his water gourd to Geourdai. 'The Bardineto

valley is just ahead of us. Around the town is a glow of campfires. Far more than a battalion, a regiment at least.'

Geourdai coughed as he drank too fast. 'If the kaiserliks took Finale Ligure today, then they aim to take Loano tomorrow. This Bardineto regiment is only three hours from Loano's flank. Will our wounded lads clear Loano?'

Jobert shuffled to stretch a cramp in his thigh. 'Our wounded ought to be safe in Oneglia tonight.' A growl of success hummed in the throats around the fire. *At least we got that right.* 'Yinot, with Bardineto taken, where does our peasant suggest next?'

'Another two, maybe three, hours to Rocca Barbena on the Garessio road, sir,' said Yinot. 'From there we either press onto the coast or push across the next valley to Pieve di Teco.'

'Reveille at three o'clock and let us see what tomorrow brings.'

The stockinged feet of sleeping men were squeezed and shaken. Waking moans were given the whispered response 'Reveille. Stand to.'

Four half-section patrols pressed further out into the fog-shrouded darkness and listened to the forest. Men sat up and pulled on boots, then stood and attached their belts, cross-belts with cartridge box and musketoon, and sword belts.

Having slept under their horses' noses whilst tethered to the platoon horse-line, the chasseurs moved in beside their horses' ribs and urinated under their horses' bellies, then folded back their horses' canvas rugs and placed them on the saddle pad of their folded paillasse and blankets.

The saddle pad was followed by the timber and iron saddle frame. Once girth, breastplate and crupper secured the frame to the horse, a roll of horse rug and cape was strapped over the pistol holsters on the saddle bow. Across this arrangement, the grimy woollen shabraques were fastened with a surcingle. Finally, the chasseurs attached their portmanteau to the rear of their saddles, all within fifteen minutes of waking.

As sentries stared into the night listening, groups of chasseurs formed work parties and either relieved the outposts, so the sentries could saddle their mounts, or stowed the ropes and staves of the horse-lines, or saddled and loaded packhorses.

By four o'clock, in the dim grey light before dawn and to the twitter of the day's first birdsong, 2nd Squadron, standing at the shoulders of their remounts, began walking down the dim trails under the heavy, black branches towards the forest's edge.

'The east-running road to Loano is in front of us in the centre of the valley beside the stream.' Yinot interpreted the peasant's description for Jobert and Neilage. 'Bardineto is one thousand metres up the road to our right. He says we seek a road running south from Bardineto into the forested slopes on the far side of the valley towards Rocca Barbena.'

Jobert closed his telescope. 'We aim to arrive at Rocca Barbena by six o'clock. If we are hunted by chevau-léger, they will pick up our tracks where we departed the Melogno road. With the trail churned by four hundred hooves, they will have no problems pursuing us at the trot. If they have our scent in this light, they will stand here where we are standing in one hour, and they ought to arrive just behind us at Rocca Barbena.'

In the predawn light, 2nd Squadron departed the tree cover and entered the summer stubble of the Bardineto's harvested pastures. Horses took their time to drink at the tumbling stream in the centre of the valley while the men filled their gourds and flasks, and sergeants had larger casks on packhorses replenished.

Thirsty horses are at risk of colic by drinking too much cold water. But these scruffy remounts, hardened through the last three years of their service to France by drinking from puddles and gobbling the bleakest of dried grass, were inured to the circumstances which presented a real risk to well-cared-for, stabled mounts. Nevertheless, Koschak stood mid-stream and waved the troopers forward to ensure each horse did not over-indulge and for the march to continue.

Everyone's heads spun towards Bardineto when, through the valley's thick summer fog, Austrian drums were beating.

Flanking scouts reported to Jobert that a white-jacketed battalion column was approaching the chasseurs on the road to Loano. Another battalion was on the road south to Rocca Barbena and disappearing as the road curved into the sloping treeline on the other side of the valley.

'We need to get ahead of that far battalion,' said Jobert.

'Our guide says once inside the treeline,' said Yinot, 'we follow forest trails up onto the far ridge and intercept the road on the far side of the ridge.'

Once it was clear the drumming was a steady marching beat, not the insistent pounding of orders, the chasseur column, disguised by fog, focused on crossing the stream and the Loano-Bardineto road then continuing their march up the forested slopes. As the column crested the southern ridgeline above Bardineto's vale, the sun was just above the eastern peaks.

They listened to the progress of the Austrian battalion on the Rocca Barbena road beneath them. Over the crunch of marching boots on gravel, came the creak and clank of wheels and chains, and steady clatter of hooves.

'The kaiserliks have a battery with them,' said Jobert.

Peugeot trotted up the column from 2nd Company's rear guard. 'Captain Geourdai sends his compliments, sir, and reports chevau-léger entering the Bardineto valley from the far treeline.'

The news caused the chasseurs to press their horses down the crumbling paths until they arrived on the single-lane gravel road.

Rocca Barbena was less than an hour to their left.

To their right, the drums of the advancing Austrians sounded through the trees.

The threat of avenging chevau-léger sabres, hot on their ridgeline trail, hung above them.

Musket fire sounded from their front.

Jobert squeezed Bleu to canter the two hundred metres to Neilage at the head of the halted mounted column.

'There is French line infantry in the village of Rocca Barbena,' said Neilage.

Now clear of the trees in the paddocks surrounding Rocca Barbena, the faint sound of distant, intense gunfire reverberated.

Jobert reached into his jacket for his watch. 'Six o'clock. The Austrians are attacking Loano. Yinot, canter forward under a flag of truce. Find their commander. Warn them of the Austrians approaching on this road. Neilage, keep the column marching.'

Within ten minutes, Jobert met the company commander in the village square. Jobert recognised that the officer belonged to a line infantry regiment from General Masséna's division. 'Describe your situation, captain, so I know how best to support your battalion.'

The young infantry commander drew himself up, his eyes revealing his nervousness to the cavalry audience. 'The road network around Rocca Barbena is like a capital letter H, sir. The right upright of the H is this ridge-line road connecting

Bardineto to Loano. The left upright is a road set low in a sharp valley connecting Garessio to Albenga via the village of Zuccarello. The interconnecting crossbar of the H is a steep, twisting road. My chief of battalion holds the upper junction. My regimental commander holds the junction in the valley floor.'

The clatter of iron-shod hooves on village cobblestones, rebounding off tight-packed stone walls, cracked the morning calm. Jobert winced as an infantry captain, a regimental aide de camp, jerked his horse to a clumsy stop in the plaza.

The surprised aide saluted Jobert. 'Forgive me, sir, I had no idea we had cavalry in support. Gentlemen, an Austrian regiment supported by guns, approaches from Garessio on the lower road. Our chief of battalion has orders to withdraw to the valley floor.'

'On your return, sir,' said Jobert to the infantry aide de camp, 'inform your commanders there is another Austrian battalion, with guns and a squadron of cavalry, on the upper road from Bardineto. They will reach Rocca Barbena in half-an-hour.'

The infantry aide saluted, executed a harsh turn and gouged his mount to a canter.

The infantry company commander spun towards his drummers lounging against the walls. 'Beat *Assembly* and *Outposts In!*'

'We will hold them, sir,' said Jobert. 'Depart at the double-march without drums. It will lead the kaiserliks to believe infantry still hold the village, and that will slow their advance.'

Jobert turned to address Neilage, Geourdai and Koschak. 'We will cover the infantry's withdrawal but avoid crossing sabres with the chevau-léger. Our men performed well skirmishing above Finale Ligure, yet I hesitate to test the lads' resolve so soon after that bastard of a frigate. Is my assessment of their ardour amiss?'

'I think the men need to regather themselves, sir,' said Geourdai. 'Since the ambush two mornings ago, the lads have not had time to scratch their arses.'

'I agree, sir,' said Koschak.

'There we have it.' Jobert thumped his shabraque. 'But we must move fast as I do not want to be cut off again by this lower enemy battalion. Neilage, have 5th Company continue the advance behind the infantry. Identify this junction that leads to the lower Garessio-Zuccarello-Albenga road. I will take one platoon from 2nd Company and the marksmen to set a dismounted ambush at the edge of the village. Geourdai, set flanking outposts and hold a mounted reserve.'

'Release the peasant and his son, sir?' asked Yinot.

'No. Release him once we have quit this village.'

Jobert watched the lead file from the chevau-léger column.

The mounted enemy held short of the village on the far side of the harvested fields. Following the sound of French drums and trumpets as they approached, the wariness of the Austrian horse scouts was heightened when they observed the complete absence of any movement within the village.

'Do you have the range, lads?' Jobert asked riflemen Duval and Tulloc at his side.

Duval breathed as he settled his aim.

'Drop them!' said Jobert.

Duval and Tulloc fired, then their mates passed their second rifles, and they fired again. Three of the four Austrians snapped back in the saddles as if struck in the chest by a sledgehammer at full force.

'They have withdrawn, sir,' cried Tulloc.

Jobert lowered his glass and allowed the gun smoke to clear from under the olive branch that concealed their position. 'Bullshit. They are watching. The sun is behind them so no tell-tale reflections this morning. Watch for movement in the trees beside the road. The next observers will be their officers.'

Duval jerked his chin at the far meadow walls. 'Drums, sir. The kaiserliks are bringing their infantry forward.'

A chasseur coughed behind Jobert. 'Sir, Captain Geourdai reports there is cavalry on the slopes above the village flanks.'

'Their skirmishers are deploying, sir,' said Tulloc over his rifle's sights.

'Drop the skirmishers, lads, as our work here is done. Moench, sound *Assembly*!'

Within five minutes, the dismounted men of 2nd Company had jogged back to their waiting horses, mounted, and in column of fours, trotted from the village to catch 5th Company somewhere on the road ahead.

Jobert held an impatient Bleu long enough for him to take a pinch of francs from his calf-skin purse and pass them to the sullen peasant from Melogno.

Rubbing the chafed skin of unbound wrists and gripping his child, the peasant spat at Jobert's feet.

On the ridgeline above Jobert, small, dark figures of the enemy cavalry peered over the edge.

The Garessio-Zucarello-Albenga road ran at the base of a sharp ravine, now blocked by a French battalion fire line, some two hundred metres long. A pair of French cannon boomed at the approaching Austrian infantry.

At Koschak's insistence, chasseurs pressed forward to the swift stream and watered desperate horses.

Jobert approached the infantry colonel. 'Sir, Major Jobert, 24th Chasseurs. The enemy have a battalion with a battery above you, supported by a squadron of chevau-léger. I have a company of chasseurs at your service. If it accords with your plan, my company is well able to hold this junction, if you wish to press on to Zuccarello.'

The colonel's eyes narrowed at the appalling state of Jobert's uniform. 'Ah, the 24th Chasseurs. I am obliged, sir. I have ordered my regiment to concentrate at Zuccarello. These upper and lower road junctions are too widespread. My first battalion is well up to the task of stepping back our fire line. So, thank you, sir, but I have no need for your immediate support, except to convey my report to General Masséna at Pieve di Teco twenty-five kilometres away.'

Jobert clenched his teeth at the remaining distance that his exhausted soldiers and remounts must travel.

'It is now half-past seven o'clock, sir, your message shall be delivered in Pieve di Teco by one o'clock. Moench, sound *Advance*. We are going home.'

Chapter Twenty-Three
July-October 1795, Oneglia, Italy

3rd July 1795
Oneglia, Italy

To the family of Second Lieutenant Michel Pultiere,

It is my sorrowful duty to inform you that your son, Second Lieutenant Michel Pultiere, has died in battle near Savona, Italy, on the 29th of June 1795.

It is a singular honour for me to have served alongside your son for the last two and a half years as his commander. During that period, Michel was devoted to the Republic, loyal to his regiment and a firm and dedicated leader for his chasseurs. Every soldier in the regiment's 2nd Company mourns his passing.

At the time he was taken from us, Michel commanded a vital element in a crucial supply convoy. Despite our force wickedly ambushed by the Republic's enemies, much of their destructive effort was thwarted by

Second Lieutenant Pultiere's fierce counterattack. An inspiration to us all, your son died a brave hero in the heat of battle, sabre and pistol in hand, surrounded by his slain foes. With us, his name will remain a byword for courage.

On behalf of the regiment which loved him, I impart our deepest condolences for your loss.

Your loyal servant,
Chief of Squadron André Jobert,
24ᵗʰ Chasseurs à Cheval

Lieutenant Colonel Clemusat, second-in-command of the 24ᵗʰ Chasseurs, arranged blank sheets of paper under his elbow before dipping his quill into a glass-and-silver inkpot.

'Major Jobert, the aim of this investigation is to determine the nature of the incident 2ⁿᵈ Squadron was engaged in on the morning of the 29ᵗʰ of June this year. I received your written report. Your diagrams of the ambush were most illuminating, thank you. I am now obliged, under General Masséna's terms of reference, to ask further questions. Did you receive written orders to undertake this escort?'

Jobert rearranged himself to relax on the hard-backed dining chair in the warm, stuffy room. 'No, sir. Verbal orders only from Colonel Raive, of General Masséna's staff, sir, in the presence of Colonel Spiccard.'

Clemusat skimmed Jobert's report. 'Acting as an ammunition convoy, you escorted eight empty regimental wagons from Oneglia to Toulon. Then your convoy proceeded from Toulon to Savona and then returned to Toulon. During this period, you conducted all your road movement by day. How did you utilise the time whilst travelling to prepare for the next two escorts?'

'I conducted route reconnaissance and the siting of ambushes with the squadron, sir. During the escorts east to Savona, we maintained our routes on the coastal road capable of wagon traffic. During any movement west to Toulon, patrols were dispatched to assess alternative parallel routes for vehicle movement, and, failing that, flank guards.'

'Why did you task the squadron to site ambushes?'

'To evaluate the opportunities and difficulties of our enemies, sir. That insight was discussed with the junior leaders of the squadron, and countermeasures were prepared based on that shared experience.'

Go on, ask me directly 'Were we prepared?' Jobert stifled his irritation by wriggling on his uncomfortable seat.

'Once in Toulon on the second occasion,' said Clemusat, 'you escorted eight gun-limbers to Savona. You travelled by night on the coast road. Why?'

'We timed our travel to coincide with the setting moon, sir, a time of darkness aimed at decreasing the effectiveness of our enemies' fire. Colonels Raive and Spiccard agreed to the tactic.'

'What use of alternative routes did you make?'

'Flank guards only travelled on alternative routes, sir, as and when they became available. Over the three-hundred-kilometre route the squadron was directed to traverse, there are multiple lengths of the coast road where no alternative routes exist.'

'What alternative routes were available to you on the coast where the squadron was ambushed?'

'One other inland route existed capable of wagons, sir.' Jobert reached forward and pointed to Clemusat's charts. 'Having evaluated both roads four times, consensus between the officers and sergeant majors of the squadron preferred the coastal route as the more difficult for infantry to ambush. One flank of the road was protected by the sea and the sharp escarpment had a path along its top edge which was cleared by a flank guard. It was the poorest of ambush sites with no location to site artillery. After their first volley from the beach, the enemy was trapped beneath us with no place to disperse or form square.'

'You describe in your report how 2nd Squadron was an extended convoy —'

'Target, sir.'

Clemusat glanced up from his notes. 'I beg your pardon?'

'It was not a convoy, sir, the squadron was a deliberate target paraded in front of the enemy, whether they chose to ambush it or not. The appearance of a convoy was a charade.'

Clemusat gave Jobert a weary look. 'Quite so. What were your considerations if you were attacked by light infantry?'

'The enemy's trump card was the shock to us that their surprise generated, and any obstruction of the road by horse casualties created with their first volley. The enemy infantry needed to be thirty to seventy metres from the path over which we travelled. We exploited the fact that the squadron could concentrate one hundred and fifty sabres within the time it takes to reload a musket.'

Clemusat's nib tapped an annoying rhythm to lose excess ink. Jobert sighed. *Should I ever excel, then I shall be elevated to be a scribbler of reports.* Somewhere outside, a trumpet called chasseurs to their stable duties.

Clemusat dipped, tapped and was poised to scratch once more. 'How effective were the counter ambush drills displayed by the squadron's advance and rear guards to the enemy's blocking forces on this particular evening? Did your men fail in their duties?'

Jobert's face spasmed with anger. *You bastard!* 'Each chasseur was well acquainted with the requirement of his section should he lose his commander. Safety of the horses trapped in the ambush was the greatest single motivator for every man to succeed. The darkness was a boon. Whilst enemy musket fire revealed their location, the darkness, combined with the resultant gun smoke, covered our approach. What is more, darkness ensured our horses did not shy at their bayonets. My chasseurs were exemplary in the conduct of their duties, sir.'

'I am satisfied with your views of the enemy infantry. What were your considerations of enemy artillery prior to the ambush?'

'Again, sir, Colonels Raive, Spiccard and I were of the same opinion that light guns, three-pounders, would be dismantled and brought in by packhorses. Infiltration through French screens over mountain paths was difficult, but a determined enemy force supported by the Italian partisans could achieve it. Through previous route reconnaissance, the 5th Company advance guard became aware of every potential gun position.' Jobert imagined his chair beginning to sink as Vert had collapsed that evening. His pulse was rapid and his breathing shallow. *What I want to know is whatever happened to that Inoubli bastard?* 'At no time, sir, did Colonels Raive, Spiccard or I ever discuss a warship engaging us. What the *Romulus* contrived was unprecedented. What knowledge have you gained about the *Romulus*, sir?'

Clemusat tapped his quill on the rim of the pot. 'Indeed. Assisted by the number and size of the shot you collected, our naval colleagues in Toulon conclude she was a thirty-six-gun frigate. Your squadron was ... complimented by eighteen guns on one side of the gun deck, thirteen eighteen-pounders and five nine-pounders.'

'That is obscene, sir! That is the army equivalent of receiving the flanking fire of eight fucking six-pound batteries at less than one thousand metres whilst stationary.'

Aghast, Clemusat sat upright, before his face drooped to empathy. 'Jobert, the column was struck by fifty-four rounds in five minutes, along four hundred metres of its length. You say your men complied with their orders, was it your plan that failed?'

Jobert trembled to control his seething rage.

'We were struck, sir, with a phenomenal weight of fire. Despite taking one-third casualties, sir, 2nd Squadron succeeded in pushing three hundred infantry back down onto the beach. We held our ground as they withdrew. 2nd Squadron most certainly did not fail, sir.'

With no breeze to ease the smell of raw sewerage, Jobert gained slight relief as he flapped his notebook against the whine of mosquitoes. Insects and frogs serenaded his dinner. Little nourishment was forthcoming from the watery bean and onion soup on the table in front of him, not even a pinch of flour to thicken it.

'Did the water boil before you added the ingredients, Tulloc? Is there enough in the kettle for Sergeant Major Koschak?'

'Yes, sir. Sorry —'

Beside Jobert, Chabenac curved his sunken cheeks to encourage their cook for this evening. 'You have prepared a fine meal from what was available, Tulloc. Take rest from your labours and enjoy your repast.'

Dribbles ran down his chin as Jobert scoffed his single meal of the day. 'So, the Army of Italy is to be reinforced?'

Chabenac slurped his spoon with more enthusiasm than the meal deserved. 'Quite so. With the dividend of peace with

Prussia and Spain, the War Committee has released troops from the Rhine and the Pyrenees to join us. Wherever I go, the chatter centres on us striking towards the River Po.'

Jobert gouged his bowl for an elusive sliver of onion. 'Strength? Huh! Whilst Minister Carnot focuses France's efforts north of the Alps, I restrain any expectation that we feast upon the bounty of Piedmont any time soon. Furthermore, with Savona now back in Austrian control, the British can base their fleet's actions closer to the mouth of the Rhône.'

Jobert gulped at his watered brandy as his frustrations surfaced. 'Reinforcements mean more mouths to feed over winter. From what I hear, another seven or eight regiments of cavalry are to arrive. Good grief! The coastal valleys from Nice to Oneglia were grazed to dust by the current four under-strength regiments. With the rise of sickness, in both men and animals, due to the poor supply and summer's harvest already consumed, we will emerge in a pitiable shape when winter comes.'

Chabenac sloshed more from an earthenware jug into his friend's wooden cup. 'I have heard numbers as high as twenty thousand men are hospitalised between here and Avignon. The countryside ravaged to desolation. Villages overcrowded with infantry. The ports full of displaced villagers. No one growing or harvesting food. The waterways are fouled with contagion. Supply of rations and medicines abominably corrupted. Criminal supply contractors not providing even the basics of flour, brandy, beef and grain. Then the dribble of supply that reaches Marseille, the British capture or sink the balance.'

Jobert tugged at the collar of his shirt to wipe the sweat from his brow. A pungent waft from within his shirt reminded him of the need to return to Savona and bathe in the sea. Water for laundry was a rare luxury.

Jobert drained his cup. 'Is Spiccard still furious?'

'Yes. Spiccard has not taken the losses from 2ⁿᵈ Squadron's

ambush well. He seeks someone to blame, either you or Raive. Distributing sections to make up for the losses will bring every company down to around eighty men per company.'

'Is 2nd Squadron and the surviving wounded still in reserve in Nice?'

Chabenac nodded as he chased the flies gathering on the rim of his cup.

Jobert's face soured as he ran grimy fingers through his matted hair. 'Spiccard denied me leave to visit them in Nice. He made the point that Geourdai and Neilage are paid to look after their own wounded. I asked Geourdai to list the needs of the two companies as I wished to contribute and make their ... recovery a little more ...'

A wave of sadness flushed Jobert's chest and face with an unexpected memory of Vert. The bay gelding never needed constant scratching as did Rouge, nor was impatient to move like Bleu. Jobert loved how Vert would lower his great head to Jobert's thighs so Jobert could tickle his ears.

Chabenac's chair squeaked as he reached to grip Jobert's slumped shoulder. 'Quite so. Has Voreille settled in at Masséna's headquarters with Raive? I never understood that business with Voreille in Garessio. In late May, you arrested the man for writing to a harlot. Six weeks later he is a divisional aide de camp. The situation confounds me.'

Jobert forced upon himself an image of Vert under a shady tree at the bottom of a lush paddock to focus on avoiding any discussion of Voreille. 'Ah, a misunderstanding on my part. Raive straightened it all out. You know I have sent Orlande and Moench to Avignon for a month.' Jobert's eyes slid across his friend's face as Chabenac attempted to resume the thread of thought concerning Voreille.

Chabenac tapped his bowl. 'Ah, that explains Orlande's absence.'

'I have sent Moench back to Avignon to spend time with his family following the loss of his brother,' said Jobert. 'Orlande has a long list of equipment repairs and purchases for Avignon.'

Chabenac looked down at his bowl now crawling with flies. 'I, for one, look forward to Orlande's safe return.'

Stockinged toes extended towards the fire, Jobert rolled the local *rossese* around his mouth as he re-read his cousin's latest letter.

6th October 1795
Paris

Darling André,

Two months have elapsed since the excitement and alarm of the royalist landings in support of the Brittany uprising. In the last few days the city again explodes with drama. Literally explodes! Extraordinary days, indeed.

In the transition from the detested Committee of Public Safety to the new five-man Directory at the end of the month, the royalists have attempted another coup. Barras, one of the key personalities within the Directory, turned out the army and the Parisian National Guard to eradicate the royalist fools. It is all so confusing here. From what I hear, Barras' general, Bonaparte, directed the army to fire artillery point-blank into crowds in the streets. The result was yet another massacre of six hundred people dead or wounded. A law has passed to disarm the citizens. There are moves afoot to bring the governance of Paris under the control of the new Council of Five Hundred. My friends who know such, believe this ends the dominance of the sans-culottes.

My friends also say that Barras and Bonaparte met during the siege of Toulon. Did you happen to meet them whilst you were all there?

The combination of the ruby wine and a sardonic 'Hah!' caused Jobert an eruption of coughing.

Such bloody excitement distracts us from the misery of the economy. In better days, one exchanged a gold louis for fifty francs. With the rampant use of these horrid paper assignats, no one will exchange a gold louis for anything less than a two thousand franc note. The immediate impact of these worthless pieces of paper here in the city is the total lack of cooking oil, eggs, meat, wine and flour.

One financial note of good cheer is, thanks to you, my darling cousin, our family now holds the title papers to the farm. With interest rates rampant, your annuity is delivering a healthy return. Doubly so with your choice to compound the interest.

Jobert raised his eyes to the fire and took a sip. *With the income of a major and a situation where there is nothing to spend it all on but boot repairs and grain for horses, what will I do with a compounding annuity of a lieutenant colonel?* Neither cup nor flames provided any immediate clarity.

Duque, of course, comes to our rescue in this regard. The family's wagons add these desperately needed commodities to their loads, sufficient to maintain the meanest of meals for both ourselves and our families in the workhouses. Duque sends you and all your fellows his warm wishes. He finds it difficult to adjust to academic routine, but he delights at the knowledge that is shared with him. As for us ladies here, we are overjoyed to spoil him when he visits, after, of course, he has completed the interminable repairs that our antiquated apartment brings.

The other distraction from inflated prices and the uncertainty on the streets is the company of dear friends. Madame de Chabenac, Valmai and I are enjoying a full card of balls, games evenings and garden parties. There is a new dance I adore, the 'waltz', which is wonderfully fun. The gentleman takes the lady in his arms. How delightfully scandalous. Would you believe it is now fashionable to meet with friends in restaurants, of all places?

The weather here in Paris has started its descent into winter. Does the warmth linger there on the Mediterranean? Do you bathe in the sea? With so many handsome officers in Nice, is the season there quite lively? If so, you must try the 'waltz'.

All the ladies here send their warmest regards,
Write to us as soon as you can …

To waltz. To attend parties. Jobert drifted with the music of the hearth. As he watched the entwined flames pirouette, his fingers caressed the pages as if it were the lace on the back of a ball gown.

'Hah,' he whispered to the flickering dancers, 'if only I had the freedom to bathe.'

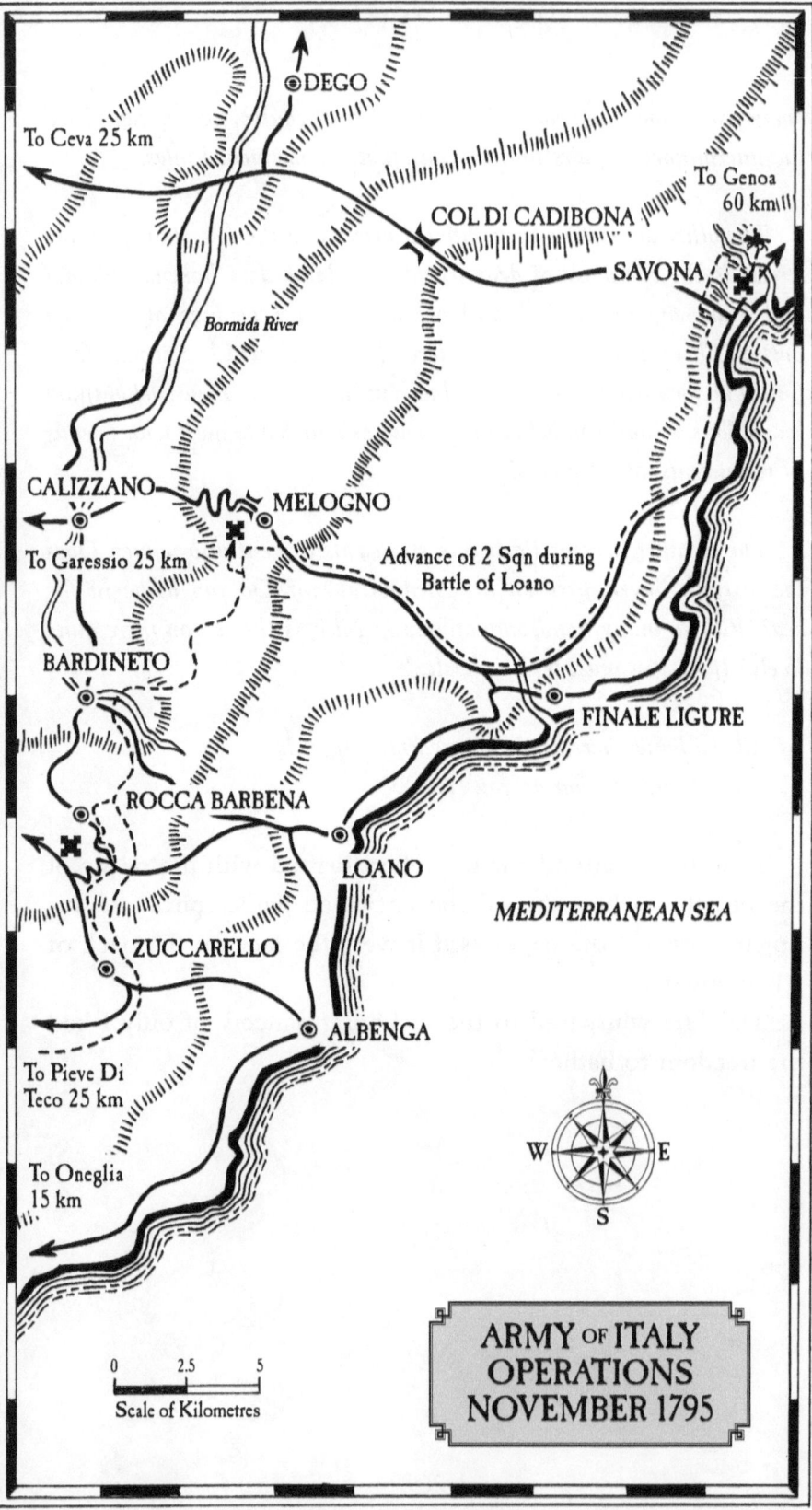

DEGO

To Ceva 25 km

COL DI CADIBONA

To Genoa 60 km

SAVONA

Bormida River

CALIZZANO

MELOGNO

To Garessio 25 km

Advance of 2 Sqn during Battle of Loano

BARDINETO

FINALE LIGURE

ROCCA BARBENA

LOANO

MEDITERRANEAN SEA

ZUCCARELLO

ALBENGA

To Pieve Di Teco 25 km

To Oneglia 15 km

W E

S

0   2.5   5

Scale of Kilometres

ARMY OF ITALY OPERATIONS NOVEMBER 1795

Chapter Twenty-Four
October 1795, Zuccarello, Italy

On a high ridge above Zuccarello, a bitter drizzle blew in off the Mediterranean. The wind whipped away the notes of a mournful tune from Moench's fife. The chasseurs of 2nd and 5th Companies watched their horses graze on the last of the season's pasture. Amongst the horses, a work party stripped leafless shrubs for firewood into the squadron's wagons. Madame Quandalle moved amongst the soldiers selling diluted local *eau de vie* from the cask slung over her shoulder.

Behind a rocky outcrop, Jobert, Geourdai and Neilage sat huddled in their capes watching wind-whipped flames do little to boil a tea kettle than dry the ashen mud smeared on the kettle's base. Chabenac hitched his horse to the squadron's horse-line.

'To what do we owe the pleasure?' asked Jobert.

'General Kellermann no longer commands the Army of Italy,' said Chabenac, gathering his cape about him as he sat on the ground.

'Yet another general,' said Geourdai.

'Has Masséna taken command?' asked Neilage.

'No, General Schérer is reappointed as the Army's commander,' said Chabenac.

'Schérer is back again?' asked Geourdai. 'Is this part of the
new Directory-led government?'

'The Directory have certainly made their mark in Paris with
a raft of new policies,' said Chabenac. 'For example, mass executions are to cease. Five hundred people awaiting execution were
released. Even measures against priests and royalists are softened.'

Looks of puzzlement were exchanged.

'Government support to the clerics is aimed at reducing the
agitation of the peasants,' said Chabenac. 'It removes a point of
leverage from the royalists.'

'But will the new Directory, or Schérer's return, relieve us
of this supply nightmare?' asked Geourdai. 'The influx of new
troops has crammed every village.'

'I have seen infantry stripping cottages for firewood and
sleeping in pits thatched with thorns,' said Neilage.

'We still await such relief,' said Chabenac. 'General Jourdan,
of Fleurus fame, has struck across the Rhine and captured
Dusseldorf, Mannheim and Heidelberg, and the vast stores
contained therein.'

'Captured food on the Rhine will not fill our bellies here.'
Geourdai dropped a meagre pinch of tea into the boiling kettle.
'Can you see Schérer doing that?'

Jobert and Chabenac exchanged a look of resignation at
Geourdai's melancholy.

'Speaking of stripping bare,' said Chabenac, 'with the lack
of winter forage, the regiment is to retire to winter quarters in
Oneglia.'

'Oneglia?' Geourdai spat. 'There is not a blade of grass in
Oneglia. Why not winter at our depot near Nice?'

Chabenac raised his hands to deflect any anticipated outburst.

'Fergnes will bring the regimental depot forward to Oneglia to make room for another new cavalry regiment.'

'Mark my words.' Geourdai plucked at his loose-hanging uniform. 'Our horses and ourselves are poorly now. With no grain for them and one meal a day for us, we will lose men and horses over winter, you will see. We were well served by our depot in Nice. Sufficient fodder, access to limited grain, fresh water, sea-bathing, brandy, vinegar and fresh milk for the wounded. Now that the rains have arrived, the mud of Oneglia will swallow us.'

A musket shot rang out. The four officers' heads jerked around. Cheering from the chasseurs indicated that someone had bagged a skinny hare for the platoon's soup kettle.

Neilage poured the tea into four wooden cups perched in the mud beyond the ash. 'Has Huin returned from Avignon?'

'He has,' said Chabenac. 'I have just taken my leave from his quick wit in Nice. Huin is as cool and calm as ever. The Avignon doctors saved his eye. Sadly, he has lost much of his vision and now wears a patch. He is to serve Colonel Spiccard as an aide de camp.'

Jobert saw that Neilage's smile did little to cover his concern for his wounded friend.

Geourdai poked at something floating in his tea. 'Who will remain to inspire our empty bellies over winter?'

Jobert cupped the steam of the tea to his pinched face. 'Clemusat is to take his first leave in two years in November and December. Spiccard is on leave in January and February. Fergnes will act as regimental second-in-command whilst we are in winter quarters.'

'Fergnes is not happy, as Marguerite has just given birth to their first child,' said Chabenac.

'Fergnes is not happy?' Geourdai raised a scornful eye from his tea. 'We have not had leave in two years and Fergnes has spent a year with his gorgeous wife in Nice. A pox on bloody Fergnes.'

Jobert shifted his gaze away from Spiccard's nonchalant air.

Spiccard lounged to one side of his armchair. 'We are to launch a winter offensive to recapture Savona.'

Jobert glanced toward Fergnes.

Fergnes' jaw clenched as he stared at the glowing logs crumbling in the hearth. 'I assume, sir, an initiative from our new Directory?'

'The provision of food throughout the country continues as the single largest economic and political challenge for France,' said Spiccard. 'The value of the franc continues to fall which exacerbates the ability to grow and sell food.'

'And printing more assignats has not assisted the situation,' said Fergnes.

'True,' said Spiccard. 'As internal and external threats remain, the army continues at its inordinate size. To feed the army, Minister of War Carnot, a member of the Directory, has set the policy of "make war pay for war". There is now great pressure from Paris for General Schérer to advance into Piedmont and secure the Austrian magazines to feed us.'

'But we know General Schérer resists, sir,' said Fergnes.

Spiccard sneered. 'He is now willing to advance along the coast to re-establish the grain trade with Genoa.'

Jobert frowned over his notebook. 'General Schérer resists Deputy Saliceti, sir? General Dumerbion would have been executed if he had refused to comply with a Deputy.'

'In a Republic without Robespierre,' said Fergnes, 'the opinion of the Deputies of the People, although they hold weight, are no longer a death sentence if disregarded.'

'The Austrians are not expecting a winter offensive,' said Spiccard. 'We strike as the Austrian troops settle into their comfortable winter quarters, and most of their senior commanders have retired back into Lombardy for Christmas. We want Savona. We want Tuscan grain from Genoa.'

'I daresay, sir,' said Fergnes, 'we want the stores the Austrian troops have put aside for winter.'

'Quite so. General Schérer will attack with three divisional columns. In the north, the first column will attack down the Tanaro River valley to occupy the Piedmontese reserves. Along the coast, the second column will secure the ports of Loano and Finale Ligure. In the centre, General Masséna's divisional column is to strike through the mountains threatening the flanks of both Garessio and the ports.'

Fergnes sucked in his breath. 'An advance along limited, narrow roads in an alpine winter.'

'Indeed,' said Spiccard. 'The terrain forces General Masséna to advance in a column of four infantry regiments. One regiment, the 16th Légère, will advance from our outposts at Zuccarello to secure Rocca Barbena, Bardineto and Melogno, thus breaking the flanks of the Austrian coastal defence. Jobert, with knowledge gained from your July meanderings in that area, you are to lead the 16th Légère. Moreover, Jobert, ...'

Jobert watched Spiccard's face for the expected opprobrium and imagined Spiccard rolling a potentially derisive comment around in his mind. *Go on, say it.*

Spiccard shrugged. 'Moreover, Jobert, Colonel Raive has asked you to escort him this evening on an inspection of the outlying piquet.'

'I beg your pardon, sir? Colonel Raive? This evening?'

'Yes, Colonel Raive this evening, Jobert.' Spiccard slapped

the desktop. 'Make it so, and do not disappoint. We are to march the day after tomorrow. Gentlemen, any final thoughts?'

'Bread and grain, sir?' asked Fergnes. 'How has General Masséna allocated bread and grain?'

The frosted slopes reflected the glint of a dull November moon. Clouds of exhaled breaths, human and equine, hung and sank on the still night air.

Jobert rubbed the hilt of the dagger he carried in his jacket cuff. *Why am I sitting here? I should gut the miserable bastards.*

Koschak's cape-draped form halted beside Jobert and Raive. 'Our sentries have withdrawn, sir.'

'And the enemy piquet?' asked Raive.

'They patrol the valley by day, sir,' said Jobert, 'but they do not maintain a watch by night.'

'Then, if we have no witnesses ...' Raive turned to the indistinct lumps on the seat of Jobert's cart. 'Ready? Off you go.'

The soft outlines of the Inoubli brothers slid down from the cart. Starlight revealed the shawl-wrapped shoulders of a peasant couple, a middle-aged woman and an older man, a father, or an uncle perhaps. Without a backwards glance at Raive and Jobert, the pair drifted down the slope, blending into the gloom, leaving no discernible tracks in the icy grass.

'I am sure we will never again see them both in the same place,' said Raive.

The weight of Jobert's sabre tugged at his waist. *Then I should cut them down now for the suffering they —*

'You are too silent, Jobert,' said Raive. 'I hope you are not brooding.'

Jobert continued to stare at the darkness of the valley below. 'What motivates their shift in loyalties?'

'The same as yours and mine, I suspect. Desire to escape hunger. Why?'

Greed, you mean. Are they and I the same? Jobert shifted his weight in the saddle. *I think not.* 'And when will Anissa hang, sir?'

'Not hang,' said Raive. 'She is also in our pocket. I am keeping her close.'

Jobert scowled towards Raive.

'Why ever not?' said Raive. 'Inoubli – I cannot help speaking of them in the singular, probably because only one is ever in view, the other gliding in the shadows – is now our spider. His web now trembles for the Republic. Anissa, too, has valued skills that must be nurtured.'

No, Raive, the web now trembles for you. Jobert glanced at Raive's grey-lit torso, expecting a glimpse of an unguarded exposure of some arachnid feature. *They are now your pet insects. And you gamble on their newfound loyalty?*

'And you feel confident they will return?'

'Quite confident,' said Raive. 'You, Jobert, are to be one of their contacts for returning messages.' A cold spasm gripped Jobert's spine. 'They have been in-structed to seek out Orlande. At some time in the future, be ready for an unfamiliar face at your hearth.'

Chapter Twenty-Five
November 1795, Zuccarello, Italy

Ten kilometres to the south, Jobert heard the opening salvoes of the French assault on Loano crisp on the breeze. In the grey light, the low thunder of distant guns appeared to firm the resolve of Masséna's divisional column, winding up the road from Zuccarello to the lower junction then climbing the steep zigzag to the upper junction. With Rocca Barbena held by a single Austrian battalion, the defence succumbed to the surprise attack and the defenders either surrendered or fled.

By midday, Masséna stood by a roaring brazier in the village square of Rocca Barbena surrounded by his two dozen commanders and staff.

'We press on to Bardineto,' said Masséna. 'Major Jobert, what of the roads?'

'The road north to Bardineto is tight against the slope, sir. There is no bypass. If the Austrians choose to hold the road, a pair of guns will force it.'

'What of the mountain which dominates the country between Rocca Barbena and Bardineto?'

'I descended the mountain in summer, sir,' said Jobert. 'But it cannot now be ascended with this snowfall.'

Masséna folded his arms and stroked his chin as he considered his division's options.

'Sir, I suggest an alternate,' said Jobert. 'Although I have not travelled this path, if I were to lead a flanking battalion east across the face of the high country to the Bardineto-Loano road, that force will assemble outside of Bardineto by sunset if we march in the next hour.'

Masséna's eyes glided around Rocca Barbena's square at the infantry forage parties emerging from homes and shops with their arms full of bags, kegs and chickens. Masséna's roving gaze locked onto the commander of the 16th Légère. 'Colonel, have your regiment ready to march. Two of your battalions will advance to Bardineto by the road. Your other battalion is to follow the 24th Chasseurs.'

Soon after, 2nd Squadron filed out of the village. The two companies of horsemen and the eight companies of infantry climbed the paths to the ridge above the village, then struck out by the snow-clogged pathways east. The chasseurs' disgruntled mutterings deplored their lack of a share of Rocca Barbena's pillage but they hid their sullen faces from the iron-hard stares of Jobert, Koschak and Geourdai.

In two hours, Geourdai's lead patrols found the Bardineto-Loano road. In the slush were fresh hoof-prints. Geourdai leant out of the saddle and inspected the mud around him. A body of cavalry had passed down the road towards Loano. 'Column of fours. A troop patrol. More than a courier's escort.'

Jobert fumbled in his waistcoat for his pocket-watch.

'Bardineto is another hour along this road. Neilage, have 5th Company lead the battalion forward. Geourdai, hold 2nd Company as rear-guard and watch the road behind us to Loano.'

The sun was just setting on the tops of the western peaks when the battalion column and Jobert's light cavalry escort drew up outside of Bardineto. The town was already under fire from the sister battalion and Masséna's foot battery that had forced the road from Rocca Barbena. At sunset, the eight guns of the foot artillery roared from their gun line astride the Rocca-Bardineto road and signalled the regimental attack on Bardineto.

With a thunder of drums and a roar of hungry desire, from all sides of the town the French assault companies trudged through the gun smoke generated by their skirmishers, across the snow-bound gardens and the frost-covered walls into the determined Austrian fire from the windows of the town.

Pistol fire from the vedettes caused Jobert to twist in the saddle.

Chasseurs from 2nd Company's outlying piquet were cantering their weary mounts up the Loano road towards Geourdai's mounted inlying piquet.

At the edge of the icy meadows, a troop of Austrian chevau-léger formed a battleline of over sixty sabres. In the dusk, the steam exhaled by their horses blended their outline with the snow, just as their dark caped shoulders and oil-skin wrapped helmets melded with the black leafless groves behind them.

'Lieutenant Bredieux, mount the reserve troop. Moench, sound *Assembly.*'

Jobert squeezed Bleu into a trot through the fetlock-deep snow, pulled his sheepskin shabraque back to reveal his pistols, drew his sabre and watched Geourdai form Peugeot's inlying piquet in battleline.

'Sabres! Bredieux, form troop line on the left.'

A trumpet call sounded from the far side of the meadow. The Austrian cavalry surged forward at the trot, sabres drawn, Peugeot's forty horsemen their obvious target.

Jobert saw Geourdai twist in his saddle seeking Bredieux's reserve troop. 'Moench, sound *Charge*,'

Jobert did not want Peugeot's forty men to be caught at the halt by the chevau-léger. Bredieux's line was forming slowly and still well behind Peugeot's left rear as the chasseurs weaved around the trees and low hedges that peppered the landscape. Moench's call was soon repeated by Geourdai's trumpeter.

The two ranks of Peugeot's troop lifted to a slow canter, horses hampered by fatigue and snow.

Bleu was bringing Jobert abreast of the 2nd Company's sergeant-major at the rear of the forward troop. A space was opening on the left of Peugeot's troop, through which Jobert saw the chevau-léger front rank lift their own exhausted horses to a canter.

As Jobert came in line with Peugeot's front rank, from behind he heard Koschak urging Bredieux's troop forward. 'Moench, sound *Charge* again.'

Over one hundred metres away, the Austrian troopers snarled at their horses labouring over the frozen clods.

As Moench's call faded, an abrupt call sounded from the Austrian line. The leading Austrian officer was not more than fifty metres from Geourdai when he raised his sabre. In a flurry of ice, the chevau-léger ceased their arduous charge to wheel their horses about.

Now was the chance to cut the chevau-léger down. Geourdai looked to his left towards Jobert, stood in his stirrups, stabbed his sabre at the snow-churning horses just to his front and roared.

Looking along the front rank of Peugeot's troop, it was obvious to Jobert how strenuous it was for the snorting horses to canter in the snow. 'No! Moench sound *Halt*!'

Geourdai was a mere ten metres away from the rump of an Austrian horse, sabre arm outstretched, when the shrill call split the air.

Horses propped from canter to halt. Expletives burst from the chasseurs in the battleline.

'Silence!' yelled Koschak. 'Not a bloody word.'

Jobert watched the chevau-léger rally with some difficulty due to negotiating roadside stone walls in the failing light, then form column and move back down to Loano. *The lads are rightfully angry that their effort came to nought, and their horses wasted energy.* Jobert trotted Bleu to face the company's centre and stood in his stirrups.

'Shut up, 2nd Company, and listen in. You saw the bastards off and protected our infantry. I made the decision to halt because our horses were climbing mountains since before dawn.'

Jobert watched them huff in reluctant agreement. *Thwarted from glory and loot, I expect.*

'Today was not the day. General Masséna still has much for us to do. Our opportunity will come.'

The next day, Masséna's division continued its advance through the mountains. Before dawn, Jobert was responsible for guiding the 16th Légère along forest trails to a small fort that sat in the pass above Melogno, securing the road beyond Melogno as it descended to Finale Ligure.

With tasks allocated to Geourdai and his two troop commanders, Jobert had no pressing commitments but to ride with Bredieux's troop. Jobert straightened his slumping figure, knowing his drowsy posture was not assisting Rouge climb the icy slope. At the front of the 2nd Squadron column for two nights now, Jobert had slept little and, without the stimulus that comes with supervising the chasseurs, he found his weariness irritating. With less than four hours sleep, a hot meal of rock-hard artillery biscuit soaked in tea and a half-ration of grain for the remounts, 2nd Company had plodded their remounts single file up the mountain tracks for six hours. His gloved fingers fumbled to remove his cape as he rode, letting the bracing air sharpen his wits.

The calm of the November morning was shattered by the crash of drumming and a roar of voices as the French infantry assaulted Melogno's fort. The exchange of musketry built in ferocity and was answered by three blasts from guns sited high on the fort's ramparts.

The assault roused the village roosters, and their crowing identified the spread of the cottages surrounding the settlement.

Austrian fusiliers, billeted in those cottages, emerged onto the paths in response to the beat of the drums from within the village. Musket fire was exchanged with patrolling chasseurs. Surprised Austrians scampered into the relative shelter of the leafless orchards.

Tinges of pink striped the Mediterranean horizon, when Geourdai halted 2nd Company on the empty Melogno road, high on the ridgeline, just south of the village outskirts. Musket fire still cracked the morning air from the vicinity of Melogno's small fort, but its intensity was fading. A French light battalion struggled onto the road behind the chasseurs.

Jobert approved Geourdai's request to dismount the company. The order to dismount was received with a relieved grumble from the men and groans of urinating horses. As distant gunfire roared in the grey light, grunted expletives encouraged the assault on Loano by the coastal division twelve kilometres away. Many chasseurs declared they smelt gun smoke on the breeze.

'That is better,' said Koschak, buttoning his over-breeches as he crunched across the snow from behind nearby shrubbery. 'Deep in thought, sir?'

'I am tired,' said Jobert. 'I am thinking bullshit.'

'Your thinking keeps us alive. Come now, sir, spill the beans.'

Jobert wriggled in his sheepskin saddle. 'It is the same old question. Are we ready? I reflect on our time here in Italy. The kaiserliks put us on our arse at Ponte di Nava, we went for a lucky gallop at Dego, we were gutted on the beach outside of Savona. The charge by the chevau-léger yesterday evening reminds me the Austrians are not afraid of us. This winter advance is bringing us swiftly towards something larger. I cannot help asking myself have we done enough.'

Jobert and Koschak rode past the huddled cottages and bleak garden plots wreathed in a haze from kitchen fireplaces. The sharp breeze blowing up from the coast enlivened their horses as they splashed through the icy slop behind Bredieux's advance guard platoon down toward Finale Ligure.

'The question you should ask yourself, sir ... are you ready?' said Koschak.

Jobert searched Koschak's green eyes. Koschak's grim stare was unyielding.

'Yes, I believe I am,' said Jobert.

'Then, whatever state we are in, if you are ready for what comes, we will follow you.'

It was past nine o'clock, further down the Melogno-Finale Ligure road, when a musket shot sounded ahead.

Jobert and Geourdai rode behind the lead file of four 2nd Company chasseurs when the troopers reined in their horses, brought their musketoons to their shoulders and fired, before wheeling about and cantering back.

A ragged volley fired out of sight through the trees. A foreign trumpet call pealed.

'A platoon or so of chevau-léger on the road, sir,' said Corporal Duval.

Hearing enemy horsemen trotting away, Jobert sensed an opportunity. 'Geourdai, I want to know if I have found the flank of the Austrians on the headland above Finale Ligure. By my reckoning we are close to the 'grenadier' farm with its three-way junction. Remember? Sabres! Column of platoon, trot, march! Moench, sound *Advance.*'

Jobert and Geourdai led the trotting chasseur column, with Moench tucked in behind the two officers. The density of the bare-limbed trees thinned, allowing glimpses of the grey Mediterranean through the leafless branches. Fallow fields within their stone walls hemmed in the jostling chasseurs and pressed their horses nine or ten abreast to form column of platoon.

Local men, women and children screamed as they raced to remove lowing cattle and honking geese from the barns to safety in the orchards.

Unseen ahead, beyond the retiring chevau-léger column, many drums beat *To Arms.* The trees along the entire ridgeline quivered with the repeated order. Jobert winced at insistent tattoo. *That many drums infer a sizeable force on the headland separating Finale Ligure from Loano. But how many?*

Two hundred metres ahead, on the road flanked by two stone barns, the curtain of chevau-léger withdrew and revealed a company of over one hundred grim Austrian fusiliers standing their ground. Their officers and sergeants strode behind their third rank bellowing at them to prepare for the fight.

Jobert twisted in the saddle to confirm the leading troop commander. 'Bredieux, dismounted skirmish order from the left.' Jobert pointed to an orchard full of fleeing livestock. 'That troop of chevau-léger are somewhere behind the infantry, so watch our flanks.'

Bredieux grunted with his pipestem clamped firmly between his teeth. A roadside timber gate shattered as Bredieux's troop forced their way into a fallow field. Chasseurs scrambled to sheath their sabres, repack their musketoons' charges and hand over their reins to their horse-holding mates. At Bredieux's bellowed commands, an eruption of musket fire from his dismounted skirmishers ripped through the olive grove, cracking off the low stone walls.

Less than a dozen Austrian skirmishers on Bredieux's side of the road fired in response at the darting green-jackets amongst the gnarled trunks. The enemy retreated to the side of a barn dragging wounded comrades.

Jobert spun his scar-chested warhorse on its hocks to face Geourdai's remaining troop, Peugeot's troop. 'Fancy a kaiserlik for breakfast?' yelled Jobert. 'Today is your day, 2nd Company!'

Geourdai, Peugeot, Koschak and the four ranks of troopers roared back and shook their sabres at the Austrian line.

Using the low stone walls as cover, Bredieux's dismounted chasseurs poured fire into the packed ranks of the Austrian company. Obscured by Bredieux's gun smoke, the disciplined Austrians held their volley. Just beyond the smoke, massed drums pounded again.

Jobert spun Rouge towards the Austrian company and stretched out his sabre's tip. 'Charge!'

Bredieux's chasseurs raced to reload their musketoons and fire one last ball. The noise reverberated off the rough-hewn walls adding to the pounding hooves and the screaming trumpet.

The Austrians, engulfed in the cloud between the farmhouses, raised their muskets to fire. A ragged volley exploded between the stone walls.

Jobert's face was wrenched upwards, as he felt his reins

slacken. *Am I hit?* An Austrian ball cut a rein, dug through his rolled cape and horse-rug, ricocheted off his iron saddle bow and continued its trajectory upwards through the visor of his helmet.

Only aware that Rouge had extended his gallop in response to the looser rein, and feeling no immediate pain, Jobert tightened his core, pressed down his heels and hissed as he was consumed in the cloying smoke. Rouge leapt over the fallen Austrians in the road. No faces at knee level in the smog. The freezing air on the far side of the barns struck him. *Where are the kaiserliks?*

Whipping his head around, Jobert saw Peugeot and Moench emerge from the trapped smog with tendrils of gun smoke twirling in their thundering wake. In his peripheral vision, Jobert glimpsed white uniforms tumbling across the snow-topped clods in the fields behind them.

The piquet company was no longer his problem. Jobert had a new concern. Around the next corner, an uncomfortable two hundred metres away, a white-jacketed battalion was racing to form square.

Jobert reefed his remaining three reins high as he tilted his hips, and gripping his saddle with his knees, twisted a toe of his boot outwards, causing a spur to cut into the muscular gut churning beneath to check Rouge's racing gait. Rouge, despite his exhilaration at the race he was winning over the horses thundering from behind, bent his ribs, skipped his hindquarters across the road and slowed his momentum into a sideways trot. Rouge dropped his head as the pressure of bit, knees and spur were removed.

Jobert raised his sabre above his helmet to signal halt. 'Peugeot, halt! Moench, *Rally!*'

On the slope above the square, Jobert had seen all he needed to see.

Beyond the immediate wall of bayonets and bawling infantry challenging the chasseurs to continue their charge lay three hundred metres of packed disciplined mass. The other two battalions of an Austrian regiment on either side of a battery of foot artillery, a force of two and a half thousand men, in a three-rank arc facing south-west towards Loano.

Further beyond the Austrian rear-guard, along the road beside the 'grenadier' farm, a long, plodding column of wagons filled with wounded crested the rise from Loano and disappeared over the lip towards Finale Ligure below.

Chapter Twenty-Six
November 1795, Savona, Italy

Upon completing his report, Jobert stepped back amongst Masséna's commanders.

Masséna's eyes never lifted from the map stretched in front of him. 'One infantry regiment and a battery of six-pounders defend the ridgeline above Finale Ligure. Here we are on their flank but constricted by the narrowness of the crest. I foresee us marching into the muzzles of their guns. A tough fight, but we will prevail. Will we not, gentlemen?'

The gathered senior infantry commanders rumbled in their assent.

Jobert remembered his river bath after the frigate's ambush. 'Sir, what if this force was bypassed?'

Masséna flashed Jobert a glare. 'How?'

'The Austrians' lines of communication run along the coastal road covered by British warships. There is an inland route that is wagon capable and bypasses the coastal route. There are paths down this promontory that will keep us clear of Finale Ligure. There is a ford that crosses the stream at the base of these heights, that is quite separate from the bridges in the town.'

Masséna's face twitched with excitement as his fingers stroked the map. 'Yes, we will do it. We will bypass Finale Ligure and establish a block north of the town. Their lines of communication will be cut and Loano's defence will crumble. That leaves the road open to Savona.' Masséna scowled at Jobert. 'How far to Savona?'

'Twenty-five kilometres, sir.'

'What a prize to retake Savona.' Masséna's eyes blazed. 'I know our lads have marched hard since Bardineto this morning. Gentlemen, I ask you, do we have the fire for another five hours?'

'Faced with the choice of sit on your arse and starve,' said the colonel of the 16th Légère, 'or march and eat, the 16th Légère vote to march.'

Despite the twenty-five-kilometre distance, the air still shuddered from the third morning's bombardment of Loano.

For five hours, 2nd Squadron followed a company of enemy chevau-léger shuffling backward in front of Masséna's surging brigade column. Now, on the outskirts of Savona, the two bodies of light cavalry stood four hundred metres apart.

The Austrian chevau-léger, extended into line, protected the tail of a wagon convoy full of Austrian wounded as it crossed a bridge leading into the town. The gentle snow falling from the low black clouds muffled the interminable screech of wagon axles, and the occasional whimper from the wounded.

The French chasseurs also formed in line on a slight knoll overlooking a snow-choked river.

'Am I correct, Jobert, that there lies the road ascending to the Col di Cadibona away to our left?' said Spiccard, pointing to a path of mud branching west up the slopes.

'Yes, sir,' said Jobert.

'Excellent. Then while we stand above the chevau-léger here, they are unable to move along it.'

The forbidding shadow of ancient Fort Priamar, nestled within the port city, dominated Colonel Spiccard's and Jobert's evaluation of the enemy's defences. Voreille, tasked with reporting back to Masséna, stood to their rear.

Spiccard jerked. 'My word, who is that crossing the bridge?' An Austrian horseman, in a light-blue uniform and tall, red, peakless shako, cantered towards the line of chevau-léger. Colonel Spiccard stared through his telescope. 'A hussar, I believe. No distinctive pelisse across his left shoulder, though.'

For Jobert, memories returned of such enemies at the battle of Jemappes three years ago. 'It is a hussar, sir. He is wearing his pelisse due to the weather. He is probably a divisional aide.'

'What would a divisional commander order a company of chevau-léger to do? These fellows represent the only cavalry available to Savona's commander.'

As snow fell in wet, downy blobs, Spiccard and Jobert considered how the cheval-léger might act upon receipt of the hussar's message.

'Sir, the hussar is coming towards us,' said Voreille.

'No escort, no white flag, his sabre drawn,' said Spiccard. 'My goodness, he is actually challenging us. He cannot be serious? A duel between the lines?'

Jobert drew his sabre. *This will put to right my losses on the beach.* 'I claim him.'

'No, sir, I claim him,' cried Voreille.

Spiccard and Jobert turned in their saddles to look hard at Voreille.

'Please, sir,' said Voreille, 'I need to make good. I need to redeem my reputation. This man is mine.'

'Very well, Voreille,' said Spiccard. 'Have at him.'

Voreille gulped at the frozen air. Drawing his sabre, Voreille pressed his mare forward down the slope.

Jobert sheathed his sabre to follow Voreille forward at the trot. 'Voreille, what would fencing-master Fergnes advise?'

Voreille sank in his saddle bringing his mare to a halt, closed his eyes and sucked on the air. 'The cut is an extension of the horse's posture. Watch the rump to predict the stroke. In turn, relax the seat and soften the heels.'

'Correct. Observe how the hussar's charger steps too high.' The hussar's charger pranced on a flat area at the base of the slope mid-way between the opposing lines. 'Your man is nervous. His energy affects his horse. Can Juno trot sideways?'

'Yes, sir.' A slight smile curved Voreille's cheek.

'Then I look forward to observing her gait.' Jobert cantered Rouge back to the chasseur line.

Voreille squeezed Juno into a calm walk and watched his opponent. The hussar was a long-legged, thick-set blond man in his late twenties, with a crushed nose smeared across his face.

They saluted each other with their sabres.

Jobert's mind raced as he watched. *Slow your breathing, lad. Shortened your reins. Focus on his horse.*

The hussar sprang at Voreille on a right canter-lead, his wrist high, the point of his gleaming curved sabre arcing down at Voreille's face.

Voreille shuffled Juno two steps to the left.

A disapproving smirk flashed across the hussar's face at the fumbled horsemanship. In response, the hussar tipped his horse's shoulder and aligned on Voreille again.

Voreille then side-stepped further across toward the left as the hussar swung his blade down onto the right of his horse for an offside cut. Voreille swept his blade tip up, rolled his wrist back and parried the hussar's blade clear of his right thigh.

Loud hurrahs exploded from the ranks on both sides of the field.

Jobert set his teeth. *Remember Fergnes. Exploit impetuosity.*

Having bounded past Voreille without landing his cut, the hussar sat back in his saddle, recovered his blade in a wide sweep, and reined in his frothing horse.

In that time Voreille spun Juno over her hocks to the right before a squeeze leapt her forward toward the hussar's left side.

The hussar, his back to Voreille, glanced rapidly over both shoulders.

Take advantage of the bastard's indecision, boy.

Voreille bounded past the hussar's rump, now positioning himself behind the hussar's right shoulder.

Watch out for his extended rearward slash to the right.

Voreille checked Juno's pace. With his blade thrust forward across his body on Juno's nearside, Voreille aimed to pierce his opponent's extended right hand or wrist before the hussar's sabre sliced across Voreille's chest.

The hussar twisted with great force to the right, his flashing blade hissing just over Juno's ears. As he twisted, the hussar's spur raked his horse, and the charger stepped away to the left.

Voreille's outstretched sabre missed the targeted right fore-arm, the tip of his blade catching the hussar's sabre just under the hilt. Both blades squealed before the hilts struck each other with a jarring clang. With a high swing, Voreille guided the Austrian blade's formidable energy over his crested helmet.

The opposing audiences roared with the sizzle of metal on metal.

Voreille lifted Juno onto her left canter lead, bringing her into a tight left arc.

The hussar regathered his reins.

From his vantage point, Jobert considered Voreille's options. With Voreille moving right to left across his stationary front, the hussar could attack forward across Juno's hindquarters and make the shorter nearside thrust at Voreille's kidneys. Or he might spring forward of Juno's face and slash out to the right. Or wait for Voreille to approach him.

Voreille checked Juno's pace. The solid little mare followed the pressure of Voreille's thighs and faced the black charger. Voreille twisted in the saddle to the right, brought his hilt back past his shoulder and gripped Juno's ribs with his calves. Juno pranced on the spot.

The hussar launched his horse at Voreille. As they raced to close, the hussar leant out to his right, prepared to turn his wrist over, drop his blade and cut under Voreille's parry into Voreille's abdomen.

The cock expects you to fumble to your left again. Come on, lad, now is your moment.

As the growling hussar flew at him, Voreille released his right calf for Juno to step across into the hussar horse's face.

The Austrian horse shied away to the left. The hussar was extended well out of balance, his weight heavily on his right stirrup.

They collided at the canter, Voreille's torso smashing into the outstretched hussar's face and chest. The hussar's sabre deflected off Voreille's rolled cape across his pistol holsters and thrust out beyond the far side of Voreille's hip.

In the instant the hussar's horse strode past Juno, Voreille punched down at the man impacting with his chest, his knuckle guard crunching behind the ear of his opponent.

Both crowds roared again at the simultaneous grunt of the duellists and their horses.

As the hussar fell between the horses' bodies, he reefed back on the reins, ripping his cantering horse to a stop. Fearing his arm dislocating, the hussar twisted as he fell.

With his right foot wedged in his stirrup and his right shoulder extended across Voreille's saddle bow, the hussar was able to retract his right sabre arm, only to fall heavily and crack his skull, The sabre hilt, trapped under his ribs, caused both his ribs and wrist to snap. With his right foot still trapped in his stirrup as his horse shied from the collision, the hussar screamed in pain as he was dragged face down.

Voreille scooped a flapping rein with his sabre tip and tugged the hussar's horse to a halt. Holding both horses' reins in his left hand, with a half-stroke from his sabre Voreille severed the taut stirrup leather, releasing the hussar's suspended leg.

As the hussar moaned in pain and attempted to rise, the Austrian audience sagged.

An exultant French roar erupted from the knoll.

An Austrian chevau-léger officer approached Voreille at the canter. 'The gentleman had his face broken by a chasseur on the field at Jemappes. He had hoped to repay the compliment. But you have the honour today, sir. You may retire.'

Voreille gathered his reins, backed Juno and saluted the fallen hussar. Voreille cantered Juno back up the hill toward the jubilant cheers from 2nd Squadron's ranks.

'Moench,' called Jobert, 'sound *To Mess*.'

As Voreille cantered upwards patting his mare as he rode, a wide, freckled grin was plastered on his young face and a nervous laugh erupted from his lungs.

Jobert snorted. *With a sideways trot, lad, Juno has reclaimed your reputation. But where does my redemption lie?*

The chevau-léger withdrew into the city, leaving Austrian fusiliers to hold the bridge.

A sentry's warning pistol shot cracked through the air. It alerted the chasseurs on the knoll to the dull beat of marching drums.

Chabenac and a four-chasseur escort joined Spiccard and Jobert at the front of the 2nd Squadron line.

'Good afternoon, gentlemen.' Chabenac saluted. 'General Masséna presents his compliments and wishes you informed that Loano has fallen. His brigade blocking position still secures the coast road. He has released our 3rd Company and the 16th Légère. General Masséna requests that Colonel Spiccard continues to secure the southern approaches to the port until the arrival of the 16th Légère and establish a screen on the northern approaches to Savona.'

The beating of drums became louder. Surrounded by a company of green-caped chasseurs in skirmish order, a French light infantry battalion crested the last rise and descended towards Savona's southern bridge.

From within Savona, Austrian drums exploded and trumpets shrilled.

Another pistol shot warning fired from within the sloping treeline that encased the road to the Col di Cadibona.

Corporal Duval's four-man patrol cantered down the slushy road then up the slope towards the cluster of officers in front of the chasseur line.

'Squadron strength column of kaiserlik dragoons marching down the Col di Cadibona road, sir,' said Duval. 'When they saw us break cover to return, we were not pursued. They just stood there.'

'Voreille, message for General Masséna,' said Spiccard. 'Time is now ... three o'clock. Savona is held by an Austrian infantry regiment supported by a foot battery and a company of chevau-léger. A squadron of Austrian dragoons marches down the Col di Cadibona road to reinforce Savona. I have secured the southern approach to Savona with the 16th Légère and will establish a screen north of the port with a squadron of chasseurs. If we act with determination, Savona and Genoa's grain is ours.'

Voreille departed at the canter.

'We met a squadron of dragoons, sir, last year at Dego,' said Jobert. *Are these the same who froze?*

'Quite so,' said Spiccard, 'with, we must assume, the rest of their regiment marching close behind. Jobert, take 2nd Squadron to screen north of Savona. You have less than two hours until dusk.' Spiccard pummelled his reins against his shabraque. 'Jobert, do you understand what is at stake?'

Jobert frowned at Spiccard's restless hands as memories of horse corpses heaving in the waves became a fast-stepping Austrian gunner with an outstretched fizzing quickmatch fuse. 'Yes, sir, I understand.'

'Whatever you find on the north side of Savona, do not fail again, Jobert,' said Spiccard. 'I have not reconciled myself to the losses you incurred at Ponte di Nava and on the beach just yonder. Crippling your command for a third time is unacceptable. Ride swiftly now, before the dragoons close your path. We shall have a tricolour fly from Fort Priamar yet.'

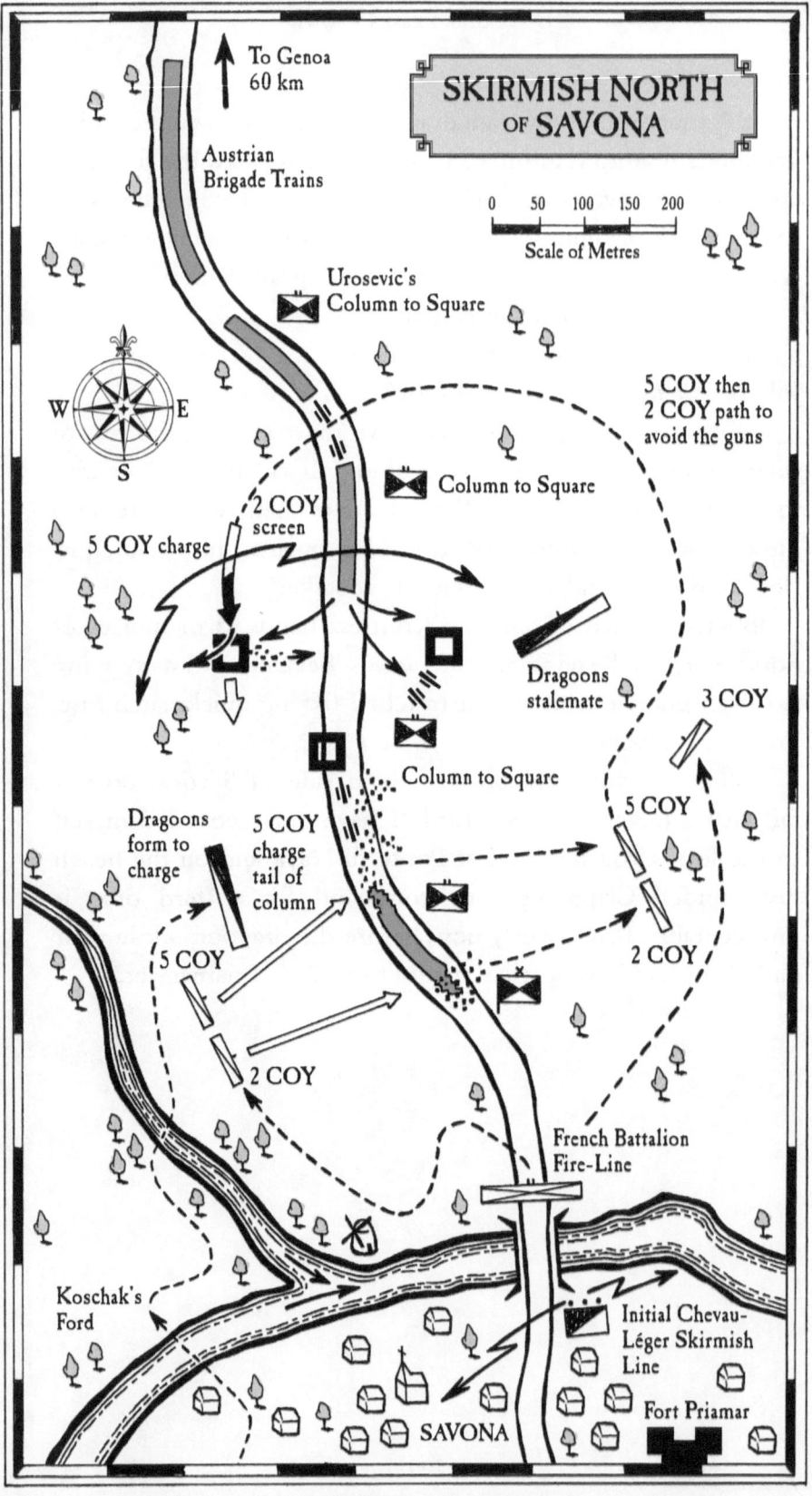

SKIRMISH NORTH OF SAVONA

To Genoa 60 km

Austrian Brigade Trains

Urosevic's Column to Square

0   50   100 150 200
Scale of Metres

5 COY then 2 COY path to avoid the guns

Column to Square

2 COY screen

5 COY charge

Dragoons stalemate

3 COY

5 COY

Column to Square

Dragoons form to charge

5 COY charge tail of column

5 COY

2 COY

5 COY

2 COY

French Battalion Fire-Line

Koschak's Ford

Initial Chevau-Léger Skirmish Line

SAVONA

Fort Priamar

Chapter Twenty-Seven

On the northern side of the port, under the guns of Fort Priamar, lay a bridge across an ice-grey stream gushing to empty into the Mediterranean. The road across the bridge led sixty kilometres from the northern gates of Savona toward the Republic of Genoa. Amongst the leafless groves and snow-covered furrows of winter fields, a troop of sixty chevau-léger maintained a vedette line. In the city's outer farmsteads, companies of white-jacketed Austrian fusiliers barricaded the roads, strengthening the neglected northern defences of Savona.

Jobert raised his gaze to the ramparts of the medieval fort. 'The fort's guns will have the range to the bridge. Canter across the bridge by platoons. 2nd Company, once across, skirmish screen facing north. 5th Company, company battleline facing back towards the bridge.'

A colossal boom erupted from the top of the fort.

Everyone, French and Austrian, looked up at Priamar's smoke-engulfed gunports. The reverberating thud of the falling iron ball was faint.

'A target on the southern side of the city,' said Jobert. 'Perhaps our infantry moving forward are the target?'

'Patrol approaches, sir,' said Koschak.

Bredieux reined in his blowing mount. 'Austrian infantry approaching from the north, sir. Battalion column on the road, and more behind. I did not expose myself to see any more. They are wearing dark capes, not white overcoats.'

'Grenzers!' Jobert soured at the memory of the Balkan frontiersmen. 'The pricks hid under their capes before the beach ambush, remember. Those arseholes must not reinforce Savona.'

Jobert stared into the middle distance as he considered his options, then back to the Genoa road rising up from the stream's banks to a low crest.

'Lads, we cannot defend a bridge, but we can delay them in square. We have not a second to lose.' Jobert pointed to the sloping banks alongside the stream. 'Form squadron battleline in the low ground in silence. Move!'

Geourdai and Neilage squeezed their mounts to the trot, they and their company trumpeters waving for the chasseurs to assemble in the ranks.

'Chabenac,' said Jobert, 'pass my compliments to Colonel Spiccard. An Austrian infantry regiment is marching to reinforce Savona from the north. 2nd Squadron is unable to defend the bridge but will delay the enemy's arrival at Savona's northern gate. Their infantry can sally out from the town to support the arrival of the reinforcements.'

Chabenac raised his eyebrows as he looked at the outskirts of the port teeming with highly capable Austrian defenders.

Koschak twisted in the saddle to identify the nearest section commander. 'Corporal Duval, provide an escort for Captain Chabenac to return to Colonel Spiccard.'

As Chabenac and his escort cantered away south, Jobert, followed by Moench and Tulloc leading Bleu, trotted through the fetlock-deep snow onto the banks of a narrow creek which joined the larger snow-fed stream.

'Sir, the chevau-léger have retaken the bridge,' said Koschak. 'I will take a patrol and confirm a ford back across the stream.'

Jobert gave Koschak a grim wink of acknowledgement and thanks.

Jobert, Geourdai, Neilage and their attendant trumpeters dismounted and jogged toward the crest line, only to fall to their knees once they had spied the long, dark column trudging three hundred metres away in the falling snow. Jobert looked back to confirm his dark silhouette above the snow-white crest was camouflaged by trees lining the creek line behind him.

Taking his glass out from his jacket, Jobert scanned the approaching enemy. A taste of bitter iron filled his mouth. 'Fucking grenzers.'

Judging by the length of, and the spacing within, the column of hunched, dark-clad infantry, Jobert believed he was observing three battalions and a detachment of four small calibre guns. Jobert sensed that further troops and trains were following just beyond what he saw. Out in the fields that lined the road, protective enemy skirmishers roamed. The drifting, clotted snow kept the sentries' heads bent low as they trudged across the frozen furrows through the ankle-deep snow.

As Jobert lowered his telescope, he noticed steam from Neilage's breathing was emitted in small puffs. Neilage looked back towards the chasseurs tamping their musketoon charges and ensuring the steel blades of the sabres were not trapped in the brass mouths of their scabbards from the cold.

'Neilage, listen to me,' said Jobert, 'we are not trapped. We can ride into the hills and sleep the night. The Austrians have just lost Loano and are about to lose Savona. We are irrelevant to them. But right now, we are going to catch these bastards flank on in column. Remember what these miserable pricks did to us? Do your scars still ache? Because mine fucking do!'

Geourdai bumped Neilage with a reassuring nudge. Neilage rubbed the wound within his jacket's sleeve with resolution.

'Horsemen lead the infantry column,' said Jobert. 'Regimental commander, battalion commanders, battery commander, aides. White jacket, red breeches, see him. A general of some sort. Geourdai, take 2nd Company through the head of the lead battalion and that command group.'

Geourdai watched the column through his glass, mouth characteristically tight with fortitude. 'Will the snow affect their muskets?'

'Since their muskets are cradled under their capes,' said Jobert, 'probably not their first volley. But not long after their fire will be for naught. If we are quick about it, their commander will not order them into square fast enough for a volley. Neilage, you and I will take the rear of the lead battalion and the two guns following.'

'Spike the guns with horse-shoe nails, sir?' asked Neilage.

With the reference to spiking guns, Jobert's vision clouded to a rocking red flare in a smoke-filled night. His gloved fingers flexed to tickle the imaginary withers of Vert.

'Not unless we have secured the guns, no. You will only be cut down by the infantry for your troubles. Instead, shoot the horse-teams so the guns cannot travel, whatever crews survive your onslaught will have to serve them from where they stand. As the centre point of your company, aim for the last file of the battalion. Take your troop on your left flank into the small battery. I will stay on the right of your line and lead Yinot through the back-quarter of the battalion. Lads, our squadron will rally to form on the far side, facing back at the column.'

Bent in a crouched shuffle, the officers returned to the chasseurs mounted in the low ground. There Jobert found Tulloc forward of the battleline holding Rouge and Bleu.

Mounted beside Tulloc was a grim Koschak and an unsettled Corporal Duval. Koschak appraised Geourdai and Neilage with steely determination for the coming assault. Both captains held the sergeant major's fierce eye, their faces set for the task ahead.

'Those kaiserlik dragoons on the Col di Cadibona road have followed our path around the city,' said Koschak.

Geourdai's and Neilage's eyes jerked towards the forested slopes on the far side of the stream. A column of Austrian dragoons emerged from the forest on the far-side of the gurgling brook, their black bicornes and tall, black boots highlighting their white jackets and trousers.

Jobert mounted Rouge then pulled back his shabraque to reveal his silver-inlaid pistols. 'Duval, did Captain Chabenac get through?'

'Yes, sir.'

'Gentlemen, we are gifted with a column of grenzers flank-on. Those dragoons are the key to allowing the grenzers to reinforce Savona. This is for Pultiere and all those bloody good men they took.' Jobert raised his voice to the chasseurs in the ranks. 'Lads, want revenge for our brothers lost to that mongrel frigate?'

A long, low hiss of angry determination rippled along the one hundred and forty men in two ranks, as they rolled their arses further into their saddles and tightened their rein lengths.

'Front rank, sabres! Second rank, musketoons ready! Canter, march!'

Slowed by the snow and the frozen ruts, the distance of three hundred metres to the side of the Austrian infantry was galloped in forty-five seconds.

The squadron had no single point of aim, it had two separate company targets. The length of each chasseur company battleline was only forty metres, so the two companies drew further and further apart as the chasseurs screamed at each other to maintain their dressing, or straightness, behind their galloping captains. Committed to collide with their targets at either end of the one hundred and fifty metre-long grenzer column, 2nd and 5th Companies would impact one hundred metres distant from each other.

It was standard practice for the chasseur officers to leap far ahead of the charging line. Apart from imbuing the following chasseurs with confidence in their leaders, it allowed the sergeants on the end of the first rank to orient to the line of the charge, and then adjust the dressing of the line accordingly. As the point of impact came closer, it was usual for the officers to check their horses, allowing the line to close up behind them, so the avalanche of horsemen collided into the wall of infantryman with greater effect.

Satisfied that Neilage was urging his excited horse at the last Austrian fusilier in the battalion column, and Geourdai's company was angling away to his right, Jobert twisted in the saddle and pointed his sabre at Yinot. Yinot's flapping hussar-plaits streamed away from either temple of his helmet's brim, his eyes bulged with violence.

'Yinot, on me! Moench, sound *Charge!*'

Rouge's great brown body stretched, head extended, as he was given his freedom, his stride so fast Jobert no longer heard his footfall. Gripping his saddle with every muscle from one knee through his pelvic floor to the other knee, hardening every fibre through his abdomen and lower back, Jobert concentrated on the power coming through his right shoulder and locked right elbow, guiding his floating sabre's tip toward his enemy. With his heart swollen by the trumpet's demand, the physical preparation for impact caused Jobert's lips to curl back from his bared teeth and scream.

Moench's shrieking trumpet was answered soon after by the thrashing of Austrian drums.

For the Serbian soldiers on the road to Savona, those forty-five seconds passed differently.

Across the width of the road, marched six men side-by-side, three from one company and the other three from another, ready to swing out in great wings when the drums demanded. Weary from marching in frozen slush and stumbling on unseen ruts, the grenzers' spirits had risen with the proximity of cannon fire from Savona just ahead. Apart from the snarls resulting from someone farting in the packed, steamy confines of the closed ranks, rest, hot soup and then the chance to slaughter those bastard French was the hubbub of conversation along the length of the line. Added to the low mumble of snatched conversation, the jangle of slung equipment, kettles, water flasks, bayonet scabbards and musket butts was the song of their march.

The marching men were oblivious to the deep rumble of the charging French cavalry.

The grenzer skirmishers heard it. Their heads jerked up to see a black, wavering line rising above the crest. They blinked to comprehend. They screamed when the French trumpet call demanded they understand.

The trumpet, the yelling, and perhaps a musket shot or two, caused the leading Austrian officers to swing their vision across the field to the right of their column. Despite guts turning to ice, someone in command had the presence to roar 'Beat *To Square!*'

The shrill rat-a-tat-tat from the drumheads gripped the hearts of the well-drilled column. Their bodies were trained to move in an instant, yet their brains had not yet assimilated what was happening. The soldiers screamed at each other to unwrap their capes from their cherished muskets and move onto their practised paths.

Where is the fucking cavalry? How far away are the bastards?

Their rage and fear mounted.

Animal screams from the men on the outside of the column closest to the charging French caused men to look and stumble and sergeants to explode with invective to maintain the desired manoeuvre. For those who saw the racing black tide, the overwhelming desire was to unsling their musket and just shoot the approaching monster.

Do not look at the pricks. Do not freeze. Shoulder that musket, you dumb bastard. Keep fucking moving. Stop fucking pushing me ...

Predicting Rouge's path a few metres ahead, Jobert's frantic eyes sought any small obstacle that caused him to adjust Rouge's explosive stride with his knees. Thus, within those forty-five seconds of violent rhythm, there was only limited mental capacity to reflect on anything else. Jobert was aware of the end of the line to which Neilage was galloping, and his own point of aim. There was no time to think about those skirmishers who chose to turn and run or kneel and fire. The zip of a ball passing, whether metres above his head or within a whisker of his body, could not be contemplated.

At twenty metres from the mass of shuffling shapes in front of him, satisfied Rouge had delivered his blade cleanly, Jobert offered himself wholeheartedly to the god of war.

In the two strides before impact, Jobert flicked his wrist, dropped the tip of his sabre down and over, giving it a downward scything momentum. His practised timing was perfect as Rouge's footfall dispensed the sabre's razor edge to someone's neck just above the rolled blanket. Jobert's wrist felt the bite into the flesh and then the sudden freedom of the arcing blade.

In a stride, he rolled his wrist up and over and allowed the speed of the sabre tip to accomplish its nasty work. The collision of Rouge's chest and Jobert's knees into the bodies beneath him caused a cacophonic ripple of brown-jackets and bobbling black leather helmets. The rapid deceleration had Jobert's pelvis slam into his high saddle bow lashed with holsters, horse-rugs and cape. Jobert's focus leapt from maintaining his seat to not having the crush of bodies around him knock his feet from his stirrups, scanning the faces to his left to identify any emerging threat on his nearside, and, on his right, what was the required path for his scything sabre tip.

A sound not unlike the metallic, crackling strike of a giant hammer initiated a monstrous groan from a vast beast.

Within a second of Jobert's arrival amongst the packed infantry, the converging paths of twenty horses of Yinot's front rank intersected with around one hundred and twenty infantrymen. French or Austrian, those who survived started bellowing and shrieking.

Muskets fired into faces above.

Sabres cut into faces below.

Moench's grey mare crashed into Rouge's rump. The mare threw her face to avoid the collision, delivering a powerful blow into Jobert's left kidney, ribs and shoulder-blade. Jobert was thrown forward moaning with pain. He recognised the clear far side of the road only two horse lengths ahead. Bitter from the shock of receiving a galloping horse's head to the ribs, Jobert continued to press Rouge into the gaps he cut.

Within seconds of arriving, he was clear of the grenzers on the far side of the road.

Jobert checked Rouge's desire to escape the unpleasant throng and race across the crisp snow. Only fifty metres away on his immediate left, Jobert saw Neilage's other troop turn their horses in tight arcs, cutting down the artillery drivers and shooting the horse-teams in their traces.

A roar of musketry exploded behind him as Yinot's second rank discharged their musketoons into the cringing, staggering, brown-jacketed puppets emerging from the rumps of their front-rank mates. Applying a touch of right spur to cause Rouge to skip his hips away, Jobert looked behind into the mass of screams and grunts of men locked in close combat. The groans of labouring horses, the hissing of sabres on bayonets and muzzles was punctuated by the odd musket blast.

Jobert scowled at a frightened Moench, the mouthpiece of his trumpet close to his trembling lips. 'Moench, *Rally!*'

The long notes of *Rally* were repeated by the company trumpeters. Neilage's troopers swirling within the relative freedom of the artillery limbers and caissons, thundered across the hard-packed snow. In a surge of effort, Yinot's chasseurs trapped within the press of Austrians, obedient to the trumpet and stimulated by the drumming hooves of their sister troop, swung their sabres and carved a path to freedom.

It had taken less time for the charge to pass through the Austrian ranks than it had to move from the battleline to contact. Soon after, Yinot's jabbering horsemen and snorting, blown horses were reforming on the flank of Neilage's exuberant chasseurs.

That exhilaration faded as the chasseurs watched loose horses gallop from the grenzers' midst, dragging corpses on their backs, arms flailing in the snow-spray from the hooves to rejoin the long line of equine mates.

'Reload!' roared Koschak, as he sliced at straining stirrup leathers to cut free those dragged, whether dead or dying.

Neilage's own elation evaporated when he saw a dozen empty saddles rejoin the company line. 'Yinot, parade state!'

The French battleline cheered as two or three chasseurs emerged on foot from the battalion's human debris.

Silence descended as they watched their brothers shot in the back. In an instant, only the deep puffs of horses regathering their breathing was the singular sound emitted from the angry, green-jacketed line.

Two hundred metres away, the leading grenzer battalion was in a shambles. The centre of the column straggled to create a tiny square. Both ends of the column were a mass of distraught men, crawling on hands and knees or sitting slumped. Trained to avoid a trapped blade impaled within a torso, the chasseurs' sabre cuts were cruelly peripheral, so very few dead were seen lying still.

Jobert watched those who did lie in the slush, writhing to stem the flow of blood from the gashes on their necks. *Where is your British frigate now, you bastards?*

Three hundred metres away on the squadron's half-right, the next Austrian battalion had formed square. As the base of a triangle, the final two battalions had formed stationary squares a further two hundred metres distant. Within that triangle, lay the assured destruction of any body of cavalry foolish to traverse the interlocking fire of the battalions' volleys.

Yet Jobert gave the brown-black squares only a glance.

'Tulloc!' Jobert waved his arm causing a painful spasm in his left ribs. 'Bleu! Now!'

A far more serious threat had arisen.

Chapter Twenty-Eight

Beyond the trail of grenzer wounded, sat the snorting, steam-ing, squat line of Austrian dragoons, easily identifiable in the drizzling snow by their tall, black bicornes topping their white jackets and massive black chargers.

The dragoons had formed as the chasseurs had charged. Jobert realised they had followed the tracks in the snow and had forded the stream and dressed their ranks close to where the chasseurs had first assembled.

'Gentlemen, well fought,' said Jobert. 'We have gone some way to repaying the compliment to those bastard grenzers. Now focus on the dragoons.' Close to three hundred men, Jobert estimated the full-strength dragoon squadron was twice the current strength of 2nd Squadron. He knew 2nd Squadron must avoid these big, disciplined men on their powerful, well-schooled mounts.

From the dragoons' line, a rider cantered across the space to the closest square. *What scheme is the dragoon commander concocting with his grenzer mate?*

'Why let our horses catch their breath?' asked Geourdai. 'Why not charge us?'

'Do you remember at Dego last year, sir,' said Neilage, 'how that squadron of dragoons sat behind the horse artillery and froze when we threatened their flank. And, this morning, having disturbed our patrol on the Col di Cadibona road they paused. Is it the same squadron?'

Geourdai raised the hilt of his sabre to rub drying blood off his nose with his glove cuff. 'Perhaps the same hesitant commander. A young nobleman given command responsibilities based on his family connections, yet well beyond his experience.'

'I care not,' said Jobert. 'The idiot is giving us time to breathe, whilst those grenzer cocks are locked in square. The dragoons will charge uphill, and we will meet them on top of their wounded to our advantage.'

Behind Jobert and his captains, Koschak and his sergeants snarled to prepare the chasseurs for further combat.

'Look north down the road,' said Geourdai with a lop-sided grin. 'Our dinner awaits.'

Beyond the squares, obscured by the snowfall, stood a long horse column. Since it was neither deploying into cavalry battle-line nor gun battery fire line, it must be the grenzers' trains. Austrian logistic rigour inferred the wagons would be packed with food, drink and clothing ripe for the taking.

'We want that grenzer train.' Jobert's face twisted with malignancy. 'That prize settles the debt between us.'

Their heads spun again to the left as guns fired from Fort Priamar within Savona. The great iron balls crashed into the forested slopes to the west of the town.

Jobert squinted as he contemplated the potential target. 'Something worth firing at is moving around the town.'

A far trumpet sounded. A crackle of distant musket fire. The troop of chevau-léger cantered off the bridge. Dark horsemen emerged from the treeline. Then a brown-blue column emerged from the forested tracks and approached the bridge, their marching drumbeat muffled by the snow.

'Look, it is our tricolour, lads,' called Koschak, trotting along the rear of the ranks. 'It is Colonel Spiccard, 3rd Company and the 16th Légère.'

The chasseurs erupted with cheering, causing panting horses to jerk their heads with surprise.

The grenzer drums started to rattle. Jobert scanned for a change in formation as ordered by the drums.

'There!' Geourdai cried. 'The far square is marching. Perhaps they are stepping the squares forward to meet our battalion at the bridge.'

'What of their battalion guns, sir?' asked Neilage. 'Are they not three-pounders? The same as Ponte di Nava.'

Scanning through the drifting blobs of snow, Jobert saw, in the gap between the lead battalion's wounded and the face of the closest square, a pair of guns being man-handled so that the muzzles pointed towards them, an uncomfortable two hundred metres away. Further, at three hundred metres, a small battery of four guns was coming into action by the second square. Furthest of all, the third square had no guns close by that Jobert saw.

'Sir, the guns by the closest square are preparing to fire,' said Neilage.

The dragoon rider was seen returning to the squadron line. A foreign trumpet sounded. The dragoons advanced at a walk.

'Listen to me!' Jobert's head jerked at the opportunity. 'We are going to walk forward then trot away to our right. We are going to stay well clear of the guns. We are going to feint towards their trains and then we will turn back behind at that furthest square to cease its march forward. On my signal, double back from the trains. Sabres! Walk, march! Moench, sound *Advance*!'

As sabres were already drawn, there was no squeal of steel on scabbards but the chasseurs were rocked back into the serious business of preparing to fight.

Wounded grenzers struggling between the closing lines of horsemen started to cry out as the two lines of horsemen trudged closer.

'Neilage,' called Jobert, 'march to their trains.'

Neilage spun his remount to the right and cantered across the face of his company. '5th Company, form column of fours to the right, trot, march!'

The three hundred dragoons roared as they watched half the French line flee.

A half-hearted cheer rose from the square, as those in the ranks watched the heartless horsemen about to crush their wounded Serbian and Croatian brothers under iron-shod hooves. The wounded started to bellow as the dragoons lifted to a trot with an evil crashing beat, the long dragoon-musket of one man clacking against the scabbard of the next.

Within thirty-seconds of impacting with the dragoons, Geourdai, spun his horse across Bleu's rump. '2nd Company, column of fours to the right, canter, march!'

'Follow!' screamed Koschak. 'Follow fast, lads! Follow!'

A desultory ripple of muskets from the broken square was not the only zipping salute to the departing French cavalry. Two Austrian guns fired at the fleeing horsemen. Double-shotted, the three-pounder's canister barely made the distance of two hundred metres, but the hurtling three-pound balls struck their target.

One ball punched through the leg of a chasseur and into the ribs of his horse, both horse and rider flung to one-side like dolls. The second ball removed a foreleg, the horse crashing to the ground and the chasseur crunching heavily into the churned ice. Bleu skipped around the floundering, groaning remount.

Jobert gave a grim nod to the downed chasseur, whose face was etched with anguish as he scrabbled in the scarlet snow.

The sergeants screamed to close the files. Jobert squinted through the spray of icy mud thrown up by the leading horses. The column raced on.

Across the top of the infantry squares Jobert had lost sight of the dragoons. Seeking any sign, Jobert twisted in the saddle, aware the dragoons were able to take the short cut between the squares with impunity. He saw the far square still marching forward. It was certainly not a simple activity for the mounted battalion commander to coordinate six hundred men in four ranks, facing all the points of the compass, to march in a single direction.

As 2nd Squadron curved well out from the square behind him, the chasseurs were now shielded by the infantry square from the three-pounders' firing arcs. A simultaneous roar erupted from the Austrians, of anger from the nearest square and of fear from their trains, as the French cavalry's target became obvious.

'Moench, sound *To Mess!*' The first distinct notes of the call caused the squadron column, led by 5th Company, to wheel about at the trot.

The Austrian roar of anger changed tone to one of alarm.

Their drums thrashed out a new beat.

Their gunners burst into action.

Jobert watched the Austrian gunners, brown-jacketed grenzers from their battalions in their Hungarian tight, blue trousers, not the usual brown-jacketed, white-trousered gunners in their distinct black bicornes, struggle to man-handle their small guns rearward to face the new cavalry threat.

The 5th Company trumpeter blew *Skirmishers Out*. Neilage led his chasseurs in a trotting swarm within one hundred metres of the westernmost square, as 2nd Company formed battleline behind Jobert.

The marching square halted, faced outwards with the front-rank kneeling, driving the butts of their muskets firm into the icy slush. Yelling broke out within the square as sergeants closed gaps and fusiliers were reminded to hold their fire. The grenzers swore taunts at the skirmish screen at the top of their lungs. These disciplined Balkan veterans, well-enough experienced with the murderous Ottoman cavalry, were not fooled by these French farm-boys.

Above the squat black leather caps of the grenzers, Jobert spied the mounted battalion commander. *Urosevic? It is Urosevic!* Skirmisher musketoon balls punched into the dense infantry target. Belching French gun smoke screened any movement beyond the noose of skirmishers and obscured Jobert's view of Urosevic.

'Geourdai! Koschak!' cried Jobert, wheeling Bleu to face 2nd Company. 'The square is commanded by the prick who had our wounded bayoneted on the beach.'

Geourdai, Koschak, Bredieux stiffened in their saddles.

'Having the bastards stand is not enough.' Jobert's heart pounded to be free of his chest. Tears stung his eyes. '2nd Company will charge the square. Peugeot, take your troop down the outside flank, fire into the corner, then form in line as our rally point. Geourdai, I will take forward Bredieux's lead platoon. Follow in echelon with the other platoon. 2nd Company, for our absent brothers, canter, march!'

Geourdai screamed to his trumpeter for *Charge*. Koschak spun his horse towards the ranks and screamed to shorten reins.

Howling like a demon, Peugeot led his troop charging in column of fours. As the cantering horses pounded past Jobert, their riders knew full well the danger they rode toward, and the slaughter that would be inflicted on their sister-troop if they failed.

The chasseurs shrieked their fury at Jobert as they thudded

past him. He bellowed his wild-eyed rage back at them. 'They butchered us at the beach. Now they pay.'

As they had practised, Peugeot's troop cantered straight down the side of the square in column, skimming along the face. In a detonation of fire, the chasseurs discharged their pistols and musketoons into the faces of the infantry in the right-most corner of the square. Those grenzers not struck and flung backwards into the bodies of their mates bawled in alarm. Many in the rear face of the square looked back into the centre to see if the order to fire was given or if the battalion commander was aware of the thundering menace on their western flank.

Jobert looked to Moench. Moench was pale with fear. 'Moench, this is for your little brother. Sound *To Mess*, then *Charge!*'

Moench, shortening his reins to follow his mad officer once more into the fray, raised his face to blink away his tears and play the call his brothers needed.

Jobert pointed his sabre at 2nd Company's remaining troop, Bredieux's troop. 'Koschak! Bredieux! Without a warship, they are nothing. For Pultiere! On me!'

Bredieux's men bellowed as one, pumping their sabres in the air as they followed a racing Jobert through Neilage's skirmish pairs. Knowing what duty had fallen to them, their sergeants roared to check their excited horses and give space to the men in front. Otherwise, there was no chance to exploit the gap in the square the fellows created in front.

Within ten seconds of passing through the skirmisher swarm, with two strides to go, Jobert saw the muskets come off the shoulders of the Austrians. The battalion yelled something in unison as the muskets levelled outwards, bayonets rattling beyond the muzzles.

Neilage's skirmishers skittered out of the way, emptying their barrels into the massed brown-jackets, and screamed encouragement to their squadron brothers as they reloaded.

A struck grenzer reeled backwards. Bleu saw the gap in the line and felt Jobert's guiding squeeze. Bleu stretched his neck and leapt into the gap knowing from previous experience that he would stop all this cantering, catch his breath and perhaps receive a gobble of bread or apple.

As Jobert and Bleu, with a combined weight of seven hundred kilograms, hit the packed mass of men at forty kilometres-per-hour, over one hundred muskets discharged outwards within twenty-five metres of each other.

As Bleu leapt, Jobert's eyes flickered between his sabre's target, the neck of the Austrian on the right of the gap, and the grenzer on the left to determine the likelihood of a bayonet thrust from that quarter. Squinting through the stinging smoke cloud, Jobert guided his blade beyond his man's upraised musket barrel, carving through his cheek and ear and across the top of his rolled blanket. That his sabre was not caught in the soldier's straps was of more importance than knowing his target had wrenched away from the burning steel.

Knocking another man down under his folded forelegs, Bleu completed his jump with a lurch. Jobert's skimming blade pierced the chest of the following grenzer in the dense ranks. As he felt Bleu stumble to his knees beneath him, Jobert slipped his feet from his stirrups. *Not you, Bleu, my beautiful boy, not today.*

For a moment, Jobert sat astride his saddle, his feet firmly on snow or bodies, his face the same height as the astonished Austrians floundering to close the gap around him. Jobert's right arm was outstretched behind him, the hilt deep in a grenzer's chest, his embedded sabre unlikely to draw free. Jobert tugged at the sabre, and the impaled grenzer bawled in pain and teetered forward to lean against him. Bleu struggled to lift Jobert, and the yowling Austrian, and place his front hooves back underneath himself.

Jobert looked left and saw a terrified young grenzer, working hard to reload his musket beside him, looking up and over Jobert's left shoulder at whatever was making an almighty animal roar. *Probably Koschak or Bredieux cutting their way in.*

The sound of whooshing steel thwacking on leather, meat and bone.

On his right, Jobert easily parried a clumsy bayonet thrust by the next man across with his brass hilt, before checking, with a flick of his eyes, his pistols were still firmly tucked into their holsters at the front of his saddle.

If a grenzer battalion was approximately six hundred men, then each side of the cavalry-proof square was manned by one hundred and sixty infantrymen, in four ranks, with half-a-metre shoulder-to-shoulder. The face of the square was about twenty metres long, with the chasseurs having broken in close to the outer corner.

Jobert rocked his hips urging Bleu to stand whilst nearly one hundred and sixty brown-jacketed Austrians behind him attempted to broach the tide of incoming, green-jacketed horsemen. Another wall of grenzers on his right faced out towards Peugeot's troop forming on their flank.

Within the smog of cloying gun smoke, the clouds of stale breath, human and horse, the stench of fear and faeces, the cacophony of hoarse growls and laboured grunts, against the sharp rattle of drums, the metallic crash of stirrups and sabres impacting on bayonets and belt-buckles, punctuated by the occasional musket shot, Jobert twisted his face to identify a clear scream of rage directed at him.

Jobert looked up into the eyes of Urosevic. 'You arsehole!' screamed Jobert. 'Stand, Bleu! For Vert, fucking stand up.'

With immense strength, Bleu surged upwards and regained his feet, pushing deeper amongst the packed men, his heave wrenching Jobert's sabre clear, and in doing so, pulled the reins from Jobert's gloved grip. In a moment, Jobert swung his blade up, foregoing the overwhelming desire to cut at those around him, extended his little finger from the grip, hooked his loose reins, and, as if he was drawing a bowstring, shortened his reins. His ankles rolled so his toes might snag his stirrups, but to no avail. Although he had a firm seat, without stirrups, Jobert could neither reach far with his sabre nor generate the power in his core for an arcing slice.

As Bleu raised Jobert's green-clad torso clear of the brown-jacketed throng, Urosevic brought his infantry sword *en garde*, and pressed his stout chestnut forward, through the drummer-boys and the wounded in the middle of the square, to thrust at Jobert. Jobert appraised in an instant Urosevic was not skilled in mounted fencing, and in the press of the square, the horse was not trained as a cavalry mount.

'The beach, you bastard,' Jobert screamed at Urosevic in German. 'Do you remember the beach?'

Urosevic bellowed something unintelligible back.

Extending the sweep of his blade, from his kill's chest to drawing his reins shorter, Jobert maintained the sabre's momentum by cocking his elbow and rolling his wrist to sweep his blade over his head and parry Urosevic's blade forward. At the extremity of his swing, Jobert flicked the tip of his sabre to slice open Urosevic's horse's right eye.

Urosevic's horse squealed, throwing its head away from the pain.

Although Bleu had regained his feet, his shoulders were squeezed, by Jobert, to halt. No sooner had Jobert brought his sabre back to the recover, a grenzer, low on his right, thrust a bayonet up at him. Jobert let his sabre fall forward, knocking the bayonet onto his thigh across his gut. Jobert grabbed at the hot muzzle with his rein hand, and, to gain momentum for his cut he swept the blade back, up and over and brought it down onto the soldier's neck. Conscious of Urosevic gaining control of his wounded horse, as the fusilier fell, Jobert allowed the sabre to continue its swing back past his heel.

Urosevic spurred his horse forward once more, the one or two steps he needed to reach Jobert. With a powerful thrust, Urosevic stabbed at Jobert.

With no stirrups and his right arm again mid-swing down by Bleu's right hip, Jobert threw himself back to lie across his saddle portmanteau, his feet flicking up and grabbing Bleu with spurred heels. Urosevic's outstretched razor-sharp blade cut through both of Jobert's thick cross-belts and into his dolman jacket and waistcoat. Searing pain sliced across Jobert's chest.

With the sharp rowels gouging his lower throat Bleu reared slightly, sitting low on his hocks with both front hooves just off the ground. Jobert was falling backwards out of the saddle as his extended sword-arm had completed its loop and was slicing back at Urosevic.

Bleu leapt out of his half-rear, with both Urosevic's blade and the dying grenzer's bayonet scissoring towards Jobert's throat. With his fist full of reins, Jobert grasped Urosevic's razor-sharp sword menacing his collar. With Bleu's bounding energy, combined with Jobert's overarm swing across his head, the sabre cut left-to-right on Jobert's left side.

The blade sliced through Urosevic's left ear and would have removed the top half of his skull, but Bleu's leap took the blade away for the tip to exit out through the bridge of Urosevic's nose.

As Urosevic slumped, and with the limp bayonet falling away on his right, Jobert was left holding Urosevic's short infantry sword.

The roar of the six hundred grenzers and the forty chasseurs entering the square was deafening. Jobert looked to his right to see Koschak cutting his way out of the square's flanking face.

'On me! On me!' Koschak bellowed, as he hacked a path

through the wall of men. Koschak's whirling blade, cleaved through necks, heads and shoulders, leaving an arc of hot, dark gore.

The far sides of the square were melting away towards the other squares. Those tight-packed grenzers were thrusting their way across the square, across Jobert from right to left.

The grenzers' screams fuelled the chasseurs' lust for blood.

The chasseurs' faces were twisted horribly with revenge and murder as they rocked and kicked their jammed horses forward, sabres raised high, slicing down onto any and all brown-jacketed shoulders or high, black caps. Here was their revenge for the frigate ambush, let alone the square's volley for those who had survived it.

'Moench, *Rally*! *Rally*!'

The demonic chasseurs screamed 'Rally!' at each other as Moench's unsteady trumpet call rang out.

Holding his dripping blade high, clamping his severed cross-belts under his left elbow and gripping tight with his knees, Jobert let Bleu have his head and follow the flow of horses eager to run clear of the distressing confines of the square, towards the assured comfort of 2nd Company's line of snorting, steaming remounts.

Upon Bleu reaching 2nd Company's line, Jobert reached down, untwisted his stirrup leather that was avoiding his searching toe, and stood in his stirrups and searched beyond the remaining two squares. 'Geourdai, where are the dragoons?'

'Where we left them, sir. They have Colonel Spiccard and 3rd Company threatening their flank.'

Beyond the dragoon's mounted stalemate, Jobert saw the French light infantry, brown and grey blobs in their greatcoats and blankets, forming a long fire line to protect the bridge.

'Charge another square, sir?' Neilage's glazed eyes twitched with nervous energy, grinning like a demonic imbecile at the bloodied slash across Jobert's heavily braided jacket.

Jobert recognised the moment of critical vulnerability, whereby charging the other squares while the fields of fire were choked with survivors of the two previous charges, was passing. 'No! Stand fast. The dragoons will catch us disordered. Tulloc! Give me Rouge. Take these cross-belts and sword.' Jobert pointed at Urosevic's blinded chestnut with its rider draped over its withers. 'And catch that wounded Austrian horse.'

Confirming that Bleu was not wounded, Jobert mounted Rouge and surveyed the sea of carnage. The air reeked of blood and shit and was filled with the ululations of pain and drums. A howling grenzer crowd scrambled to thrust into the faces of the remaining two squares. The stoic gunners kept their posts by their beloved guns. Loose 2nd Company horses trotted up from the shattered square to stand close-by, snuffling to seek their friends.

'Sergeants,' called Koschak, 'parade states!'

'Peugeot,' called Jobert, fumbling in his waistcoat for his notebook, 'select an escort and take this message to Colonel Spiccard.'

Jobert scribbled. *Dear Colonel, two enemy battalions crippled with minimal casualties to 2nd Squadron. One for Ponte di Nava. One for the ambush at Savona. I hope you find this acceptable. Jobert.*

Jobert lifted Rouge and faced the steaming, panting, gibbering line of 2nd Company.

'Lads, two of their battalions have repaid the debt. Those dragoon shitheads are befuddled to a standstill.' Jobert stretched his legs in his stirrups, his face twisted with malice. 'Now for pay day! Secure their trains! Cut down any bastard that attempts to stop us, for it is ours by right. With that prize long owed, the 24th Chasseurs will feast tonight.'

In the rapidly fading light of this long day, Jobert watched the gentle blobs of snow touch, then rest on, the frozen blocks of brown earth. The spade-long slabs hewn from the ground had been stacked to create the burial mound. Good men, naked and bloodied, now sheltered beneath, far from cold, fatigue and hunger.

Bleu dropped his head and pawed the slushy ruts, tugging pain through Jobert's rein arm into his injured chest.

'Has the surgeon seen that?' asked Koschak.

'It is nothing. A long scratch at best. My cross belts took the worst of it. I certainly will not burden the surgeon with ...' Jobert expanded his bound chest against the encircling bandages. 'How do your tasks progress? How diminished is the inlying piquet?'

'The prisoners have stripped and buried our ...' Koschak nodded toward the long mound. 'Our dead horses have been stripped and equipment stacked. The grenzers' wagons are being catalogued, including the prisoners' weapons, ammunition, capes, blankets and satchels. I have a platoon roasting salted goat and baking loaves. The outlying piquet's share has been delivered forward. Orlande has a ham and bean broth ready for the wounded.'

'Then, excuse me, as I shall attend the surgeon.' Jobert shortened his reins with a grunt.

'Sir, ...,' said Koschak.

Jobert turned.

'It has taken three years, or two since Toulon,' said Koschak, 'but ... they are ready, sir.'

'Who are?' Jobert scowled at the fresh grave. 'For what?'

'Our men, sir,' said Koschak. '2nd Company, in fact all of 2nd Squadron. They have proved themselves ready for what lies ahead.'

Jobert's face turned to the mound. 'Yes, indeed they are. But they are no longer "our" men ... they are Geourdai's, Neilage's ...'

The creak of wagon wheels, and the whimpers of the jolted wounded within, announced the approach of a chasseur column delivering grenzer casualties to the gates of Savona.

'Platoon, eyes right!' cried Bredieux, pipe clenched between his teeth, a wreath of blue smoke about his head as he saluted Jobert. 'Fucking lovely day for it, sir.'

Jobert returned the compliment. 'Thank you, Lieutenant Bredieux. Carry on.'

'No longer our men?' asked Koschak. 'Bullshit, sir. They will always be our men.'

Chapter Twenty-Nine
February 1796, Oneglia, Italy

Two months later, Jobert, Koschak, Moench and Tulloc awaited their only meal of the day.

'Apologies for beans again,' said Orlande, ladling soup, fragrant with onion and herbs, into five wooden bowls. 'I saved some horse tailbones for the broth. The last of our flour will yield a small pancake each.'

'Indeed, my apologies also, lads,' said Jobert. 'My last coins secured that little grain for our six horses. Orlande, was the honey replaced that we used on Grenzer's eye?'

'Sadly no, sir. Even if we had more coin, there is simply nothing to buy, medicine nor food.'

'We have gone a second month without pay,' said Tulloc into his soup bowl. 'It is not right.'

'And if the army paid us, no one accepts those worthless assignat notes,' said Moench. 'Perhaps a change of circumstances with our next commander? Major Jobert, sir, what are the implications of General Schérer's resignation?'

Jobert rolled his hot soup around his mouth. 'I imagine General Masséna will take command of the Army of Italy. Our fifth commander in two years. Why? When does your book close, Moench?'

'Another week, sir. As General Masséna is the favourite, I have him on quite short odds. General Augereau is a possible and I have General Sérurier further out. I have even taken bets on Jourdan, Moreau and Hoche.'

'There you have it,' said Koschak. 'One implication of Schérer's departure is you will make a little money.'

'Will we ever receive the rations the regulations say we are entitled to, sir?' asked Moench, scoffing his small pancake. 'Horse is the only meat we have eaten since mid-December. It is not right, sir.'

Jobert lowered his spoon and sipped at his watered wine.

'We recaptured Savona to maintain the grain trade with Genoa. I am unaware if Genoa has any grain, or if they are indeed selling it to France. But with Savona in our hands, the British now sail from ports further away to interdict our coastal freighters. I have no idea what state our coastal fleet is in, or if any supplies are reaching the mouth of the Rhône, let alone if any trade is occurring between Marseille and Savona.'

'Then, sir,' asked Moench, 'if the generals are reporting to Paris the alarming supply situation over which they have no control, why maintain the crush of troops along the coast that they do control? Why are regiments not placed in reserve around Marseille where resupply is better?'

Jobert drew a simple map with his finger in a dribble of wine.

'If the natural ramparts of the Alps are our border with Austria, then that border meets the coast at Nice. So, we arrive back at our original conundrum of being unable to access Genoa's grain due to interdiction by the British navy. It is the promise of Italian grain that forces us to maintain our tenuous grip on this strip of coastline forward to Savona. While the

Austrians and the Piedmontese threaten to pour through the Col di Tende, Col di Nava and the Col di Cadibona to crush us against the sea, our army is maintained at a certain size to hold the coast.'

'Moench,' said Koschak, scraping his bowl, 'run a book on the likelihood of General Masséna taking us into Piedmont in April.'

Moench's face tightened at the financial possibilities. 'What would that likelihood be, sir, of us marching into Piedmont?'

Jobert passed his empty bowl to Tulloc. 'I know we all want that to happen. We were inspired by the legends emanating from the Rhine of the food and equipment captured. We have teased ourselves throughout the winter with the bounty contained within the kaiserlik magazines only a few days' march away. Following our capture of Garessio, Loano and Savona, the supplies that two Austrian divisions had put aside for four months in winter quarters, filled our bellies for only a few weeks.'

'They say we defeated two Austrian divisions last November, sir,' said Moench. 'One and a half thousand Austrian dead, four thousand men and over ninety guns captured in four days. If we achieved that, why would we not be just as good north of the mountains?'

'In November we surprised them,' said Jobert. 'With no forage in winter, the Austrians had neither cavalry nor teams to transport their guns. Once we find ourselves north of the Maritime Alps in the spring, our Army of Italy becomes vulnerable to the massive armies of Austria. If we face them on Piedmont's plains, where tight mountain paths no longer protect our unproven patriotic volunteers, the Austrian generals and their troops will prove their experience in fighting in massive formations. Sergeant Major and I have seen more than once our green French regiments break once they have received their first volley, screaming "treason and betrayal", only to be slaughtered by the kaiserlik hussars and dragoons. General Schérer would have been executed if he had failed.'

'But is not the bulk of the Austrian army arrayed against France on the Rhine, sir?' asked Moench.

Jobert stretched back in his chair. 'Some part of it is, certainly. I imagine the Holy Roman Empire's forces are stretched against us godless French on the Rhine, the protestant Prussians to their north, the orthodox Russians to the north-east and the Muslim Turks to their south-east. But Lombardy has long been a bountiful food bowl for the Austrians and a gateway to Mediterranean trade. With the Kingdom of Sardinia having lost the province of Savoy, Piedmont, Austria's protective barrier to Lombardy, is sure to be savagely contested.'

Koschak held up his battered pipe in a gnarled hand to intercept Moench's next question. 'Enough, Moench! See to the pots, lad.'

Moench suppressed his impatience and joined Tulloc at the frothy wash tub.

Koschak leaned forward on the rickety table. 'If Masséna is the most likely candidate for our new commander, sir, does he have what it takes to lead us into Piedmont?'

Jobert contemplated his half-empty wine cup, his mouth twisting in a grimace. 'I am sure Paris' orders for the transfer of command are galloping towards us as we speak. We will know soon enough.'

Jobert's adventures, in 1796 and 1797, continue in
'*Yet Another General*'.

Visit **www.jobert.site**
to learn more of Jobert's adventures.

Author's Note

This story is a work of fiction, set within historical events. A chronology, incidents that are referred to within the story, is included as an appendix to this book.

During the Revolutionary period (1789-1799) the French army was in chaos. New government bodies changed the military's descriptive nomenclature with alarming regularity. This was done, not only so the army stepped away from its royal past, but also in response to the furious changes demanded in the face of prodigious enemies, both internal and external. I have chosen not to burden the reader with the dizzying array of changes to ranks and organisations. By the time Napoleon Bonaparte comes to power, the names used by the old, royal army were returned, terminology that we still use in our armies today. Acknowledging most of Jobert's audience are broadly, some intimately, aligned with the modern military structures of the United States, the British Commonwealth and Europe, I have maintained a degree of consistency to uphold the vibe of the period without irritating the reader with the changes that occurred.

I leave it to the reader to determine the overwhelming number of people, not just those of 'noble' birth, executed during the revolution, by the iconic guillotine, decapitation by more manual means as well as being shot and hung. Maintaining a focus on the military context, in the period of revolutionary wars, my research indicates that seven hundred men of the rank of general were dismissed of which nearly four hundred were executed. This purge removed the distrusted and 'treacherous' nobles, those who proved incompetent in the field, some 'as encouragement to others', as well as to cover the government's embarrassment for racing woefully prepared levies en masse into the enemies' volleys. My research found that less than a third of families of noble birth emigrated from France. The overwhelming majority determined, despite suffering tremendous discrimination, to remain in France and uphold the ideals of the new Republic.

I utilised a Kickstarter.com project (**www.kickstarter.com/ projects/jobert**) to launch the first and second books of the Jobert series, prior to making the books available to the wider public. There were several exclusive offerings, such as signed hard-cover editions and exquisitely painted Jobert collectable models, only available through the Kickstarter.com project. You are welcome to visit **www.jobert.site** to learn how you benefit from exclusive offers during Jobert's next Kickstarter. com project.

Rob McLaren
Veresdale, Queensland
September 2021

Bibliography

Bourgeot, V., *Les Tresors de l'Emperi*, Paris, 2009.

Bucquoy, E., *Les Uniformes Du Premier Empire, La Cavalerie Légère*, Paris, 1980.

Bukhari, E., *Napoleon's Cavalry*, London, 1979

Calvert, M., Young, P., *A Dictionary of Battles*, 1715-1815, New York, 1979

Chandler, D.G., *Napoleon's Marshals*, London, 1987

Chartrand, R., *Napoleon's Guns 1792-1815*, Oxford, 2003

Chandler, D.G., *The Campaigns of Napoleon*, New York, 1966

De Marbot, JB.A.M., *The Memoirs of General the Baron de Marbot*, London, 1892.

Dodge, T.A., *Warfare in the Age of Napoleon, Vol. 1,* 2011.

Doisy de Villargennes, Chuquet, A., *Soldiers of Napoleon, The Experiences of the Men of the First French Empire,* 2008.

Duffy, C., *The Military Experience in the Age of Reason, 1715-1789,* New York, 1987.

Dupuy, R.E., Dupuy T.N., *The Encyclopaedia of Military History,* London, 1970.

Devereux, F.L., *The Cavalry Manual of Horse Management,* Cranbury, NJ, 1979.

Elting, J.R., *Swords Around A Throne,* London, 1988.

Erkmann, E., Chatrian, A., *The History of a Conscript of 1813,* London, 1946.

Fuller, J.F.C., *The Decisive Battles of the Western World,* London, 1970.

Fremont-Barnes, G., *The French Revolutionary Wars,* London, 2001.

Glover, G., *The Forgotten War Against Napoleon – Conflict in the Mediterranean 1793-1815,* London, 2017.

Haythornthwaite, P., *Austrian Specialist Troops of the Napoleonic Wars,* London, 1990.

Haythornthwaite, P., *Napoleonic Light Cavalry Tactics,* London, 2013.

Haythornthwaite, P., *Uniforms of the French Revolutionary Wars 1789-1802,* Poole, 1981.

Letrun, L., Mongin, J., *Chasseurs à Cheval, 1779-1815, Vol. 1-3,* Paris, 2013.

Maughan, S.E., *Napoleon's Line Cavalry – Recreated in Colour Photographs,* London, 1997.

Muir, R., *Tactics and the Experience of Battle in the Age of Napoleon,* Bury St Edmunds, 1998.

Napier, C.J., *Lights and Shades of Military Life; The Memoirs of Captain Elzear Blaze,* London, 1850.

Petard-Rigo, M., *La Cavalerie Légère du Premier Empire,* 1993.

Smith, D., *Napoleon's Regiments, Battle Histories of the Regiments of the French Army, 1792-1815,* London, 2000.

Walter, J., *The Diary of a Napoleonic Foot Soldier,* London, 1991.

Wise, T., *Artillery Equipments of the Napoleonic Wars,* London, 1979.

I also acknowledge the insights and detail provided by the Wikipedia, Google Maps and YouTube websites.

Chronology of Events

The following chronology lists the historical events that are referred to within the story, with particular focus on France's Army of Italy's operations in Piedmont.

1792

7 Feb   Urged on by French emigres to exploit the current chaos in France, Prussia, Austria and Sardinia (including Savoy and Piedmont) form an alliance, known to history as the First Coalition.

20 Apr   Proposed by the Republican government to galvanise and control the populace, France declares war on Prussia, Austria and Sardinia. King Louis XVI agrees. Louis hopes that the subsequent military campaign fails, the French government is overthrown, and France is returned to absolute monarchy.

10 Aug   With the immediate threat of Prussian invasion, the Parisian mob storm Louis' place and massacre his royal guard. The Constitution of 1791, which provided for a constitutional monarchy, is abolished. Louis is deprived of all power and universal suffrage is established.

19 Aug   In response, Prussia invades France and captures frontier fortresses.

20 Sep   In northern France, Dumouriez and Kellermann defeat the Prussians at the battle of Valmy.

21 Sep   Delivered from crushing defeat, the next day France is declared a republic, the monarchy is abolished, and the National Convention established.

21-27 Sep	Sardinian province of Savoy invaded and captured by French forces. The French fail to secure the fortress at Saorgio and the Col di Tende.
6 Nov	Invading Austrian Belgium, Dumouriez defeats Austria at the battle of Jemappes.

1793

21 Jan	Tried for collusion with the enemy, Louis XVI is executed. In response, Britain, the Netherlands and Spain declare war on France.
23 Feb	As the threat increases, a levee-en-masse is declared. An extra twelve chasseur à cheval regiments are raised, including the 24th Chasseur à Cheval.
6 Apr	The National Convention forms the Committee of Public Safety, sowing the seeds for the period known as 'the Terror'. The Deputies, or Representatives, of the People are established by the Committee of Public Safety.
30 Apr	Naples, Portugal and the Papal States declare war on France.
May-Dec	Revolts in the cities of Marseille (29 Apr), Lyon (29 May), Avignon (25 Jun) and Toulon (27 Aug) disrupts critical supplies to the Army if Italy.
8-12 Jun	Attempting to capture the fortress at Saorgio, French forces are defeated due to the Piedmontese superiority in mountain warfare.
27 Jul	Jacobin control of the government is enhanced as Robespierre is elected to the Committee of Public Safety.

27 Aug	British and Spanish fleets secure the port of Toulon, capturing the French Mediterranean Fleet. Elements of France's Army of the Alps and Army of Italy besiege the allies holding the forts of Toulon
5 Sep	Robespierre promulgates 'Make terror the order of the day' causing a further surge of executions of people suspected of opposing the government.
9 Sep	The National Convention enacts laws that force farmers to surrender grain.
17 Sep	The National Convention enacts the Law of Suspects, allowing anyone to be imprisoned and executed without trial.
28 Sep	Subsidised by Britain, the Kingdom of Sardinia contributes four Piedmontese battalions to support allied operations at Toulon.
16 Oct	Queen Marie Antoinette is executed, which incites Russia to declare war on France.
7-18 Oct	Attempting to capitalise on the distraction of operations around Toulon a lacklustre Piedmontese offensive fails to recapture Savoy.
17-19 Dec	Based on a plan devised by Bonaparte, Republican forces attack the allied fleet at Toulon then enter the evacuated port.

1794

6-28 Apr	As a result of the battle of Saorgio, another plan devised by Bonaparte, the Army of Italy captures the strategic Col di Tende and the ports of Loano and Savona.

Apr-May   The Prussians, Austrians and British advance into northern France. The allies have great difficulty coordinating their attacking forces, despite brilliant Allied cavalry actions at Villers-en-Cauchies, Beaumont and Willems. On the other hand, whatever success the French gain at Tourcoing and Tournai is unable to be exploited. By 30 Apr, the vital fortress of Landrecies in northern France is captured by the allies.

1 Jun   The Glorious First of June is the first and largest naval battle between the naval forces of Britain and republican France, a battle where both sides claimed victory.

5 Jun   Based on a plan of Bonaparte's, the French Armies of the Alps and Italy capture the Col de l'Argentiéres. Minister of War Carnot's vetoes any further advance into Piedmont due to the precarious strategic situation in northern France.

12-26 Jun   Republican General Jourdan invests the allied fortress of Charleroi. The campaign results in the decisive battle of Fleurus (the first battle at which an aircraft, an observation balloon, is used in warfare). The battle causes Austria to withdraw from the Netherlands, Britain to withdraw their forces to Hanover and the return of Belgium once more to French rule.

27 Jul   Robespierre overthrown in coup d'état.

6-20 Aug   Bonaparte is arrested on the charge of treason by Saliceti, then released two weeks later.

19-24 Sep   In response to an Austrian move against Savona, and taking advantage of the political tumult in Paris, the commanders of the Army of Italy claim victory at the first battle of Dego and reinforce their lines prior to winter.

| 20 Nov | Dumerbion is reprimanded for not advancing deeper into Piedmont. Command of the Army of Italy passes from Dumerbion to Schérer. |

1795

23 Jan	As part of France's capture of the Netherlands, the French 8th Hussars charge across the iced Den Helder, supported by the 15th Ligne, to capture the Dutch fleet. The fall of the Netherlands causes Prussia to withdraw from the First Coalition.
11–14 Mar	A French Mediterranean fleet, to which Bonaparte is attached, sails to recapture Corsica. The British Mediterranean fleet disperses the French covering fleet thus defeating the operation.
6 Apr	France and Prussia sign the Peace of Basel at which Prussia withdraws from the First Coalition.
6 May	Command of the Army of Italy passes from Schérer to Kellermann.
22 Jun	France and Spain sign the Peace of Basel at which Spain withdraws from the First Coalition.
27 Jun– 21 Jul	In response to royalist uprisings in Brittany, the British support a landing of French royalist emigres. The force is defeated at Quiberon with 3,600 French royalists killed and 1,800 captured.
29 Jun– 3 Jul	A swift Austrian summer offensive recaptures the ports of Savona and Loano.
Aug–Oct	As a result of the Peace of Basel treaties, the Army of Italy is reinforced by troops from the Rhine and the Pyrenees.
29 Sep	Command of the Army of Italy passes from Kellermann to Schérer.

5 Oct   As the Republic establishes the Directory, under Barras, monarchist uprisings in Paris are suppressed by Bonaparte.

23-26 Nov   Delayed by heavy snowstorms, a French surprise winter offensive results in a resounding French victory at the battle of Loano and the recapture of Savona.

Ready Reference – Military Organisations

A very simple overview of military organisations in this period:

Squad/File/Patrol – Cavalry soldiers were grouped together in threes or fours to patrol, cook and sleep together as well as ride together in larger formations.

Section – Twelve men, when at full-strength, or three squads/files, commanded by a corporal.

Platoon – Two sections, twenty-four men at full-strength, commanded by a sergeant.

Troop – Two platoons, fifty men at full strength, commanded by a second lieutenant.

Company – Two troops, one hundred men at full strength, commanded by a captain.

Squadron – Two companies, commanded by the senior captain of the two companies.

Battalion - Six to eight companies of infantry, commanded by a chief of battalion (major).

Regiment – Three or more squadrons of cavalry or battalions of infantry commanded by a colonel. A cavalry regimental commander had two chiefs of squadron (major) who assisted him by commanding squadrons on independent tasks.

Brigade – Two or more regiments of infantry or cavalry, with supporting artillery, engineers and logistic support, commanded by a brigadier (a rank of general).

Division – Two or more brigades, with associated support, commanded by a major general.

Corps – Two or more divisions, capable of significant independent operations, commanded by a lieutenant general.

Army, or Army Wing – Two or more corps, commanded by a general.

Ready Reference – Measurement Conversion

An approximate conversion of metric measurements:

One inch is approximately two and a half centimetres. Ten centimetres is approximately four inches.

One metre is approximately one yard, or three feet.

One thousand metres, or one kilometre, is approximately two-thirds of a mile (five-eighths). One mile is approximately one and a half kilometres.

One kilogram is approximately two pounds.

One litre, or one kilogram of water, is approximately two pints.

Dramatis Personae

This story is a work of fiction within a historical setting.
In the list below, those characters with their names underlined
existed, otherwise the character is an author's creation.

Army of Italy
(Napoleonic ranks in brackets)

Saliceti   A Jacobin Deputy of the People assigned
                     to observe the performance of the Army.
                     A friend and sponsor of Napoleon Bonaparte.

Dumerbion,   Commanders of the Army of Italy.
Schérer and
Kellermann

Bonaparte   Brigadier (général de brigade) and Chief of
                     Artillery on the headquarters of the Army of
                     Italy. Future Napoleon I, Emperor of France.

Masséna   Divisional commander (général de division)
                     within the Army of Italy. Future Marshal of
                     France under Emperor Napoleon.

Raive   A staff officer on General Masséna's head-
                     quarters. Previously the regimental second-
                     in-command of the 24th Chasseurs à Cheval.

The 24th Regiment of Chasseurs à Cheval
(Napoleonic ranks in brackets)

Morin   Colonel and Commanding Officer
                     of the regiment until November 1794.

Spiccard	Lieutenant Colonel (major) and second-in-command of the regiment. Assumes command of the regiment in December 1794.
Fergnes	Major (chef d'escadron). Marries Marguerite of Avignon.
Chabenac	Captain, regimental aide de camp.

2nd Squadron
(Napoleonic ranks in brackets)

André Jobert	Captain, commander of 2nd Company and 2nd Squadron. Promoted to major (chef d'escadron) in December 1794.
Koschak	Company sergeant major (marechel des logis chef). Upon Jobert's promotion, becomes 2nd Squadron's sergeant major (adjutant major).
Moench	Jobert's trumpeter.
Geourdai	Captain, commander of 5th Company, the junior company within 2nd Squadron. Upon Jobert's promotion, commands 2nd Company, the senior company within 2nd Squadron.
Neilage	Lieutenant and second-in-command of Jobert's 2nd Company. Promoted captain to command 5th Company within 2nd Squadron.

Voreille   Second Lieutenant (sous lieutenant) in 2nd Company. Promoted Lieutenant company second-in-command in Geourdai's 2nd Company.

Huin   Second Lieutenant (sous lieutenant) in 2nd Company. Promoted Lieutenant company second-in-command in Neilage's 5th Company.

Pultiere   Sergeant (marechel des logis) in Voreille's troop. Promoted second lieutenant in Geourdai's 2nd Company.

Bredieux   Sergeant (marechel des logis) in Voreille's troop. Promoted second lieutenant in Geourdai's 2nd Company.

Peugeot   Recent graduate of the École Militaire, Paris, is a second lieutenant (sous lieutenant) in Geourdai's 2nd Company.

Yinot   Sergeant (marechel des logis) in Huin's troop. Promoted second lieutenant in Neilage's 5th Company.

Orlande   Jobert's valet and cook.

Duque   Corporal (brigadier), Jobert's groom. Attends France's veterinary school at Alfort, near Paris.

Tulloc — Company apprentice farrier and marksman/sniper. Becomes Jobert's groom.

Duval — A corporal chasseur.

Madame Quandalle — 2nd Company's cantinière.

André Jobert's Family

Jacques Chauvel — André Jobert's grandfather. Ex-artilleryman and horse breeder.

Sophie Chauvel — André Jobert's great aunt and sister of Jacques. Seamstress.

Yann Chauvel — André Jobert's uncle and son of Jacques. Ex-sergeant-veterinarian. Manages the family horse breeding farm in the high country of the Auvergne.

Didier Jobert-Chauvel — André Jobert's brother. Chief of squadron in the 1st Hussars.

Michelle Chauvel — André Jobert's cousin, daughter of Yann. Seamstress.

Others

Madame de Chabenac and Valmai de Chabenac Mother and sister of Captain Chabenac

Avriol Ex-chief of squadron of the 24th Chasseurs, now promoted brigadier general.

Inoubli Avignon dance master

Anissa Voreille's sweetheart

www.ingramcontent.com/pod-product-compliance
Lightning Source LLC
Chambersburg PA
CBHW022205010726
47493CB00002B/428